IT HAD TO BE YOU

David Nobbs was born in Orpington and educated at Marlborough, Cambridge and the Royal Corps of Signals, where he reached the lofty rank of Signalman. His first job was as a reporter on the *Sheffield Star*, and his first break as a comedy writer came on the iconic satire show *That Was The Week, That Was*, hosted by David Frost. Later he wrote for *The Frost Report*, *The Two Ronnies* and many top comedians. *It Had To Be You* is his eighteenth novel, no less than six of which he has adapted for TV, including his two hit series *A Bit Of A Do* and *The Fall and Rise of Reginald Perrin*. His first three novels, *The Itinerant Lodger*, *Ostrich Country* and *A Piece Of The Sky Is Missing*, are now available through Print On Demand. David lives in North Yorkshire with his second wife, Susan.

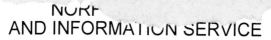

Also by David Nobbs:

Novels

Obstacles to Young Love
Cupid's Dart
Sex and Other Changes
Going Gently
Fair Do's
A Bit Of A Do
A Piece Of The Sky Is Missing
Ostrich Country
The Itinerant Lodger

Reginald Perrin Series

The Legacy of Reginald Perrin
The Better World of Reginald Perrin
The Return of Reginald Perrin
The Fall and Rise of Reginald Perrin
The Death of Reginald Perrin: a novel

Pratt

Pratt à Manger
The Cucumber Man
Pratt of the Argus
Second from Last in the Sack Race

Non Fiction

I Didn't Get Where I am Today

DAVID NOBBS

It Had to be You

HARPER

This novel is entirely a work of fiction.
The names, characters and incidents portrayed in it are
the work of the author's imagination. Any resemblance to
actual persons, living or dead, events or localities is
entirely coincidental.

Harper
An imprint of HarperCollins*Publishers*
77–85 Fulham Palace Road,
Hammersmith, London W6 8JB

www.harpercollins.co.uk

A Paperback Original 2011
1

A catalogue record for this book
is available from the British Library

ISBN: 978 0 00 728629 4

Set in Meridien by Palimpsest Book Production Limited,
Falkirk, Stirlingshire

Printed and bound in Great Britain by
Clays Ltd, St Ives plc

Mixed Sources
Product group from well-managed
forests and other controlled sources
www.fsc.org Cert no. SW-COC-001806
© 1996 Forest Stewardship Council

FSC is a non-profit international organisation established
to promote the responsible management of the world's forests.
Products carrying the FSC label are independently certified
to assure consumers that they come from forests that are managed
to meet the social, economic and ecological needs
of present and future generations.

Find out more about HarperCollins and the environment at
www.harpercollins.co.uk/green

For the Goddard and Stubbs families, who have brought
so much pleasure into my life

Acknowledgements

I must thank my agents Jonathan and Ann Clowes, Nemonie Craven Roderick and Olivia Guest for their ever helpful suggestions, Lynne Drew, Victoria Hughes-Williams, Liz Dawson and Elinor Fewster for all their support since I joined the Harper list, and my wife Susan for her unfailing help, patience and support.

Thanks also to the composer Matthew Taylor for his guidance with the pieces that Charles plays on the piano in the last two chapters.

But my greatest thanks must go to my editor, Mary Chamberlain. Her suggestions were extremely detailed, sometimes quite harsh, but almost always utterly right. I owe her a great debt of gratitude for whatever quality the book has.

Wednesday

A husband and wife were driving, in separate cars, towards two very different luncheon appointments. It was a glorious June morning, quite unsuitable for sudden death, yet only one of them would arrive.

Deborah Hollinghurst was driving along a quiet country road. She was in danger of being early, and she really didn't think it would be stylish to be early, not today, not yet. So she was driving sedately, at a steady forty-five miles an hour along the winding road, to the irritation of the drivers of a couple of vans that had once been white. Her car was a convertible, but the roof was not down. She didn't want the wind in her hair, not today. Next month she would be forty-seven. She was still lovely, but she was beginning to feel that her loveliness needed all the help it could get. Especially today. She felt excited, but also a little fearful. The fear was only faint, but it was getting stronger with every mile that she drove. She felt as if she was about to step off the edge of the world. Her world, anyway. She told herself that she didn't have to step off. Nothing had been decided. She didn't believe herself. She knew that everything had been decided.

3

A rabbit with myxomatosis stood at the side of the road, blind, impervious, a stone statue, like a ghastly garden sculpture of a rabbit. Deborah swerved to put it out of its misery, shuddered at the squelch of the tiny impact, on that glorious June morning, so unsuitable for sudden death.

A heron flapped slowly, contentedly across a field beside the road. Soon, if it had its way, a fish would meet *its* sudden death. The calm of the morning was illusory, its beauty marred by a thousand little tragedies.

To James Hollinghurst the morning had no beauty. The windows of the totally unnecessary 4 x 4 were closed, the air conditioning was on, his world was a mobile fridge, summer had no place in it, summer had been banished as a frivolous nuisance. He was on the M1, in the middle lane. He was in danger of being late, and he didn't think it would be wise to be late, not today.

He was anxious. It was not going to be an easy meeting. He put his foot down. Eighty-five. Ninety. Ninety-five. He didn't want to be caught on a speed camera, but anything was better than being late today.

He was listening to Classic FM. The adverts began, and he leant forward and pressed a button, which switched the radio over to another channel. He didn't like the adverts. Their repetition irritated him. He had dark, unruly hair, thick untamed eyebrows, a high forehead and a low boredom threshold.

The next station that he found had music on it, or what passed for music. 'Call that music,' he shouted. He shouted at the radio a lot. It was what he had it on for. He was forty-eight. He was on quinapril, amlodipine and bisoprolol hemifumerate for his blood pressure, and simvastatins for his cholesterol.

Unfortunately the music stopped, and the DJ announced that he was going to speak to Tracey from Doncaster. James groaned. It was very possible that Tracey from Doncaster was a lovely girl. He often met people who were much nicer than the towns they lived in. But he didn't think Tracey could tell him anything that he really needed to know at this moment. He switched back to Classic FM. The adverts were almost over.

'We've more relaxing music for you in the next hour,' purred the presenter in the honeyed, reassuring, faintly patronising tone adopted by almost all the announcers on Classic FM.

'Relaxing?' groaned James. He desperately needed to relax. Packaging was the first thing to suffer in a recession. If people had bought less, they had fewer things to pack. But he didn't want to listen to relaxing music. He wanted to be transported into another world by *great* music. 'I know you've done a lot for classical music,' he told the presenter sorrowfully. After all, the man sounded nice and was probably kind to his wife. 'But really, is that what you think great music is about? Did Beethoven say, "Darling, I think I created something memorably relaxing this morning"? Did Mrs Mahler find Mahler spark out as she brought him his morning coffee? "Sorry, Ingeborg, this symphony I'm writing is so relaxing I must have nodded off." Give me great music. Stirring music. Please.'

He reached forward to press the button again, feeling a stab of pleasure at reducing the announcer to impotence. How he wished people could feel it when he switched them off. 'Bad news, Monty. We've lost James Hollinghurst. The bastard was distinctly unimpressed. He's switched over to BBC Radio 3.'

He accelerated with a sudden surge of impotent anger, and swung out into the fast lane. Surely, the way James was driving, if one of the Hollinghursts was to have a fatal accident that day, it would be him?

Not so.

Deborah came to a rare straight stretch of road. Four cars were proceeding smoothly in the opposite direction. A fifth, a Porsche, was overtaking them at speed. Suddenly she realised that it was going to be a close-run thing, if she didn't slow down to let the driver through. Why should she, though? He was the one at fault, arrogant, rich, spoilt, in his expensive car. He deserved to have a moment of shock, of doubt, of fear. She'd brake, of course she would, she'd have to, but not for a couple of seconds.

It was the worst decision she ever made in her life.

It was also the last decision she ever made in her life.

A tall man, elegant in white linen, sat at a window table in the pink and cream restaurant, toyed with a glass of rather average house white and looked out over the gardens, which sloped down towards the gently flowing water. He wouldn't like his name to be revealed. He shouldn't be there. He'd chosen the place because he wasn't known there. He'd kept his wits about him, and he was certain that nobody had followed him. The only private dick he needed to be concerned with was the one in his sharply creased trousers, which was so stimulated that he was finding it hard to keep it private. Let us allow him his precious anonymity – for the moment, at least.

There's no need to name the hotel either. One of the things that had most attracted him to it was its obscurity. It was a long way from anybody he knew, and a long way from anybody whom the woman he was expecting knew. Let's just say it was the Whatsit Arms, prettily situated on the banks of the River Thingamayjig, just outside the pleasant but not distinguished little village of Somewhere-juxta-Nowhere. It was mentioned in no guidebooks. It had no Michelin stars. It was perfect.

He had the table furthest from the door. He sat facing the door. Every time anybody entered he felt a frisson of excitement, soon dashed. My God, he said to himself with a wry internal smile, as he watched the lunchers enter, we're an ugly race.

He wasn't surprised that she was late. He'd expected her to be late. It was stylish for a woman to arrive late, and she was very stylish. He'd guessed that she would be eight, nine, perhaps ten minutes late. It was correct, and he always liked to be correct, which was why he'd had to be so secretive. There was no way what he was doing today was correct. A clandestine lunch with a married woman. Not his style at all. And, of all married women, this one.

Not just lunch, either. Or so he hoped. Not half an hour ago he had booked a double room for the night, just in case. He could hardly believe that he had been so bold. But if things went well, and if the mood was right, and if he did manage to persuade her, it might be disastrous to have to go through all the business of booking, of pretending to be a married couple, of giving false names. Do you need any help with your luggage? We have no luggage. Only baggage.

He'd had to give a name of course, fill in a form. Mr and Mrs Rivers, Lake View, 69 Pond Street, Poole. Utterly unbelievable, but it had aroused no suspicion from the Hungarian receptionist, whose skin was like a white pudding he had once eaten in the Languedoc. He'd blushed slightly at the boldness, the wild optimism of his choice of house number. He couldn't remember ever having been even remotely risqué before. What had got into him? Love? Madness? The girl hadn't reacted. Perhaps they didn't use that term in the villages around Lake Balaton.

Suddenly he realised that he was wearing his wedding ring, and that might be tactless. He stood up abruptly, then calmed himself down and walked out of the restaurant, trying to look insouciant. He went to the Gents and forced the ring off his finger. He had never taken it off before, and it didn't come easily, this was taking time, she would arrive before he got back, he began to panic. His finger felt trapped inside the ring.

At last it came off, and he breathed more easily again. But now he needed a pee, his third in the last hour. He had rarely been so nervous. Oh, hurry, hurry, lazy prick. She'll be there. She'll have arrived and found him absent, the great moment ruined.

He walked back, trying to look calm and carefree. She wasn't there yet. For a moment he was glad.

Twelve minutes late. Thirteen. He began to feel just faintly uneasy.

James *was* late. The traffic had been heavy, but he should have allowed for that. And the BWC (Big White Chief) was a stickler for punctuality. The summons to the head office in Birmingham would have been unnerving at any time, but the recession was beginning to bite, the coalition's threatened cuts hung heavily, and he felt very nervous. It shamed him to feel so nervous.

He drove past the ugly, glass and stained concrete building that housed the world HQ of Globpack. He turned right at the side of the building, then at the back turned left. A bar blocked his way into the car park. It irritated him that the intercom was so inconveniently placed that he had to get out of the car to speak into it. The intense heat of the city was a shock after the iciness of his car.

8

'The car park's full,' announced a crackly disembodied Birmingham voice with barely concealed delight.

He gave his registration number, and added, 'I have a space reserved.'

'I have no record of this, I'm afraid,' said the voice, sounding more pleased than afraid.

James swallowed. He found it difficult to be assertive to people when they weren't on the radio.

'I think you'd better find me a space,' he said. 'I'm the Managing Director of the London office.'

The bar rose. James got back into his car. Its iciness was a shock after the intense heat of the city. He drove in. The car park *was* full. He managed to squeeze his Subaru into a corner, at a somewhat humiliatingly awkward angle. Every little setback was making him feel even worse about the day's prospects. He strode towards the ugly back of the building, which was called, as it deserved to be, Packaging House.

He had forgotten the four-figure security number that would unlock the back door. He would have to go round the front. He was getting later and later. This was bad. He didn't feel like the Managing Director of the London office. He felt like an underling. And that was what he was, in reality, when he was meeting the Managing Director of the whole global venture.

He longed to break into a run, but in this heat it would have brought him out in a sweat, and that would have been disastrous. The BWC was a stickler for hygiene. Americans usually are.

As he walked towards the main entrance, James remembered something his father had said. This tended to happen at moments of stress. The voice came clearly to him from that Christmas fifteen years ago.

'I feel guilty about you, James. I haven't dealt with my

children fairly. I've given Charles my artistry, Philip my brains, and you my eyebrows.'

How typical of his father, to have wrapped a grenade in a coating of sympathy. Fifteen years, and it still rankled. If only Deborah was with him, striding beside him on her long, strong, fleshy farmer's daughter's legs. He closed his eyes for a second in a sudden revulsion at how he had treated her, and almost fell as his foot caught the raised edge of a paving stone.

Careful, James. Get a grip.

Easily said, but in a few minutes he would know what this summons was all about. Surely it couldn't be the sack? He'd been chosen to make the speech on behalf of the company at the big luncheon next Wednesday to mark the fiftieth anniversary of the formation of Globpack UK. They'd hardly do that and then sack him.

Or would they? Maybe that would give out a sign of the company's ruthlessness very effectively. No, he wasn't secure.

Nobody was.

And even if it wasn't the sack, it might be the dreaded news that the London office was to move to share premises with the global HQ – in Birmingham. That would be almost as bad.

Globpack! How had they come up with that? He had inherited a bit of his dad's artistic taste, and he found it hard to believe that a career that had begun in the Basingstoke Box Company had led him, inexorably, to being employed by a firm called Globpack.

Another intercom outside the main entrance.

'James Hollinghurst to see Mr Schenkman.'

The doors opened, with, it seemed to James, a sigh of resignation. We don't want to let him in, but we can find no reason not to.

'I have an appointment with Mr Schenkman. I'm afraid I'm late.'

The receptionist winced sympathetically, phoned Mr Schenkman's office, and then said, to James's surprise, 'He's coming down.'

Did this mean . . . could it mean . . . lunch? His spirits rose.

In the early years of their relationship, James had enjoyed many lunches, lunches marred only by the fact that the giant American was so abstemious that James had felt like an alcoholic every time he took a sip of his wine.

And now here the man was striding gigantically and rather aggressively over the even more gigantic foyer.

'I'm so sorry I'm late,' said James, just before he was enveloped in Mr Schenkman's global handshake. 'The traffic!'

Dwight Schenkman the Third frowned. James felt that the frown said, Anticipation of difficulty is halfway towards success in the intensely competitive world of global packaging. No. He was becoming paranoid. The man was addicted to verbosity, but he must stop attributing quite such pompous words to him.

'Could I have a taxi, please, to go to the Hotel du Vin?' said Mr Schenkman to the receptionist.

The Hotel du Vin. James's spirits took another cautious leap, then plummeted. When you feel insecure, no signs are good, and this could be a way of saying goodbye, and thank you.

A taxi pulled in almost immediately. James felt that they always would, for Dwight Schenkman the Third.

'Hotel du Vin, please.'

The moment the taxi had slid away from the main entrance, the immaculately groomed American leant forward and said, 'Driver, we're actually going to the Pizza Express.'

James raised his bushy eyebrows, those unwelcome gifts from his father.

'Couldn't let them know that in the office,' explained

11

Dwight Schenkman the Third. 'One word out of place, and the shares could slide. Confidence is fragile in the intensely competitive world of global packaging.'

The man in the white linen suit studied the menu for the third time. There were two misprints. There was 'loin of God', which was careless, and 'expresso coffee', which was ominously ignorant.

Thirty minutes. Thirty-one. Thirty-two. The serious doubts began.

At the next table they noticed 'loin of God', and the conversation turned to misprints on menus.

'In a restaurant I went to in the Ardeche,' said a crayfish cocktail, 'there was a starter of "*avocat farci*". It was translated in the English version as "stuffed lawyer".'

There was laughter.

'I wouldn't have ordered that,' said a soup of the day. 'Too tough.'

There was more laughter.

'Too expensive,' added a chicken liver pâté, and there was yet more laughter.

All this laughter hit the man in the white linen suit like a punch in the stomach. He was in a state of anxiety that no laughter could penetrate. Suddenly he was convinced that something serious had happened.

He still didn't think of an accident, though. He certainly didn't think of death. It was the third day of Wimbledon. The day smelt of strawberries and cream. It wasn't a time for accidents.

His first thought was that she had fallen ill, was in hospital, couldn't phone, hadn't dared to reveal their secret plans. That would be surprising, though. She was very fit.

He shook his head, to rid it of these speculations. A rather plump, middle-aged woman, lunching with a woman of similar age, caught his eye, and he tried not to look as if he was waiting for someone who hadn't turned up. This irritated him. Why should he care? No wonder she hadn't come, if that was the amount of confidence and poise he had.

No . . . on second thoughts . . . on second thoughts that was exactly what he thought she had had . . . second thoughts. She had seen the road ahead. The clandestine meetings. The lies. The deceptions. The hurt. She had decided that she didn't want to have to be Mrs Rivers, of Lake View, 69 Pond Street, Poole.

He wasn't worth it.

This was ridiculous. There was some utterly trivial explanation. Any minute now she would breeze in, smiling her apologies with that memorable wide smile of hers.

But she didn't.

The Pizza Express was like . . . well, it was like every other Pizza Express. Just about Italian enough to be acceptable to the sophisticated, not so Italian that it discomfited the gauche. Warm enough to be pleasant to enter, cool enough to discourage a long stay.

A Polish waiter approached, trying to look Italian, trying to pretend to be really rather excited to see them. His insufficiently practised Eastern European smile foundered on the rock of Dwight Schenkman's face.

'Anything to drink, gentlemen?'

God, I could sink a Peroni.

'Just a small sparkling water, please,' said Dwight Schenkman.

Maybe a glass of the Montepulciano, thought James. A large one. But the words died in his throat.

'Still water, please.'

James studied the menu. How, when the main course

13

was mainly pizza, could there be dough balls as a starter? How much dough could a man consume?

'How's the lovely Deborah?'

'Very well. Very well indeed.'

'You're a lucky son of a gun.'

'I know I am. More than I deserve.'

'And Max?'

'Great.'

'And Charlotte? The absent Charlotte?'

'Still absent.'

The tension grew with every devastating drip of politeness. Now he had to take his turn at asking questions, and there was a problem. The names of Dwight's wife and family escaped him entirely. He had once begun a correspondence course to improve his memory. 'That'll be a futile gesture,' Deborah had predicted, and she'd been right. Halfway through the course he'd forgotten all about it.

'Everything all right with your family?' he enquired.

Pathetic. The lack of detail was blatant. But the BWC didn't seem to notice. He took a photograph from his wallet.

'We have our very first grandchild.' He handed James a photo of an ugly, podgy baby being held in the excessively ample arms of an unrealistically blonde lady with slightly stick-out teeth. In the background was a bungalow of quite spectacular dreariness. 'Who do you think that is?'

Inspiration, that rare visitor to his life, struck James.

'Dwight Schenkman the Fifth?'

'Yessir!' This was said so loudly that several people in the vicinity turned to look.

'Lovely,' said James. 'They make a lovely couple. And is that their home? It looks . . . cosy.'

'James, that is exactly what it is. Dwight's very New York, but Howard's a real home bird. That's his wife, Josie. James,

14

it gives me great pleasure that you, my old friend, my trusted manager of the London office, think that Josie and Howard make a lovely couple. Thank you.'

James looked desperately for sarcasm and found none. But 'old friend', 'trusted manager'. Maybe things weren't so bad after all.

The waiter scurried across with their water, and asked if they were ready to order.

'Absolutely,' said Dwight Schenkman the third without consulting James. 'James?'

'I'll have the capricciosa, please.'

'Great choice, James. I'll have the Veneziana. I like to feel I'm giving 25p to Venice. It's a great little town. And those dough balls sound nice to start. You going for the dough balls, James?'

'No, thank you.' How thankful he was that he hadn't made any comment about them.

'We've had some great lunches, haven't we? Le Gavroche. Le Manoir aux Quat'Saisons with Claire and the lovely Deborah.'

Claire! Must remember that. Claire. An éclair with the e on the end instead of the beginning. Easy-peasy.

'And now the Pizza Express.'

'Hard times?'

'Got it in one. What's your view of the state of the packaging industry, James?'

'Difficult, Dwight. We pack what people buy. We can't pack more or less than that. We're a kind of barometer of the economy.'

'I like that.' The BWC rolled the phrase round his mouth as if it was a glass of *premier cru* Chateau Margaux. God, James could do with a glass of wine. Any wine. 'A barometer of the economy. I'll remember that.'

Of course you will. You remember everything, you bastard.

Dwight Schenkman the Third leant so far forward that James could smell his toothpaste and his aftershave.

'To business,' he said.

James's heart began to pump very fast. Thank goodness he'd remembered to take all his pills.

'There are two elements to this, James. A global element and a UK element.'

The pumping of James's heart began to slow just a little. It didn't sound like the sack.

'In the short term, James, I am requiring every element of our global operation to make a fifteen per cent cut across the board. Across the board, James, from personnel to toilet paper via water coolers and stationery. I need your specific proposal as to how this target may be met in Bridgend and Kilmarnock, and I need it within six months.'

James knew how difficult this would be, but all he could feel was relief, immense, shattering relief. He had been given a job to do. He had not been sacked.

Dwight's dough balls arrived. Since he was far too well bred to talk with his mouth full, and since he was an exhaustive chewer, his outlining of James's greatest challenge came with long interruptions.

'There is a real possibility, James, that we might have to consider transferring some, if not most, of our total British production capacity to . . .'

James tried not to watch the curiously sterile rhythmic movement of Dwight's jaw as he chewed.

'. . . Taiwan. Well, there are other possibilities, but Taiwan is favourite as of this moment in time.'

As opposed to this moment in space, thought James irreverently.

'In six months I will have received estimates of the saving that we can achieve by moving production to Taiwan. I want you to set up a committee to give me another report producing equal . . .'

James took a sip of his water and tried to pretend it was gin.

'. . . savings in the UK. Otherwise, Taiwan it is. In which case we could . . .'

He chewed on his next morsel of dough ball as if he couldn't bear the pleasure to end.

'. . . close the London office and you could all join us here in Birming-ham.'

Dwight Schenkman pronounced England's second city as if it was a type of meat.

James's heart sank. Even the arrival of his pizza capricciosa couldn't lift it.

She was more than three-quarters of an hour late now. He was in turmoil. He stared wildly at the door, willing her to hurry in. But he knew in his heart that she wouldn't.

He had ruled out the possibility that she had had second thoughts. Apart from the fact that there was no reason why she should – they had talked about it and talked about it and she had committed herself and told him how much she loved him and told him of James's lack of real passion in recent years – there was also his knowledge of her character. She was a woman of courage, of spirit, of compassion, of style. If she *had* had second thoughts, she would have phoned to tell him.

He began to think about the possibility of an accident. He could barely allow himself to believe that she would have had a bad accident. His happiness, his utterly unexpected happiness, was not to be taken away so cruelly. But a minor accident, that would be what it was.

If it was a very minor accident, though, she would have been able to phone.

17

So why didn't he phone her? Not in the restaurant, though. It was too quiet. Too many people were eating in whispers, in that strange, overawed English way.

He strolled out into the garden, slowly, trying to look casual.

He had chosen this remote spot so well that there was no network coverage.

He returned to his table, smiled at the lunchers and sat down, trying to look as if he hadn't a care in the world.

Round and round went his mind.

He told himself that he had lived without her reasonably happily for fifty-one years. Surely he could manage another thirty or so?

He knew that this was nonsense.

He caught the eye of the plump, plain woman. She had a stern, stiff look on her face, and traces of tiramisu on both her chins. He had a sudden fear that he knew her, and that, therefore, she knew him. He smiled at her, trying to make the smile look casual and relaxed. She gave a defensive half-smile in response, as if she wasn't sure whether she knew him.

What did it matter, anyway? Deborah hadn't come. Nothing had happened.

A waitress lumbered over towards him, English, local, with inelegant legs and not a shred of style.

'Would you like to order, sir?' she asked. 'Only the chef's got the hospital at two forty-five, with his boils.'

'Well, he could hardly go there without them, could he?'

'Sorry, sir?'

'I'll have the chicken liver pâté and then the loin of God.'

'Good?'

'Fine, Dwight. It was fine.'

'You're an unusual eater. I was watching you.'

Too right. Like a hawk. Disconcerting. Very.

'I make sure that I don't run out of the things I particularly like, which in this case were the egg, the anchovy, the capers,' explained James. 'There must be a bit of those left at the end. Not too much, though. That would be childish.'

'I see,' said Dwight, not seeing at all. 'Right. So there we are, James. A simple task. Not too frightening, is it?'

It's terrifying.

'Not at all.'

'I could have just phoned you, James, but we go back a long way. I wanted to establish the continuation of a relationship that is a substantial part of the bedrock that has helped to cement the British sphere of the Globpack operation over the years, not to say the decades.'

'Thank you.'

'Coffee? No. Back to work. Quite right, James. Time is money.' He summoned a waiter and asked for the bill. It came instantly.

'Thank you very much for lunch,' said James.

'My pleasure. We must do it properly soon. The four of us. Not on the company, though. Those days are over, never to return.' The waiter moved off and Dwight leant forward. 'One other matter, James. Sack your PA. Immediately. She's incompetent. She's a liability to the company image.'

'I know, but . . .'

'You're not having . . . ?'

'Of course I'm not.'

'I know. I'm sorry.'

'It's just . . .'

It's just that she's so useless she'll never get another job. And I like her. I'm comfortable with her.

Can't say any of that.

'Immediately. Absolutely.'

Oh, God.

19

'How would Deborah feel if one day your whole operation did move to Birmingham?'

She'd go ape-shit.

'I don't say she'd be thrilled, Dwight, she's a London lady through and through, despite her farming background, but she'd accept it without complaint if it was necessary.'

Dwight stood up. James rose with him as if they were tied together.

They got a taxi back to Globpack. The two men stood outside the main entrance for a moment, in the stifling sunshine.

'My very best to the marvellous Deborah,' said Dwight Schenkman the Third, shaking James's hand ferociously.

'Thank you. And my very best to . . .' Oh, God. What was it? Ah! Cake. That was the clue. And ending in an e. Got it. '. . . Madeleine.'

'Madeleine?'

Oh, shit. That was Proust.

He could feel the eyes of Dwight Schenkman the Third, those piercing yet strangely unseeing eyes, boring into his back as he strode towards the car park.

The man in the white linen suit cancelled his room.

'We not charge. You not use,' said the Hungarian receptionist.

'Thank you.'

'I hoping you finding your wife very all right, Mr Rivers.'

'Thank you.'

As he walked slowly, sadly, exhaustedly to his car through a wall of heat, the man who had called himself Mr Rivers realised that he had indeed been hoping that this lunch would be the first stage in the long process of finding a wife, and that Deborah as his wife would indeed be very all right, although the whole thing was so very all wrong.

20

What on earth had happened to her? He found it almost intolerable that he had no idea.

'That was a twenty-three-stroke rally. I wonder when there was last a twenty-three-stroke rally at Wimbledon on the twenty-third of June,' said the commentator.

'Do you really? How sad is that?' called out James.

'Interestingly enough—'

James pressed the button. He smiled internally at the thought that he would never know whether the commentator's remark would have been interesting enough. He was already far away, on Radio 2, listening to *Steve Wright in the Afternoon*.

His phone rang almost immediately. Sadly, Steve Wright spent only twelve seconds in James's afternoon.

It was Marcia, his PA. At the sound of her posh Benenden voice his heart sank. Dwight wanted him to sack her tomorrow. He wasn't sure if he had the power to sack her any more. Didn't he have to give her a warning, maybe several warnings? He didn't want to sack her, but he didn't want not to have the power to sack her if he wanted to. It was odd being a boss these days.

'Hello. It's me.' So bright and warm and innocent and naive. She hadn't been to Benenden. She'd been to an obscure private school, now defunct, where they taught you to talk as if you *had* been to Benenden. James sometimes thought that it was the only thing they had taught her.

'Hello, Marcia.'

'How did it go? Do I still have you as my boss?'

Marcia, that really is a little bit forward.

'Sorry. Am I being a bit cheeky?'

'No. Not at all. It went well. You still have me as your boss.' Not for long, though. Poor girl. 'No, we just have to make savings. Fifteen per cent across the board.'

'Heavens.'

'Quite.'

'And we have to produce a report stating why we shouldn't move all our production to Taiwan.'

'Oops.'

'Exactly.'

'Are you coming back in?'

'No. The traffic's terrible. I'm crawling at forty in the fast lane.'

'Oh, poor you.'

'Always nice to hear your cheerful voice, Marcia, but was there any particular reason for ringing?'

'Yes. There was.'

Silence.

A Vauxhall Corsa pulled into the space between James and the car in front. He hooted angrily. It happened all the time if you tried to keep your distance. Keep two chevrons' distance? Impossible. Had anybody in the government ever driven on a motorway? No, they had chauffeurs and slept, dreaming of their expenses.

It was yet another irritation on an irritating day.

'Are you still there, Marcia?'

'Yes. Sorry, it's gone. Oh, lorks, maybe I'm going to have to be a bit more on the ball if you're having to make these savings.'

It's too late, darling.

'Oh, yes. It's come back. The police rang.'

'The police?'

'Yes. Sorry. I should have written it down, 'cause I usually do, but I thought it was so important and unusual that I couldn't possibly forget it.'

'Quite. What did they want?'

'He didn't say. He sounded nice, though. Quite young, I think.'

22

'Yes, I don't care what age he was, Marcia, but didn't he say anything?'

'He asked for your home number and your address. I didn't think it would sound good to be too inquisitive. I think they'll be in touch with you this evening.'

'Thank you.'

'James?'

'Yes?'

'I hope it's nothing serious.'

'Thank you. Probably some scrape my bloody daughter's got into.'

'I guess. James?'

'Yes, Marcia?'

'I'll be in all evening. Will you ring and let me know? 'Cause I'll worry.'

'That's very sweet of you.'

'Well, you know I . . .'

'What? What, Marcia?'

'No. Nothing. Sorry.'

She rang off. Oh, how how how could he sack her tomorrow? Or even give her a warning. How could he bear to witness the hurt that she would have no ability to conceal?

It was his barely admitted wish that he had been born as his brother Charles that had led James to choose to live in a three-storey Georgian end-of-terrace house in one of the more fashionable parts of Islington rather than in the five-bedroom two-garage four-bathroom suburban home with conservatory, summer house, tree house and large lawn hidden from the envious by leylandii that might have seemed more suitable for the Managing Director of the London office. The only real drawback was the absence of those two garages. Even with his residents' pass he often had to park quite a

23

way from the house, and on this day of irritations it was no surprise that this should be so.

As he dragged himself through the poisoned early-evening heat past the reticent charms of the nicely proportioned brick-built houses in the modestly elegant, understated street he longed for a drink, but even more than that, he craved the peace of his home. Every visitor commented on how restful and quietly artistic the house was, and he was always generous in admitting how much of this achievement was down to Deborah, his style guru.

His legs were leaden. The heavy traffic, the tense meeting, the fear of sacking the lovely, useless Marcia, and the news that he was going to get a call from the police all contributed to a debilitating unease.

He couldn't find his front-door key, so he rang the bell, but there was no reply. That was odd. He had expected Deborah to be in.

Thank goodness the house *was* on the end of the terrace. He took the narrow path on the eastern side of the house, picked up the back-door key from under the third stone behind the statue of Diana (Greek goddess, not princess), and entered the house through the garden door.

Perhaps it was just as well that Deborah wasn't home. She would have raised her eyebrows at the sight of him going to the gin bottle before he even took his tie off.

He poured himself a gin and Noilly Prat with ice and a slice, sniffed it eagerly, and took the first of many sips.

He sat in a green eighteenth-century armchair – no three-piece suites for Deborah – and stretched his body and his legs into full relaxing mode. He gazed with pleasure, as he did almost every day, at the carefully chosen semi-abstract landscapes by little-known modern artists that decorated the most serene living room of this man who hardly knew what the word 'serenity' meant.

At last, he gave a deep sigh, stood up carefully – his back was not something to be relied upon, especially after a long drive – and strode with sudden resolution towards the telephone. As he passed the piano, he ran his hand along the smooth walnut lid. It was a most beautiful piano. Neither he nor Deborah played. They had bought it for his brother Charles to play when he visited. James may have wished that he was Charles, but there was no envy in him. He was very proud of his brother.

He picked up the telephone, paused for a moment, summoning up his strength, then dialled his daughter's number. Well, he wasn't sure if it was her number. He'd been given it by someone at a number which had previously been said to be her number. Deborah had tried it a few times, at moments when she'd felt brave, he standing beside her and touching her to give her the strength he hadn't quite got. There had never been a reply. He felt brave now, his resolve stiffened by the task and the challenge set him by Dwight Schenkman the Third, and even more by the gin and Noilly Prat. But his chest was contracting, and his heart was beating as if it was a swallow trapped in a bedroom.

He almost rang off. He should ring off. It wasn't right to do this when Deborah wasn't here. It would be a great moment, a historic moment, and she should be part of it.

Just as he was about to ring off, there was a voice. A man's voice.

'Yep?'

The shock was immense. He had to sit down.

'Oh, hello. Um . . .' He felt foolish. 'Does . . . um . . . have I got the right number for . . .' He could barely say it. '. . . Charlotte Hollinghurst?'

Even as he spoke it the name seemed all wrong, so middle class, so . . . serene, satisfied.

25

'Who is this?'

'I'm her father. Charlotte Hollinghurst's father. She . . . um . . .' It was difficult to say the words. They made the fact of it so real. '. . . She . . . um . . . she disappeared from home a . . . um . . . long ago. Does . . . um . . .' Oh, Lord. What answer did he want? 'Is she . . . does she . . . live there?'

'Yeah, she sure does.'

Hope, fear but mainly astonishment surged through James. He had slowly become certain that he would never find her, that all alleys were blind, all clues imagined.

'Wow.'

'Yep. Wow.'

'Um . . . who am I speaking to?'

'Chuck.'

'Pardon?'

'I'm Chuck.'

'Ah.'

'Sorry.'

'No, no. Not at all. Um . . . is Charlotte there, by any chance . . . Chuck?'

'Absolutely.'

An electric current ran through James, as if he had been struck by lightning. She was there, alive and at the end of a phone line. He could barely bring himself to speak.

'Um . . . could I speak to her, please?'

'Absolutely.'

As easy as that.

James heard the phone being put down and heard Chuck call out, 'Babe, it's your old man.' Then there was silence.

He was desperately trying to control his breathing. He was deeply shaken. Chuck and Babe? Babe and Chuck. What had happened in the last five years? How had Charlotte met Chuck? How had she become Babe? Oh, Charlotte, my . . . no.

He heard nothing for a couple of minutes and wondered if he'd been cut off. How hard it would be to ring back. Then Chuck's voice came again, and he was catapulted into sorrow that it wasn't Charlotte speaking and relief that somebody was and, strangely, almost into a feeling that Chuck was his friend.

'Hi.'

'Hi, Chuck.'

'She says she has nothing to say to you. Sorry.'

How naive to have even dreamt that it would be easy.

'Not your fault, Chuck. Chuck, is she all right? Is everything all right?'

'Yeah, man. Cool. Everything's cool.'

'Good. Good. That's good. Chuck, will you try again? Could you tell her for me that she may have nothing to say to me but I have something to say to her? Could you tell her that I agree with her that it's a wicked world and that the values of our civilisation are fucking crap and will destroy our planet unless we do something about it pretty quickly?'

'Wow. Cool, man.'

'Thank you. I'm . . . um . . . I'm quoting her actually. Um . . . so would you say to her that *because* it's such a wicked world it's all the more important for people who love each other as much as her mother and I love her to stick together and support each other. We just want to see her, Chuck.'

Saying 'we' made him feel slightly better about making the call on his own.

'Yeah. Right. Cool. Got that. Will do.'

It was five years since he'd heard his daughter's voice. She had rung, once, about two years ago, to say she was all right, but it was Deborah who had answered. Charlotte had left them a phone number, but had said that she would disappear for ever if they rang except in emergencies. They

27

had phoned when a favourite godmother died, but by that time Charlotte had moved on. He wondered how much of what she had experienced in those five years would be reflected in her voice. But, when the voice came, it was Chuck's again.

'Hi there. Sorry. No dice,' he said.

James found himself nodding his head in acknowledgement that this was what he had expected, as if Chuck was in the room with him. He almost felt that Chuck *was* in the room with him.

'Well, thank you for trying.'

'No probs. Um . . .'

'Yes?'

'She didn't sound angry. She didn't say anything negative about you.'

'Are you saying that that's . . . surprising . . . unusual?'

'Well, it is a bit, yeah. Sorry.'

'No, no. Thank you. I . . .' What? Nothing. This was all too difficult. 'Well, thank you, Chuck. That's something, I suppose.'

'I think it might be.'

Chuck's reply surprised James, but his own next remark surprised him even more. He found himself saying, 'Chuck? Look after my baby.'

'I do try, Mr Hollinghurst.'

'Do you know something, Chuck? I actually believe you.'

As he'd talked to Chuck, James had almost felt relieved that he was talking about Charlotte rather than to her. But as soon as he had rung off he felt devastated that he had been so close to his daughter but still had not spoken to her.

He looked at his glass indecisively, then went to the gin bottle and added quite a slurp of gin, but no more Noilly Prat.

28

Why hadn't he asked more? Why hadn't he probed?

Because he sensed that of all the courses he could take, probing would annoy her the most. He would have to wait till she was ready.

If she was ever ready.

'Oh, Debs, where are you?' He realised that he had actually said the words out loud. He needed her there. He needed to tell her what was emerging as the most important, the most amazing point of all. Charlotte was alive and at least to a certain extent well and things were good enough to be described as cool and she was at the end of a telephone line and he knew the number and she was with a man and for no reason whatsoever and against all probability he trusted this man.

He tried to rehearse the words he would use, but no words fitted. 'Debs, there's great news.' Well, was it 'great'? Was that the word? 'Debs, I've found Charlotte.' Well, not entirely. The words would come when he saw her, the strength of her presence would dictate the words. He stood at the window and looked for her car as she tried to find a parking place. The roof would be down and her straw-coloured hair would be streaming behind her and he would pour her a drink and within minutes they would be talking about their beloved, lost daughter. He was amazed to find how clearly he imagined her, how deeply he needed her, at this visceral moment. He took several sips of his drink in his excitement. It was a long while since he had wanted to share anything with Deborah as much as he wanted to share this news. It was really annoying of her to be late this day of all days. It was the Irish in her. He drowned his irritation with another sip. This was no time to be irritated. This . . . conditional though it might be, strange though it might be, terrifying though it might still be . . . was joy.

He had completely forgotten Marcia's remark about the police, but the moment the knock came, he remembered, and from the nature of the ring he knew that a policeman was calling. This ring said, 'Hello. Police,' not, 'Sorry, darling, I've lost my key again,' or, 'Kathy and I wondered if you felt like popping to the pub for a quickie.'

And he suddenly knew, because the call could now not be about Charlotte, that it would be about Deborah, it would explain why she was late, something had happened.

As he walked towards the small entrance hall, James took a swallow of his drink and then hid the glass on the top of the piano behind the large photograph of Deborah and him on their wedding day twenty-four years ago.

The policeman looked absurdly young.

'Good evening, sir,' said the officer. 'It's . . . um . . . it's about your wife. Does she drive . . .' he looked down at his notes. '. . . a silver Renault Mégane hard-top convertible?'

'You'd better come in.'

As he entered the living room, the policeman took off his helmet, revealing hair so close-cropped that he looked almost bald. He had the air of a man who had joined the force to bully members of the underclass, not to be offered a comfortable chair in a living room of the well-heeled.

'What's all this about, officer?'

'I'm afraid your wife's car has been involved in a serious accident, sir.' He looked huge and wretched in his delicate chair. 'I'm afraid the . . . um . . . the driver had no chance. I'm sorry.'

He had often dreamt of this moment, in his fantasies, often when half awake, sometimes even when lying beside her in bed. Deborah dying suddenly, without pain, leaving him free, free, free.

But this wasn't fantasy. It wasn't right that a man's fantasy should suddenly become real. He was deeply shocked. He sat down heavily. He wondered if the officer could see into his thoughts – his dreadful thoughts.

Of course he hadn't really wanted Deborah to die. Only in make-believe.

He was shocked that she had died.

But, the fact remained, he had dreamt of being free and now he was free.

He heard himself say, 'Is there no chance, officer?' and to him it was the voice of a man acting out the role of a grieving husband, and acting it badly. It was dreadful.

'I wonder if you could get me a glass of water, officer,' he said, to buy himself time. 'The kitchen's through there.'

'Of course, sir.'

The officer looked delighted to have something practical to do.

As soon as he was alone, James closed his eyes and groaned. He couldn't have explained what he was groaning about, whether he was groaning because Deborah had died or because he had dreamt of her dying or because he was dismayed at the confusion of his emotions or because it was so appalling that a man should have to face his fantasies in real life or because he was a worthless shit who was going to find it very difficult to live with himself.

He had been glad to get the officer out of the room. Now he was glad to see him back. His dreary normality was comforting.

'Glass of water, sir,' said the officer, not without a glimmer of satisfaction at his success in carrying out this simple task.

The water tasted quite wonderful. It really was the most magnificent drink. He couldn't think why he ever drank gin or Noilly Prat or whisky or vodka or port or wine or beer or sherry or Madeira or Ricard or Campari or Manhattans or dry

31

Martinis or Negronis or Harvey Wallbangers or Deborah's damson gin. Deborah? He was never going to see her again, never feel the warmth of her smile. Never. He was free to marry the woman he loved, but never to see Deborah again, that really was a heavy price to pay.

'What exactly happened, officer?'

The officer consulted his notes, frowning with concentration. Reading didn't come naturally to him.

'It was on a road just outside Diss, sir.'

'Diss?'

'It's a town in Norfolk, sir.'

'I know it's a town in Norfolk, but what was she doing there?'

'I have no idea, sir.'

'No, of course you don't. Silly of me. Sorry. Carry on.'

'She hit a Porsche head on, sir. Both cars are write-offs. Both drivers dead.'

'I suppose I'll have to go and identify her.'

'I . . . um . . . I'm afraid that probably won't be possible, sir. There's . . . um . . .'

The young officer began to break out into a sweat. What had he been on the verge of saying? There's not enough of her left, sir?

'It's my understanding that it will be done with dental records, sir. Shouldn't be too long.'

'So the car might have been stolen? It might not be her.'

'I suppose it's possible, sir, but there was the remains of a handbag on the back seat, sir, with two credit cards of Mrs DJ Hollinghurst, and . . . um . . . on the floor at the back, a pair of high-heeled red Prada shoes, sir.'

'I see. Thank you.'

Cry, damn you.

'It seems, sir, that the accident was entirely the fault of the other driver. He was overtaking. A witness said that there just wasn't room. There was nothing that your wife . . . if it was your wife . . . could have done.'

'It was my wife, officer. Nobody else would have had those red shoes in the car.'

It was the shoes that puzzled him. Why should she have been taking them? She had God knows how many other pairs she could have taken. Why had she taken her very favourite pair, and to Diss?

The policeman had gone half an hour ago, and he had done nothing, except think about having another wonderful glass of water, and then pour more Noilly Prat into his drink instead. He shouldn't have poured himself any more. He had a lot of phone calls to make, and he didn't want to end the evening slurring his words. He wanted to be dignified. He would need to have his wits about him. But he had persuaded himself that in pouring more Noilly Prat he was weakening the overall alcoholic content of his drink, since Noilly Prat was less alcoholic than gin, so that was all right.

He'd wished that he hadn't hidden the drink behind his wedding photograph. It had been difficult to recover it without looking at the photograph, and he could hardly bear to do that. Those smiles. That radiance. Those hopes. He waited for the tears to come. He waited in vain.

So many phone calls. Oh, the burden of those calls. He felt so alone, so desperately alone. That was ridiculous. He had two devoted brothers, many friends he could rely on for support. And Helen. There was no need to be alone. He could ask Helen to come round. No, Helen here? How insensitive would that be?

He could go round to be with her, though. He needed her. He must phone her first. But what could he say? Bad news, Helen. No. Wonderful news, Helen.' No!

Hello, darling. We've often talked about what we'd do if we were free, you've urged me to divorce Deborah, and I've said I just couldn't, I couldn't bear to hurt her that much, well, fate has taken a hand, she's been killed, instantly, outright, thank goodness for that. We're free, my darling, to spend the rest of our life together. Isn't that wonderful?

Couldn't do it. Not yet anyway. Certainly couldn't do it in this room, in front of that photograph.

Probably he'd need another drink before he rang her, and that thought struck him as very odd.

No. It wasn't odd. It was . . . seemly. He had loved Deborah for, oh, almost twenty-five years. Only in the last few years had he . . . after he'd met Helen . . . and even then he and Deborah had had good loving times. He didn't think that she had suspected anything. She had continued to look after him most splendidly. He owed her a seemly death, a respected death. He . . . he loved her. In his way. Yes, he did. Despite . . . although . . . oh, God.

No, he must ring Max first. Except he couldn't. Max didn't like being phoned at work. His bosses frowned upon personal calls. We were six hours ahead of Canada. Max usually finished work at about five-thirty. He'd try him on his mobile at twenty to six Canadian time.

That meant that he'd have to stay at least reasonably sober until twenty to twelve British time. Oh, Lord.

It had to be Charlotte. Oh, God.

He forced himself to dial the dreaded number. He hoped he'd get straight through to her, so that in an instant the whole problem of speaking to each other after all those years would have been solved.

'Yep?'

'Oh, hello, Chuck. When I rang you earlier it was because I'd had a message that the police wanted to see me.'

'You thought Charlie'd screwed up again.'

'Yes. I have to say I wondered. But it wasn't that. No, it was . . . there's been a car crash. Charlotte's mum's been killed, Chuck.'

'Oh, my God.'

'Yes. Can I speak to her, please?'

'Trouble is, Mr Hollinghurst . . .'

'Yes?'

'Trouble is . . . oh, and I'm sorry. Real sorry. That's a cunt of a thing to happen. Sorry. Bad language.'

'Hardly matters under the circumstances.'

'No. Quite. Trouble is, Mr Hollinghurst, I'll have to tell her what's happened or she won't come to the phone. She'll be so, Tell him to go fuck himself. Oh, sorry.'

'No. I have a pretty good idea how she talks about me, Chuck. OK, Chuck. Tell her.'

'Shit, man, I'm not looking forward to this.'

'Take your time. I'll wait.'

While he waited, James hurried over to his gin and Noilly Prat and took it back to the phone. He sat on the purple chaise longue and waited. The silence went on and on. It was awful to be so close to her and yet so far away. He longed to hear her voice. She was a woman now. How much would her voice have changed in five years? How much suffering would there be in it? How much evidence of . . . abuse, frailty, self-harm? He couldn't face up to the word 'drugs' even in his thoughts. But nothing could be worse than her silence. Oh, Charlotte, my darling, speak to me, please.

'Hi.'

He nodded sadly at the invisible Chuck.

'Hi.'

'No go, I'm afraid.'

'Oh, shit, Chuck.'

'I know. I know.'

'How's she . . . taken it?'

'Floods of tears. Floods of tears, Mr Hollinghurst.'

James envied her.

'Didn't she say anything?'

'She said to tell you she's sorry.'

James felt absurdly pleased, and embarrassed at feeling so pleased. It seemed inexcusably self-centred at this moment. Even to be aware that he was being self-centred seemed self-centred. But he was always hard on himself.

Besides, what she had said, it was nothing.

But it was also everything.

He put the phone down very slowly. He decided that it would do him no harm to have just one more drink. Just Noilly Prat, though. No gin. He picked up the Noilly Prat bottle, looked at it with unseeing eyes and put it down again. Just gin would make more sense, because gin could be diluted with tonic.

He walked slowly back to the phone, taking a sip of the drink as he did so. He realised that he hadn't done a very good job with the dilution. Diluting drinks had never been one of his strong points. And a gin, Noilly Prat and tonic just wasn't quite right. What did it matter? What did the taste of a drink matter compared with . . . with the enormity . . .

He decided not to dilute it further. He would sip it slowly instead.

Who should he ring next? Helen? He still wasn't ready for that. Someone on Deborah's side? Have to be her sister. Couldn't face that yet either. Couldn't face being the messenger of such terrible news. A whole family, a close family, all in tears. Couldn't bear the thought.

Couldn't bear telling the terrible news, when to him it wasn't terrible, that was what was so terrible.

Have to be Charles, his eldest brother, his hero, his mentor, his inspiration, his guide, his lodestone.

*   *   *

36

'That's the phone.'

'Don't answer it. Valerie, please. Don't.'

'I should. It might be somebody.'

'It might be a call centre in India offering me free balance transfers. Don't go.'

It was too late anyway. It had gone onto the answer machine.

'Darling, I really want this meal uninterrupted. This oxtail is awesome. Awesome.'

'I can't believe you wanted oxtail in June, in a heatwave.'

'Well, I did. I get salads everywhere I go. Thank goodness I'm not going to America this summer. I hate those salads as starters. So pointless.'

'Can I at least go and listen to see if there's a message?'

'You sound as if you think you need my permission.'

'I do when you're like this. I do when your stomach's involved.'

They were eating in the dining room. The mullioned windows were open, a light breeze from the east was wafting in, rippling Charles's luxuriant beard ever so gently, and it was pleasantly cool in the dark elegant sixteenth-century room.

Valerie – Charles didn't permit her to be called Val by anyone – was seated at the head of the table, with Charles at her left hand. The table was so large that to have each sat at one end would have been to risk seeming like a scene in a comedy, and Charles, for all his virtues, didn't much like being an object of amusement.

'Honestly, if it's an emergency, they'll ring back straight away. Go if you must, darling, I'm not stopping you, but I really don't want you to. These next days are going to be a logistical nightmare, the oxtail is quite beautiful, these sweet young turnips are little poems, it isn't just a question of my stomach, it's a question of respect, Valerie. Respect for your wonderful cooking. Please. I need this evening.'

'All right.'

Charles ate more slowly with each passing year, and every mouthful of this was worth savouring. The carrots were bursting with flavour, the meat clung gelatinously to the bone, the sauce was rich and deep. The thought of five concerts in six days in Europe, planned by a madman, faded. And then, three days' holiday in lovely, much-mocked Belgium, in Ghent, which was Bruges without the crowds, the reflections of the spires and gables shimmering on the canals, the choice of cold beers, the marvellous food, French quality, German quantity. His first break for four months. He could hardly wait. Poor Valerie. She didn't really like cities. Poor Valerie, she found his long meals tedious. She was still itching to listen to their message. He chewed even more slowly, and he was going to have seconds.

It wasn't that he was cruel, but this was his day, his space, his renewal.

Valerie didn't understand.

Deborah would understand.

Sometimes – how James would laugh if he mentioned it – he envied his youngest brother.

Philip, the middle brother, was sitting outside the little wooden summer house in his pleasant garden on the outskirts of Leighton Buzzard, reading in the evening sunshine. He had taken his massage chair outside and was gently manipulating himself on it as he read. He was finding it hard to concentrate this evening, in this heat, and the book was hardly a page turner. It was a comparative study of acidity in the oceans.

The cordless phone sounded shrill and invasive in this suburban setting. It gave him quite a shock.

Not as great a shock as James's news, though.

'Deborah!'

'I know.'

'Of all people.'

'Exactly.'

'How?'

Philip listened to the story of the car crash in silence. Then he said, 'Oh, James, I am so sorry. Bloody bastard young men with too much money. Bloody Jeremy Clarkson has a lot to answer for.'

'Oh, Philip, that's so unfair. That's ridiculous. Why drag him in? Anyway, who cares? She's dead, Philip.'

'Shall I come over?'

'This sounds awful, Philip, but . . . I don't think I could cope . . . not tonight.'

'No, no. No problem. Tomorrow, maybe. I'm supposed to be at work, but I can come any time if you'd like it.'

'I don't know. I just don't know, Philip.'

Philip said that he would ring in the morning about eight, before he set off, to see if James needed him.

'Thanks.'

'James?'

'Yes?'

'Love you.'

Who next? Mum? Oh, God. She'd blame him. I knew something like this would happen. You haven't looked after her.

He went to the gin bottle, held it over his glass, thought of his mum listening for signs of thickening in his speech, sighed deeply, put it down again, and, on an impulse, phoned Deborah's sister.

'Fliss Parkington-Baines.'

'Hello, Fliss, it's James.'

'Hello, James!!' This in her two-exclamation-marks voice,

39

as if she was really delighted to hear from him, as if there was nobody in the world she'd rather hear from, and perhaps there wasn't, except the Queen, David Cameron and James Blunt.

Her good cheer didn't make James's task any easier.

'I'm afraid I've got bad news, Fliss.' Already the words were beginning to hang heavy, burdened by all the repetition that was to come. 'Very bad news. Um . . .' How could he say the monstrous words, cut through her good cheer, with Dominic in Indonesia on business as he suddenly remembered. He swallowed. 'Deborah's dead.'

'No!'

It was a cry of pain from a wounded animal, a yell of protest from a middle-class sister, a scream of disbelief and yet of instant understanding.

He started telling her about the car crash, the driver of the Porsche, the fact that it had happened near Diss.

'Diss? We don't know anyone near Diss. Do you?'

It was as if she was clinging to the hope that, since the location was unbelievable, the whole story was untrue.

When he had finished his sad tale, Fliss asked if there was anything she could do, and he asked her if she could break the news to the Harcourt clan. She agreed, but reluctantly.

'No, look, Fliss,' he said, 'you don't want to, it'll be very difficult, it was unfair to ask, I'll do it.'

'I'll do it, James,' she said grimly, through gritted teeth. 'I said I'll do it and I'll do it.'

He groaned inwardly. Why did so many of their conversations end with gritted teeth?

'Oh, dear,' said Fliss. 'Oh, dear. I think I'm going to cry.'

'Do. Do, Fliss. I have.'

How many lies was he going to have to tell in the days ahead?

* * *

Mum. Mum next.

He looked at the gin bottle on the sideboard, but didn't dare go near it.

His mother was shocked, very shocked. With every telling the irresponsibility of the driver of the Porsche grew slightly greater. With every telling the fact of Deborah's having been near Diss grew more mysterious. When he had finished, she said, 'I'm so sorry, James. First Philip and now this.'

Philip's wife had died three years ago. James felt a spasm of irritation, swiftly quenched. It was natural for his mother to see it all from her point of view. That's two sons who've put me through pain and suffering because I love them so much. It'll be Charles next, you mark my words. Valerie'll fall off a cliff path on one of their walks or something.

Sometimes James felt that he could see right into his mother's subconscious.

'I loved her, James,' she said. 'I hope you know that. Well, how could you not love her?'

He was already beginning to ask himself that question. Although he did, didn't he, in his . . .

'Am I interrupting a programme?' he asked, hoping to find an excuse to ring off.

'No. It's all right. I've lost the thread. Another girl's been strangled while we've been talking, but I won't know who or why.'

They talked on for a bit, both of them coming slowly to terms with the enormity of what had happened, and then his mother suddenly came out with one of those devastating remarks of hers which showed that she was incapable of believing that her youngest son was not responsible to some extent for whatever had happened.

'You had had her car properly serviced, hadn't you?' she asked.

*   *   *

'You are going to ring him, aren't you?'

Charles knew that to a certain extent it was his fault that Valerie was like this. He went away so much and she didn't like travelling. She was quite pleased that he was famous but she had no desire to move in the world of celebrity.

'I'm going to speak to him the moment I've finished this wine, which is bursting with hints of vanilla and raspberry and even, dare I say, a distant intimation of saffron?'

He took another sip. She gave the faintest sigh because his sip had been so small. He decided to speed up, without giving her the satisfaction of seeing that he was speeding up. But it would be cruel to tease her any more.

At last the glass was finished, and he went to the phone, and dialled James's number.

'Hello, James, it's me. Got your message. What's up? . . .'

Valerie saw Charles's face go very serious. Suddenly she felt cold all over. She walked slowly towards him, as if by being closer to him she might divine what had happened.

'No. Oh, James, James. How . . . Oh, my God . . . Oh, James . . . Diss? . . . No, nor do we . . . That'll be it. Oh, James, this is so terrible.'

He turned towards Valerie and mouthed, 'Deborah.'

'I'd say I'd come over, James . . . oh, I do wish Surrey wasn't the wrong side of London . . . but the awful thing is . . . well, I suppose death is never exactly convenient, but I'm off to Copenhagen first thing in the morning, I've got this ridiculous six-day tour, so here I am completely unable to even provide a shoulder to cry on . . . Well, the last concert's Tuesday night in Dresden but then next Wednesday . . . no . . . no, nothing . . . Well, I was going to say that Valerie and I were going to have a couple of days in Ghent . . . Ghent. You know, where they took the bad news to from Aix . . . No, a long time ago, and in a poem, nothing to worry about. Look, I can get back Wednesday, so

42

Thursday or Friday next week would be fine . . . It was only a couple of days, little chance to relax, it's no big deal . . . Well it *is* actually a bigger shame that your wife has died. And James, have you been drinking? . . . Not slurring exactly, but I can tell . . . Don't get upset, James, I'm saying it because I think you'd be sorry if you felt you hadn't been dignified throughout . . . Yes, goodb . . . Wait a minute, Valerie's waving.'

'What is it?' he whispered.

'Ask him if I can do anything. Anything.'

'You know he'll say no.'

'Ask.'

'Hello. Yes, Valerie wonders if she can do anything . . . anything . . . I thought that's what you'd say but don't try to be a hero. Well, she's here, waiting, ready . . . Fine. James, I'll phone every day. And James. I'm doing the Schumann in Helsinki, the one she loves, the piano concerto. I'll be dedicating it to her now.'

Charles put the phone down abruptly and burst into tears. Valerie went to him and held him tight. They stood there, motionless, sharing silent tears as they had rarely shared anything in recent years. Behind them, unnoticed, beyond the mullioned windows, the horizon rose slowly towards the evening sun.

James didn't want to phone Helen from the living room. It would be tactless, tonight, to speak to her with Deborah's radiant wedding photo smiling at him from the top of the piano. Also, the sight of his two older brothers, one at each side of the wedding photo, would have unnerved him. He decided to use the main guest bedroom, which he regarded as neutral ground.

He took his glass with him, topped up with a little gin and quite a lot of tonic. He'd been shaken by Charles's knowing that he'd been drinking. It didn't matter so much with Helen, but still . . . he didn't want to seem weak. He did feel weak, though. He needed the glass at his side.

The sky was beginning to turn a soft, faint, misty pink. He went into the guest bedroom. It smelt of emptiness and perfection. Over the bed there was a beautiful long mirror which made the room look quite large. The walls were salmon pink. On the bed there was a profusion of cushions, and beside the bed there was a carefully chosen selection of books. How Charlotte would snort. He flinched at the thought of Charlotte snorting. The thought of what she might be snorting terrified him.

His heart was pumping. What a day this had been for the pumping of his heart.

He thought, just for a few seconds, about taking all his clothes off. It was a habit they had, to talk on the phone stark naked. It was one of the things that turned them on. There popped into his mind unbidden and unwelcome, the picture of that time, in his office, under the Hammersmith Flyover, when he'd stayed late to plan his polystyrene presentation and had taken all his clothes off and sat there starkers in the dark, the slatted blinds down on his windows and only the faint sodium glow from the street lamps shining on the filing cabinets, and he had phoned her and they had chatted and he'd had the most enormous hard-on, and suddenly the office had been flooded with light and there had been Marcia staring at him and blushing like a beetroot, and she had said, 'Oh, sorry. I've left my diary somewhere. Golly.'

His erection had slowly subsided, and he had said, 'Sorry, Marcia. It's a thing Deborah and I do to keep our marriage exciting,' and she had repeated, 'Golly.'

How could he sack the only woman in England who still said 'Golly'?

He abandoned the thought immediately. Helen wouldn't be expecting him to ring so she wouldn't be naked, and, in any case, it would be utterly bad form, it wouldn't be – that word again – seemly. He broke out into a cold sweat at the very thought of it, took a steadying sip of his drink, and dialled Helen's number.

'Hello.'

'Hello, darling, it's me.'

'Are you all right?'

'Yes, why?'

'You sound . . . I don't know . . . breathless. Tense. Shaky.'

It always amazed him how sensitive she was to every nuance of his existence.

'Yes, well . . . something's happened, Helen.' Adjectives flew through his mind like a flock of starlings. Good news. Bad news. Sad news. Amazing news. Shocking news. Startling news. Incredible news. None of them suitable, none of them quite right. Stick to the facts. 'Helen, Deborah's dead.'

Silence. Words whirring through her mind. Thoughts and emotions churning uncontrollably. No social formula in which to clothe her naked feelings. He sensed it all, and he felt for her. He knew what it was like.

'Are you still there?'

'Yes, sorry, I . . . I'm dumbfounded, James. Deborah, dead? How?'

'Car crash. Head on. Instant.'

'Well, I'm glad of that.'

'Yes, so am I. That it was instant.'

'Yes, that's good.'

'She won't have suffered.'

'No, that's good.'

'I don't expect she even had time to know it was happening.'

'Well, I hope not.'

It was the only aspect of the thing on which they could express any pleasure or agreement, so it wasn't surprising that they laboured the point.

He didn't know what else to say, and it was clear that she didn't either. Well, what could she say? That she was sorry? That she was glad?

'How exactly did it happen?'

She didn't want to know. It was irrelevant. And he didn't want to tell her. It was pointless. But there was no other way to deal with it, and he heard himself starting off on the tale yet again. The Porsche. Diss.

'One odd thing, she—'

Suddenly he realised that he didn't want to tell Helen about the mystery of the red Prada shoes.

'She what?'

'Nothing.'

To tell her would seem like a betrayal of Deborah, a revelation of a secret. This surprised him.

'It doesn't sound like nothing.'

Oh, God.

'No, I was just going to say that she always thought East Anglia was flat and boring, so I'm surprised she was going there.'

It sounded lame, but he just couldn't mention the shoes.

'Oh. Right.'

She knew that he hadn't been going to say that. He could hear it in her voice. He could even sense that she was thinking of saying, 'Maybe she has a lover there,' but had decided not to say it. And, in thinking that she was thinking of saying that, he articulated the thought to himself for the first time. There really was no other explanation for the red shoes.

One of them had to say something pretty quickly, or this conversation was going to be a disaster.

46

If only she was there. If only he could kiss that small, slightly pouty, deeply sexy mouth. If only they didn't need words. For this emotional situation, there were no words.

'Can you come over?' she asked.

'Darling, I'd love to see you, of course, God, I long . . .' to unroll your tights and kiss your slender thighs, to fondle your pert little breasts, to gently bite your stiff nipples, '. . . to see you. But . . . it's not possible tonight. I have phone calls to make. It's just not possible.'

'Tomorrow, then?'

'I think tomorrow's going to be very difficult too, sweetheart.' He began to tell her all the things he would have to do tomorrow. The thought of them all, at the end of this long day, exhausted him. He was going to yawn. No. No. He mustn't.

'I do so want to see you, darling, but you must see that it's difficult.'

'Oh, I do. I do. It's just . . . it seems a shame. I want to help you through this.'

'And I want your help. It's just . . .'

It's just that there's no acceptable formula for appropriate social behaviour in such circumstances. Couldn't say that.

'Look. You finish at lunchtime, don't you, Fridays? Let's . . . I know. I'll meet you for afternoon tea at Whistler's Hotel.'

That wouldn't be too dangerous if somebody saw them. He could take a folder with him and put it on the end of the table, ready to pretend to be discussing business in the unlikely event of anybody he knew being in that slightly raffish hotel.

'Afternoon tea?'

'Well, yes. It seems . . . I don't know . . . appropriate.'

'Well, OK. Yes. Fine. Oh, James.'

So many things in that 'Oh, James.' Shock. Sympathy. Amazement. Hope. Frustration. Love. Fear. Desire. Self-doubt.

Sorrow too, because she was not a cruel person. So many things, and he could sense them all.

'Whistler's at four, then, Friday.'

The light was fading. Wispy clouds were floating very slowly across the sky. They were tinged with subtle colours, mauves and pale yellows and salmon that matched the walls of the spare bedroom. In the north-west the sky was beginning to darken to a fiery red. Islington glowed. Three small boys, normal bedtime suspended, were kicking a football among the parked Audis as they drifted homewards. How could everything be so normal, and so beautiful, on this of all days? He took a large gulp of his drink. He needed it.

It was past ten o'clock now, too early to phone Max and too late to phone anybody else. He realised that he was very hungry. He went to the fridge-freezer, Deborah's pride and joy – Deborah! Oh, God. He would never see her again.

There were so many bits of things in the fridge section. Delicious leftovers hidden under foil and cling film. He couldn't cope, couldn't choose.

He raised his glass to his lips and found that it was empty. He pressed the glass against the fridge freezer and it filled with an avalanche of ice. No. He mustn't. There was Max to ring.

He dropped the ice into the Belfast sink in the crowded utility room – my God, he'd have to learn to use the washer and the dryer. And the ironing board. He could take things round to Helen but was she an ironer? She didn't look like an ironer. Five years, five years of sex, and so much he didn't know about her.

He uncorked a bottle of Brouilly. Well, it was less dangerous than spirits.

He opened a tin of tomato soup, heated it rapidly, began

to eat it eagerly. Lovely. There was something in it, some secret ingredient, that made the thought of it irresistible to men. Halfway through, as always, it began to disgust him. He struggled on for a bit, then poured water into the soup to weaken the mixture, and poured it down the sink.

Sardines. He had a craving for sardines. A bit strong for the Brouilly, but this wasn't an evening for purists.

Halfway through the tin he suddenly felt absolutely disgusted by the taste of tinned sardines. He chucked the tin into the elegantly concealed waste bin.

He began to feel very uncomfortable in the kitchen. It was Deborah's room, friendly, lived-in, foody, attractive but unpretentious and rather higgledy-piggledy.

He remembered that there was a box of chocolates in the living room. It was up to him to finish them now.

No need now to defer to Deborah's wants. He chose the marzipan one from both levels, chewed them greedily, not popping them into his mouth whole as Deborah insisted. Manners hardly mattered now.

Half a tin of tomato soup, half a tin of sardines, two chocolates filled with marzipan. It was not the best three-course meal he had ever eaten.

He went to the phone. He would ring Helen, go straight round, fuck her most tremendously.

He dialled her number, then put the phone down hurriedly.

He decided to make a list of everything he had to do tomorrow. That calmed him. That brought a bit of instant order into his life.

He sat at the mahogany table in the small dining room with the burgundy walls which were just a little darker than the Brouilly, and there, where they had hosted so many little dinner parties over the years, he began his list.

Vicar. (*Never met him. Will he be cross because I never ever went to church?*)

Funeral Director. (*The Hutchinsons used Ferris's Funeral Services.*)

The Hutchinsons. (*Were Ferris's Funeral Services any good?*)

Marcia. (*Tell her the bad news. Cut her off if she offers help i.e. her body.*)

Vernon and Ursula Norris. Tom and Jen . . .

Oh, sod it. Do it tomorrow.

He dropped the list into the waste bin.

He switched the television on, flicked though the channels, saw a pathologist cutting out the left eye of a middle-aged man and dropping it into a bottle, a panellist in a panic as he thought of the ridicule he was going to get from his workmates after he'd failed to name the capital of Hungary, a C-list fashion designer eating leeches in a mangrove swamp, an audience roaring as an overpaid chat show host held out a box of chocolates to a pretty actress and said, 'Can I give you one?', a pathologist cutting up a pretty girl, a celebrity chef cutting up a bulb of fennel, blood pouring from the stomach of a woman in a crypt, an ugly twenty-two-stone man with a horrendous paunch throwing a dart at a board, a lion eating a cheetah, a pathologist cutting up a gay young man, a manly Rock Hudson trying to seduce a virginal Doris Day, a pathologist cutting up a very obese man, a celebrity chef cutting up a loin of pork, and two sloths copulating very . . . well . . . slothfully.

He switched off, poured himself another glass of Brouilly, went to the waste bin, rescued his list, went back to the dining room, stretched the list out on the kitchen table, trying to iron it with his hands, added one more name, Mike . . . Oh God, should he invite Mike, how would he behave? . . . He began to think about Mike, once his best friend, now a wreck. Memories of happier times with Mike. Lots of drinking. He took a couple more sips of the Brouilly. His head dropped.

He woke suddenly, to find himself face down on a crumpled piece of paper covered in traces of tomato soup and sardine oil. He had no idea where he was. At first he felt that Deborah's death was part of a dream. Then he was wide awake and standing up and knocking his red wine all over the carpet.

'Oh, shit,' he shouted to nobody.

What did you put on red wine? White wine? Salt? Lavatory paper? He tore off some toilet rolls and stamped around on them, watching them go red. Then he remembered that Deborah had some stuff that worked wonders. He rummaged around under the sink, found the stuff, stood up, bashed his head on the edge of the cupboard door, swore violently to the empty room, and worked away on the stain, with moderate success.

Max. He was supposed to be ringing Max.

He felt as though he had been asleep for several hours, but it was only twenty to twelve. He dialled his son's mobile number very carefully, feeling dismayingly drunk.

'Hi, Dad. How are you?'

He'd never get used to phones that showed you who was ringing. He didn't like them. It cut into the preliminaries, the careful approach to difficult subjects. He was thrown by Max's cheeriness. How could he destroy that carefree youthful happiness? He felt about a hundred and five.

'I'm fine, Max. Bit drunk . . .' get that in before Max did, '. . . but fine.'

'Great to hear from you, Dad.'

'Not really.'

'What?'

'I've got some terribly bad news, Max. It's your mum. She's . . .'

He couldn't say the word.

'What? Not . . . ?'

Max couldn't say the word either.

'She was in a very bad car crash, Max. I'm afraid . . . I'm afraid she was killed.'

'No!'

James shuddered. He had fantasised about something that could cause his son such grief. In that moment he realised just how much he loved Max.

'I'm afraid so, Max. Max, at least it was instant. She didn't suffer.'

But Max was clearly too shocked, too bereft, to even care about that at that moment, and as he heard the sorrow of his distant son, James felt real sorrow too. He told Max a few more details. By now the driver of the Porsche was a homicidal villain. They needed a villain, father and son, separated by thousands of miles.

James told Max about his conversation with Chuck, but he could tell that his long-lost sister hardly registered in the ghastly slipstream of his mother's death. Max was in deep shock. He told Max who he'd rung (omitting Helen) and Max wasn't interested. He asked Max if there was anyone he'd like him to ring, and he was too numb to care.

'So when's the funeral?' he asked eventually.

'I don't know. Rather dependent on when you can come.'

'I'll phone Mr Jellico tonight, and then I'll check the airlines. Oh, Dad, I can't believe this. Not Mum.'

'I know. If anyone was indestructible, it was her.'

'Dad?' Suddenly Max sounded young, younger than his twenty-two years. Suddenly he sounded like a boy who needed his father. 'I've got some leave owing. I could stay a bit after the funeral. Like a week maybe.'

A week. A whole week with Max. James felt dismayed. He felt dismayed that there would be a whole week in which it would be very hard, even downright dangerous, to see Helen. He felt dismayed that his behaviour, his desire, his love had led him into becoming a man who was dismayed at the thought of his son's staying for a week.

'A week. That would be wonderful, Max. That would be simply great.'

James was beginning to realise that things were not going to be as easy as he had thought. If only life was a fantasy.

Thursday

The alarm woke James at half past seven, as usual. He woke slowly, and from a long way off. His head was heavy. His sleep had been deep but troubled.

He turned to face Deborah, reached out with his right hand to stroke the ample curve of her admired and envied buttocks, very very gently, so gently that he wouldn't wake her if she was fast asleep, but would stimulate her to a faint moan of yawned pleasure if she was sleeping lightly, and, if she was already awake, would reassure her that he was still fond of her, even though he was no longer interested in the glories that had once banished all thoughts of early-morning tea from the first minutes of the day.

There were no curves. There were no buttocks. His arm felt only space, and suddenly all the events of the day before came flooding back. His head was heavy because he had drunk too much, and because he had taken a temazepam tablet when sleep wouldn't come, when the empty bed that he had dreamt about had been more than he could bear.

Philip had said that he would ring at eight. He hoped he would. He would ask him to come and help. He couldn't face everything that had to be done without some form of support. And Philip was easy, reliable, calm, methodical. In his adoration and admiration of Charles he sometimes forgot how much he liked Philip.

He took a shower, and washed his hair, removing any traces of tomato soup and sardine oil that he might have picked up when he'd fallen asleep on his list.

If only he could just leave, just pack a suitcase and go to Helen's.

He looked out of the window. It was another stunning Wimbledon and barbecue day, so beautiful even in Islington, so inappropriate. A faint residue of mist softened the sunlight.

He shaved, cleaned his teeth; his gums were bleeding, it was the tension, but he must check to see if he'd remembered to make another appointment at the hygienist's.

He dressed for work, remembered that he wasn't going to work, took off his suit and put on jeans and a denim shirt, decided they weren't respectable enough or sad enough, took them off and was naked except for his purple pants when Philip rang.

'How are you?'

'Fine. Well, you know.'

'I can imagine. James, would you like me to come over?'

'Do you know, Philip, I really would. Can you? Is it all right?'

'No problem. My statistics will all still be there tomorrow, and I'm pretty much my own boss, you know.'

'There's such a lot to do and I think I'm still in shock.'

'You will be. You must be.'

Yes, I must, thought James. Even if I'm not, and I'm not sure if I am, I must seem to be. God, this is going to be hard.

He selected a pair of black trousers and a dark blue shirt. With a black belt and black shoes he would look sad and dignified without actually looking as though he was in mourning.

It dawned on him that Helen might ring while Philip was there. For years she had been unable to ring him at his home. It had upset her occasionally, although most of the time she had accepted it as sensible and inevitable. Today she would feel that she could ring, and so she would. It would be a defining moment for her. How awful it would be if she did.

He started to put on his shirt and then stopped. He was almost naked, it was early morning, it wouldn't be so terrible, this morning, to phone her in the altogether.

He took off his shirt and his purple pants, picked up the cordless phone, and went into the spare bedroom, far from prying photographs. He sat on the bed and dialled.

Her voice was sleepy.

'You've woken me up.'

It was a rebuke.

'You know I don't work Thursday mornings.'

Helen and her friend Fiona ran a smart little dress shop in Chelsea. It was quiet enough for them to take it in turns to attend, except on Saturdays. James thought they were playing at it, and had been unwise enough to say so once. It was not a thing you would say twice.

'Sorry, darling, but I needed to speak to you.' He amended the sentence hurriedly. 'I wanted to speak to you.'

'That's nice.'

She was mollified. He breathed a sigh of relief. He began to be glad that he had taken his pants off. Things would have been tight.

'Are you naked?' he asked.

'Of course. Are you?'

'Yes.'

'Oh, James. Oh, James, my darling. Are you . . . ?'

'Very. Oh, Helen.'

Her pouty mouth. Her pert breasts. Her slim arms. Her

disturbingly neat bottom. Her pale soft skin. Her wide green eyes.

'Oh, Helen. Oh, my God.'

It was so quick. Absurdly quick. Fierce, painful, glorious, uncontrollable yet perfectly synchronised.

'God, that was good. Oh, Helen darling, you are so unbelievably lovely, my darling. Um . . .' The gear change was going to be difficult, very difficult. 'Um . . . well, I'd better get dressed, I suppose. My brother Philip's coming round to help. There's such a lot to do.'

'Poor you. I wish I could be with you.'

'I know. So do I. Um . . . the . . . um . . . the thing is, Helen . . . oh, God, I wish you could be with me, but the thing is . . .' Oh, Lord, this was difficult. 'The thing is . . . I thought maybe you might phone me today, but Philip's going to be here and . . . um . . . it could be awkward . . . a bit.'

There was a moment's silence.

'Is that why you rang?'

'No. Well, I mean . . . no, I really wanted to . . . you know . . . what we did . . . but yes, I knew I had to talk to you about this. Obviously Philip doesn't know anything about us, and it would be very hard to explain.'

'I understand.'

'But you're not happy. I can tell you're not happy.'

'Well . . . I do understand, James. I can see the difficulties. It's just . . . nothing's changed.'

'It's early days. I want these next days to be dignified in memory of Deborah. She deserves that.'

'I know. I agree. I never wanted to hurt her, James. You know that. That's why I accepted . . . everything. But now . . . well, it's a bit galling to find that nothing has changed.'

'Everything's changed. I want to marry you and live the rest of my life with you and soon I'll be able to. We just have to be patient.'

'I know. I know you're right. I know how dreadfully difficult this is for you. I really do, darling. It's just that I've been patient for so long. And now . . .'

'We'll talk about it tomorrow, over tea.'

'Yes. We'll talk about it tomorrow.'

From her repetition of his words he sensed how vulnerable she felt.

'Bye, James.'

From the abrupt way she rang off he knew that she had been about to cry.

He couldn't cry. He just felt . . . flat. Flat, in his situation? He shook his head in disbelief at himself.

His first phone call, and already he was exhausted.

He opened the window of the spare bedroom, for fear that Philip would detect a faint odour of semen. In came the smell of heat, grass and petrol.

He took another shower, then went back into the master bedroom, tried not to look at the smiling photo of Deborah on the dressing table, kissed the photo of a fourteen-year-old Charlotte, and dressed.

He made himself his usual breakfast: two slices of toast which he cut into halves and covered with spreadable butter on its own, or marmalade, or honey, in a different order every day, lest he should feel that he was becoming a creature of habit. The order this morning was marmalade (Seville orange), butter, honey, and marmalade again (three-fruit).

At ten past nine – give her time in case she was a few minutes late and punctuality wasn't one of her virtues, but come to think of it, what were her virtues? – he phoned Marcia.

'It's me. Marcia, I'm not coming in today.'

'Crikey. Are you ill?'

'No. Marcia, you remember that police message.'

'I remember. The one I almost forgot and then remembered.'

A feeling of dread shuddered through his body, dread of all the sympathy he was going to get, from Marcia, from everyone at Globpack UK, from his friends, from his fitness trainer, from his acupuncturist. Sympathy and pity.

'It was to tell me . . . Deborah's been killed.'

'What??? Oh no!! James! Oh, James!! Oh, that's . . . awful!! That's . . . terrible!!!'

There were a lot of exclamation marks in Marcia's young life.

'How?'

'Car crash. Head on.'

'Oh, well, I suppose . . . Oh, God, though.'

'Yes.'

Through it all he went. How many times was he going to have to go through all this today?

'Oh, James, I am so very, very sorry. Is there anything I can do?'

'Well, tell everybody who needs to know.'

'I sort of meant . . . is there anything personal? I mean . . . this evening, for instance. I don't like to think of you all alone.'

'That's very sweet of you, Marcia.' Oh, give me strength. 'But my brother's going to be here.' Philip would have long gone, no doubt, but there was no need to add that.

'The concert pianist?'

'The other one.'

'Well, that's all right, then. I . . . p'r'aps I shouldn't say this but I . . . you're more than a boss to me, Mr Hollinghurst, and I . . .'

Oh, no. Oh, suffering serpents and suppurating sores, this was terrible. Interrupt, quickly. No time to lose.

'Thank you, Marcia. That's very sweet of you.'

Thank God, the doorbell. His sweet sweet friend the doorbell.

'Philip's here. I've got to go.'

A gust of brotherly love disturbed the still, windless morning. 'The other one.' Poor Philip, clever scientist, esteemed statistician, conducting vital research into climate change, a nobody in celebrity Britain.

They hugged. James always hugged Charles, you had to, Charles was a hugger, but he didn't remember Philip ever hugging him before.

James and Charles had broad, almost round faces from their mother. Philip had his father's long, narrow, slightly beaky face. It was a face that suggested that he might also have his father's caustic tongue. It was not a relaxing face. But Philip was kind and much more easy-going than he looked. James felt so very pleased that he was there. Philip met his eyes, shook his head as if to rid himself of the bad news, and looked away.

'The accident's made the nationals,' he said, and he handed James a paper. 'Page seven.'

'*Tragic death of joy-ride war hero*,' read James. What?

'*Craig Wilson came back to England from Afghanistan just three days ago, delighted to be alive after seeing two of his friends killed in Helmand Province.*' Oh, no. '*Now he too is dead, killed in a head-on car crash in a borrowed Porsche on the A143 near Diss.*

'*The driver of the other car, a 46-year-old woman, also died.*

'*"I feel so guilty," said Craig's best friend, local skip magnate Ben Postgate (30) yesterday. "There hasn't been much joy in his life recently, and I lent him my Porsche for a joy ride. He was all properly insured and stuff, and he was a very good driver, but I think the fun of it, after what he'd been through, must have gone to his head. I keep saying to myself, "Oh, if only I hadn't."*

'*"Craig was a brave committed soldier and a thoroughly nice lad who had a great life in front of him," commented his commanding officer, Colonel Brian McIntyre. "We're all devastated."'*

James shared a grimace with Philip.

'I know,' said Philip. 'All Deborah's vitality, her beauty, her kindness, her energy, all described as *"the driver of the other car"*.' He wasn't aware that he was sometimes called 'the other brother'. 'Upstaged in death. Mind you, she had no shred of pomposity or self-importance. She wouldn't have minded.'

'No. A fitting obituary, then, perhaps.'

James didn't tell Philip why he had been grimacing. He had lost his villain. He no longer had anybody to blame.

He gave Philip a list of tasks. Look on the web for information about funeral directors in Islington and how much they cost. Look for any comment pages, if there were such things. *First-rate service. Will definitely use them next time. Snotty-nosed, supercilious and extortionate. Wouldn't touch them with a barge pole.* Find a vicar. How did you do that? Look up 'Vicars' in Yellow Pages? Use the web again. Vicars, Islington, search. Try to begin to fix the date of the funeral. Try to avoid Tuesday and Wednesday, Charles wouldn't be able to make it. Make morning coffee. Make lunch. Answer phone and door as required.

'I so appreciate this, Philip.'

'No probs.'

He left Philip indoors with the land line, got his mobile, went out into the garden, sat on the white William Morris chair Deborah had picked up in a little shop in Winchcombe, placed his address book and a glass of chilled water on the cast-iron table she had spotted in Much Wenlock, wondered briefly if there was one single thing in the whole house and garden, except stains, for which he was responsible.

He looked round the garden, delaying the moment when he would have to begin. It was broken up into little gravelled areas and small, irregular flower beds, which cleverly hid its narrowness and its uninspiring rectangular shape. There were cyclamens and lilies and attractive green ferns whose names he couldn't remember. The smell from the pots of lavender brought back memories of lunches taken outdoors in weather such as this. The passiflora growing up the back wall was in full flower. Giant grasses were used as windbreaks. And all this, the ingenuity, the elegance, the restraint, had all been created by Deborah.

He sat in the middle of this living memorial to her artistry, and he felt awkward and ashamed. He sensed that he was about to miss her deeply, and so, in the end, he picked up the telephone almost eagerly.

And began.

'All right, all right, I'm coming as fast as I can.'

Stanley Hollinghurst, James's uncle, his father's brother, talked to himself quite a lot now. He didn't care. Charles had once pointed it out, and that evening he had caught himself saying, 'So, you're talking to yourself, are you? Well, Charles, you're wrong. It isn't the first sign of madness. It's the first sign that there are sod all other people to talk to. It's all right for you, you're surrounded by people, you complacent young fool, but I talk to myself because it's someone to listen to, all right?' And then the humour of his talking to himself about his habit of talking to himself had struck him, and he'd laughed till his teeth came out.

'Don't ring off. I'm on my way.'

He didn't have an answer machine. He was a Luddite. Well, he was an anthropologist. The past was his business. Or had been. All that was in the past now. Ha ha! Ironic!

He got to the phone while it was still ringing. Must be somebody he knew, making allowances.

'Stanley Hollinghurst, OBE.'

'Stanley! You haven't got an OBE.'

'No, but very few people round here know that. How are you, James?'

'Fine. Stanley, I—'

'How are Charles and Philip?'

'Fine. Charles is on a concert tour and Philip's here.'

'Is he? Well, tell him not to worry about all that global warming stuff. I think it's great.'

'Stanley, I've got—'

'Human race deserves it. Can't hurt me. I'll be gone.'

'Stanley, I've got some—'

'Spaniards sizzling. French frying. What's the problem?'

'Stanley, I've got some bad—'

'Brighton under six feet of water. All those homos and lesbians shitting themselves.'

'Stanley! That's terrible.'

'I know. I do so enjoy saying things like that, though. People are so bloody self-righteous, James.'

'Stanley, has it occurred to you that I might have rung you because I have something to tell you?'

'Ah. Yes. Sorry. Like the sound of my voice. You will when you live alone.'

'Stanley, I do live alone.'

'What? What are you on about?'

'Stanley, Deborah's dead.'

Stanley remained silent throughout the whole sad story, and when James had finished, he said, in the soft, sincere, real voice he hadn't used since Mollie died thirty-three years ago, 'James, I'm so sorry. I really am. Deborah, of all people. She was the best of the whole bunch, James.'

Mike next. No, difficult. Gordon Tollington first. Easier. Gordon and he went right back to the Dorking days. He was the only man who liked food even more than James did. Fifty-three years old, sold out for millions. Rich, idle and fat. Good company, though. Haven't seen them for far too long.

Gordon Tollington listened in almost total silence, only interrupting, as it seemed most people did, to say, 'Diss?', as if Diss was just outside Timbuktu. When he rang off, Gordon's face was grim.

He went out into the spacious garden, with its long sloping lawns.

Stephanie was sliding broad beans out of their pods in the shade.

He slumped down beside her and told her the bad news. They sat in silent shock.

'Oh, my God,' he said suddenly.

'I know. It's just sunk in, hasn't it? It's so awful.'

'Not that. Well, that too, of course. But . . . I bet the funeral will be next Wednesday. It'll take that long to organise.'

'So?'

'That's the day we're going to the Fat Duck.'

'For shame, Gordon. Is a meal more important than Deborah's death?'

'It isn't *a* meal. It's *the* meal. We booked months ago.'

'Gordon, I don't believe what I'm hearing.'

'I know, but . . . I loved Deborah, Steph . . . loved her, wonderful woman, I'm very sad. But we can't bring her back, and you have to book months in advance.'

'I think we have to go.'

'Well, I don't know that it's that cut and dried. I think they'll be used to people cancelling. They'll have a cancellation list.'

'I meant, "We have to go to the funeral . . ."'

'Yes. Yes, of course we do. No, I really want to. Of course I do. What do you think I am?'

'It may not be next Wednesday.'

'It will be. Death is never convenient. Do you know, I think I'm fated to die without ever having tasted snail porridge.'

Edward and Jane Winterburn. He'd been quite close to them once. Well, very close to Jane, for a while. Well, she'd been his very first proper girlfriend. She had legs that went on for ever. He'd thought he loved her. He'd thought she loved him. Definitely wrong on the second count, she went off with Ed the day after James had taken her to his college's May Ball. Probably wrong on the first count too, because he got over it pretty quickly. They had stayed friends at first. Then Ed did something he really didn't approve of. Twice, to his knowledge. Went bankrupt, opened up under a new name, owing vast sums that nobody would ever receive. Mocked James for his disapproval, called him naive and stuffy and unrealistically idealistic. After that it had been Christmas cards only. But they had both liked Deborah. Yes, he decided that he'd let them know.

Jane answered. He was pleased about that.

'Bad news, I'm afraid, Jane.'

'Yes. How did you know?'

'What?'

'Has it been on the news?'

'What are you talking about?'

'Ed.'

'Ed?'

'His disappearance. Isn't that what you're ringing about?'

'Ed's disappeared?'

'Yes. Into thin air. I haven't seen him since Tuesday.'

'I don't believe this.'

'He went off to a party in some pub somewhere, round Chelsea, well, it was Roger Dodds's actually, you remember him? I didn't go. He never came back, hasn't been seen since.'

'Good God.'

'I thought that's what you were ringing about.'

'No. I had no idea. I'm so sorry.'

'Thanks. So what *are* you ringing up about, James?'

'Um . . . I've got some news too.'

'Well, I hope yours is a bit more cheerful. I need cheering up.'

'A light went out of the world yesterday morning, James.'

Yes, yes, Tom, but don't overdo it.

He had been surprised to find Tom at home, but Tom had explained that he worked from home two days a week now. All right for some.

'James, I think I'm probably your oldest friend.'

'Undoubtedly. I don't have any other friends from that dreadful prep school.'

'So please, please, feel you can rely on Jen and me for support twenty-four seven.'

'Thank you.'

'Um . . . about the funeral. About the date. Is it decided?'

'Not yet. These things are complicated.'

'The fact is . . .'

'I can only just hear you, Tom.'

'I don't want Jen to hear. She'd be livid if she knew I was asking this. Livid.'

'What are you asking, Tom?'

'The fact is . . . I have two tickets for the Centre Court at Wimbledon for next Thursday. I mean, don't get me wrong, James, that isn't important, isn't remotely important, compared to . . . your tragedy. However . . . James, I've never told another human being this, except the doctors, but I have . . . um . . . a bit of a problem. I . . . not to put too fine a point on it . . . I suffer from premature . . . um . . .'

James knew he shouldn't interrupt but really there had been no scope for fun all morning.

'Ejaculation?'

'No!'

'Baldness?'

'No. Well, yes, but . . . um . . . that's not the . . . and that annoys Jen, actually. The way baldness is said to be a sign of . . . um . . . virility in male mythology. Nonsense, of course.'

James ran his fingers through his thick, riotous hair.

'Absolute nonsense, Tom.'

'Everybody comments on my baldness. "Jen's a lucky woman." "Jen's obviously getting plenty." People can be surprisingly coarse in Godalming.'

'So what you suffer from is . . .'

'Yes. Impotence at an unusually young age. I mean, I was never a several-times-a-night man, if you know what I mean.'

Too much information, Tom.

'Not by a long chalk. I mean, Jen's very sympathetic. She's behind me all the way. As it were. Anyway, the point is . . .'

Ah! At last.

'. . . The point is, I've tried for Centre Court tickets for eighteen years at the tennis club draw. Never got them. Every year Margaret Insole gets two, and she prefers golf. Goes, though, and don't we hear about it? Every sodding serve. Over these last few years as my . . . my problem . . . has got worse, the tickets have become a kind of symbol of my impotence, my general uselessness, James. And this year, bingo, two tickets, ladies' semi-final day. I'd rather a men's day, I find women's tennis boring, but Jen doesn't, of course, and that's what it's all about. So, all I'm saying is, if there

70

is any scope for choice, I'd be enormously grateful if you could avoid today week.'

'I'll do my best, Tom.'

Oh, give me strength, he thought. And he couldn't continue delaying the call to Mike.

Mike was feeling quite depressed and wondered whether to answer the phone. Just before it went onto the answer machine, he found himself picking it up.

'Mike, it's James.'

The contradictory feelings surged. Well, they would have done if he'd had enough energy for surging.

Affection. Only James of the old mob kept in touch. Only James ever took him out and bought him food and drink. The others had smelt his failure, called him less and less often, eventually dropped out of his orbit altogether. His orbit! He didn't have a house any more. He didn't have a wife any more. He didn't have an orbit any more.

Irritation. James never invited him to his home any more, never invited him to meet any of his friends, never wanted to spend more than two minutes in his horrid little pad, always took him to a pub or restaurant. So kind. So demeaning.

Anger. It was never far from the surface. It wasn't so much anger at James himself as at his situation and the way James reminded him of his situation. By phoning him James reminded him of all those people who never phoned. By being kind to him, even in the limited manner of his kindness, James brought home to him that the rest of the world was not kind.

'Well, hello, James. Long time no hear.'

'I know. I'm sorry. You know how things are.'

Only too well.

Mike was shocked at James's news.

'I'm really sorry, James.'

'Thanks. Maybe we could have a drink this weekend.'

'I'm not going anywhere.'

'I'll be glad to get out of the house, to be honest. Mike, I've rung you first of all my friends because I know I've rather let you down. Anyway, mate, how about Saturday evening? Hang a few on. Sup some lotion, as your dad used to say.'

That's right. Remind me I'm working class.

'Fine. Great.'

'I'll need it by then. And by then I'll know the funeral date. Mike, I hope you can come. And for drinks afterwards. At the house.'

When James had rung off, Mike looked at himself in the mirror. His stained T-shirt was a map of his recent pauper's meals. He was unwashed and unshaven. His hair was a tangled jungle. He shuddered.

At the house! It was years since he'd been invited to the house. Maybe it was Deborah who hadn't wanted him anywhere near her. He looked at himself again. Nothing a haircut and a good shave and a clean shirt wouldn't cure. But perhaps he wouldn't bother. Perhaps he'd go like this and embarrass the bastard.

Not a bad bastard, though. He wondered whether to ring his ex-wife and suggest that she came too. Melanie had always liked Deborah. If he could see her again, just once, who knew? He looked in the mirror again. No. No chance. Be good to see her, though. Perhaps. Or awful. Oh, hell.

Fuck them all.

He felt a rivulet of sweat running down his back. There were spreading dark stains under his arms. The sun had moved round, and he'd no longer been sitting in the shade, and he hadn't even noticed. His face was burning, and he had no protection on it. How angry Deborah would have been. 'Do you *want* skin cancer?'

He tried to stand up. The chair came with him. He was stuck to the chair. He had to prise it off.

And even then it was agonising to stand up straight. His back was so stiff.

He went, very cautiously, through one or two of the stretching exercises that Gareth had prescribed. Gareth. Should he cancel him on Saturday? And the acupuncturist? No. If they were any use, if they weren't a waste of money, it was at times like this that they'd be needed. He'd stick to his routine.

He walked slowly into the blessed darkness of the house, the wonderful coolness of the kitchen, then went into the utility room and drank two glasses of chilled water from the fridge-freezer.

He entered the sitting room just as Philip was saying, 'Thank you. Thank you very much for your help,' and putting the phone down.

'I've had enough for one morning,' said James. He couldn't believe that it was only two minutes to twelve. He seemed to have been talking for hours. 'Still a few people to ring, but I can't take any more. Um . . . I never drink before twelve, it's one of my rules, but it'll take two minutes to pour. Would you like something, Philip?'

'Actually a G and T would go down quite well.'

'Fine. I won't drink. I'll only start falling asleep this afternoon if I do.'

'Well, no, if you're not having one . . .'

'No, no. You want one. You must. I'm very grateful.'

He poured Philip's G and T and opened a bottle of German beer for himself.

'I thought you weren't drinking.'

'I don't count beer.'

73

Philip raised his eyebrows, which were scanty affairs compared to James's.

'No need to give me a look. I usually drink too much and in the days to come I'm probably going to drink much too much. Cheers. Thanks for coming.'

'Cheers. Really glad to help.'

'How's it gone?'

'Not bad. I don't think there'll be any real problems. The Hutchinsons were perfectly satisfied with Ferris's. Well, "efficient and only slightly greasily subservient" were the actual words. It looks as if it'll have to be Thursday. The vicar can't do Friday. We could have twelve-thirty or three-thirty. Ferris's recommend that we get back to them pretty quickly. "Experience shows, Mr Hollinghurst, that we do tend to have a bit of a rush in heatwaves."'

'Oh, grab twelve-thirty. The sooner the better, on the day. You said "the vicar". You've found one, then.'

'Your local man is the Reverend Martin Vigar. I told him you weren't religious and he said, "I'm a pretty flexible sort of chap. I was actually thirty-two years with Allied Dunbar before I took up this lark." I didn't quite see that that followed, but I didn't press the point.'

'This "lark"!'

'I know. Not sure I'd want him if I was a fervent believer but he sounds pretty convenient for our job. He asked if you wanted burial or cremation and I had to say I didn't know. He pushed me very strongly towards cremation – apparently graveyards are bursting at the seams in London. I mean, what do you feel?'

'Oh, Lord. Let me think. I need to think about that. Could you . . . um . . . start getting a bit of lunch, anything, just ferret around and see what you can find, and I'll take my beer and . . . think. I'm also going to have a shower. I've sweated rather.'

Upstairs, the house was like a furnace. James had his third shower of the day, the nearest thing to a cold shower that was possible without feeling shock, then sat in the shade in the marital bedroom looking at the photo of Deborah on the dressing table. What would she want? Cremation, surely, her ashes strewn over a field on the family farm, an end to it all. To be somewhere for ever, as bones, that wouldn't be her style at all.

He put on a pair of mauve pants and matching socks. It was so hot in the bedroom. If he wasn't careful he'd need a fourth shower, so he carried his shoes, a pair of grey flannel trousers and a dark green shirt downstairs, where he dressed in the dark cool of the kitchen. Philip gave him quite a long look, and he realised that there was admiration in it. With his hairy chest, his flat (ish) stomach and his muscular legs, he achieved something quite rare in an Englishman in his forties. He didn't look obscene with no clothes on.

'I'm making a Spanish omelette,' said Philip.

'Perfect. I've decided on cremation.'

'Good. That makes it easier. Now, the thing is, it's normal when there isn't what the vicar called "a specific congregational element" – in other words, in English, you didn't attend a particular church – to use the nearest crematorium chapel.'

'Oh, I hate those. The mechanism starting up, the coffin sliding away. If you've watched too much television you expect three pathologists to rush in and shout, "Stop!"'

'I know, but you've never been to any church in Islington, you're not in a strong position.'

'No, you're right. Oh, Lord. Oh, Philip, I dread the day.'

'As of now the vicar can do both of Ferris's times, but he also would like a swift decision. "It's strange," he said, "but deaths tend to come in batches, rather like London buses."'

'Do we really want this man?'

'He'll be perfect for our purposes. I'll book him for the twelve-thirty slot. Oh, and he's booked himself in provisionally to come round at four-thirty on Tuesday for a chat with you about Deborah. "So that I can introduce that personal element that I think is so all-important."'

'I dread it more and more, Philip.'

He whipped the top off another bottle of beer.

Max rang at ten past one, just as James was eating the very last mouthful of the Spanish omelette that Philip had cooked, delicious, the egg with just a faint moistness still, the onions as sweet as blossom, the tiny pieces of potato soft but with just a touch of crispness.

'Hello, Dad. It's ten past seven here but I thought I'd better catch you.'

'Thanks. How are you, Max?'

'I cried myself to sleep.'

James wanted to say, 'So did I,' but he found it hard to lie to Max.

'How are you, Dad?'

'I'm all right. Keeping busy. Philip's here helping. He's just made the most marvellous Spanish omelette. I felt guilty about enjoying it, but the body's a funny thing. My heart's aching, but my taste buds are unmoved. So, what's happening? When are you coming?'

'Well, I've booked my flight provisionally for Tuesday. I'd have liked to have come sooner, but the thing is, Dad . . .' Max hesitated. He sounded embarrassed. 'Dad, something very important is happening here on Monday. Well, it may not seem important to you, but it is to my work and I'd just like to be here. I hope you don't think that sounds awful. Obviously if you really need me before Tuesday I can cancel.'

'No, no, it looks as though the funeral's going to be on Thursday. Tuesday's fine.'

'Are you sure, Dad?'

'Absolutely sure. So . . . what's happening on Monday?'

'It may not seem much to you, Dad, and I mean, Mum's death, I've hardly slept a wink, I'm devastated, but I can't bring her back, and this is . . . well . . . to me it's important, but I don't want not to be with you if you need me . . .'

'I'm all right, Max. Don't tear yourself apart. Come on. Tell me. What's happening on Monday?'

'It probably won't seem important.'

'Tell me.'

James wished he hadn't sounded so abrupt. Max was clearly finding this very difficult.

'It's a big planning meeting about some very important woodland that I care about very much. I've grown to love the Canadian woodlands and I want to be there to support our case.'

It's a relief when your children care about anything, but to care that much about woodlands. And a planning meeting. At twenty-two. Emotion flooded through James.

'I think that's wonderful,' he said, and his voice cracked and at last he felt that he might be able to cry. Philip slipped out of the kitchen so tactfully that it almost seemed tactless. 'Your mum would too.'

'Well, that's what I hope. Anyway, I can stay on afterwards, as I said. I think actually I can stay till Tuesday fortnight.'

A whole fortnight when he'd still have to be secretive about seeing Helen. Stop it.

'Great. That's terrific. I'm delighted you can stay so long.'

And he was. He really was.

'Dad, you mentioned about Charlotte. Be fantastic to see her.'

'Yes, well. Let's hope.'

'Got to rush, Dad. Work.'

'Course. Can't . . .'James's voice began to crack again, '. . . wait to see you.'

At last the tears came. He could cry with pride for his son, but not for the death of his wife.

Philip went off to work after lunch, but offered to come back at half past seven to take James out for a meal. James accepted, and Philip looked pleased.

He was surprised to find how much he wanted Philip to stay all afternoon. He went upstairs and watched him walk down the street to his car. Philip must have sensed that he had done this, because he turned, looked up and gave a short but affectionate, almost emotional wave. This surprised James. Philip was the scientist, the reserved one, the cool one, intelligent rather than intuitive. He found himself waving back as if Philip was emigrating to New Zealand, not popping up to Cambridge for a few hours.

He went out into the airless garden, careful to be well in the shade this time, just in front of the jacuzzi, which had been cleverly squeezed into a corner right at the back of the garden. Those lovely moments in the jacuzzi, over the years, each with a G and T if it was before supper, a brandy if it was after, and, just occasionally, without any alcohol at all, it was known.

He carried the chair and table over, settled himself, opened the address book, stiffened his resolve, reached for the telephone, and dialled.

'Yep?'

'It's me, Chuck. The despised dad.'

'Oh, hi there.'

'Is Charlotte there?'

'Yep, she's here.'

James's desire to hear her voice was almost irresistible. She was probably only a few feet from the phone. It was awful not to know how she looked now, how she would sound now. But he didn't ask to speak to her. She had to be the one to make the move.

'I won't ask to speak to her, but I have a message. The funeral's at twelve-thirty next Thursday.'

James shuddered as he said those words for the first of many times. It brought home to him how final death was.

'A week today.'

'Yep.'

'Got it.'

'Listen to me, Chuck. I love my daughter very very much.'

'I believe that, Mr Hollinghurst.'

'Thank you. And please call me James. I feel I know you.'

'OK. Cool.'

'Chuck, her brother Max is coming back from Canada. They used to get on so well. The thing is, Max would just love to see Charlotte again. And so would I. And so would everyone in the family. She was a lovely girl.'

'She still is, James.'

'Yes, sorry.'

A pigeon, plumped up with pride and passion, was stalking a female very warily.

'I'm so glad that she . . . that you think that she's . . . anyway, all of us would love her to come to the funeral . . . We won't be upset if she doesn't, but we'd be so pleased if she did. She loved her mother once.'

'She still does, Mr . . . James.'

'Oh, Lord, that past tense again. Sorry.'

The pigeon made his move. The object of his desire flew away at top speed. He looked comically deflated.

'Oh, and Chuck, you'll be very welcome too.'

'Thank you, James. That's real neat of you.'

'And at the house afterwards, for the wake.'

'OK. Thanks. Cool.'

'Oh, and Chuck?'

'Yep?'

'There'll be no recriminations. What I mean is, she will be accepted for what she is and the past will not be dragged in.'

'I know what recriminations mean, James.'

'I'm so sorry, Chuck. Of course you do. And if she can't face the house, just the crematorium would be fine.'

'Cool.'

'And vice versa. If she can't face—'

'I know what vice versa means, James.'

'Sorry. Oh, dear, I seem to be having to say sorry a lot, don't I?'

'You sure do, yep.'

'Sorry.'

'I think that could be one of the problems, James.'

'Sorry?'

'All that bourgeois politeness thing. I think that's one of the things Charlie could have been running away from.'

Gordon Tollington walked slowly across the lawn. The air was shimmering with heat. The afternoon was still, but not silent. A woodpecker was drumming nearby, there was the calm, soft drone of a light aircraft, and the reassuring sound of a lawnmower manicuring this safe suburb. The hot weather had brought out the butterflies. Gordon Tollington was a relieved man. And a shamed one.

Steph was half asleep over a John Grisham. She looked up as he approached. His was not a light tread. Unbeknown to them, well beneath the surface of the lawn, moles were panicking.

'Good book?'

'Riveting.'

'That was James.'

80

'Oh.'

'Funeral's a week today.'

He watched her working it out. He hadn't married her for her brains.

'Thursday,' she said.

'Yes. We don't need to cancel the Fat Duck.'

'You look so pleased,' she said. 'I'm ashamed of you, Gordon.'

'I'm ashamed of myself, Steph,' he said, 'but I can't help it.'

He tried Callum, the son of an old school friend who lived in Argentina. He liked Callum, in fact he had sponsored him to help him through art college, and not just so that he could slip a reference to it into a conversation with Charles. He had just graduated, and had been tipped, in one national newspaper, as the one to watch this year. They had been to supper with him and his much tattooed girlfriend Erica. Erica had been so beautiful that he had almost overcome his revulsion to tattoos. The vegetarian moussaka had been a revelation. Callum took his art seriously. Their crazy single-roomed beanbag-bursting sex-smelling apartment had been overflowing with avant-garde pictures and sculptures and posters, but in the surprisingly modern loo there had been just two pictures, exquisite, nicely framed still lifes, each picture consisting of just one fig, so realistic and ripe that you wanted to pluck it out and eat it. Under the pictures were the words *Fig 1* and *Fig 2*. James had loved that.

'Callum. Hello. It's James.'

The story again. The shock again. Oh, God.

'I'm devastated. I cannot believe it,' said Callum. 'She was so lovely, James. I shouldn't say this, but Erica knows it. She was the only woman over thirty I've ever fancied. I've dreamt about her several times.'

* * *

81

His second call to Tom and Jen Preston. He was dreading this one.

He was relieved that it was Jen who answered.

'Oh, hello, Jen. It's James.'

After a few polite exchanges, he braced himself to give the bad news.

'I'm afraid, Jen, the funeral's going to have to be next Thursday. A week today.'

Her silence spoke volumes.

'I really am very sorry, but it is literally the only day that everyone vital can do.'

'So we're not vital!'

'Yes, you are, Jen, but you can do it. I know it's your Wimbledon day, but you *can* do it and there are days that people like the vicar just literally cannot do.'

'He told you. I told him not to tell you, and he told you. He begged, I suppose.'

'He didn't beg, he just asked, quite strongly, yes, but very reasonably.'

'He's useless, James. This is typical of him.'

'Oh, come on, Jen. It's hardly his fault.'

'You aren't married to him.'

'Very true.'

'He never wins anything, and if he ever does, there's guaranteed to be a snag. We buy Friday-afternoon cars. The boiler fails on the coldest day of the winter. The double-glazing firm goes bankrupt halfway through. That's the sort of character he is.'

'You can't blame him for that.'

'I can, James. He's a loser.'

'Look, Jen, may I say something? I don't think Deborah would mind one whit if you went to Wimbledon. Go. Enjoy yourselves. Come over another day and remember Deborah with me. On our own, just the three of us. Much more

82

effective than just being a member of the crowded crematorium chapel, and it will be crowded, Jen. Go, Jen. Honestly. Please.'

'Deborah was my closest friend. She was the most wonderful woman I ever met in my life. The strawberries would rot in my mouth.'

He sat in a stupor in the soupy London air. There were still quite a lot of people to ring. A couple of Cambridge friends, the Hammonds and Roger Dodds – James hadn't shone at Cambridge in the way that Charles and Philip had at Oxford, but his social life had been good. Declan O'Connor and Rod Avery, two escapees from packaging; Sandra Horsfall from the Dorking days, now widowed; Amanda Castlebridge, one of the Glebeland girls. Deborah had still attended occasional girlie reunions with some of the more glamorous alumni of Glebeland School, though she had lost contact with others, including Denise Naylor, Constance Thrabnot (with delight, but we needn't go into that) and Grace Farsley with regret that deepened over the years.

Amanda would round up as many girls as she could. Philip would contact his four children (two of each). Charles was childless. That was about it – for the moment, at any rate. It was enough. How many more times could he describe that wretched accident?

He would start making the calls again soon, but for the moment he was done in. A dreadful feeling was creeping up on him, a debilitating unease that was grabbing him by the throat and making him feel trapped, claustrophobic, as if the garden was a cage in a zoo.

The best of the whole bunch. Lady Deborah. So very special. The only woman over thirty that Callum had ever fancied. The most wonderful woman that Jen Preston had ever met. A light went out of the world yesterday morning.

Was he the only person in the whole world who had forgotten how to appreciate her?

Friday

The alarm woke James at half past seven, as usual. He woke slowly, and from a long way off. His head was heavy. His sleep had been deep but troubled.

He turned to face Deborah, reached out with his right hand to stroke the ample curves of her admired and envied buttocks.

There were no curves. There were no buttocks. His arm felt only space, and suddenly all the events of the last two days came flooding back. His head was heavy because he had drunk too much, and because he had taken a temazepam tablet when sleep wouldn't come, when the empty bed that he had dreamt about had been more than he could bear.

A sickening thud of memory struck him, just as he was summoning up the strength to get out of bed. Today he would have to sack Marcia.

The phone rang while he was in the middle of shaving. He knew it was his mother. The tone was shrill with mother-hood. He would have to answer.

'Are you all right?'

'Yes, Mum. I'm fine. Just shaving.'

'Oh. Sorry.'

'No, no, it's all right.'

'I was a bit worried when you didn't phone yesterday. I thought you would have done. Charles phoned from . . . somewhere, it was raining. Philip phoned. He said you'd probably phone later.'

Yes. It entirely slipped my mind.

'I know. I meant to, but the phone kept going, and then Philip came round to take me out to dinner.'

'I know. He told me he was going to. He's very kind. He's always been kind. He's reserved but actually he's very warm-hearted.'

'I know that, Mum.'

The subtext was, You might try taking a leaf out of his book.

'He really appreciated everything Deborah did for you.'

'I know that, Mum.'

The subtext was, You didn't, always, not sufficiently, anyway.

'You could always have rung me, Mum.'

'I can't hear you, James. You're speaking very quietly.'

'Sorry. I'm holding the phone a bit away from me, so that it doesn't get smothered in shaving cream.'

'Is it the almond one I gave you for Christmas? That makes a good lather, the man said.'

No, I haven't got round to that yet. I find the smell of almond in the morning vaguely sickening.

'Yes. It's lovely. Mum, I have to get ready for work, I'll ring you when I get there.'

'Your father used to sack people if they made too many personal calls.'

The subtext was, You be careful now. I can't believe that the least talented of my three sons can be secure in his employment. The sack now would just put the tin lid on it.

'I am the boss, you know, Mum.'

'Yes, but Americans are sticklers for the rules.'

The subtext was, Of the London office, yes, but you aren't the boss globally, are you?

Why on earth had he told her that?

He chose a pair of green underpants that Helen had once said she liked. Not that tea at Whistler's Hotel was likely to lead on to a sight of his underpants, it wasn't the time, it was too soon, but you never knew. After much hesitation he plumped for a striped shirt full of reds and purples. It wouldn't look good with a tie, but when he took the tie off and went for tea he wouldn't look as if he had just come from work. He also chose the least stuffy of his many dark suits.

After a quick breakfast – honey first, today, then spreadable butter only, then marmalade (three fruits) and finally marmalade (Seville orange thick-cut, not to be confused with the other Seville orange one that he'd chosen yesterday) – he walked briskly to his car. The glory of the morning gave him no pleasure. It was dreadful to have to attempt to sack a pretty young woman on such a morning.

He set off on his tortuous journey across London to Globpack UK. As he drove he thought about his meal with Philip last night. They had reminisced about their childhood in a way they had never done before, as if the shock of Deborah's death had unlocked their tongues. When James had said that he was beginning to find their mother deeply irritating, Philip had reminded him how often she had protected them from their father's wrath. 'She's beginning to be difficult because she's starting to panic about old age, that's all.'

James had been surprised to find how strongly Philip had also felt that in his parents' eyes he had been a disappointment compared to Charles.

'Well, if that's so, since I was a disappointment compared

to you, think how much of a disappointment I was compared to Charles. I think they may have stopped after me because they feared the next one would be a greater disappointment still. A sliding scale of ever less prepossessing children.'

'Father . . . It's funny, isn't it? Nobody calls their father "Father" any more, but he just was a father, there was no way you could call him "Dad".' James had signalled to the waiter to bring another bottle of Margaux so efficiently that it hadn't even interrupted Philip's flow. Ordering bottles of wine was one of the few things he was really good at, he had thought wryly. 'Father was grumpy and cruel because he hated himself for not having the courage to become a painter. He hated banking. He might have resented Charles because Charles had the courage to do what he never did. But instead he admired him and lived his own ambitions through Charles's success.'

Philip had insisted on paying for the meal, had driven James home, and his farewell hug had been rib-threatening.

The pleasure of reminiscence faded in the face of the morning rush-hour traffic on the unlovely eastern stretch of Euston Road, with its budget hotels and run-down Irish pubs. Something was missing. Suddenly James realised what it was. He had forgotten to switch the radio on.

As luck would have it, he found himself in the middle of a discussion about soldiers in Afghanistan. A grieving mother was protesting about the paltry salary her son had earned for doing the job that had cost him his promising young life. A politician with a voice like a foggy day tried to console her with the thought that he so respected our boys and what they were doing for their country that he knew no rewards would be sufficient. Etna erupted in the Subaru. Stromboli spat fire. James's emotional confusion fed his resentment. The fact that the other driver in Deborah's crash had just come back from Afghanistan lit the fuse of his anger. The need to confront Marcia fuelled his emotion.

'You illogical inhuman hypocritical mass of slowly decaying food wrapped in a boring dark suit,' yelled James. 'Is that an argument for not giving them more? I never heard such rot. That's the argument Mrs Thatcher used about the nurses. Can't pay them more or we'll get the wrong kind of people. Well, look what's happened. We've paid our bankers more, and what have we got? The wrong kind of bankers. We've paid our lawyers more and what have we got? The wrong kind of lawyers. We should pay our soldiers like lawyers. Three hundred pounds an hour, and get paid for every letter home. God, our world is financially obscene. And you call yourself a radio presenter, you pasty-faced nonentity. You've let the swine off the hook. And how do I know you're pasty-faced? Because you're pasty-voiced.'

He didn't feel as much better after his rant as he had hoped he would. Every slow stop and start irritated him, and then, when he was on Western Avenue, he felt that he was rushing towards Globpack UK too fast.

Then he was in thick traffic again and an impulse grabbed him by the throat. Why not swerve over into the path of the oncoming traffic? It wasn't the first time he'd experienced this sudden illogical death wish. It had happened before in traffic, and of course he hadn't done it, because he might kill innocent people. But it had also happened once on their only cruise. He'd been standing by the rail at the stern of the ship and he'd suddenly wanted to climb the rail and jump overboard into the seething wake, for no reason other than because it was possible. It had so frightened him then that he had never dared look over the rail again, and this frightened him now. He had to pull in to the side to regain his equanimity, before driving the last half-mile to Marcia.

She came towards him impulsively and hugged him,

without even a thought that it might be inappropriate behaviour from an inexperienced PA to the Managing Director of the London office.

'Oh, I'm so very sorry about your wife, James,' she said. Usually she called him 'Mr Hollinghurst'.

She was wearing a low top and a short skirt. Her legs were a little on the broad side, her knees were ungainly, her greatest admirer couldn't have denied that at times she looked slightly lumpy but her ample flesh was the colour of summer and her lively young breasts were two invitations that would look well on anybody's mantelpiece. In this weather young men should be undressing her with their eyes outside every pub in South Kensington. She should not be showing barely suppressed sexual desire for a boss with bushy eyebrows almost twenty years older than her, and especially for one who would be beginning the elaborate process of sacking her in less than half an hour, and who recognised her charms but did not desire her at all, because the only woman he desired in the whole world was one who was gloriously, triumphantly, not his type at all.

'No. No. Thanks. Please. Thanks,' he said as he tried to disentangle himself from her without causing offence.

At last he was free from her and he'd thought of a good excuse for delaying his confrontation with her for a few minutes.

'I'll send for you in a few minutes,' he said, 'I just need to phone my mother,' and he disappeared into his inner sanctum.

He sat in his large swivel chair at his large desk in his large office and felt very small indeed. That was the trouble with size. It was a double-edged weapon.

He dialled his mother.

'Hello, Mum.'

'There was no need to ring back, you know. How are you, dear?'

'I'm all right, Mum. How are you?'

'Well, I'm fine. Why shouldn't I be? I mean, I'm shocked and saddened. You know how fond I always was of Deborah. I said to your father, "You're wrong about her, you know."'

'He didn't like her?'

'Oh, sorry. I forgot you didn't know that.'

'What was there that he didn't like?'

'I don't think it was really about her. He . . . no.'

'What?'

'I was going to say something I shouldn't.'

'Well, you can't not now you've started.'

'Oh. Well, for some reason . . . you know what he was like, I loved him dearly, but he drove me to despair the way he thought so little of people . . . for some reason he didn't think you were capable of making a good choice.'

'Of women?'

'Of pretty well everything, actually, really, come to think of it.'

'I see.'

'I knew I shouldn't have said it. You shouldn't have made me say it. Anyway, let's change the subject.'

Good idea.

'It was so sad, James, about that war hero. Poor boy. Just wanted to have a bit of fun after everything he'd been through. Poor lamb.'

'Yes. Awful.'

'I do hope Deborah wasn't driving too fast. She did rather, you know.'

Don't scream, James. Let it wash over you. And, admit it, you wondered too.

'So, when am I going to see you?'

His brain became a diary, whipped through all the possibilities.

'I'll come to tea on Saturday.'

93

'Good. You'd better go now. I don't want you getting into trouble.'

'I can't get into trouble, Mum.' No, don't grit your teeth. Learn to be calm, James. It's not too late. It's never too late. 'I run the place.'

'I know you do, darling, and I'm very proud of you. Saturday, then. I think I'll make a walnut sponge. You like walnuts.'

If you say so.

He put the phone down slowly. He gulped. He sighed. His throat was dry. He didn't think even Alan Sugar would find it easy to sack Marcia.

He picked up the phone again, hesitated, then rang Sandra Clipstone in Human Resources.

'Sandra, if I wanted to sack somebody, and I'm not saying I do, how do I go about it in this modern age?'

'Ah. If you're the maverick type and ruthless and don't give too much of a damn about the consequences you just sack them and hope to get away with it.'

'Right. If I'm not, and I'm not saying I am and I'm not saying I'm not, I'm not sure actually that I know whether I am or not, but if I'm not, what do I do?'

'You give her a verbal warning.'

'I see.'

'Which has to be in writing.'

'That's a bit ridiculous.'

'It's a government decision.'

'That explains it. You said "her". How do you know it's a woman?'

'Nobody can believe you've kept Marcia on so long, James. You're too soft-hearted to be a Managing Director, you know.'

'I suppose that's a compliment. Well, I'm not saying it is Marcia or it isn't. So carry on.'

'You have to give your reasons. And then if things still aren't satisfactory you have to give two more written warnings, with further reasons. And then if things still aren't satisfactory you can sack her . . . them.'

'Right. Thank you, Sandra.'

'My pleasure. Any time.'

He called Marcia in. She came so eagerly. It was dreadful.

'Marcia . . .'

He could see that she was surprised by his tone of voice. So she wasn't entirely insensitive.

'Marcia, you know we have to make cuts. I think I told you. Fifteen per cent across the board.'

She looked at him with slowly growing horror, fear, disbelief, more horror. It was as bad as he'd feared.

'I'm afraid . . . and, believe me, Marcia, this is one of the most difficult and awful things I've had to do in the whole of my forty-eight years.' He threw his age in to try to distance her from him emotionally. 'I'm going to have to consider your future here.'

All the colour drained from her face. She couldn't go white, she was too sunburnt. She just looked . . . muddy. And so shocked. So bereft. She looked as if a bolt of lightning was coursing through her, pinning her to the top-of-the-range-wood-effect plastic floor.

'I'm very, very sorry, Marcia.'

'But . . .' Slowly she regained the power of speech. 'You'll still need a PA. That'll cost you. It may cost you more. Probably I'm cheap.' For a moment she seemed more in control of herself. 'I can't see how this fits in with your fifteen per cent savings.'

He sighed.

'I'm sorry, Marcia. You're too clever for me. It doesn't. The truth is . . . Sit down, please, you look dreadful standing up. I mean, not dreadful, you couldn't look dreadful if you tried, I mean, it looks a dreadful ordeal for you to stay standing. Please, Marcia dear, sit.'

She sat down at the other side of his desk, pulling her skirt over her large knees. There was a look of resigned disappointment and disillusion on her face, as if she was a dog that was being taken to the vet by its beloved master to be put down.

'I was trying to spare you the truth, Marcia. I have actually been told by Mr Schenkman to sack you.'

'I see.'

'The actual words he used, if I recall them correctly, were that you are "a liability to the company image".'

'If only you'd told me what it was,' she said with a hint of reproof.

'I couldn't. I didn't know there was one.'

He tried to smile, but gave up the attempt. He had rarely known a moment when a smile would have been less useful.

'And you have to do what Mr Schenkman tells you, do you?'

She gave him a nervous look, wondering if she had gone too far. She blushed under her suntan. For a few moments she didn't look so muddy.

But he welcomed this spark of spirit.

'Not at all,' he said, 'but in this case, sadly, I didn't think I had the weapons with which to launch a serious attack upon him.'

She gave a brave half-smile.

'I know,' she said. 'I'm crap, aren't I?'

'I wouldn't put it quite like that, Marcia. In my eyes you have great virtues. You're very good to look at.'

She blushed.

Careful, James, or you'll have a stalker on your hands.

'You make a good cup of tea.'

Lousy coffee, but we won't go into that.

'You have a warm heart, which to me is an essential qualification, but which regrettably doesn't register on Mr Schenkman's radar. Unfortunately, you have punctuality problems, your memory isn't great, you aren't methodical, and you're weak on certain points – spelling, punctuation, meanings of words, spacing and I don't think you were ever taught apostrophes, were you? I could live with it all, but Dwight Schenkman the Third couldn't. Anyway, I'm not going to do what he asked. I'm merely going to give you a verbal warning, which I have to give in writing, with my reasons, which I have tried to express very mildly, because I . . . anyway, there we are.'

He handed her the verbal warning and she read it but he could see that she was too shocked and shaken to take it in.

'So what happens next?'

'Your work improves out of all recognition and I'm thrilled.'

'And if it doesn't?'

'I give you a written warning with my reasons.'

'And if it still doesn't improve?'

'I give you another written warning with my reasons, and if it still doesn't improve I sack you. Reluctantly. Truly reluctantly, Marcia.'

'I . . . um . . .' She blushed. 'I don't honestly think my work will improve that much. My school was shit. I can't believe the government is as cruel as to want to put me through all those terrible warnings and reasons. I couldn't stand it. I resign. I'll give you a month's notice.'

'Right . . . well . . . if you're absolutely sure . . . right.'

'I am sure. I do have . . . other ideas.'

'Right. Well . . . there we are then.'

He stood up and held out his hand. She stood up too and shook his hand very awkwardly.

'Oh, incidentally, Marcia,' he said, 'before you go, you know the comments I made on the problem of the EU rules for global disposal of unwanted styrofoam, there is one error still.'

'Oh, lorks, sorry.'

'Paragraph eight. "We must make sure that there are no barristers between China and the United States." That should be "barriers".'

'Oh, sorry. I'm rubbish, aren't I?'

She had her hand on the handle of the door but it was as if she'd forgotten how to open it.

'You said you had other ideas,' he said. 'Would you like to tell me about them? Because, I mean, obviously if you need a reference I'll . . .'

His voice faded out as he began to think about the difficulty of writing a truthful yet effective reference for her.

'I thought I might try something utterly different,' she said. 'I've always wanted to be a writer.'

The man who was no longer in a white linen suit recognised the voice of the Hungarian receptionist.

'Hello,' he said. 'I . . . um . . . I came to your hotel to . . . um . . . meet . . . um . . . my wife, and if you remember I booked a room.'

'I . . .'

'It was a couple of days ago. Lunchtime. I had lunch on my own. She . . . um . . .'

'Oh, yes. She not come, and you book out before you book in, and I not charge.'

'Thank you.'

'No problem. And you have lunch.'

'Yes.'

'No problem, I hope.'

'No. Very nice. But I think I may have left a ring in the

Gents. A wedding ring. When I got home I realised I hadn't got it. I took it off in there, because it was hurting, and I think I must have just left it.'

'Oh, yes. We have.'

'Oh, that's marvellous. Thank you.'

'We will send.'

'Oh, great. That's fabulous. My address—'

'I have the address, Mr Rivers. Lake View, 69 Pond Street, Poole.'

'Yes. On second thoughts, I'm actually away from home at the moment, not far from your area, I'll collect it myself.'

'As you wish, Mr Rivers.'

'Thank you very much.'

'No problem.'

He put the phone down, and sighed deeply. It was about a hundred miles each way. Why hadn't he just said, 'Look, to be honest, the lady was a married woman, I gave a false address,' and given his real address?

He still could.

But he couldn't. Couldn't do it. It was a question of style. And pride. Couldn't bring himself to lose face that way. Couldn't sully Deborah's reputation by revealing that he had involved her in such a charade, even though neither he nor anyone else would ever see her again.

He began to cry.

People talk about the pressure of routine, the stultifying boredom of routine, but sometimes routine can be very comforting. It was so for James that day, suspended as he was between two difficult meetings with women, between making Marcia resign and having afternoon tea with Helen. He was looking forward to that, of course he was, increasingly so. There was a pain in his balls, a faraway pain, but it was growing and getting nearer with every hour. No, it was the end of the tea that was worrying him. To go back with her to her bed, just two days after Deborah's death, deceiving his mother, and Philip, and Charles, and just four days before he discussed Deborah's virtues with the vicar, it wouldn't be right, but she wouldn't see it that way. The parting would be strained. They just must not argue. The fallout from it, if they did at this emotional time, could be extremely dangerous.

He made internal calls to several people. Lindsay Gibb. Lindsey Wellingborough. Annoying that, a Lindsay and a Lindsey sitting on the same committee, but they were the best people. Duncan Bailey. Tim Campagnetto (his mother married an Italian POW). Boris Eckhart. Jean Forrester. That should do it.

The pattern of the call was the same with all of them. Sympathy, stoically borne, with closure as swift as possible. A brief résumé of the accident, getting more brief with each telling. Sadness about the young soldier's tragic death. Astonishment that he was already back at his desk, the reasons for which he explained as briefly as possible and taking care not to use words that might precipitate a return to sympathy. A very brief résumé of the tasks set him, in the gloomy financial climate, by Dwight Schenkman the Third. An explanation of why he thought each of them in turn was the best man, or woman, in the whole company to contribute to the necessary process of identifying huge potential savings in Bridgend and Kilmarnock. A request that each of them should attend a meeting in the Small Conference Room on Monday. Discussion of availability. A promise to get back to each of them after considering all their availabilities. A second call to Duncan Bailey asking him to reschedule his meeting with Health and Safety. On his successfully managing to do so, a second call to all the others setting the meeting for 11.30 on Monday. All good, calming, boring stuff.

100

For lunch he got Marcia to bring him a tandoori chicken sandwich and a bottle of still water. He didn't want much to eat, because he wanted to do justice to his afternoon tea, and he didn't want to go to the canteen, because it would be awash with staring and sympathy, and it would be hot and he might sweat, and he didn't want to go to Whistler's Hotel with dark stains under his armpits.

He threw half the sandwich in the bin. He was too nervous to be hungry.

He had an inspiration, rang Fliss, and offered to take her out to dinner in Guildford that evening to discuss the composition of the funeral service. This would kill a whole flock of birds. It would show due deference to Deborah's side, it would relieve him of some of the responsibility for the composition of the service, it would provide him with something to do, taking his mind off things, it would be company for Fliss on Dominic's last night away, it would give her a wonderful chance to get her feelings about Dominic off her chest, it would give him lots of opportunities to shout at radio programmes on the way there and back, and it would furnish him with a cast-iron reason not to go back to Helen's place after their tea.

At first she said that she couldn't go, but he sensed that she wanted to, and he persisted. In the end she came out with the truth. She was having her hair done the next morning. It was awful. She couldn't risk meeting somebody she knew when her hair was such a mess. He pointed out that she definitely would meet somebody she knew. She would meet him. She told him that he didn't count where hair was concerned. He didn't notice such things. Deborah had often expressed regret over this. He pointed out that this evening his shortcoming would be a virtue. He wouldn't notice that her hair was a mess.

She allowed herself to be persuaded.

There was still an hour to go before his tea with Helen. The time hung heavily. How could he fill it? On an impulse he rang Jane Winterburn. He would wonder, afterwards, if he'd had some instinct that Ed's disappearance was going to turn out to be more important to him than he could possibly have foreseen.

'Hello, Jane. It's James. I was just wondering if there was any news.'

'Not a sausage. He's disappeared without trace. It's very good of you to care, James, with your problems.'

'Mine's not a problem, Jane. It's just . . . a sad event. I can't spend all day and night thinking about it. Has anybody any idea what's happened?'

'Well, no. I mean, the police have dragged the Thames near where he was supposed to have gone, but they can hardly drag the whole thing when . . .'

'When what, Jane?'

'Well, when he might just have . . . pissed off. I mean, he fucks for England. He's not really a very nice man at all, James.'

'No, well, I . . . I'm just really sorry, Jane.'

'That's nice of you.'

'I'm fond of you. You were my first proper girlfriend, you know.'

He wished he hadn't said that. God, it sounded so naive. He'd been twenty! And it suggested . . . well, it suggested that he might still be interested. Which he wasn't.

He wished he hadn't rung her.

'Well, Jane,' he said, 'I know this is a bad time for me, but for you, the not knowing, that must be far worse, it must be hell.'

'It is. Well, thank you so much for ringing. I think that's amazing of you.'

'Let me know if . . . when anything happens.'

'I will. And keep in touch.'

Not a chance. This was a big mistake.

'I will.'

The Palm Court of Whistler's Hotel was a room of slightly faded gilded magnificence, decorated with murals of Henley, Lord's and Wimbledon. Every table was taken. The ladies had dressed for the occasion. Waiters and waitresses in starched black and white bustled about, without seeming to bustle. It was seven minutes to four, and it looked as if it would be seven minutes to four for all eternity.

James was glad that he had managed to be early. He didn't think he was a control freak, but it had been important that he should arrive before Helen. This was his moment, his big scene, his first encounter with his beloved since they had become free. He was feeling sexually stimulated in a way few men are as they sit waiting for egg-and-cress sandwiches. It seemed senseless now that he wasn't going back to her flat to make love. Senseless. What had he been thinking of?

It occurred to him that in the last two years they had only twice met without going to bed together at some stage. And on one of those two occasions they had still managed to have sex, in her MG, not a car designed for sexual intercourse. He'd needed four visits to his osteopath, and he hoped he'd been convincing when he'd told Deborah that he'd slipped on the office stairs.

And there Helen was, standing on the wide, shallow stairs that led into the Palm Court from the foyer, her small mouth pouting and smiling at the same time. She was dressed in lime green, and she looked cool enough and fresh enough to drink. His heart almost stopped. She could halt traffic when she pulled out all the stops, but, equally, you could come across her in the supermarket and wonder why anybody should ever fancy her.

He stood up, smiled, moved towards her, kissed her demurely, held her chair out for her to sit down, slid it gently back in. This was not a man who had devoted his life to packaging. This was an English gentleman.

'Well,' she said, 'this is different.'

'Exactly. That's what I thought. Our life has changed. Let's do something different.'

He persuaded himself that he *had* thought this.

They ordered a full tea. They weren't hungry, but it was what you did. The surroundings demanded it. From the huge list of teas he chose lapsang souchong, she Earl Grey.

There was a moment's silence, then they both smiled at exactly the same time. This made them both laugh, and each of them realised that the other was shy. Shy, after all the times that they had met, after all the times they had made love. But this was different. They could be a couple now. Could be? They were.

'So, poor old Deborah,' she said, somewhat tentatively. She had to mention it, but James could see that she didn't know quite what to say.

'Yes, who'd have thought it?'

Armies of waiters brought things – a plate of tiny, manicured sandwiches, two scones, pots of cream and strawberry jam, two silver teapots and two silver water jugs. They smiled at each other again, and Helen said 'Thank you' to the waiters so fervently that they all smiled.

James tried to look round the room without Helen noticing, but it turned out to be one of his futile gestures.

'Anyone you know?' she asked.

'Don't think so.'

'Wouldn't matter now, would it?'

'Well, I suppose not, but . . . it's better that there isn't.'

'No, I agree.'

She took a smoked salmon sandwich. The crusts had been

cut off. James chose a cucumber sandwich. Its faint crunch seemed quite loud to him in the silence of that moment.

'This is very, very nice,' she said.

'I hoped it would be.'

She finished her tiny sandwich, chewing daintily.

'Well, well, I never really thought this day would come,' she said.

'No. Nor me.'

He hoped that the two blue-rinsed, green-tea, scarlet-lipped ladies at the next table weren't listening to this banal conversation. They wouldn't realise that the occasion itself was so momentous that no words could add to it, and only banality was possible.

But the over-permed duo *were* listening. He guessed that this was their hobby, having tea and listening. He knew they were listening because their ears stiffened like cats' when Helen asked, 'Are you coming back afterwards?'

His heart sank. They had reached this point so soon.

'It's a shame,' he said. 'I can't. I have to go down to Guildford to see Deborah's sister and discuss the service.'

'Oh.'

'There's such a lot to organise.'

'I'm sure, but . . . it seems a shame, Friday night.'

'I know.'

'When will you come?'

He took a few moments to choose his words. This was difficult.

'I've been wondering if it's entirely appropriate for me to come between the death and the funeral, actually.'

The two women were riveted.

'You said our life has changed. It hasn't changed all that much.'

'Not yet, no, but it will. We're free, free to . . .' He didn't want to articulate what they were free to do. They were free to do anything, so why stipulate, why commit, why – well, he didn't know why he didn't want to say any more and he was surprised that he didn't want to and he couldn't just let the sentence hang there, he had to say something. 'I mean, it's all so . . . it's been such a . . .' He drew back from saying 'shock', it seemed tactless, and he didn't want to say 'surprise', it seemed heartless, and he thought of saying 'mess', but that would be disastrous, so in the end he just stopped and let another sentence just hang there. Hardly a conversational triumph, and at such an important moment.

He put his right hand on her left hand and squeezed it.

'I love you,' he said. 'I love you so much.'

'Well, I love you too.'

She gave him a strange look, a mischievous look that made him feel uneasy. There was a glitter in those deep, subtle green eyes, as if she had a touch of fever. She gave a stern glance towards the two women, and they looked away hurriedly, and one of them said to her companion, 'Have you seen the new season's stock at Debenham's yet?'

Helen leant forward and said, in a very low, slow voice, 'I'm going to complain to the head waiter. This table's too big. I can't reach across and stroke your cock.'

He gawped. He was shocked.

'Helen!' he hissed.

He looked at the two ladies but they were leaning forward towards each other and talking in low voices about how long it would be before mauve made a comeback. Only when they had proved that they weren't listening would they dare to listen again.

'Helen!' he repeated.

'When are we going to go to bed together?'

'It's difficult. It's a really difficult time.'

She called out to a passing waiter.

106

'Excuse me.'

The waiter turned smoothly towards them, like a skater. 'Yes, madam?'

'I have a complaint to make. I'd like to see the head waiter.'

'I'm so sorry, madam? Are you sure I can't . . .?'

'No. I want the head waiter.'

'Certainly, madam.'

The waiter slid off towards the kitchens. The two ladies were now riveted once again.

Helen turned to them, smiled, and said, 'Can't get the staff.'

'Oh,' said one of the ladies. 'We think they're very good here, don't we, Doris?'

James, ashen-faced, leant forward and said, in a low voice, 'What the hell are you up to?'

She gave him the sweetest smile.

'Absolutely nothing, darling.'

He wanted to say that he was free all day Sunday, but he was damned if he was going to negotiate under duress.

The head waiter approached cautiously.

'You wished to see me, madam?' he asked.

'I did indeed,' said Helen. 'I just wanted to say, this tea is so delicious. It's perfect. I've had tea at the Ritz, but this surpasses it. I just wanted that message to go straight to the top.'

'Oh. Oh, thank you, madam,' said the head waiter. 'I . . . the waiter told me you had a complaint.'

'I did,' said Helen, 'but the antibiotics were effective, I'm glad to say.'

'I'm so pleased, madam. And thank you. Thank you so much.'

He beetled off in much confusion.

James raised those great eyebrows, glad of them at that moment.

'I know,' said Helen. 'Rather melodramatic. Not to say childish.' She leant forward, and spoke in such a low voice that the two ladies would only be able to hear if they listened very carefully. 'I'm sorry about that, but I'm actually a bit desperate. For five years, James, I have been discreet. I've been hidden away. I've known that you would never leave your wife. I've accepted the situation, because I've been so very much in love with you. I've ignored all my friends' advice, my own doubts, the findings of my brain, which kept reminding me that I was an attractive woman throwing my life away on a man who wouldn't commit . . .' She took a tiny mouthful of sandwich. 'I do believe this is bloater paste! How retro . . .' She smiled, then looked suddenly serious. '. . . or couldn't commit. The thing that I thought would never happen has happened and . . . James, I wish it hadn't happened in this way. I can't rejoice that a lovely woman like Deborah clearly was has been killed. I'd have rathered that she'd left you or had an affair.'

'She never would.'

He thought of the red shoes and gave her a brief, uneasy glance. Her eyes held the gaze for a few seconds, and then she looked away. She took another dainty mouthful.

'It's quite tasty, actually. No, I dare say she wouldn't, but here we are, we are free, or we're going to be, and we have to keep seeing each other or wanting to see each other, otherwise . . . otherwise the situation could destroy us. I'm just warning you, darling, and I really don't mean this as a threat, but I am not prepared to be hidden away for months and months. I know you can't suddenly produce me to your family out of a hat, but we've taken risks, all sorts of risks, huge risks actually, really, and I'm not having you going totally cautious on me now. I long for you to be in my bed so much, hence my little joke over the waiter, which I'm rather ashamed of already. You didn't really think I'd embarrass you that much, did you?'

'I suddenly wondered how well I knew you.'

'Oh, James. Well, it was a mistake, then. I wish I hadn't done it, it was stupid, but I'm feeling . . . I can't help it . . . excited. How can I not be? We can be free. We can marry. I'll accept it if I can't see you. Of course I will. It's very difficult socially and we do still have to be very secretive, I accept that, I feel awkward too, I feel very uneasy about being happy at all, I've always thought Deborah sounded like a lovely person, but I suppose . . . I suppose I just wanted to exert myself a bit, frighten you a bit, give the message that things must change at least a bit. Mustn't they?'

'Of course they must. Have a scone.'

'I'm not hungry.'

'Nor am I, but I'm paying twenty-nine pounds ninety-five a head.'

'Your silly idea.'

'We must eat some of it. One or two of the waiters are from the Third World. Share a scone?'

'OK.'

'I'll come on Sunday. Sunday lunch in one of those nice pubs near you, and then . . . one of the most fantastic fucks of all time.'

There was a crash of breaking china. A waiter hurried over.

'So sorry,' said one of the ladies at the next table. 'So clumsy of me.'

James and Helen couldn't look at each other, for fear they would laugh.

Saturday

The alarm woke James at seven-thirty, as usual. For the first time since Deborah's death he knew immediately that he was alone. It was no less a shock.

He put on his dressing gown, went downstairs, made himself a cup of coffee and just one round of toast. He ate the first half with three-fruit marmalade and the second half with New Zealand honey.

He took his coffee through into the sitting room, put it on top of the piano on a Scottish crafts coaster – it showed basket weaving, as it chanced – that Deborah had picked up for a song near Loch Lomond. The song had been the 'Skye Boat Song'. She had sung it beautifully, and had been given the set of coasters gratis as a reward. James gasped with sudden shock and sorrow at the memory of Deborah's voice. Charles at that very piano, Deborah singing Schubert so charmingly, Valerie mortified that Deborah was singing Schubert so charmingly, everyone thinking how well it would have worked if Charles had married Deborah. Don't. Don't go down that road, James, or, for that matter, down any road.

Suddenly he felt very weak. How on earth was he going to cope with Gareth?

He began the simple process of moving the furniture away from the middle of the room, not quite touching the walls, no marks on the paintwork, please. After each mini-labour of Hercules he took a sip of coffee. Why was he so exhausted?

Partly because he'd taken another temazepam. He really must stop that tonight. No good would come of starting to rely on sleeping pills.

At last all the furniture had been moved to his satisfaction. There was a wide expanse of carpet for Gareth to torment him on.

He went into the kitchen, finishing his coffee as he did so. He washed up his breakfast things. Gareth was a very precise man. Gays often were.

He thought about his dinner with Fliss as he struggled upstairs. God, his legs were weak. It hadn't gone too badly, on the whole. He had picked her up, which had pleased her. She had apologised unnecessarily for the state of her hair, which had looked fine to him, and the Chinese meal had been perfectly all right without touching the heights. In fact, it had been wonderful to see how much she had enjoyed her food and drink, especially drink, when Dominic hadn't been there to frown.

He assembled his fitness outfit. Jogging pants, trainers and his grey Champneys T-shirt. He smiled as he thought of his visit to Champneys with Deborah. He hadn't wanted to go, but he'd gone along with it and to his surprise he'd enjoyed it. It had all been a bit of a turn-on, being given treatment by attractive young women. He'd enjoyed feeling naughty by having a bottle of wine at dinner, and they'd made love twice in the five days, which was unusual in those later years.

Fliss had agreed that they didn't want the service to be overly religious. She wasn't religious, and James was a bit less religious than that. She'd told him that the Willoughby-Daltons

114

had gone for a humanist funeral and a woodland burial. He had thought that was typical of her, to give good advice too late, so that it became a rebuke.

When he'd said that he intended to say a few words, she'd looked a bit put out, and had said, 'I thought the vicar was doing the eulogy.'

'He's never met her,' he'd said. 'I'll give the personal touch.'

'Can you do it? Won't you break down? Elspeth Fothergill-Haynes thought she could do it, and she broke down in floods of tears.'

Fliss always had examples from among her friends to warn you off anything she didn't want. More than half of them were double-barrelled. James wondered if she chose them as friends *because* they were double-barrelled.

'I can do it.'

'In that case, why bother to have the vicar do it? Why bother to have a vicar at all?'

Good point, but he wasn't going to admit it. Anyway, he didn't want the responsibility of arranging the whole thing, and his mum would disapprove if there wasn't a vicar, she would say, 'This is a funny carry-on, James.' And it might be a step too far for Deborah's and Fliss's parents, who were cutting short their pre-harvest holiday in Italy, and who were traditionally religious in the feudal manner of farmers in villages.

'Well, if you're going to speak I want to say something too,' Fliss had said. She had always been competitive. Playing against her at tennis was hell. Partnering her was worse.

'That's fine, but three eulogies is quite a lot,' he had said cautiously. 'Could you find some other way? Do a reading?'

'I'll read a poem. Deborah loved poetry.'

'Fine. That's a really good idea. Two eulogies, a poem, two hymns, do you think? Both fairly cheerful, both singable by the tone deaf. Or do we want some non-religious music? A song, perhaps?'

The obvious thought had occurred to him. If they could get a piano, Charles could play. But if he'd suggested that, she'd have become competitive again, and found a long-lost cousin who could play the accordion. He'd decided that it was probably better not to mention it. Shame, though.

'What about a James Blunt song?' she had asked hopefully.

'Deborah didn't like James Blunt.'

Fliss couldn't have looked more astonished if James had told her that Deborah was a member of a terrorist cell. But then she had suddenly grown excited. 'I know,' she'd said. 'I'll tell you what would go down really well. If we could have a piano, and Charles could play.'

'Yes!' he'd enthused. It was perfect now that Fliss had thought of it. 'Yes. That's a great idea, Fliss. I'd never have thought of that. Oh, well done. Do you know, I think together we've cracked it.'

'I think we have.'

Agreement. Togetherness. Cracking it. Not experiences that had been common in the relationship between James and Deborah's sister. She had once suggested a walking holiday for the two couples.

'Where would we be walking?' James had asked. 'On eggshells?'

She had looked puzzled and said, 'No. On Mull.'

The rest of the evening had passed peacefully and easily. Fliss had dissected Dominic's many character flaws, and James had listened. Just in time, he had remembered that he had a photograph for her. He'd found it in a drawer in the bedroom, and had thought immediately that she would like it. It showed her with Deborah on the Rialto Bridge in Venice, with the Grand Canal an exquisite and animated background.

'Oh, thank you,' she'd said. 'Thank you, James, that's lovely.'

She'd looked at it for quite a long while.

'I quite like the way I had my hair in those days,' she'd commented.

He'd driven her home. She'd asked him in for a nightcap, but he'd refused on breathalyser grounds. They'd kissed quite warmly.

It had been a job well done.

The doorbell rang. Gareth. He hurried downstairs.

'Double parked,' said Gareth. 'Can you help?'

James helped Gareth unload his instruments of torture from his garish red van – rowing machine, Pilates machine, exercise ball, three smaller balls, stability whatsit, and those things that he didn't know what they were called, but you pulled and stretched with them. Then Gareth drove off to park, and James fitted the watch that told his heart-rate and tried to fit the black belt monitor that went tight round his chest and fed heart rate readings to the watch. Just as Gareth returned, whistling, the two ends of the belt sprang loose.

'Shit,' said James, lifting his T-shirt. 'Can you do it?'

This moment of closeness embarrassed Gareth, because he was gay. Not being gay, it didn't worry James at all.

Gareth slotted the two ends together, taking great care not to touch James's flesh and give out a misleading signal.

Gareth set up the rowing machine in the kitchen. 'Right, five minutes rowing while I set up the Pilates', he said as he strapped James's trainers onto the plates of the machine. 'Nothing too severe now, nothing too severe at all, just a nice, gentle warm-up, twenty-one, twenty-two strokes a minute, steer very close to the Surrey bank round Mortlake. The lovely Deborah not up yet?'

James felt exhausted at the thought of beginning all that again. He was tempted to say that she'd gone to the shops, set off early to beat the crowds. Maybe he could keep up that fiction for months, throw in a couple of long weekends with her parents. But no, he felt even more exhausted at the thought of all the excuses he would have to make. No, there was no escaping it. He would have to drop his bombshell, shock and embarrass this nice young Welshman, tell the story that now bored him stiff, accept yet more sympathy, and all while exerting himself in unnatural and unpleasant ways.

'She's . . . um . . . Deborah's dead, Gareth.'

Gareth turned and looked at him and was silent for at least twenty seconds, making it the longest silence there had ever been in their eight years of Saturday mornings.

'Dead?'

He began the story on the rowing machine, and finished it on the Pilates machine. It was difficult to tell it amid all this exertion, and by the end he was fighting for breath as he lay there, pushing with first both legs and then each leg singly.

'Oh, I'm so, so sorry,' said Gareth, when he'd finished. 'I can't believe it, actually. She was always so . . . so full of life. I always used to say . . . now the circles, ten in each direction slow . . . slow, James, quality not quantity . . . I always used to say, "You should see James Hollinghurst's wife. The lovely Deborah. She has more life in her little finger than some women have in their whole . . ." wider, James, stretch, make those circles really wide, really stretch those legs and height, let's have some height . . . "their whole body." I always used to say, "She doesn't use my services, she doesn't need to. Supple? There's supple. She could have been . . ." that's the ten, other direction now . . . "a limbo dancer." Oh, I always loved it when she came in the room and we had a little chat, and to think that I'll never see her again, I can't hardly believe it, but listen

118

to me going on and on about it and you have to deal with it every day, how much worse must it be for you, right, that's your ten, off you come slowly and safely, very good, well done, James, are you sure you want to go through with any more of this, when you must be choked up with the tragedy of it all, I think you're very brave.'

'I'm fine.'

'Right. Good man. Right, let's carry on the usual routine, you know it, that's right, standing as straight as you can and push back with both legs. Oh, I still can't bloody believe it. Last week I was having a lovely chat with her about immigration in this very room, and now seven days later she's with the angels, because she was an angel, well, you don't need me to tell you that, I tell you, I tell you, James, it's hard for me to believe, how much harder must it be for you?'

'Gareth? May I ask you something?'

'Of course. Ask anything you . . . that's right, left leg now . . . you want.'

'Gareth, I'm . . .' He could hardly get the words out, he was so breathless, all the drinking these last few days had really affected his fitness levels. '. . . I'm very grateful for all your sympathy.'

'Don't mention it. Wouldn't be human if I wasn't sympathetic, would I, when a tragedy like this has burst through the—'

'Gareth, please. That's what I want to ask you.'

'I'm sorry?'

'To . . . well . . . to shut up about my tragedy.'

Gareth went brick red. He always blushed easily. He wasn't at home in his body. His mouth opened and shut, just as it did almost all the time, but now no sounds were emerging. It was absurd. It was as if Dylan Thomas had been struck by laryngitis.

'I'm sorry, you weren't to know, but I just don't want to talk about it any more. I've had three days talking about nothing else.'

'Oh. I see.'

'I'm sorry. I really didn't want to be abrupt.'

'No. That's all right. I understand. I should have known. I should have thought. Off you come now. Slowly and safely. That's right. How's your heart rate?'

'Twenty past two.'

'What?'

'The watch isn't working properly.'

'Do you know, I had one watch for seven years, no problem with it, I've had this a fortnight and it's knackered. Probably made in Taiwan. Oh, well. Don't really need it, I s'pose. You aren't going to die. Except I'd have said that about— Sorry.'

He went brick red again.

'Sorry. Right. Back on the rowing machine, while I dismantle this Pilates machine.'

James rowed faster this time. He rowed angrily, taking it out on himself. He was angry with himself for having taken pity on Mike. He was angry with himself for not having arranged to see Helen tonight. He could have been in bed with his gorgeous, gamine lover, their legs wrapped round each other, and he'd chosen to spend the evening with a whining, self-centred loser. What was wrong with him? He could still change it. He would change it.

And all the while Gareth talked, and he didn't listen. Then there was a brief silence.

'Oh, dear. Somebody must have walked over a grave,' said Gareth. 'Oops. Sorry.'

He went even redder than before.

Now there was silence again. James relished it. Gareth hated it. He could see the young Welshman, brought up on rivers of chat, searching for a new subject to broach.

'So,' said Gareth conversationally, 'this German Pope, he's had a few years at it now, how do you think he's making out?'

After Gareth had gone James had the other half of his breakfast – another cup of coffee and the second round of toast. On the first half of the slice he put Seville orange marmalade and the second half – unusual, this, he usually liked a touch of sweetness on the last bit – was the one on which he had only spreadable butter.

Then he had a shower and dressed to please his mum – chinos and a pink cotton shirt. She liked him in pink. She said it showed that he didn't have any fear of appearing effeminate.

He went to the phone, lifted it, moved his hand towards the dials, decided to go for his acupuncture before deciding whether to phone Helen, and hurriedly put the phone down again. He felt that he was being indecisive because he was worried, and indecision always worried him, so he felt doubly worried.

This was not being a good day, and it was his belief that days that began badly usually continued badly. It was not his belief that days that began well usually finished well, so his often stated claim that he was an optimist was based on very flimsy evidence.

The drive up to Hampstead wasn't good either. The world and his wife were taking advantage of this sunny weekend, and Hampstead was a natural target. The drive took the best part of forty-five minutes. His hour with Gareth had exhausted him. His attempt to find something interesting to say about the German Pope had exhausted him. He didn't even switch the radio on, because he knew that he wouldn't have the energy to shout at it.

It was difficult to park outside the alternative health clinic, and he felt very claustrophobic as he manoeuvred the ridiculously bulky Subaru into a tight corner.

'Holly's running a bit late, but she won't be long,' the receptionist with the birthmark told him.

'Thank you.'

That was a relief. He needed to relax. He didn't want Holly telling him that his pulses were really bad. He went to her and to his doctor to be told that nothing was wrong and that any problems were in his imagination.

He picked up the top magazine. It looked suitably boring. He opened it at random and found himself looking at the interior of a house which was so expensively furnished that none of the magazine's readers could possibly have afforded to follow the style. Good. This looked really dull and pulse-calming.

'*Tamsin told me that her aim,*' he read, '*was "to create a house that contained no element that one would be ashamed to show to one's friends in Chelsea, but whose style made more than a cursory nod to the fact that it was actually just outside Diss."*'

Yes, it was indeed a bad day. Now there was no chance of relaxation. Now his mind was churning with those old worries. What had she been doing near Diss? Why the red Prada shoes?

A lesbian relationship? Her, Tamsin and an elegant, upmarket, semi-urban, semi-rustic antique dildo that she'd spotted in an antique shop in Pimlico?

A party at Tamsin's? London people streaming out to Diss for rustic raves?

He turned the pages and there was a picture of Tamsin. Smug, snobbish yet succulent, as he had known she would be.

'Hello, James. Sorry to keep you.'

He put the magazine back and followed Holly into her

surgery on weary legs but with angry, racing, humiliating pulses.

'Sit down.'

He sat at the side of her desk, at an angle of ninety degrees to her. Holly was about thirty-five, pleasant to look at but with no trace of glamour. She smiled. It was a smile that promised a pleasant hour, but could she offer anything more? How did you know if your acupuncturist was any good? How did you know how you would have felt if you hadn't been going to her? He had no idea whether these fortnightly visits achieved anything.

'So, how have you been?'

The story yet again.

The sympathy yet again.

'Right. Let's get you on the couch.'

He took off his shoes, socks and shirt, rolled up his trousers, and lay on the couch, on the hygienic paper covering.

'How are things with you?' he asked. He didn't want all the questions to be one way, as they usually tended to be in any doctor-patient relationship.

'Not bad,' she said, as she began to feel his pulses. 'Den is surviving, and in two thousand and ten that can't be bad.'

'I don't think I know what line he's in exactly.'

'Preserves. He sells preserves. Well, your pulses aren't good, the liver is particularly angry.'

'I have been drinking rather more than usual.'

'I'd be very worried if I hadn't known what you've told me. Even so I'm mildly worried. Try to pull back on your drinking and, hard though it will be, try to relax.'

'I will.'

She began to stick the needles into him. He never asked her why she put what where. He just accepted her decisions and assumed that she knew what she was doing. He sometimes wondered if he had a curiosity deficiency.

'What sort of preserves?'

Talking about her life was so much more relaxing than talking about his. Why hadn't he realised this before?

'Jams. Marmalade. Chutneys. Sauces. Jellies. Relishes.'

'Would I have heard of the names?'

'Well, he's got a big new range with cosy, personal names that's doing rather well. Mrs Wilson's Tangerine Marmalade. Granny Copgrove's Spicy Plum Chutney. Ma Bakewell's Apricot Jam. Cousin Annie's Tomato Relish.'

'Oh, that's nice. Using local small-time people. Very nice.'

Holly gave a shamefaced little smile.

'All made in his factory in Kuala Lumpur, actually,' she admitted. 'Right. Now try to relax.'

'I will. I'll probably fall asleep.'

She put a chair at either side of the couch, so that he could lay his arms upon them, and then she left him to it. He would now lie there for some forty minutes, with his arms stretched out, like a man being crucified on a horizontal cross, alone with his thoughts, in that cool, utilitarian room.

In front of him was Holly's desk and the chair on which he had put his shirt, and under which he'd left his socks and shoes. On his left were shelves full of opaque jars containing unattractively coloured herbal products. Holly was a medical herbalist as well as an acupuncturist. On his right were more shelves full of smaller, empty brown bottles with blank labels, and two small windows, affording a view of the still, pale unchanging blue of the summer sky.

Behind him . . . he had no idea what was behind him. He was never facing that way.

He lay there, half naked and studded with needles. He felt like the onion studded with cloves that he put with the kidney beans in the rather superior chilli con carne that he occasionally made. A rush of affection and nostalgia swept over him as he thought of all the cosy winter meals he'd enjoyed with Deborah, and of her delight when, just occasionally, he turned his hand to the stove. He closed his eyes and let his weariness drift over him. He wondered if Helen would enjoy his chilli, his curry, his spaghetti Bolognese, his occasional man food. He thought about tomorrow. About tomorrow after lunch. Sunday afternoon in a king-sized bed in South Kensington. Sunday afternoon with the woman with whom he would spend the rest of his life. It would be their first time in their new circumstances. He thought of their first time ever. The first time he had seen that pale, slender, boyish but exquisite frame.

The Travelodge, Bridgend.

He thought about another heatwave, four years ago, or was it five? Just a few days of sun, but in the sea as the tide came in the water had been warm. They had lain side by side in the shallows and very gently, under the water, given each other orgasms, within a few feet of children building sandcastles with total innocence. Other people could be quite rude about it, but he had a real affection for Porthcawl.

This wouldn't do. This wouldn't calm those pulses. Maybe – it was a sinister thought – Holly would be able to tell what he'd been thinking about. 'Who's been a naughty boy, then?'

His nose began to itch, as it so often did on these occasions. There was no real reason why it should itch. It was in his mind. There was therefore no reason to scratch, since he couldn't scratch his mind. So, believing himself to be a logical kind of man, he tried not to scratch. But the logic didn't work. The itch grew intolerable. Very carefully, very anxiously, worried that one or two of the needles would fall out and disturb the whole balance of the thing, he moved his right arm towards his nose, and gave his right nostril a good scratch. Oh, what a blissful cocktail of pain and pleasure a good scratch was. And none of the needles fell out.

But that little episode had not exactly been relaxing. He

must relax. He let his arms and legs flop. He closed his eyes more firmly. He was going, going, slipping away.

The door was opening, very slowly. Deborah was standing there, smiling. Of course. He'd given her the key. She stood there, so lovely. Her smile was such a direct, uncomplicated affair. Nobody had looked upon the prospect of him with such utter joy before. She let her nightshirt drop to the floor and there she was in all her naked magnificence in the middle of the Maltese night. The full thighs, the luscious bush, the generous breasts, the rounded stomach, the wide mouth, the multitude of white teeth. Oh, the joy of it, and the danger too, with all four of their parents asleep in nearby rooms on that very corridor. He looked at the rows of bottles of herbal medicines and wondered what they were doing there. And then he wasn't in Malta and Deborah was dead and he had a great bulge in his rolled-up trousers and in a few hours he would be eating walnut sponge with his mother. He'd needed to get rid of his bulge but he was sorry to see it go quite so quickly.

But this vision of his first time with Deborah had unnerved him. For goodness' sake, he was supposed to lie here and relax.

He must try to think about something other than sex.

The disappearance of Ed. He'd asked Jane to phone if there were any developments, but would she? Could she? Did he want her to? Should he give her another ring? Supposing . . . supposing Ed was dead.

He wondered if he would still find her attractive. How many years was it since he'd last seen her? Ten? Maybe even more.

He remembered her long legs and her wide mouth and her green eyes. No, he didn't. He remembered that her legs were long, that her mouth was wide, that her eyes were green. He remembered the words, the facts, but he couldn't see the pictures.

126

There would be no point in seeing her again. He was going to live with Helen.

It would be interesting, though.

But he didn't think he could possibly like her. How could you like someone who had managed to live for almost twenty-five years with Ed? And mustn't she have been in cahoots with him, to have lent her name to the revived businesses?

Why was he thinking about Jane? He might just as well be thinking about the girl at the fruit-and-vegetable stall in the market, the one with a touch of Gypsy in her, the sheen on her dark skin, this aubergine of a girl, the bright challenging eyes, the feline grace, the black hair made to be tossed like a flamenco dancer's, the sumptuous sexiness, to slowly peel this Spanish onion . . .

Help. There was an itch in his soul and he couldn't reach it to scratch it.

Think Mike. Think this evening in the pub. Bitter beer and bitter thoughts.

Think packaging. Think styrofoam. Think Bridgend and Kilmarnock.

There was a barmaid in that pub in Bridgend, with Celtic mystery in her dark eyes as she pulled the pints . . . no!

Forty minutes was a long time for a man to be left on his own lying down and festooned with needles, especially in the middle of such a stressful and emotional week. All those thoughts, and there were still sixteen minutes to go.

And then the door was opening and Holly was sliding in like a nervous rabbit, and he realised that he had fallen into a deep sleep. He needed more sleep, much more, hours of it.

'How are we?'

'I must have fallen asleep.'

'Good. That's good.'

Sometimes she was talkative, but this morning she moved

round him in silence, removing the needles, occasionally dabbing away a bit of blood. He was grateful for the silence.

She pumped the couch up a couple of feet with her foot, and began to take his pulses. He could feel himself getting anxious. This was awful. It was ridiculously important to him that she should give him a good report. But if she did, might it not mean that she didn't actually know what she was talking about?

After she'd read his pulses she gave him a searching look, and he could feel himself coming out in goose pimples. You dirty old man. You sick soul. You poor, wretched, confused individual. Porthcawl indeed!

What was she thinking? What had his pulses told her?

'Mm,' she said. 'Not as improved as I'd hoped. Not as rested as I would have expected. The right kidney, in particular, is not happy.'

She lowered the couch with her foot. He put his shirt back on, rolled his trousers down, put on his socks and shoes. As he bent down he felt distinctly dizzy. Not good.

He paid. She gave him a receipt. He couldn't meet her eyes.

'Go carefully, James,' she said. 'Be sensible.'

The man who was no longer in his white linen suit approached the reception desk. Last time he had approached that desk there had been love and hope in his soul. Now there was emptiness.

The Hungarian receptionist wasn't there. A man was on duty.

'Can I help you, sir?'

'Yes. I spoke to your Hungarian receptionist on the phone yesterday.'

'Ah, Magda, yes. She not on. Day off.'

'Ah.'

'Magda, nice girl.'

'I'm delighted to hear that. Well, no doubt you can help. I left a ring here.'

'Ring? You want use phone?'

'No, no. A ring. I left it in the toilet.'

'No phone in toilet.'

'No. A ring. My wedding ring. On my finger.'

'Ah. I understand. Sorry. I no English spoken much. I learn.'

Not quickly enough.

'I came here . . . Wednesday. Left my . . .' He prodded the finger. '. . . ring. I telephoned . . .' He mimed the act of phoning '. . . nice Magda. She said you have the . . .' He prodded the finger again. '. . . ring.'

'I go. I find manager.'

'Thank you.'

The manager arrived almost immediately.

'Sorry about that, sir,' he smiled. 'Stefan hasn't been here long. You telephoned Magda and she confirmed that we had found your ring, is that right?'

'Yes.'

'I'm afraid you've had a wasted journey, sir. We've posted it to you.'

'Posted it? But Magda said you would keep it for me.'

'I'm so sorry, sir. There's been a misunderstanding.'

'I can't say I'm surprised. Some of your staff don't speak much English.'

'Don't I know it, sir.'

'Wouldn't it be a good idea to employ staff who do speak English?'

'Would you like to recruit staff for me, sir, around Diss? Most of the locals don't want to know. I really am sorry, sir.'

'I've travelled the best part of a hundred miles to get here.'

'We do a two-course set lunch for eleven ninety-five on

a Saturday, sir. I can offer you that on the house, with my apologies.'

'Thank you. Thank you, but no . . .' Couldn't bear another lunch on my own, remembering that awful day. 'I have to get back.'

'So sorry, sir.'

As he walked towards the door, a thought struck him, and he turned.

'Excuse me.'

The manager, who was about to disappear to safer pastures, stopped, turned, forced a smile.

'Yes, sir?'

'Did you get my address from the residents' book?'

'Yes, Mr Rivers. You had filled in your address, even though of course you later cancelled when the lady didn't turn up.'

'So my wedding ring, with a considerable financial value, and a far greater emotional value, especially now that . . . ' Now that Deborah was dead. Now that it was the most treasured relic of the only other great passion in his life. Now that he felt ashamed of having taken it off in the first place. How could he possibly have forgotten it. He needed it back. He needed to repair this betrayal. '. . . especially now that my . . . um . . . my wife is dead, has been sent by post, and not presumably by Special Delivery, to Poole in Dorset?'

'Yes, sir.'

'I see. Thank you.'

He stormed through the revolving doors, had a thought, stormed back in.

The manager had already disappeared. Stefan was back.

'Mr Rivers,' he said. 'How I help?'

God knows.

'The address I gave, in your book, was not my address.'

130

'Book? You lost book? I not find book.'

'Could I speak to the manager again, please?'

'Yes, sir. I go. I am fetching.'

Not very, to be honest. He almost made the stupid joke out loud. Anything to take out a little of his frustration.

The manager returned. His smile was getting tired.

'Yes, Mr Rivers?'

'The address I gave, and to which the ring is going, it's a long story . . .'

Their eyes met. It was not a happy meeting.

'. . . is not actually my address.'

Why can I not just tell the truth? Because of those eyes.

'It's the address of a holiday cottage I was booked to go to after leaving here, and I thought, if any problems did arise, that would be the best place to contact me.'

'Very sensible, sir.'

He doesn't believe a word of it.

'But I cancelled due to . . . well, it turns out the lady . . . my wife . . . was killed in a car crash.'

'Oh, no, sir. I read about that. I'm so sorry.'

'Thank you. So, I cancelled the booking.'

'Not surprisingly.'

'No. But I can't remember the exact address. To contact them. To get my ring back.'

'I understand completely, sir.'

I know you do. That's what makes this all so pathetic.

The manager opened the residents' book. Oh, God, he could have just done that himself.

'Easy to find, sir. We're very quiet at the moment.'

I'm not surprised.

'I'll write it out for you, sir. Lake View, 69 . . .'

Their eyes met again. It was an even unhappier meeting.

'. . . Pond Street, Poole. No postcode, sir.'

'Oh, dear.'

'You should always put the postcode, if I may make so bold as to advise you, Mr Rivers. I do hope the ring arrives safely, but without the postcode there is no guarantee.'

Fuck off.

He parked the Subaru neatly in the little visitors' parking area. It was neatly roped off by privet hedges, so that the residents' view over the manicured grounds remained unsullied. These flats were perfect. It irritated his mother that there was nothing to complain about. It was one of the many things that she complained about.

It had been another slow, tedious drive through the crowded, melting streets of North London. He was tired, so tired this day. He let his head drop down onto the steering wheel, so that he could rest a moment. He hadn't switched the ignition off completely, and the horn blared loudly. He sat up rapidly, but the damage had been done. Faces appeared at windows all over the low, bland, unblemished complex. He twisted his neck to see if his mother had come to her window. It didn't look as if she had. He would risk it. He would sit in the car for ten minutes, gathering his strength.

He shouldn't have had that fifth drink. Holly had said that he should drink less. He'd known that this was good advice, and he'd decided to put it into practice straight away. Where better to drink less than in a pub? There was a pub in Hampstead called the Holly Bush. Where better to go to put Holly's advice into practice? And now he was bushed. He smiled at the word play and wondered if he was going feeble. His mother would suggest he was if he tried the word play on her. Once, when he said he found Jack Dee funny, she had said, 'Jokes are all right, I suppose, if you like laughter.' She'd been a cheery woman once, while his father was alive. 'Somebody has to be cheery,' she'd once said, 'while that man's around.' And then, when he'd died, and she could have really led a cheery life, she'd seemed to find no use for cheeriness, nothing to set it against. Tragic, almost.

He had only drunk halves, just to prove that he could drink less. But it's tiring drinking slowly, as any true drinker knows. Sip sip sip. Drip drip drip. Wearisome. And the slow tick tick tick of the clock clock clock as he sipped sipped sipped in that long hot Hampstead afternoon, thinking in circles, thinking fondly of Deborah, thinking longingly of Helen, a fortunate man suspended between great events, a lonely man with a host of friends, but it didn't do him any good to have lots of friends if none of them were in the pub with him on that long, slow afternoon, and he felt as unhappy as his right kidney. He cursed himself for having arranged to see Mike. He cursed himself for not having arranged to see Helen. He should have eaten something, but he had to leave room for the walnut sponge. He shouldn't have had that fifth half. Two and a half pints were nothing, usually, but James this Saturday was not a strong man.

He could still ring Helen, see if she was free this evening, have a quick drink with Mike, spin him some yarn about funeral arrangements. But James this Saturday was a man riven by indecision, a weak man.

He should have gone home, as he usually did after his acupuncture, for a nice little lunch with Deborah. But there was no Deborah, there was no lunch, he was a man who couldn't face shopping, he was a man this Saturday who couldn't face himself, couldn't face the truth, would be very unwise to face Helen, no, leave things as they were. James this sunny Saturday was a man without a home, a nomad, a wanderer in the desert, a man caught betwixt and between.

He felt slightly better now that he'd made up his mind not to ring Helen.

Suddenly, without his being conscious that he'd decided to, he was getting out of the car, he was walking away from the car, he was locking the car, he was walking towards his mother's flat, he had nothing in his hands, nothing to give her, no flowers, no sweet little book of notepads, no thoughtful little gift of any kind. If he'd brought her flowers, she'd have said, 'How much did they set you back? Florists? Daylight robbery.' If he'd brought a sweet little book of notepads, she'd have said, 'You think I'm losing my memory, do you?' If he'd brought scent, she'd have said, 'Do I smell? You would tell me if I did, wouldn't you? Because sometimes old people do start to smell.'

But he should have brought something.

'Hello, Mum.'

Kiss. One cheek. Brief. Not the tactile generation. Sad.

'Why did you wait in your car?'

To give me strength to face you. No!

'What?'

'You set the horn off and I looked out because I was sure it would be you. A mother recognises her son's horn. Right in the middle of Mrs Pardoe's nap, I shouldn't wonder. That nap of hers. You'd think it was the Trooping of the Colour. Quarter of an hour you've been.'

I was wondering whether to ring the woman I love and have loved for five years and whom tomorrow I will be f— No.

'Ten minutes I'd have thought, top whack. I . . . there was a programme on the radio I wanted to hear the end of.'

'I see.'

Much more important. Your poor old mum has nothing as interesting to say as the BBC. It was in her voice, but she didn't actually say it, and for that he was grateful.

'Anyway, thank you for coming, and this is all so sad. So very sad, dear. And if I may criticise, but what's a mother for if she can't, don't you think that pink shirt's just a bit cheerful a bit soon? Oh, poor Deborah. Though of course it was sudden, and at least we know she won't end up in a home. There is that.'

'She was forty-six, Mum.'

'Oh, I know. Much too young. Tragic. I'll make the tea.'

He watched her as she made the tea, and he was very relieved. She was as brisk and efficient as ever. But she looked so small. She was shrinking slowly over the years. The dress she was wearing, the red one too thick for the weather, the one that looked as if it had been made from part of a carpet, still fitted perfectly. He wondered if the Kwality Cleaners, round the corner, were serendipitously shrinking it at exactly the same rate as she was shrinking.

'And some walnut sponge?'

'Please.'

He went to the window and looked out at the pleasant, anodyne prospect.

'There are no birds,' he said.

'We're not allowed to put food out. It's against the rules.'

'What? Why?'

'Probably the noise would disturb Mrs Pardoe's nap.'

The bitterness in his mother's voice was a physical shock to him. So small, but capable of such ferocity.

'If we ever get another bad winter I'll take no notice. I won't let my birds starve.'

'Quite right, Mum. You do that.'

He was glad to see that she poured the tea with a steady hand, and cut the cake very professionally. She was only seventy-six, which was no age these days, but still, it was best to keep a close watch. She still had her bone structure, too, though she was heavily lined, having been a sun worshipper in those Malta and Majorca days. But her grey hair was getting humiliatingly sparse.

'James, there's a fork for the cake.'

'Oh, Mum.'

'We have standards in our family, James. The Harcourts think they're posh, Fliss with all those double-barrelled friends, but we have standards too. I hope the funeral tea will be a classy affair. You can judge a family by their funerals just as much as by their weddings.'

'Mum! I just want it to be a good send-off for Deborah.'

'Of course. I hope the vicar's all right. The decline in vicars in this country is shocking. Is he all right?'

'I've no idea. I've never met him. We just have to hope.'

'Oh, dear. Is Stanley coming?'

'Yes.'

'Oh, dear.'

'I can't not invite him, Mum.'

'No. I know. I was hoping he might be the next to go. That's the only solution, really, for people like that. More tea?'

'Thanks. Nobody makes a cup of tea like you, Mum.'

She tried so hard not to show that she was pleased. Why?

'Another slice?'

'Please. It's lovely, and I'm really hungry.'

He expected that to please her, but she said, 'Now that's bad. You should make sure to eat. I bet you can't boil an egg.'

'I can cook, Mum. I have a limited range, but . . . not bad.'

'Things with rice,' she said scornfully.

'Partly. We like rice.'

'Well, that's lucky. I wouldn't thank you for it. It's fine if you're Chinese, but I'm not. And nor are you, may I remind you?'

There was silence for a moment. He could see that his mother was brooding about something, and he was happy to concentrate on not dropping crumbs.

136

'She doesn't sleep at night,' said his mother. 'Of course she doesn't. It's because of her precious nap. The whole block has to be quiet. It's Remembrance Day every afternoon.'

Her eyes had sunk into her face, but they would still be able to spot a speck of dust in a stately home at two hundred yards.

'Have you seen Philip?' he asked.

'Coming tomorrow. He's not a bad boy.'

'I come whenever I can, Mum.'

'I didn't say you didn't. You shouldn't be so touchy. Touchiness is not an attractive trait in a person. More tea?'

'I've had two.'

'You always used to be a three-cup person. In the old days.'

Ah, those tea-swilling days of yore.

'All right, then. Thanks. Seen Charles?'

Her face broke into a smile at last.

'Ah, Charles,' she said. 'He's doing so well.'

'Have you seen him?'

'Not since March. He's so busy with his concerts.'

So typical. Place the one who doesn't come on a pedestal. Make him your favourite. You were an individual once, Mum, strong, holding the family together, saving them from Dad. When he died the purpose went out of your life and now, now you're in danger of becoming a cliché. When all this is over, Helen and I are going to take you in hand, make sure you become the sort of old woman you ought to be. You won't like Helen at first, but she'll grow on you.

'He's away now, isn't he, giving his concerts? Ecuador or Iceland or somewhere like that.'

This vagueness is a new thing. I think it's put on. You're an educated woman.

'I see him on the telly, of course. I saw Philip on the telly

137

too, on that programme about global warming. It's a pity *you're* never on the telly.'

I'll make some suggestions to the BBC. *Strictly Come Packaging. I'm in a Parcel, Get Me Out of Here. Britain's Got Cardboard.*

'I'm sorry, Mum,' he said at last. 'I'm going to have to take my leave.'

'Well, thank you for coming. I do appreciate it.'

He tried to hide his astonishment.

They walked slowly towards the door. It would be a while before they reached it. Saying goodbye to his mother was never a swift affair.

'You've been a good husband, James. Take comfort from that,' said his mother. 'Do you remember Mrs Tomlinson from number forty-four, when we were in Carberry Crescent before we went up in the world?'

'No, Mum. I think I was two when we left Carberry Crescent.'

'Well, I wouldn't say Carberry Crescent was a fount of wisdom. You didn't meet your Jean-Paul Sartre slipping off to Londis. Your father used to be very scornful of the people in Carberry Crescent. But you learn in this life that wisdom sometimes comes from unexpected places.'

'So what did Mrs Tomlinson from number forty-four say?'

'Do you know, I'm not sure now if it was number forty-four. I think she might have been from number forty-two . . . Yes, I think she was, because number forty-four was right opposite the letter box and had those purple curtains, and I said to Mrs Tomlinson, "What sort of person chooses curtains that colour? Actually chooses them?"'

'Mum, what did Mrs Tomlinson say?'

'She said, "People who know no better."'

'No, no. Not about the curtains. What you were going to say before that?'

'It's gone. Don't mock.'

'I'm not mocking.'

'You'll get like it one day. You'll see.'

'I'm not mocking, Mum.'

'Where was I? Prompt me.'

Oh, God. What had she been talking about?

'You can't remember. You weren't listening.'

'I was listening. You hadn't got round to what you were talking about. You'd gone into a detour about Mrs Thingummy's curtains.'

'Tomlinson.'

'Mrs Tomlinson's curtains.'

The conversation was shaped like a maze. Would he ever escape from it?

'They weren't Mrs Tomlinson's curtains. That was the whole point of it. They were the curtains of the woman next door. I was going to tell you something about Mrs Tomlinson. Something she said. It's almost there. Oh, it *is* frustrating. I'll remember the moment you've gone.'

Gone. Eventually he would be gone. Here was a cue to begin to depart. He opened the door, very slowly, as inconspicuously as possible. But he found that he just couldn't walk through it. Not yet. Not till she'd remembered.

He tried harder, thought back over the start of the conversation, and inspiration struck.

'It was following on from your saying that I'd been a good husband.'

'That was it. Thank you. If you'd said that in the first place. Mrs Tomlinson said once, out of the blue, right out of the blue, she said, "Do you know, Kathleen, what is one of the most wonderful feelings in the whole wide world?" and I said, "No, Gladys, I do not. What is one of the most wonderful feelings in the whole wide world?" and she said, "One of the most wonderful feelings in the whole wide world, Kathleen, is when you wake up one morning and realise that you did nothing to be remotely ashamed of yesterday."'

'That's very good, Mum.'

'Isn't it? And I think you can say that, can't you? Every morning.'

Oh, Mum, Mum, how little of me you know. Or am I underestimating you? Are you being devious? Are you putting the knife in, as mothers do?

He gave her a quick kiss on the cheek, and walked through the door. He had made it. He was out.

There was still time to kill before he met Mike. He'd said seven o'clock. God, it was in danger of being a long evening. He dreaded all the drinking that he would have to do. Correction. He had the car. He dreaded all the drinking that he wouldn't be able to do. Sitting watching Mike drinking. It would be about as exciting as watching synchronised swimming. He couldn't face it without a drink.

He stopped in a cavernous pub with a car park big enough for a rugby club. The huge bar smelt of stale chips and disinfectant. There were five other customers, three sad men at the bar and a couple with just about a full set of teeth between them kissing and cuddling under the blackboard menu, on which was chalked 'Special of the Day – Burger and Chips'.

He ordered a single gin and tonic, and poured the whole bottle of tonic in. He sat opposite the clock, and decided to ration himself to a sip every two minutes. It wasn't long before he noticed that the clock had stopped. After a few moments he realised that this was actually a stroke of luck. He began to count the seconds to himself, and took a sip every time he reached a hundred and twenty. That way his mind was fully occupied. There was no room for useless anticipation of great moments with Helen or unwanted nostalgia for great moments with Deborah.

He savoured each sip, seeking out the sharp juniper taste of the gin under the sweet quinine of the tonic. God, how he longed to drink it faster.

The three men at the bar were hardly speaking, but he heard one of them say, 'Fucking bastard immigrants, they're going to destroy our whole way of life.'

He longed to shout, 'What way of life?' but managed not to.

A thought occurred to him. He would tell Mike about Ed's disappearance. Mike had known Ed. It would take up a minute or two. Any topic of conversation was welcome, to help while away the long hours of struggle.

He needed to ring Jane first to check if Ed had been found.

He dialled her number. His phone told him that there was no network coverage.

'No fucking reception in here,' called out one of the sad men, 'and that goes for that fucking cow behind the fucking bar too.'

'Thank you very much,' said James with exaggerated politeness, and the three men went, 'Ooooh! Thank you very much!' in posh unison, and the dentally challenged lovers looked up and cackled before resuming their exploration of the gaps in each other's mouths.

James drained the rest of his gin and tonic in three long, luscious gulps, and walked defiantly to the bar to hand over his empty glass.

'Thank you very much,' he said again, but this time there was no response from the men.

'Thanks,' said the barmaid. 'See you later.'

No chance.

He phoned Jane from the car park.

'Hello, Jane, I've been thinking about you. I wondered if there'd been any developments.'

'Thanks. No. Nothing.'

'Oh, Jane. I'm sorry.'

'Yeah, well, it is pretty terrible, James. The not knowing. It's . . . indescribable actually.'

'I can imagine.'

'I'm all right. The family are doing shifts of Jane-sitting. I'm coping. But how about you?'

'Bearing up. No alternative. But at least I have something to try to get over. You just don't know.'

'I know. Every time the phone rings my heart races. Will it be, "I'm afraid I have bad news, Mrs Winterburn"? or, "It's me. Sorry about this, but can we arrange a time next week when I can come round and collect my things?"'

'I'm really sorry, Jane. If there's anything I can do . . .'

'There isn't really. Thanks for ringing. I'll let you know if anything happens.'

'Thanks. Jane?'

'Yes?'

'I . . . hope you'll be all right.'

'Thanks.'

He put the phone down, and breathed a sigh of deep relief. He had been in danger of saying something unwisely personal.

He drove slowly, so slowly, to Acton and Mike's flat – well, bedsit, but people didn't seem to use that term any more.

He was pleased to see that Mike was looking slightly less slovenly than the last time he'd seen him. The way he was dressed, he looked ready for combat in Afghanistan – in fact, James thought, maybe better prepared than the troops, if rumour was anything to go by, but at least he'd assembled a full range of gear on which no food had been dropped.

He invited James in, but the smell of stale fat, stale beer and urine discouraged him.

James drove to a pub in Ealing that he said was the best

in the area, and compared to the Disinfectant Arms it was Raffles in Singapore. Horse brasses abounded though no member of staff would have dared to go near a horse. Sky Sports was on in one corner, with a loop of uninteresting facts coming round every seventy-eight seconds.

James took care to order the first round.

'Bloody Wimbledon,' said Mike aggressively as they took their pints to a corner of the beer garden. James wouldn't have dared drink a gin and tonic in Mike's presence. It would have precipitated a diatribe about going posh. 'Oh, well, only forty-two days to the new football season.'

James suffered from a great handicap in male society. He knew nothing about football and cared less. But Mike, he knew, had very little left in his life besides football, now Melanie had left him. He even had two fantasy teams with the *Daily Telegraph*. Better get the football chat over.

'How are the Arsenal going to do this year?'

Mike was contemptuous.

'Tottenham. I'm a Spurs man. Can't you see the suffering in my face?'

'Sorry.'

There followed a cluster of football jokes. Tottenham have so many Jewish supporters they're renaming it Tottenham Hutzpah. My brother knows so little about football he thinks Glenn Hoddle is a malt whisky. James laughed, but it wasn't possible to laugh sufficiently to salve Mike's insecurities. Arsenal are so dirty one of their players named his auto-biography *Mein Bergkamp*. James couldn't even pretend to laugh at this one. He had never heard of Dennis Bergkamp. The mood was uneasy. In this pub, with this man, it was James who felt the misfit. That was so unfair.

'Same again?' asked Mike, who was drinking faster than James.

'I'll get them. This evening's on me.'

'No.'

'What?'

'I don't want your charity. I have money. I get benefits.'

'Compromise. We share the rounds and then I'll take you for a curry, on me. I long for a good curry. It was one of the few things Deborah and I didn't agree about. Well, she said they put weight on. She was big framed. She had to be careful. We'll have one more, and then I'll treat you to a curry. Please. I want to.'

'OK. Agreed.'

Mike bought another round.

'Cheers.'

'Cheers.'

'I'm sorry I'm sometimes so stroppy with you,' said Mike. 'You're the only one who ever comes to see me.'

This made James feel uneasy. He was so aware that he never invited Mike into his life. It came to him in a flash now that this wasn't just because he was ashamed of how Mike was, but also because he was ashamed of how he was – his cosy life, his tasteful middle-class house, the safeness, the smugness.

'Except Roger Dodds.'

'What?'

Returning from his thoughts, James had no idea what Mike was talking about.

'He invited me to a party the other day. Private room above some pub in Chelsea. Right out of the blue. I didn't even know he still had my address. It was his fiftieth. He's a bit older than the rest of us. He didn't come to Cambridge straight from school. Some kind of health problem. Mind you, I think he'd invited anyone he could lay his hands on.'

'He didn't invite me.'

'Oops.'

A particularly noisy plane roared throatily towards Heathrow, drowning for a moment the endless murmur of traffic on the still evening air.

'So, I was invited to something and you weren't.'

It would be mean to resent Mike's little triumph, but James couldn't help being miffed. Why hadn't Roger invited him?

Then he remembered something Jane had said.

'Did you see Ed there at all?'

'Ed Winterburn?'

'Yes.'

'No.' Mike had a rather strange expression. 'Why?'

'He's disappeared.'

'Ed?'

'Yes.'

'Disappeared?'

'Yes.'

'Good God. Good God. Ed!'

'I know. Not exactly the disappearing type.'

'More the reappearing type when you don't want him. Still . . . disappeared! What's Roger Dodds got to do with it?'

'Jane said that he went up to Chelsea for Roger Dodds's party, and hasn't been seen since.'

'Hell's bells.'

'He wasn't there?'

'Absolutely not. Well, I didn't see him anyway. I suppose he could have been there. It *was* very crowded. But I put myself about quite a bit, you know, quite a lot of people I hadn't seen for years, I'd have thought I would have seen him if he'd been there.'

In no time their glasses were empty and instead of going to the restaurant James found himself buying a third pint. A helicopter added to the evening's varied traffic noises. There was just the faintest breeze, but it was still hot in the beer garden. Conversation was proving so much easier than it usually was with Mike. James told of his activities during the last few days. Mike talked proudly of his success with his fantasy football team at the pub last season, and described quite amusingly the torments Tottenham Hotspur had put him through over the years. But all the time James had the feeling that something was not quite right.

Memories of Roger Dodds led inevitably to Cambridge. People who have been to Cambridge never quite get over it, however hard they try.

Mike bought his second round. James didn't want a fourth pint, but it would be patronising to refuse. Sometimes social considerations were more important than one's own desires. He wondered how many extra drinks the rounds system caused in a year. It must have been invented by a landlord.

They found a safe subject to chat about. People with whom they had both lost contact.

'Do you remember the weekend when your parents were away and you and me and Willy Tompkins and Derek Hammond cycled over from Cambridge to your house for the weekend?'

Mike smiled at the memory.

'Yeah, it was fun.'

'We all swam in the Ouse, which seems ridiculous now, but it was hot like it is this week. I didn't know the Fens.'

'Lucky you. They're horrid. Flat and the soil's almost black, and silly straight rivers everywhere, and ugly, stunted little houses.'

'Well, what I remember is beautiful wide sunsets and distant church spires and space. And we caught all those perch in some unprepossessing little river that nobody knew was there, but it wasn't called a river, it was the something drain, picturesque Dickensian name.'

Again, James had the feeling that something was wrong. Mike seemed wary somehow.

'I don't remember that. I don't know where you mean.'

'You must. It was your secret place, you said.'

'So secret I've forgotten it. James, it's all gone. I've been drinking myself to death. My mind's shot. My memory's buggered.'

'We went to your pub, and chatted to the locals, and played dominoes and darts and shove halfpenny, and challenged the locals, and we walked, and we ate endless amounts of those perch that we'd caught, and it was wonderful. I mean, it all seems so terribly innocent now, but it was all we needed, all we wanted. We ended up drunk, but we didn't go out to get drunk. Look at these people here. Don't you sense a communal desperation? Look at that lot over there, knocking back their shots. The aim is to get pissed. We didn't go out to get pissed. We got pissed because we were enjoying ourselves. With people we didn't know. We chatted to locals, farmhands, anybody. All the people here are in self-contained groups. You couldn't break in. They wouldn't let you. And that's not what pubs are about.'

An ambulance completed Ealing's repertoire of traffic noises.

'That ambulance makes your point,' said Mike. 'Tension stalks the streets of the city today.'

Mike talked about his family, how Melanie had turned against him, how she had turned their two children against him, how he had given up on seeing them, how it felt like having one of his legs chopped off. James told him about the new development over Charlotte, his hopes, his fears, his joy, his pain.

James had the feeling that there was something important about this evening, but that it was slipping away on a tide of alcohol. Well, never mind. The slipping away was very pleasant. It seemed no time at all before they had finished their four pints and were setting off for their curry.

The restaurant was within walking distance, and he decided to leave the car where it was, and not drink with the meal. The meal would take quite a while and by the time it had ended he would be just about under the limit. With a bit of luck.

But the moment he got into the restaurant he was hit by a wave of curry nostalgia, and decided that a large bottle of Cobra would go down beautifully.

In his youth there had still been flock wallpaper and bad photographs of the Taj Mahal in Indian restaurants, but now they gleamed white and the walls were adorned with abstract art. He loved the smell of curry and incense, the bustle, the poppadums, the pickles, the eccentric spelling on the menus, the ordering too much, the sharing of the food. Mike was happy for him to order for them both. He ordered onion bhajis and tandoori king prawns, followed by chicken pathia, methi gosht, tarka dhal, boiled rice and peshwari naan. They ate themselves silly and drank two more large bottles of Cobra. James discovered that Mike admired Charles and was another Schumann man, liked Sibelius and Mahler, disliked Mozart and Strauss. They managed to argue passionately about modern art without resorting to fisticuffs. Indeed, they came to a mutual conclusion, that the debate about whether modern art was rubbish or not was itself rubbish. The point wasn't whether it was good or bad but that the criteria for judging it had become so specialist that it was impossible for inverted commas ordinary close inverted commas people to know, so that, in the end, the hated comment of 'I know what I like', considered the ultimate badge of the philistine, became the only possible reaction of anyone who wasn't an expert. They both agreed that they hated intellectual snobbery, yet believed that some work was bound by its nature to be elitist. They deplored the lack of gentleness in modern television drama, as opposed to period television drama. Why was the only choice between bonnets and blood? Was there nothing to say about the modern world that wasn't violent?

'How many pathologists a week do we see on television?' asked James rhetorically. 'I mean, we never come across murder in our own lives, do we?'

He exchanged a look with Mike, and he had a feeling that Mike's look was meaningful, though he was far too drunk by now to know its meaning.

Mike forgot that he had a chip on his shoulder and James forgot that Mike was hard work and that he met him out of a sense of duty rather than of pleasure. They were truly living for the moment. A glass of Grand Marnier seemed just the thing to finish the evening off, and, if one, why not two?

James was not so drunk as to believe that it was safe for him to drive home. He would go by taxi, and drop Mike off on his way.

However, when Mike said, 'I've got a rather odd drink that I've never dared to open, it's Belgian gin, and it's in a bottle shaped like a hand grenade – would you like to come in and try it?', James was drunk enough to say 'yes'.

Sunday

There was no alarm to wake James at seven-thirty. He awoke suddenly, from a deep sleep in a dark cave shared with a monster. He was immediately in the grip of fear and tension. Something was very wrong.

Deborah was dead. Charlotte was living in a house in South London with a man named Chuck, and there was no Deborah to discuss it with. Ed had disappeared, and there was no Deborah to share the drama.

And today he was seeing Helen.

What time was it?

He tried to sit up. A steam hammer descended from the ceiling and crashed into his forehead. The room spun. His mouth tasted the way silage smelt.

How had he got home? Had he driven? Fear coursed through his heavy, aching frame.

He began to recall the events of the evening, how something odd had remained just out of reach, but how unexpectedly enjoyable it had been, how after being tired all day he had been full of energy, hadn't wanted the day to end. He remembered going back to Mike's place. A band of ice slipped down him from his neck to his feet as he recalled Mike producing a bottle shaped like a hand grenade. He shuddered. He began to shake. He felt very cold. His coldness frightened him. The fear made him sweat. The sweat froze on the icy tundras of his chest. He remembered them swearing eternal friendship. Mike had produced an autograph book, and asked him to sign it on the same page as someone called Alan Gilzean. Apparently he had played for Spurs and so this was a great honour. Oh, God, he'd signed it with his very expensive and much-loved gold Mont Blanc pen and Mike had said, 'That's right. Remind me of the times when I could afford nice things.' But the moment must have passed. They had hugged with drunken affection on his departure. Oh and, thank God, he remembered the minicab.

He found that if he moved very very slowly the pain was just about bearable. Slowly, carefully, gradually, he twisted his body so that he could see his alarm clock. He couldn't focus. When he did manage to focus, he wished that he hadn't. The clock brought him bad news. It was already twenty-five to ten.

There was no way he was going to be well enough to be ready for lunch with Helen.

He had to be.

It must have been more than twenty years since he'd suffered a hangover like this. He'd only had one since he'd married Deborah. She had put her foot down. He'd discovered the steel that lay beneath the warmth. Everybody thought how wonderful she'd been, but . . . no, she had been wonderful. The steel had been sparingly used, wisely used, and always with affection.

He needed some steel now. He needed someone to pull him together. But this was all ridiculous. If Deborah was still here, he wouldn't need the steel, because he wouldn't be having lunch with Helen.

He shouldn't even be thinking about Deborah. This was

154

his great day, the beginning of the rest of his life, the first important step on the road to total happiness.

He was going to blow it.

Desperation gave him the courage to crawl out of bed. The floor was moving as if he was on a boat. He stood and waited for it to steady itself, then walked ever so cautiously to the tiny en-suite bathroom stolen from the Georgian proportions of the room. He bent down over the bowl of the two-flush eco-lavatory, retched, and knew that he wasn't going to be able to be sick. He didn't know if this was good news or bad news.

He walked downstairs, his head hurting at every step. He was still naked, and a streak of sunlight caught his body from the window on the landing. It was a cruelly lovely day sent by a mocking God.

He opened a cupboard door, got himself a glass, padded to the fridge-freezer, filled the glass. The first touch of the chilled water on his parched mouth gave him a huge shock of . . . he wasn't sure if it was pain or pleasure. He gulped three glasses down as fast as he dared. The fourth he sipped. It was still not possible that he would be fit to have lunch with Helen, but it was now distinctly possible that he would live. He didn't know if this was good news or bad news.

He forced himself to have a cold shower. This was make-or-break. The first shock of the icy water almost stopped him breathing, but it worked. By the time he'd shaved and cleaned his teeth and dried his hair, he felt almost human, and brave enough to try his second, and final, make-or-break move.

A bacon sandwich.

Deborah always had bacon in. He hunted for it and found it. How long had it been there? Should it be tinged with green? Did bacon usually smell that strong? His stomach turned. He felt a retch coming on. But it stopped.

This could be a very wrong move, but he wasn't going to abandon the bacon yet. He put it in the frying pan and fried it gently in its own fat. He got a loaf from the bread bin. Should it be tinged with green? No. He would give it to the birds.

He ate three rashers of bacon, slowly, savouring each mouthful. Surely, if it was off, he wouldn't be enjoying it this much?

He stood up, put his plate in the sink, decided that he wasn't yet well enough to face washing up a greasy plate, put the plate in the dishwasher, alongside plates that had been there for almost a week, made himself a cup of black coffee, and went upstairs to get dressed.

He wouldn't have described himself as 'in the pink', but he felt so much better than he had any right to feel that he was being carried along on a wave of relief that was growing into exhilaration. Suddenly, however, just as he was beginning to feel safe, he had a very disturbing experience. He was looking at his array of shirts, and was about to choose a bright red one, when he sensed that Deborah was looking over his shoulder and frowning. He went cold all over again. He knew that she wasn't, it was just a lingering effect of the hangover, but it was deeply disturbing. He chose a sober dark green shirt, and forced himself to turn round to see . . . nobody.

He came out in a sweat and had to take another shower. He was running out of time, and he would have to get a taxi to take him to his car which was hugely out of his way.

He'd have to ring Helen. He really didn't want to, it would somehow spoil the clarity of the moment when they would meet, but he had to.

In fact the phone call went well.

'Darling, I'm going to be half an hour late.'

'No problem.'

156

Easy-peasy.

Then Philip rang.

'Just wanted to see if you needed company.'

'That's so kind, Philip. Actually . . . I hope this doesn't sound awful . . . but . . . it's all been so hectic . . . I just want to be alone. I need a Greta Garbo day.'

'I understand.'

'Are you sure?'

'Absolutely. Well, I'm here if you want me, James.'

'Thanks.'

Several minutes passed before he could ring off. He couldn't say, Sorry, Philip, I'm going to be late for my lover.

At last he could put the phone down. It rang again immediately.

'Just wanted to make sure you're all right.'

'That's so kind, Charles. Where are you?'

'Trieste. Just flown in from Helsinki. I did the Schumann there last night, told them it was for Deborah.'

'Thank you. Thank you, Charles. That's . . . very touching.'

'The Finns went wild. I felt very emotional.'

'Thank you so much, Charles. Look, you'd better ring off. The call must be costing you a fortune.'

What a ridiculous thing to say. Charles was loaded. But he had to get him off the phone. He was going to be so late.

At last Charles rang off.

Thank goodness, he found a taxi almost immediately. He sat in silence. His head was beginning to hurt again. The movement of the cab was bringing back an echo of his queasiness. Thank goodness the driver didn't speak. He tipped him generously.

'Oh, thank you, sir.'

'That's for not saying a word.'

'Like that, is it, sir?'

'Yes. Yes, it is.'

He leant against his car for a moment, letting the sun soak into his soul. As he set off from Ealing towards South Kensington he felt strong enough to switch the radio on.

Within seconds he was angry. Within a minute and a half he was shouting. A Church of England clergyman was describing his anguish over the election of women priests. He was going to have to become a Catholic. Suddenly a wave of anger swept the clouds from James's head. He glowed in the hot sunshine of conviction. His thoughts had that clarity that's in the air the morning after the gale has passed.

'You tight-arsed prick,' he shouted. 'Whether global warming is going to destroy our world or not, while your God stands by and watches all his creations crumble, is almost irrelevant, because we're doomed anyway if we don't solve the population problem. We're going to run out of resources sooner or later, and the Catholic Church, my good man, has guilt on its hands. But your little literal self-important conscience cares nothing about all this, cares only about its precious integrity, its puny narrow sexist cleanliness. The world needs inspiration, leadership, generosity. Women, that glorious breed who terrify you so much, can march with you and prove that religion still has a part to play in the salvation of the planet. But it's written in the good book that they can't be priests so it must be right, just as the fact that the world was created in six days must be right. I applaud you for knowing better than every scientist and expert in the whole world, you must be a very clever man, but your interpretation of spirituality is contemptible.'

That told him.

Anticlimax followed. He still had a bit of a headache. And he had that disturbing feeling that he would never be able to recall what he had said or say it half as well again. And, although he knew that it would not have been possible for him to say it except to the inside of his car, he felt sad, now

158

that it had come out so well, that it had only been to the inside of his car. It had been utterly pointless. It was the story of his life.

They sat in a shady corner of the pub. Their knees touched. This wasn't lunch. It was foreplay. All around them upper-middle-class London met, talked, exclaimed, kissed. The sun danced on the scrubbed pine tables. The newspapers were spread around, the pints and the glasses of wine were being sunk, people were reading the papers to see if they were wearing the right things, if they were thinking the right things, if they were in the right pub, if they had chosen the right wine, if they had booked the right place for their holidays, if they were sitting with the right sort of person.

There wasn't a notice on the door of the pub, saying *'Beautiful people only'*. It wasn't needed. It was sensed.

James had a distinct love-hate feeling for places like this, but today he felt only love. His anger had been spent on a hapless cleric who didn't know that he was hapless. Today was the first day of the rest of his life. James Hollinghurst was in love. He had been in love before, and it had faded, but this love would not fade, this love was different.

There were difficulties ahead. But this Sunday he was in a bubble. This Sunday there were no difficulties.

Well, only small ones. The first sip of the Syrah Grenache, for instance. How, after last night, would his body react to the alcohol? To his relief, but also somewhat to his alarm, his body greeted it like an old friend, welcomed it in, and settled down with it for a long meeting.

James chose man food – warm black pudding salad and belly pork. Helen chose woman food – smoked salmon and chicken tagine with couscous. It was as it should be, for they were man and woman.

James caught himself on the verge of saying, 'This is

159

perfection.' Luckily, he stopped himself in time. He knew that it was impossible to say, 'This is perfection,' without at least a touch of smugness, and that it is never perfect to be smug, so to say, 'This is perfection,' is to destroy that perfection instantly. He knew that even to think, 'This is perfection,' is to endanger that perfection. He knew that perfection could be sought, anticipated, expected. It could be remembered or forgotten. It could not be experienced. Perfection lived in the past and the future, not in the present.

But this day, this Sunday, to have spoken of perfection, how awful that would have been. Without the death of a good woman, this – if not perfection, this richly enjoyable moment – would not have been possible. A flicker of shame dimmed the sun for just a moment. There was no second ghostly appearance of Deborah, but she was there, she was with James for the rest of the meal, the main course, the coffee, the Armagnac that was the final pre-coital touch.

She was with James as he walked arm in arm with his beloved through the smiling streets around the Old Brompton Road, past the smokers spilling out onto the pavements outside the pubs, past the Labradors waiting patiently for their masters to finish their fourth pints. She was there, in the sunshine, and just for a moment she was the sunshine.

She was with him on the wide steps that led up to Helen's apartment. The sun, through the stained glass of the double doors, was carpeting the stairs in blue and red. He walked just behind Helen, admiring her small, cheeky, exquisite bottom.

In the richness of his desire James forgot Deborah again, or thought that he did. She was not there as he slowly undressed Helen, kissed her bottom, her thighs, her bush, her breasts. Or was she?

She surely wasn't with him as he entered Helen, his clean,

circumcised prick long and broad and triumphant. Or was she?

He pumped and pushed, Helen began to moan, and then, slowly, like a punctured balloon, like a bubble caught in the hands, he felt the stiffness go out of him. He pumped harder, but now his penis was a sorry, shameful thing, he could hardly feel it, he couldn't feel it at all, it was almost as if it had fallen off, was that possible?

It was a horrid feeling, pulling that flaccid thing out of her, like a stillborn baby. He shuddered in horror at himself and his unwelcome thoughts.

They lay side by side, touching each other, a million miles away from each other.

He said that word that he'd had to say so often lately but never before in his life under these circumstances. 'Sorry.' He smiled wryly deep inside his unsmiling self. He was beginning to think that it was his word of the week.

'Sorry,' he said again. 'That's the first time that's ever happened to me.'

'There's a first time for everything,' she said, trying but not quite succeeding to make a little joke of it.

He thought of saying, 'I had a lot to drink last night,' but that might have led her to think that he should have prepared for this great day less carelessly, so instead he said, 'I've had a very demanding and exhausting week.'

'It doesn't matter,' she said, telling the same lie that a million women had told before. Well, probably it wasn't entirely a lie. It mattered and it didn't matter. It might turn out to matter and it might not. 'Perhaps we could try again later.'

He didn't reply. He knew that they couldn't. Not today, anyway. Besides, he shrank from that word – 'try'. He had never had to try.

He had his third shower of the day. What a week it was also turning out to be for showers.

They were fully dressed again, standing in her coolly contemporary minimalist living room, with its stylish Scandinavian furniture and fittings. It was the first day of the rest of their lives. It was the first day in which he hadn't got another woman to scurry home towards. It was twenty-seven minutes past three. He couldn't leave early, now that he didn't have to. Goddamn it, he almost wished he did have to.

'What do you fancy doing?' she asked.

Sad words. Sad words.

'I don't know.'

An even sadder reply.

'Do you fancy a walk?'

'I really don't. It's so hot.'

It wasn't just the heat. It was the image. The Sunday afternoon stroll. The whole family, or just the happy couple, out on their post-prandial but not post-coital walk. On Christmas Day they'd be wearing their new scarves, but at any time of the year they'd look like the people in adverts for mortgages.

The afternoon hung before them as if this was a hospital visit. Neither could admit the desperation of this moment.

'We could always . . .' her words almost refused to come, she couldn't look him in the eyes, '. . . play Scrabble.'

From sex to Scrabble in twenty agonising minutes. Well, why not? It would pass the time.

It would pass the time! Was that what their great day had come to?

'OK.'

'Red or white?'

'Have you got white chilled?'

'Do you really think you need to ask me that?'

They decided to play in the communal gardens. That was good, because the little expedition took some time to organise – folding table, folding chairs, bottle of New Zealand Sauvignon, wine chiller, glasses, parasol. The intrepid travellers braved the long stairs, dark and gloomy now that the sun had moved on – well, now that the apartment block had rotated somewhat. The narrow back door proved no great obstacle to these brave wanderers, and quite soon they had set up their base camp in an unexplored corner of the private gardens.

James felt about sixty-seven.

When one is playing a game of Scrabble one has to be competitive, or there really is no point. James decided to show this whippersnapper how the game should be played. But it was not his day. At one stage he had seven vowels. At another, seven consonants. He had the J, but in the course of the game Helen had the X, the Z, the Q (with a U), both blanks and three of the four Ss.

There came a delicate moment when James could make two very different words. Cunt or aunt. The word 'cunt' is a difficult one for the English middle classes, and this was a Sunday, and they were in the private garden of a very respectable apartment block, close to the spot where Kensington met Chelsea.

However, the word is in the dictionary, it is permissible and acceptable, and words in Scrabble have no meaning, no value beyond their score. And the C on a triple letter would score nine.

James decided to forgo the points and settle for 'aunt'. A decision made in the interests of decency and respectability? No. An avoidance of a word that would lead back to thoughts of what hadn't been and, today, couldn't be.

By the time they had finished the game, and the wine, and had made the return expedition to the apartment, it was eleven minutes past six. It was still far too early to depart.

'I saw a little pub round the corner,' he said. 'I couldn't half fancy a pint. I've had enough wine.'

'OK.'

They sat at the bar counter. Helen had a gin and tonic and made it last, James had two pints of bitter.

'Shall I make you a bit of supper?' she suggested.

'That'd be great.'

They wandered back, arm in arm. He was ready for some more wine now. He really wanted to get roaring drunk, dangerous though that might be. She opened a bottle of red. Fleurie. Light wine for a heavy evening.

She rustled up a bit of supper. Couscous. He'd have bet on that.

'How are you with beetroot?' she asked. 'Love it or hate it?'

'No, I quite like it.'

Five years of seeing each other, and the beetroot question had never cropped up. He didn't even know if she was for or against Marmite.

It was an interesting supper. A fiddly supper. A complicated supper. A delicate supper. It was as unlike Deborah's succulent but straightforward ham and cheese and home-made pâté suppers as could be. It was none the worse for that.

And none the better.

Helen opened another bottle of Fleurie. James had the feeling that today he could have drunk the complete output of a medium-sized vineyard and still remained sober.

He saw Charlotte, saw her as he imagined she might look now, watching him with Helen. The image disturbed him.

It was time he went away, went home, stopped feeling maudlin.

But when Helen refilled his glass he didn't protest. He just watched the red stream entering his glass, didn't say a word.

They sat at the window and watched the light fade. They didn't talk much now, they sat there like a couple who were already married, and he didn't know whether that was good or bad. He began to want to see her naked again, but he knew that it would be no use. He'd had too much to drink. He didn't want to hear her say, 'It doesn't matter' again. He didn't want to have to utter his fiftieth 'sorry' of the week.

When the bottle and both their glasses were empty, James pulled himself slowly to his feet.

'Not putting pressure on,' said Helen. 'Honestly not.'

'But?'

'But . . . how long do you think I have to remain hidden away from the rest of your life?'

It was too early to mention his plan, the plan that he had worked out the other night when sleep wouldn't come. But perhaps he was slightly drunk after all, and he found that he was telling her.

'I thought we could go on a cruise, in a couple of months, say, because I don't want to go in August, children and cruises don't mix except on kid-friendly boats, which we'd both hate. September. Perhaps even a month's cruise. To really nice places. On a good cruise line. Single-occupancy cabins, but we sleep together from the start. We go back home, and I say to people, "I've met someone," and they say it's too soon, I'm on the rebound, we shouldn't flaunt ourselves out of respect, and I say, "But I love her. I'm not hiding her away. And I'm not on the rebound. This is the real thing, and I know Deborah would give it her blessing." Admit it, darling. It's not a bad plan.'

'No, I admit it, it isn't. But it's *your* plan, not *our* plan.'

'Come up with a better plan, then. I'll listen.'

'There is no better plan, and you know it. But it means that our new life will start with a lie.'

'I'm afraid we both have to accept that that is inevitable.'

She came down the stairs with him, they held each other tight for almost a whole minute.

For the second day running, he had to leave his car and get a taxi home.

Monday

The alarm woke James at half past six. He awoke slowly, and from a long way away. His head was heavy. His sleep had been deep but troubled.

Why had the alarm gone off an hour early? That hour of missed sleep clung to his eyes.

Of course. He'd left his car near Helen's apartment. He had to pick it up before parking charges became applicable. Eight-thirty, was it? Or eight? He couldn't remember.

Helen's apartment. Memories of yesterday flooded back. Sunday with Helen. It had been like sitting on a bouncy ball that had a very slow puncture.

He immersed himself in practicalities with some relief. Very calming, sometimes, practicalities. Shower. Dry. Dress. Breakfast. Coffee. Toast. Three-fruit marmalade on the first half-slice, honey on the second, then spreadable butter only, then medium-cut Seville orange marmalade. Pills. Quinapril, amlodipine and bisoprolol hemifumarate for the blood pressure. Simvastatin for the cholesterol. Cod liver oil with glucosamine for the joints. Nothing for the confusion in his soul, no cure known for that yet.

The soft plop of the newspaper onto the floor of the narrow hall.

Just time for a quick read over the last of the coffee. No point really, never anything worth . . . what??

'Two Lincolnshire schoolboys had a surprising shock . . . [What other kinds of shock are there? Morons!] *. . . when the kite they were flying landed in the waters of the River Ouse yesterday. They found not only their kite, but the dead body of controversial businessman Edward Winterburn (48). It is believed that it had been there for several days.*

Mr Winterburn was last seen walking away, on his own, from a private party in Chelsea last Tuesday. The police were alerted, and are known to have dragged several reaches of the Thames in their search for the missing 'high-flyer'.

A police spokesman said last night, 'We have no idea how he got to the river or whether he died there. It is too early to rule out foul play.'

His widow said last night that her husband had 'made enemies. He drove a hard bargain, and inevitably will have upset some people in his career. But I don't know of anyone who disliked him enough to take his life.'

Mr Winterburn's company, Braemar and Kettlewell, is believed to have financial problems, and suicide has not been ruled out.

James sighed deeply. It wasn't a matter that really affected him, but it was one more source of tension, however slight.

He flung the newspaper into the waste bin, as if he blamed it for spoiling his coffee, and stepped out into the cool warmth of a perfect summer's morning.

Deborah would never see, never feel, never smell another summer's morning. He gasped at the wound this thought opened in his heart.

*　　*　　*

170

'I don't like burkas,' said the taxi driver, as they saw a woman wearing one outside King's Cross Station. 'It's not right, isn't women covering their faces. It's not British.'

James had a great respect for London taxi drivers, but he feared that this morning of all mornings he'd been unlucky. He hardly ever went on the underground, and never in heatwaves, when it stank. But now he wished that he had. A great weariness came over him. He felt that he was no longer capable of facing up to the world. If only the taxi driver was a radio, incapable of answering back. If only he could lean forward, grab his neck, and twist him to a music channel.

There was so much wrong in the world of immigration, yet it sounded awful to be against it. He didn't really believe in multiculturalism, didn't believe it was working, had serious doubts whether it ever could work, yet he believed passionately that all men (and women, oh, heavens, yes) were equal. He thought that in an ideal world the richer nations would help the people of every poorer country to become well-off-enough never to need to move from their homelands to the gloomy streets of places like Bradford and Peterborough. These issues were far too complicated to discuss with a taxi driver at twenty to eight in the morning. If he made the attempt there was a serious danger that he would sound like an ally. He was no ally. But if he argued against him he would be tied up in rings and get nowhere. He would never meet the taxi driver again. He would achieve nothing by arguing. And he didn't much like burkas either, on security grounds, aesthetic grounds and sexist grounds. Sometimes the politically correct genes in his body ached when racism clashed with sexism.

No, there was no point. But he felt he had to say something. He decided to steer the driver into calmer waters.

'Do you have much trouble with cyclists?' he asked.

171

'Do I have much trouble with cyclists? Them bastards. I hate 'em,' said the taxi driver.

He felt that steering the driver into calmer waters had not been a success.

'Don't talk to me about cyclists. Go through red lights, they do. Cut across in front when you've got the right of way, they do. Slip through on the inside where you can't see 'em.'

These weren't calmer waters, but they were safer waters. James realised with a wry internal smile that while he would have hated to be thought of as racist or sexist, he wouldn't much mind being thought of as cyclist. No, that would have to be cyclistist.

'Think they're above the law,' he said.

'Absolutely right,' agreed the taxi driver. '*And* . . . they don't pay no sodding road tax neither. No, don't talk to me about cyclists.'

There were a few seconds of blessed peace, while James didn't talk to him about cyclists.

'Half of them are women,' resumed the taxi driver in a tone which suggested that this too was a criticism. 'Half of them are bloody women. Have you seen 'em? Weather like this, what they're wearing. Or rather what they're not wearing. Flimsy little skirts riding up in the wind. Flimsy little tops sliding down to meet them. Long legs and arms like what they have these days, and if we takes so much as one peep it's, "What are you looking at, you dirty old man?" Don't tell me there's a God.'

James hadn't any intention of telling the driver that there was a God, but he did wonder what that had to do with it.

Keep quiet, James. You'll find out.

'I mean, I know God's supposed to test us with temptation, but he wouldn't be human if he gave us that much bleeding temptation, would he? *And* . . . one little lapse of

172

concentration, and we lose our licence. It's not fair. It is not fair.'

At this point James made a very serious tactical error, such as he would not have made if he hadn't been in a state of considerable nervous tension as the taxi drew nearer to Helen's corner of London.

'You're complaining about women showing too much flesh,' he said. 'A few minutes ago you were complaining that they were covering themselves up too much.'

'Them burkas, oh, yes. You just wait till we go past Harrods. You'll see hundreds of them. No, don't talk to me about burkas.'

But I just have. Oh, God, I just have. And it's set him off again.

'I'll tell you something else that's wrong with this country.'
Please don't. I'm so tired. So confused.

How wonderful it was to step out of that taxi. The air smelt of roses and motorbikes. James approached his Subaru and stopped, tempted to put an hour's worth of coins into the parking meter and call on Helen. She'd still be coated in sleepiness. She looked pale and frail and other-worldly in the mornings, so unlike Deborah, who had jumped into each new day with vigour.

James willed his prick to respond to the thought of Helen in the early morning. But answer came there none. He shook his head. His shoulders sagged slightly. He couldn't not phone her. He couldn't leave yesterday's failure just hanging there limply. As it were. She sounded sleepy. He felt a tinge of desire. He must see her, put things right. He consulted the mental diary in his head. 'I could see you Tuesday evening,' he said.

'Tomorrow evening.'

Oh, God, so soon.

173

'Oh, good. So soon.'

He pinged the key of his Subaru, watched the welcoming flash of the lights, stepped into the car, and switched on the engine and the radio.

He'd hardly set off towards Hammersmith when he received his first injection of irritation. A pompous male voice was in the middle of a blanket condemnation of the young people of Britain. It seemed that they were almost universally lazy and violent. This was music to James's ears.

'Come on,' he shouted. 'How can they be both couch potatoes and violent? Who ever heard of a violent potato? There are some splendid young people around.' He thought of Max and what he was. He thought of Charlotte and what she might have been and – oh, God, the pain, the hope – might still be. The pain was like lava, always there but only occasionally erupting. Oh, God, how much longer could he stand the situation? Think of something else, James. Back to your rant. Oh, blessed rant.

'Do you know what young people have to put up with? They have to put up with the prospect of our civilisation imploding before they reach the age of fifty because of the complacency and inactivity, the mental laziness and corruption of your generation, you ode to pomposity. They get exams and tests every thirty-five minutes, their school trips get cancelled due to Health and Safety in case they fall over, and if they do fall over the teacher doesn't dare to pick them up because he or she . . .' James was careful not to sound sexist even in the privacy of his Subaru, '. . . will end up on the sex offenders' register and be charged by the European Court of Human Rights so they're left there crying. There's at least one paedophile on every double-decker bus because the human race is sick, sick, sick, there are drug pushers in every street, there's cheap alcohol in every supermarket, they're bombarded by adverts telling them to spend, spend,

174

spend, and anyone who is clever enough and strong enough to avoid all these pitfalls and get decent A levels finds that the A levels have been made so easy that half of them can't get a place at university and the other half come out with a debt of thirty thousand pounds before they start their first day's work.'

Oh, how much better he felt. He just wished that the taxi driver could have heard him.

Marcia was ten minutes late, and very embarrassed by the fact.

'It's not deliberate,' she said. 'I'm not playing you up because of what's happened.'

He had a sudden desire to bend down and kiss her rather large knees. He resisted it.

'I'm sure you aren't,' he said.

The desire passed as quickly as it had arrived, and was succeeded by a spasm of pity. She was actually looking at her lumpiest this morning.

'Maybe I don't need to say this, Mr Hollinghurst, but I want to,' she said. 'I intend to work out my month as diligently as I can.'

'Thank you. I wouldn't have doubted it.'

'Thank you.' The beginning of a blush spread over her innocent face. 'I think you've been a fantastic boss, actually, James. I think I've been very lucky.'

This was terrible. If only she'd not just stand there at the door of his office, blushing and shifting from one foot to the other. If only she'd go to her desk and start sorting his mail.

'Also, I have to say this, maybe you'll think I'm saying more than I should . . .'

Yes.

'. . . but I really admire you coming to work like this after what's happened.'

175

So much blood was rushing to Marcia's face that James began to worry that there wouldn't be enough left for the rest of her body.

'I'm only in today,' he said. 'I've a very important meeting.'

'I know. Eleven-thirty in the Small Conference Room.'

'Well remembered, Marcia.'

She smiled with shy pride.

'There are things I just have to set in motion. Then I'm taking the rest of the week off.'

'I'll keep the ship afloat.'

'I'm sure you will.'

'You aren't anyway. You've got your speech on Wednesday.'

'That's not work. That's showing off.'

'I would love to hear you, but I'm not invited.'

'I'm afraid I can't help there.'

'Oh, no, I wasn't . . .' She blushed at the thought. 'Mr Hollinghurst? There's something else I want to say.'

Please don't say you long for my body. His hand snaked out and touched the Philippe Starck telephone on his large desk, as if willing it to ring.

'Yes?' he prompted cautiously.

'You've done me a favour, forcing me to give up this job.'

'How come?'

'It's woken me up. You know I told you I wanted to be a writer. I never would have been. I'd have drifted on here for ever. Well, I've started. I've written eight pages.'

'Congratulations.'

'Thank you.'

'How did it go?'

'I don't know. Maybe authors . . .' Her voice rose slightly on the word 'authors'. She was an author already, in her mind. '. . . never do.'

He wanted her to go, but he didn't know how to break

176

the conversation off without hurting her feelings, and he heard himself asking a question he might deeply regret.

'What's it about?'

She didn't reply for a moment, and he added, hopefully, 'Or perhaps you don't want to tell me.'

'No, I don't mind. I'm going to have to learn to pitch, if I'm to get anywhere. I've read all about that. It's . . .'

He could see her courage beginning to fail her. He smiled encouragingly.

'It's about a wombat.'

'A wombat?'

'It's a children's book. That's my ambition – children's books.'

'Oh, great. Good.'

'I love children,' she said wistfully. 'It's called *Willy Wombat*. Or possibly *Willy the Wombat*. I'm not sure yet. Titles are difficult.'

She spoke as if from long experience.

'And what happens to . . . *Willy Wombat*? Or *Willy the Wombat*?'

'I don't know really. It's a bit early to say yet.'

'Of course. So what are your eight pages about?'

'Well . . . you know . . . setting the scene. Mum. Dad. Wendy Wombat.'

'Or Wendy the Wombat.'

'Quite.'

Oh, dear. It's hardly J.K. Rowling.

'It's hardly J.K. Rowling, is it?' she said.

He felt impelled to phone Jane. He didn't know what he would say, but he must say something.

'Hello, Jane. I've seen the paper,' he said. 'I'm so sorry.'

'Thank you.'

'Well, at least you know.'

'Yes.'

'They suspect foul play?'

'That's all bollocks. Everything they say is bollocks. They don't *suspect* foul play. They *know* it's foul play.'

'Not suicide?'

'Not unless he plonked a carving knife into the bed of the river – which wasn't the Ouse, incidentally, just about everything's inaccurate – at a very shallow point in the river, and then jumped off the bank onto the knife with such precision that it plunged right into the centre of his heart.'

'Good God.'

'Yes. I bet the journalist from the news agency who's spread that story about Braemar and Kettlewell being in trouble is hoping the shares will plummet and he'll buy lots of them at the bottom and make a fortune.'

'What a suspicious mind you have, Jane.'

'I work in that sort of world. I must say I'm relieved it wasn't suicide. I don't think I've been a very good wife to him, and I certainly haven't liked him much for a decade or two, but I wouldn't want to think I helped to drive him to that.'

James noticed that he had begun to stroke his right nipple with his free left hand. He removed the hand. He didn't know what was going on this morning. First, Marcia's knees. Now, Jane's nipple. Because that's what his nipple had become, in his mind, as he stroked it. He didn't usually have sudden sexual feelings of this sort.

'So . . . how are you?' he asked. 'Are you all right?'

'I'm disturbingly calm, James. I . . . the awful thing is . . . well, I suppose it's not that surprising really . . . I just don't seem to be able to cry.'

'Jane, I was wondering . . .'

Marcia lumbered in with bad timing and his ten o'clock

178

coffee. She always made the coffee herself, proudly, saying that the coffee from the machine was terrible. It was, but so was the coffee she made. He had failed to tell her right at the beginning, out of his natural kindness and good manners, and then it had been too late, and he had drunk an unpleasant cup of coffee almost every weekday morning for eight and a half years. He often wondered whether any other Managing Directors behaved like that, and what was wrong with him. He didn't wonder this now, because he was more concerned that, with a talent worthy of a professional waiter, Marcia had arrived at the very worst moment.

'Are you still there, James?'

'Yes, I'm still here. Marcia – she's my PA – she's just arrived with my coffee. Thank you, Marcia. Lovely.'

'There's a—' began Marcia.

'Later, Marcia. Thank you.'

'Sorry.'

Marcia walked out, inelegantly, and flustered.

'Sorry about that,' he said to Jane.

'You didn't mention my name.'

'What?'

'You said your PA had arrived with your coffee. You didn't mention my name. You didn't want Marion to know you were talking to a woman.'

'Marcia. What a lot you read into things. You always did, I remember.'

'Anyway, before you were so rudely interrupted, you were wondering.'

'Yes. Yes. I was wondering, Jane . . .' He'd had time, during the interruption, to wonder if he should have been wondering what he'd been wondering. The thought had surprised him very much, but, also somewhat to his surprise, he had decided to go through with it. 'I was wondering . . .' He felt as if he was nineteen again, plucking up courage. '. . . I mean, here

179

we are . . . you were, you know, my first real girl-friend . . . OK, very briefly . . .'

'Yes, sorry about that.'

'Here we are, both losing our partner violently in the same week . . . odd, really.'

'Not particularly. I did a paper on probability at Cambridge. I had a theory which I called Event Batch Syndrome. I explored the phenomenon whereby similar types of happening tend to occur in clutches.'

'You always were clever. You'd have been too clever for me. Anyway, here we are, in the same boat . . .' Neither of us able to cry, though I'm not going to admit to that. 'I . . . I just wondered . . . I'm taking the rest of the week off . . . and the family hordes aren't beginning to muster until Wednesday, the funeral's Thursday, I wondered if you . . . fancied lunch tomorrow.'

'That sounds like an extraordinarily good idea, James.'

The moment he'd put the phone down, he thought that perhaps it wasn't. He thought that perhaps it was a very bad idea indeed. He'd had no intention of suggesting any such thing. It had come out of left field . . . and right nipple. He was seeing Helen in the evening. What on earth was he doing arranging lunch with Jane?

He picked up the phone, to ring her and cancel.

He put the phone down again.

The man who had decided never to wear his white linen suit again picked up the phone and rang the number he had been told to ring by the person at the number he'd been told to ring by the person whom he had first rung. God, you needed patience.

'Oh, hello, this is a little awkward, and I don't know if I'm ringing the right place, but I've been told that you're the person to ring.'

'How can I help you, sir?'

The voice sounded polite and not impatient. Promising.

'Yes. It's a little embarrassing. My name's . . . well, no, it isn't, that's the problem.'

'I don't understand.'

Impatience creeping in.

'I lost a wedding ring at a hotel. My wedding ring. They found it and sent it on to my address. But I'd given the wrong address . . . in their guest book, because . . .'

He hesitated. He didn't know this man, the man didn't know him, they would never meet, why on earth was he hesitating?

'. . . because, to be honest, I was meeting a married woman and I . . . I know her husband pretty well . . . and just to be on the safe side I gave a false name and address, and so this ring, which has some fantastic diamonds in it and was a gift from my beloved wife so it is extremely valuable both financially and sentimentally, as you can imagine, has gone off to a man who doesn't exist, living in a house that doesn't exist, in a street that doesn't exist, in Poole, which does exist, which is why I am ringing you.'

'I see. What was the address, sir?'

'Does it matter, since it doesn't exist?'

'Well, it might be similar to an address that does exist, and the postman might have used his initiative.'

'I see. Yes. All right. It was addressed to Mr J. Rivers, that's me, or rather it isn't, of Lake View, 69 Pond Street, Poole.'

'I see, sir.'

Not a flicker of amusement, making the joke address seem even more childish than ever.

'Are you still there?'

'I'm just checking in the book, sir.' A distinct note of rebuke. 'Yes, sir, there is no Pond Street in Poole.'

'So what will happen to it?'

'It will be sent, maybe has already been sent, to Belfast.'

'Belfast?'

'We have an office in Belfast, sir, to which all letters and packages with untraceable addresses are sent.'

'Why Belfast, of all places?'

'I have no idea, sir. It was not my idea.'

'No, I realise that. Pretty silly idea, though. It'll probably get blown up.'

'I understand that there is no great security crisis in Belfast as of this moment in time, sir.'

'No, I was only being . . . I'm just irritated. Maybe the Post Office has an agreement with an airline so that everybody has to fly to Belfast to get their letters back.'

'I couldn't possibly comment on that, sir.'

'Anyway, the bottom line is, to get this ring back, I'll have to go to Belfast.'

'I'm afraid so, sir.'

'Bloody hell!'

'Precisely, sir.'

At 11.30 in the Small Conference Room of the Head Offices of Globpack UK, in a dark place hidden from yet another sunny summer morning by the Hammersmith Flyover, with double glazing so efficient that the perpetual roar of traffic on the flyover was but a distant faint rumble, James Hollinghurst, just five days after the death of his wife, looked surprisingly happy. He looked like a man on top of his game. Lindsay Gibb, Lindsey Wellingborough, Duncan Bailey, Tim Campagnetto, Boris Eckhart and Jean Forrester looked at him with barely hidden amazement. Was he a man of stone, with no feelings? Yes, for an hour and a half. That was why he was so surprisingly happy. Cocooned in the conference room, he was safe from all emotion. And he realised that

Dwight Schenkman the Third had handed him not a poisoned chalice but a great opportunity. There was something almost magnificent about James that morning. Duncan Bailey and Tim Campagnetto often went for a quick pint after work, and very occasionally James would join them. This evening he would not, so one cannot know what Duncan said to Tim, but it could well have been something on the lines of 'Who did he think he was? Winston Churchill?' Yes, absurd though it might seem in the context of packaging, on the subject of saving two factories on industrial estates, this was James's 'We shall fight them on the beaches' moment.

He explained the facts briskly and pithily. Bridgend and Kilmarnock would go to Taiwan, unless huge savings could be made at Bridgend and Kilmarnock.

'Anyone fancy a coffee?' he asked.

Five of the six fancied a coffee.

'Well, we can't afford any. HQ is not immune. None of us are immune. We will all be pulling together, to save our manufacturing base. Think coffee, drink water, save.'

Much of the meeting was taken up with the minutiae of organisation. It took quite a while to decide which three of the six would take specific responsibility for Bridgend (Tim Campagnetto, Jean Forrester and Lindsay Gibb, as it happened), and which three would take on Kilmarnock (no need to tell you, unless you're not following this closely, that it was Boris Eckhart, Lindsey Wellingborough and Duncan Bailey).

James actually spoke . . . oh, perhaps you should be told, in case it becomes a worry to any of you, that it was actually Lindsey Wellingborough who hadn't wanted the coffee that none of them had . . . James actually spoke, without embarrassment, about responsibility. 'Not a fashionable word, but I have chosen the six of you because I believe you have a sense of responsibility. At the end of the day we may have to decide that there is no alternative to relocating to Taiwan, but it's our responsibility to explore every possibility of maintaining production in Bridgend and Kilmarnock, and of keeping as many of the workforce there in work as is humanly possible. We must try to remember at all times that every compulsory redundancy could be a family torn apart.'

James's concentration faltered for the first time. An image had crept uninvited into his head, an image not of sex, but of a river, the Ouse, a body being dragged out, Ed, dead, dripping with water. Strange that he had been talking about the Ouse with Mike. Strange that . . . he shook his head, tossing the image away. Where was he? He was lost. They were looking at him with sympathy, with understanding. It almost amused him to think how little understanding they could have about what he was thinking.

'Where was I?'

For a nasty moment he thought that none of them would remember either.

'Compulsory redundancy,' said Boris Eckhart.

'Families torn apart,' said Jean Forrester.

'Ah. Yes. I've also chosen the six of you because I believe that you will be able to work well with the good people of Bridgend and Kilmarnock. We must take the local people with us on this. If we can't inspire them to play their part, we can't save them. I think there's a chance that in the years to come rising transport costs, rising wages in the Third World and quality issues can begin to create a revival in British manufacturing. Slow and not very glamorous, perhaps, but I hope that we can all get satisfaction from doing our bit in this long battle.'

If they did go to the pub that evening, and if Duncan Bailey did say, 'Who did he think he was? Winston Churchill?' let's hope that Tim Campagnetto replied, 'It's easy to mock, but I thought he was rather magnificent.'

184

After a lot of discussion of dates and meetings and programmes of visits to Bridgend and Kilmarnock and lists of people in those places who would need to be consulted, James explained to them that he was taking a week off, although he would fulfil his engagement to speak at the fiftieth anniversary lunch in the Mauretania Room of the Park View Hotel on Wednesday. He would return to the office tomorrow week, and they would have a further meeting then. He hoped to see them at the lunch, and also at the funeral the following day.

The funeral. The world outside packaging beckoned. After he'd shaken hands with all six of them, and accepted their sympathy, he gathered his papers up slowly, took a long drink of water, and walked out of the cool oasis of the beige conference room into the sweltering desert of his blood-red heart.

He heard the pub before he saw it. The roar of two hundred conversations, the laughter at the latest jokes about Irishmen and Muslims and sex and Cameron and Clegg. It was elbow to elbow on the wide pavement outside the pub. It was a fight to get to the bar in the vast, marbled, mirrored interior. When you got to the bar, it was a fight to get served. When you had been served, it was a fight to get away from the bar. In a corner, unheard, unwatched, two men, both six foot six tall, served tennis balls at each other like bullets. It was London in summertime.

Four men who had once punted with girls along the calm, exquisite waters of the Cam, stood on the pavement with their pints, huddled and squashed together in the steaming crowd like four umbrellas in a stand. Roger Dodds, about whom little was known. Derek Hammond, about whom everything was known and in much too great detail. Seb Meikle, whom James hardly knew. And James himself, whose afternoon had been an anticlimax. He had phoned Dwight Schenkman the Third, to report on the progress of the morning's committee meeting, and had been told, 'Your devotion to your duties, your acceptance of your responsibilities, your energy and stamina and discipline in the face of a personal trauma that would have destroyed a lesser mortal are awesome, James. You know what you are? You're the role model that the world of packaging needs.'

God forbid. That had done it. He hadn't done a stroke of work for the company during the rest of the afternoon. He had found himself unable to concentrate on work. He had given his all at the meeting. He had spent himself.

Slowly, inevitably, Thursday had begun to loom. He'd found himself breaking off from his work to finalise arrangements. He'd rung the caterers to increase his estimate of the numbers who would come back to the house. He'd rung the undertakers to discuss the composition of the procession of cars to the crematorium. He'd finalised the arrangements for the arrival, the evening before, of the piano that Charles would play at the service. He'd rung Fliss to consider the delicate question of who should go in which car. He'd rung his mum to avoid being accused of not having rung her. He'd longed for . . . what? He hadn't known what he had longed for. He had only known that he had longed for something.

And tomorrow evening he was seeing Helen. That, too, had begun to loom.

Why was he here? Because Roger Dodds had rung back, after he'd told him of Deborah's death, and had suggested that they 'show solidarity. Take you out of yourself.' The only person, of course, who can take you out of yourself is yourself. James had almost managed to do this in the conference room. On the crowded pavement he had only been taken out of everything that was relevant to himself, but he had not been taken out of himself, so there he was, irrevocably himself, in a place which had no relevance to him and in which he didn't want to be. Oh, why had he come?

Because they meant well. Because there might come a day when he wanted their friendship. Because he didn't know what he would have done if he hadn't been there. Well, that was a good enough reason.

Seb Meikle, who was too tall and felt it, bent down slightly to talk of the great cricket matches they had played on Sundays against the villages around Cambridge, and the fine times they'd enjoyed afterwards in the village pubs before catching the last bus and rushing to the nearest Indian restaurant with empty stomachs and bursting bladders.

Derek Hammond, who was too fat and hated it, gave detailed updates on the progress of his three children, the latest developments in his battles against moles, his itinerary for his motoring holiday in Germany, and the saga of his septic tank, which an ignorant surveyor from the big city had spelt 'sceptic tank'. Every summer he invited them all to a barbecue where excellent wine flowed with immense generosity so listening to all this was a small price to pay.

Roger Dodds, who was neither too tall nor too fat and knew it, smiled and laughed and commented on everything and revealed nothing. He was very amusing on the subject of sceptic tanks, and informed them that he was the proud owner of a very cynical lavatory. The other three shared a look which stated, That's the only thing we'll ever find out about where he lives.

The thought led on in James's mind to Roger's party, which he had not held in his secret home but, typically, in a private room above a public house. He found that he needed to take this opportunity to find out more about the party. He was hooked on Ed's death.

'You had a party last week, didn't you?' he said.

'Yes. Fiftieth.'

None of them had ever known what Roger had done between leaving school and going to Cambridge at the age of twenty. This, they had felt, had been taking the principle of a gap year too far before gap years were fashionable. But Roger was fun and you had to accept him for what he was and accept that you'd never find out what he was.

'Mike was there, wasn't he?'

'Everybody was there, James.'

'I wasn't.'

'No. You weren't. Right. My round.'

Roger struggled to the bar, and Seb went with him to help. While they were gone, while James was still wondering why Roger hadn't invited him, Derek took the opportunity of imparting a little more information about his life.

'Did I ever tell you about our honeymoon in Crete?'

'Yes.'

'About the farm we stayed at and the horse that got into the loft?'

'Yes.'

'It was amazing. We'd booked into this . . .'

James had to admire Derek's masterly narrative powers. He made the tale last exactly the length of time that it took Roger and Seb to bring four more beers.

He tried to preserve his dignity and ignore the conversational itch that was assailing him, but in the end he had to scratch.

'May I ask why I wasn't invited?'

'Yes.'

'Oh, come on, Roger. Don't piss about. We're old friends. Why wasn't I invited?'

'Because three times you've accepted my invitations and not come.'

'Ah. Fair enough.'

He had taken the invitations as opportunities to have some time with Helen. How egocentric he'd been. Well, more Helenocentric, really.

Now at last they got round to the extraordinary business of Ed's murder, which none of them had wanted to be the first to mention for fear of being accused of having an interest in sensation that could not be described as cool.

'He was there, at the party, was he?' asked James. 'Only I went out with Mike on Saturday – well, I do see him occasionally, I feel sorry for him – and he said he'd been at the party and I told him about Ed's disappearance, which he knew nothing about, and he said it was a very crowded party and he hadn't run into him.'

'I hope he didn't,' said Roger. 'I had my doubts about inviting them both, to be honest. But somehow, you know, whatever you thought about Ed, it wasn't the same if you excluded him, and Mike, like you, sympathy, dreaded word.'

'I'm not with you. Why should you worry about inviting them both?'

'Well, when Ed went bankrupt that second time and opened up again in Jane's name he owed Mike thousands, nearer six figures than five, I'd say, and Mike got about five per cent. It's what really pushed Mike's business over the edge. Five years ago, I'd say it was.'

Just when he'd started seeing Helen. Lost touch with what was going on. Taken himself out of the loop.

James had been aware, as they stood on that crowded, noisy pavement, of a growing and inexplicable tension. Now the tension began to be less inexplicable. A disturbing possibility had entered his mind, the possibility that Mike had murdered Ed. It was astonishing and disturbing and at the same time curiously exciting to think that a man you knew well might have killed another man you knew well. He hoped, almost desperately, that none of them would move on to speculate about Ed's death. He wasn't ready to confront this possibility.

He needn't have worried. Derek said, 'We sat on the same table as a bankruptcy expert on one of our cruises,' and the conversation moved on to other topics, including the complete itinerary of the cruise on which Derek Hammond had sat at the same table as the bankruptcy expert. James had never felt so grateful for one of Derek's excruciatingly boring stories.

Roger said he had to leave fairly soon after that, giving no reason. Seb went off to go to the theatre. Derek returned to his memories of the bankruptcy expert, listing every item of food that the unfortunate man had been unable to eat due to the delicate state of his intestines. It wasn't riveting stuff, but it was better than sitting at home on his own, and James was quite sorry when Derek announced that he had to leave in order to catch the 8.44 to Coulsdon.

Tuesday

The first magical hint of rose was creeping over dewy Islington when James woke. The world was silent, sleeping. Only a hissing milk float, harbinger of the rumpus that would soon be London life, disturbed the uncanny calm. It was far too early to get up.

He turned over, to face the empty side of the bed. To think that he'd fantasised about Deborah's death. How he missed her now.

He couldn't bear to see the place where she wasn't. He turned back onto his right side again. But there was no peace to be had there either. His worries crowded in on him, jostling for places in his brain.

Helen, his last, long love. He was seeing her tonight. He was dreading it. Why? Jane, his brief, first love. He was seeing her for lunch. Why? Oh, James, you idiot, why? Mike, his second oldest old friend, with whom he had enjoyed a curry on Saturday. If Mike really hated Ed . . .

No. He was imagining things. He was in a heightened state of tension. He wasn't himself. Such things only happened in a parallel world, the world other people lived in. Or on television, in the land of blood and pathologists.

But pictures of Mike presented themselves to him unbidden. Horrid images that he hated. Mike plunging a knife into Ed's stomach. Mike tipping Ed out of a forklift truck into the muddy water of a Fenland river. Ridiculous. Mike was his drinking buddy. Ed had done a dreadful thing, but, damn it, they had both been to Cambridge. Mike was bitter, twisted, but . . . a killer? Never.

But somebody had murdered Ed. That much was clear. And Ed *had* done Mike out of a huge amount of money and in essence ruined his life. And Mike *had*, not surprisingly, hated Ed, according to Roger Dodds. And they *had* both been at Roger's party. And Mike said that he hadn't seen Ed there, which seemed unlikely.

This was all terribly vague. Derek Hammond had been at Roger's party. Seb Meikle had been at Roger's party. Either one of them might have hated Ed. He was being ridiculous.

Neither Derek Hammond's life nor Seb Meikle's life had been ruined, though.

Stop it. Had some great times with old Mike . . . Think of something else. Count sheep. Pretend to be making love to . . . no! Don't. None of it was any use. All of it was confusion. His thoughts churned in circles.

Cancel Jane. That was a must. There was still a question that he needed to put to her, though. He would have to have that lunch.

He could phone her. There was absolutely no need to have lunch with her.

She had been beautiful. Tall, statuesque, a little intimidating. She would still be tall. She would still be statuesque. But would she still be beautiful? He would rather like to find out. Besides, if things with Helen didn't . . . what? What was he thinking? He was rather dreading seeing her, because he was ashamed of his failure in bed on Sunday. That was all. Nothing more. Nothing serious.

No, there was absolutely no point in seeing Jane. He didn't like her. And he knew for certain now that she had been in cahoots with Ed, that she had been a partner in the activities that had ruined his best friend, who was not a killer.

He would phone and cancel.

He felt relieved that he had made a decision. He turned over onto his left side again, stretched his legs, closed his eyes and made another attempt not to think about these things. He made a map, in his mind, of the faint, feathery cracks in the ceiling. He opened his eyes to see how accurate his map had been. Hopeless. Way off the mark.

Then, against all the odds, sleep came. With it came Mike, lunging at him with a bread knife. He sat up, wide awake in the empty room. This was ridiculous. His eyes felt as though they had sunk into his head, like his mother's, but he wasn't going to get any more sleep. There was no alternative but to get up.

It was seventeen minutes past five. What on earth was he going to do?

He padded down to the kitchen, made himself a cup of builder's tea, unlocked the back door, and took his tea out into the narrow, elegant garden. The roofs of the houses were still touched with red. No leaf stirred. The dew lay silvery on every blade of the long grasses. The cast-iron bench was soaking. The gravel was darkened by moisture. The little Elizabeth Frink, their prize possession, was soaking. Diana, the huntress, was soaking. This was not the garden of a man who was big in packaging. This was Deborah's garden.

He began to shiver. The morning was still surprisingly cold. Or was he just shivering with fright?

Mist was rising from every plant and every roof. It was a fairyland. He finished his tea, and went back inside. The house smelt of tiled floors. He switched the television on, then switched it off for fear that even at this early hour the pathologists would be about. I'm developing a pathological fear of pathologists, he told himself.

He switched the radio on. '. . . but my essential point about modern Britain's decline is . . .' He switched it off. It struck him how strange, how amazing, how magical the communication systems of the modern world are. A self-important prophet is intoning, you hear none of it, you switch the radio on, you hear nine words, they depress you beyond belief, you switch it off. The man drones on, his smug pessimism unaffected by your decision, but you can hear nothing.

How silent the house was. He put the kettle on, just to hear it whistle.

He thought of switching the radio back on, the radio was his friend, there were no pathologists on it, or, if there were, they were talking about pathology and not cutting people up. But he couldn't, not here. He would need to shout at it. That was fine in the car, but if he shouted here it would wake – if not the dead – the neighbours.

He had a shower, washed his hair, dried it, got dressed. It was twenty-three minutes past six.

He actually thought about driving round and round Islington, with the radio on, shouting at it. He thought of going down to the Emirates Stadium and shouting, 'Come on, you Spurs.'

He made his breakfast, put honey on all four half-slices, shouted, 'That's surprised you, hasn't it?' He ate the toast very slowly.

He took his pills.

He drank the herbal concoction that Holly prescribed to get rid of the dry cough that was a side effect of the pills.

He made himself a cup of black coffee to get rid of the taste in his mouth that was a side effect of the herbal concoction that Holly prescribed to get rid of the dry cough that was a side effect of the pills.

It was seven minutes to seven.

He went into his study and opened his address book. He went right through the book, making a list of people whom he thought that perhaps, marginally, he should have told about the time and place of the funeral.

He decided that if he telephoned them today, giving them only two days' notice six days after Deborah's death, the brighter among them might realise that they were marginal. Besides, already more people were coming than could be coped with by the chapel and the house.

He screwed up the list and tossed it towards the waste-paper basket.

He missed.

He found himself downstairs again, rummaging in a bureau, without any recollection of having decided to go there. He found a large envelope he didn't think he had seen before. On it was written, in Deborah's generous hand, 'Glebeland, 1979'. He opened it, and found a large photo of a group of girls. There was Deborah, her beauty not yet quite formed, smiling with such vast optimism that he shuddered at the knowledge of her death. Helpfully, she had written the names of all the other girls under the photo. Amanda Castlebridge, hating to be photographed and making a silly face. Constance Thrabnot, no warmth in her narrow smile, so that her sticky end (which need not concern us) didn't seem surprising. Grace Farsley, the one that got away, whom Deborah missed so much, her niceness, her openness, the warmth of her wide smile shining through from thirty years ago. He lingered over the photo, drinking in these girls and their hopes, and all the while the funeral was like a black spot in the barbecue sky, a black spot that was growing like something in science fiction, a black spot that would slowly

197

spread all over the sky, that would bubble and suppurate and strangle.

Of course it was possible for him not to go to the funeral. He could just go to Brighton for the day. People would put it down to stress. He could get away with it.

Or he could just disappear altogether. Get away from all his tensions and escape to a new life.

These thoughts soon passed. There is no escape. Everywhere is somewhere else. Nowhere is nowhere.

At eight o'clock he wondered if it was too early to phone Jane and cancel lunch. He decided that it was.

Suddenly he remembered that he needed to transfer money from his business account to his personal account.

He dialled his bank's automated business service. He had to answer several questions asked by a recorded voice. Account number. Sort code. Date of birth. Third and sixth letter of his security code. His mind went blank for a moment, then it came to him. Helen's date of birth. 151174. He felt a sense of shock. 1974! He'd forgotten how young she was. She would still have time to find someone else.

He was impatient at the best of times, and now the voice-recognition system failed to recognise his voice three times, forcing him to repeat himself. When at last he was asked to wait for the next available advisor, he found he had to wait for more than three minutes. He was forced to listen to idiotic music constantly interrupted by another mechanical voice thanking him for the patience he hadn't got.

When at last he got a human voice it was young, adenoidal and irritatingly friendly.

'Good morning!' she said. 'My name is . . .' She knew her name so well and had announced it so often that she gabbled it so fast that he had no idea what it was. And he could barely understand her thick Black Country whine anyway. 'Do you mind if I call you James?'

He hesitated for just a moment, wondering whether to let it pass. But he was too irritated for that.

'Yes, I do mind,' he said. 'I mind very much. How dare you presume an intimacy you haven't earned? How dare you force me into sounding like the kind of pompous prig I can't abide?'

There was a brief silence.

'How can I help you, Mr Hollinghurst?' she said, in a thin, hurt voice.

He felt dreadful.

'I just want to transfer some money from my business account to my personal account.'

'Certainly, Mr Hollinghurst. I can do that for you.'

May as well try to be polite, make amends.

'Thank you very much.'

'How has your morning been so far, Mr Hollinghurst?'

Replies whizzed through his mind like combinations on a fruit machine. 'Fucking awful.' 'Mind your own business.' 'Do me a favour, get on with it, I'm paying for this call.' 'Lonely, my wife's just died.'

He couldn't. He had to make amends. This slip of a girl was forcing him, a Managing Director, to make amends. That was what was so intolerable.

'Not very good, to be honest. Which is why I was so short with you. I really don't think there's any reason why we should be on first-name terms. But then I'm from an older generation, and the generation before mine, my father's generation, didn't even call their close friends by their Christian names. But I'm sorry. I shouldn't have been so rude.'

Who's talking too much and building up the phone bill now?

'That's all right, Mr Hollinghurst. How much money do you want to transfer?'

When he had finished the call, James sat at his desk for almost four minutes, motionless. His chat with the girl at the call centre had upset him. Next week he faced another haircut. An eleven-year-old girl would wash his hair, wetting the collar of his shirt in the process, and she would ask him, 'Are you doing anything exciting this weekend?' and he would want to scream at her, and the person he should scream at was the creator of the training courses that taught these people how to deal with the public.

But he had been even more shaken by something else, by something he had thought while talking to the voice-recognition system. *He'd forgotten how young she was. She would still have time to find someone else.* What had he been thinking about? She had him. They were for ever.

He desperately needed to get out of the house. He decided to pop down to the travel agent's, get some brochures, start thinking about what cruise they could go on and pretend to have met on.

He would never forget his visit to the travel agent's, which was as hot and airless and boxlike as a holiday hotel room.

He smiled at the staff, mumbled, 'Just looking,' and set himself to work. There were so many brochures, such large ships, so many facilities. He could see within minutes that the industry was going in a way that was not for him. The latest ships were the largest. The thought of three thousand people disgorging themselves into some quiet port revolted him. He had seen big ships arriving in Venice, dwarfing the palaces, destroying the unity of the place they were bringing people to see. There were whirlpool spas, golf simulators, bungee trampolines, champagne bars, all-night food, chocolate festivals, art auctions, nightclubs, champagne fountains, casinos, posh restaurants in the names of celebrity chefs who had probably never stepped on board. The vulgarity was staggering, and, since most of the cruises began and finished in Southampton, which involved crossing Biscay twice, for much of the time the passengers would probably be staggering too. He couldn't see himself and Helen on these ships.

Then there were really smart ships, top of the range, altogether more tasteful, but, he still felt, they were dealing only in a rather more tasteful vulgarity. He could feel the soft, carpeted pampering, the anodyne background music in the lifts, the excesses on the table, the galloping consumption of the passengers, however well-bred and discreet it might be. No, somehow, for some reason, he couldn't see himself and Helen on those ships either.

There were other, altogether more promising cruise lines, smaller ships, ships for people who wanted to explore the world, ships with lecturers who knew about the places they were visiting, ships that James liked the sound of, ships that would eventually be squeezed out in an industry increasingly being run by people who thought that profit was the whole point of it all, rather than being the necessary and admittedly pleasurable ingredient that made all the other pleasures possible.

When he felt that he couldn't quite see himself and Helen performing their little charade with their separate cabins on one of these ships, he began to be worried. He realised that the charade was never going to happen, wouldn't work. He took the brochures back to the shelves. He was shaking.

When he said, 'Thank you very much,' he could hear a tremor in his voice.

He knew then that it wasn't just the cruise that wasn't going to take place. It was his life with Helen that wasn't going to take place. Perhaps, he thought, he had never truly wanted her, he had only wanted to want her.

He knew now why he had been dreading this evening so much.

When he went outside he walked into a wall of heat; the heat was already bouncing off the pavement, and it was still early morning.

He felt faint. He had to clutch at the traffic lights at the pedestrian crossing, and when the lights turned green he was afraid to cross. He felt in that moment that the lights would never be green for him again. He thought of Helen and he felt sad, scared and ashamed. He thought of the rest of his life and he felt bewildered.

He had only spoken two sentences, nobody had spoken to him at all, but he would never forget his visit to the travel agent's.

By the time he got home it was thirteen minutes past eleven. He didn't see how it could be. It didn't make sense. It hadn't been long past eight when he'd transferred his money. All he'd done was walk to the travel agent's – ten minutes? Fifteen top whack? – and back again. Well, he'd had to wait quite a while for the travel agent's to open. And he *had* looked through quite a few brochures. Oh, and then, because he'd felt so weak, he'd gone to a greasy spoon, had a cup of tea and a bacon sarnie. He must have sat there for longer than he'd thought, enjoying the banality, hiding in the crowd, wondering how to handle his meeting with Helen tonight.

What had he been thinking of, having a bacon sarnie when he was going out to lunch? Oh, of course. He had decided to cancel the lunch.

He wondered if it was too late to phone Jane and cancel lunch. He decided that it was.

Quarter past eleven. Jane had suggested an Italian restaurant that was 'a bit above the average. And Nino will look after us.' She was the sort of person who would have lots of Ninos around. She was the sort of person who made sure she was looked after. God, he hated her.

No, he didn't. That was unfair. What he hated was the fact that the first woman he had made love to was a woman like that.

Sixteen minutes past eleven. He only needed to allow forty minutes to get to the restaurant. That left sixty-four minutes unaccounted for. And they would go slowly, the bastards, you could count on that. James hated to be late, hated to be rushed, but he wasn't obsessed with time. Until today. He had never known a day when he had been so conscious of the passage of time, or one when time had behaved so capriciously, so cruelly, so teasingly.

How would he fill the next sixty-three minutes? Yes, another minute had passed with all the pace of a snail on its day off.

Calmness, James. That's the key. This is the only moment in this day when there is any real prospect of calm. Relax. Let your mind go blank.

His mind would not go blank for sixty-two minutes without help. Where would he find help?

He switched the television on.

At first he watched calmly. At first he found the tedium exquisite. He was in a time capsule. Time passed very very slowly, but it did pass, and it passed without incident. But then he felt the first stirrings of distant anger. He began to feel trapped in his capsule. The anger built. It struck him that he had rants the way other people had fits. He needed to break out of the capsule. He needed to release his anger.

He stood up.

'Who in their right mind,' he shouted, 'would want to watch a programme about a tedious badly dressed young couple with moderate IQs and charisma bypasses being shown by a smarmy young estate agent with two O levels round three very ordinary houses with cramped kitchens and brown window frames in dreary countryside on the outskirts of ugly towns and enthusing about all three and buying none of them?'

He felt better after his rant.

'Oh, well,' he said, much more quietly but still out loud, as he switched the television off, 'at least there wasn't any blood, and there wasn't a pathologist in sight.'

More than once he was tempted to ask the taxi driver to turn round. There wasn't any point in seeing Jane. It was her just as much as Ed that he had deliberately cut out of his social life. She had to have been a willing accomplice in Ed's ruthless bankruptcies.

But then, each time he was tempted, he realised that there was something inescapably intriguing in meeting again, after many years, one's first love.

Once he'd realised that he *was* going to meet her, he'd felt a growing excitement.

Could it be that he thought that he might be able to have an affair with her? Surely not? With Deborah not yet cremated. With Helen not yet dispatched. Unthinkable.

But they were both widowed and perhaps in time they would rekindle that old flame.

Then he realised why he really wanted to see her. He wanted to confess. He ached to tell her all about his affair with Helen. Pour out the guilt that sat on his stomach like a surfeit of cheese. Tell her what he had told nobody else and what he could tell nobody else. He realised, as they turned a corner by a Wren church, how powerful was the seductiveness of confession. Perhaps that was why Tony Blair had become a Catholic. He had so much to confess.

He would tell Jane of their first meeting, the first time they made love, the snatched moments in foreign cities, her lonely hotel dinners while he talked styrofoam and sex with men, how their love flourished not in Venice and Paris but mainly in Bridgend and Kilmarnock, in hotels that were not called Majestic or Splendide but Premier and Comfort Inn. He would tell her of the secrecy, the lies, the narrow escapes. He would tell her how essential those things had become to him. He would tell her how, last Sunday, he had failed for the first time in bed. Well, possibly by that time he would have told her too much.

He was going to be early. He asked the driver to pull up round the corner.

As he approached the restaurant on foot, James saw Jane striding along the pavement towards him from the opposite direction. They met just by the door. It was like a scene in a film, and he wondered if she ever imagined that she was a star in a film, and decided immediately that she didn't, that she was extremely intelligent but had no imagination at all.

In her high-heeled shoes her long legs looked slim and elegant. In her high-heeled shoes she was exactly the same height as him. He felt that this had been calculated.

She kissed him on each cheek and then on the lips. Then each stepped back to examine the other.

'You look great,' he said.

'You look tired but interesting,' she said.

They wafted into the restaurant on a tide of expensive perfume and to a chorus of dramatic and meaningless exclamations of delight. Jane was kissed on both cheeks by three handsome Italians. There were cries of, 'Ah, Mrs Winterburn,' and, 'Oh, Mrs Winterburn,' and, 'So good to have you back, Mrs Winterburn.' Men who were big in plastics sighed enviously into their pasta. James's hand was vigorously congratulated on the good fortune and good sense of being in Mrs Winterburn's company. Their chairs were pulled back, and then softly moved forward once they had sat, and their shining white napkins were opened with a flourish that might in a different environment have brought several bulls to heel.

James could sense Jane's endless firm thighs under the table. To think that he hadn't known whether he would still fancy her or not.

'So,' he smiled, 'not just Nino to look after us, but Franco and Mario and Marco and Polo. God, you look good.'

He wished that he hadn't said this, it was too much, and much too soon.

There followed a curious silence, a silence born not out of the difficulty of finding something to say, but out of the fact that there was so much to say that it was impossible to know where to begin. With their being companions in widowhood? With Ed's murder? With the question, concerning Ed's murder, that he had to ask, and to which he dreaded the answer? With memories of their brief affair in Cambridge? With the challenge to her business ethics that he would have to make?

Easier to start on menu chat.

'It's a good menu.'

'Oh, yes.' In her voice was a tone which stated, Would I be here if it wasn't?

He had forgotten just how supremely confident she always was. He was amazed, now, to think that he had ever possessed the courage to ask her out, to take her to bed, to unroll her tights, to . . . please her.

But had he pleased her? Perhaps he hadn't. Perhaps that was why she left him, so soon, all those years ago.

'Everything's good, but it's always as well to go with Nino's recommendations.'

She spoke as if she was sitting in a sedan chair being carried by two lesser mortals. You don't have to like somebody, James thought, to be seriously attracted to them.

'Now. Wine,' she said. She was taking control. He had forgotten how she took control.

When she turned to summon the wine waiter unostentatiously but in a manner that was impossible to refuse, he noticed that perhaps she didn't look quite as good as he had thought in the theatricality of their arrival. There was just the faintest beginning of a second chin, above a slight, barely detectable scrawniness to the skin of that swan-like neck. Soon it would be more turkey than swan.

That's the danger of compliments. You can never take them back. You can't ever say, You know how good I said you looked. Like to qualify it a bit, on reflection. You *are* beginning to go off just a little.

She asked the wine waiter for his recommendation. 'All the wine's good, but it's always as well to go with Paolo's recommendation.'

'The Barolo's drinking well at the moment,' said Paolo.

'So am I, to be honest,' said James.

He wished that he could take this remark back, God, how he wished that he could take it back, but Paolo laughed as if he had never heard it before and said, 'Sir is a wag.'

James met Jane's eyes, and he wanted to laugh. But he seemed to remember that she didn't do laughter, and his amusement died.

'But perhaps that is too heavy for luncheon,' said the Italian sommelier. 'I have a Valpolicella that will dispel any prejudices you may have against that wine.'

'Thank you,' said Jane. 'All right with you, James?'

'Perfect. I'm more than happy to dispel a prejudice.' Oh, how he wished she would smile.

They ordered dry Martinis.

'Carlo makes the best dry Martinis in London.'

'Of course he does,' he said, dry as the Martini.

She didn't recognise the mockery.

Nino recommended the vitello tonnato and the wild sea bass. After careful consideration they both chose the vitello tonnato and the wild sea bass.

'Well, well, poor you,' she said, clasping his hand but without warmth. 'You must be devastated.'

A sliver of sorrow flitted through James like a sparrow through a greenhouse. Yes, he missed Deborah, but this wasn't devastation. He wanted to say more, but it was still too early to confess. You confessed over brandy, not in dry Martini time.

'My feelings are very different. Ed and I had no sort of . . .'

Even in this immaculate restaurant the waiters brought the drinks in the middle of important sentences. James longed to take the first exquisite, bracing sip, but was too polite to do it till she'd finished her remark.

'. . . no sort of marriage in the last years. He went to bed with anything that moved. I lost all interest in that kind of thing. Anyway, cheers.'

He tried not to look too eager to take that first sip, but the sigh of pleasure that he gave as he rolled it round his mouth gave it all away, and he felt obliged to make some comment.

'A little voice inside me cries out for cool, clear, mountain spring water,' he said. 'It praises it as the finest, most healthy, tastiest drink on earth. But it speaks too quietly, and I hardly hear.'

They talked about Ed's death. James didn't mention his suspicions over Mike. Nor did he ask his question. It was too soon for that too. It was strange, but it was too soon for everything.

Jane said that it was only natural that Ed should have

made enemies, and James could tell that, although she no longer loved him, she couldn't quite conceal her pride.

He seized on the moment.

'After going bankrupt he opened up again once in your name, didn't he?' he asked. 'So you knew all about it?'

Her eyes challenged him.

'We did nothing illegal.'

You didn't have to admire a woman to want to go to bed with her.

'I don't think that's the point. The point is moral, not legal.'

James found himself – he could hardly believe it – talking about responsibility, talking about how he felt about his workers, about the ethics of business and indeed of all human life. Why? Did he have the faintest chance of cracking this hard nut?

'You always were naive,' said Jane. 'I remember that being what attracted me to you.'

'Oh. Terrific. What every man wants to hear. "What first attracted you to me? Was it my charm, my sense of humour, my good looks or my big prick?". "No, it was your naivety."'

'Not just your naivety.'

'Ah. There's hope. What else?'

'Your shyness.'

'Fantastic.'

The wine, though not ideal with the sea bass – black mark, Paolo – was very pleasant. The sea bass – black mark, Nino – was no more than adequate. James felt that the restaurant – black mark, Jane – was no more than average in quality. It was only outstanding in charm. Jane had fallen for the charm, perhaps because she had so little herself.

He realised now why he had gone onto his high horse about the ethics of business. He'd been trying, with words, to do what memory and appearance and the passage of time had failed to do. He'd been trying to quell the excitement in his genitals.

He'd succeeded. He'd fancied Jane because in those first moments it was exciting and glamorous to be with her. He'd fancied her because he'd fancied her long ago. He'd fancied her because she had long legs, great breasts, a wide mouth, and fine hair, as black and thick as his but softer and less rebellious.

His words, his spelling out of his disapproval, had begun to cut through his desire. Her admission – well, she didn't see it as an admission – that she had 'lost all interest in that kind of thing' had stamped on several small fires. When a woman says that she isn't interested in sex, it can be a challenge to a man, but it can also be a sign that he's wasting his time.

James, who was often very honest with himself, also reflected on the fact that an element in the cooling of his desire was his hurt pride. The revelation that Jane had fancied him for his naivety and shyness had not sent bold, brave messages to his sperm cells.

The thrill had all gone already. He'd noticed, even as she walked towards him, that her legs, though long, were charmless. They widened as if by some mathematical principle. They were severe. Her features, too, were perfect but without character. Her mouth was wide, but her lips were thin and ungiving. Already, after an hour, he was tired of her. There was no pleasure to be had from or with her. This came as an enormous relief, but also – for what real man does not have a streak of perversity in his make-up? – as a real disappointment. James felt that he was left with a scene that had ended halfway through. It had been too early to confess, and now already it was too late. There was no point in whispering intimate secrets to this woman in this restaurant. He might as well shout them to a brick wall. The meal was now like the last, dead match in Davis Cup tennis, which often featured reserve players once the result had been decided. How James wished that there was another James in reserve, to finish his meal for him, and keep Jane company, and share the bill.

It was almost too late to ask his final question, but it had to be done.

'You said that the newspaper reports were very inaccurate. You said Ed's body wasn't in the Ouse. Where was it?'

The answer was the one he didn't want, but the one he had known it would be.

'An obscure little thing called the Peckover Drain.'

The Reverend Martin Vigar had sparse hair which he had carefully combed to cover as much of his pate as possible. He was very tall, and walked with the slight stoop of a man who doesn't want to intimidate his fellow mortals.

James couldn't believe that he was so pleased to welcome a vicar to his home. But then anything that took his mind off the evening to come was welcome.

In fact the vicar fascinated him. When, on being offered a cup of tea, he replied, 'That would be quite delightful. "The cup that cheers,"' and, 'No, no, no sugar thank you, I'm sweet enough already,' he was every inch a vicar and as arch as a bishop. But, when they went into the living room and he got a wad of A4 and a ballpoint pen out of his briefcase his voice lost its trace of sing-song, and developed a hint of North Kent, and his businesslike manner led James to expect that at any moment he would say, 'Now, life insurance. Are you adequately covered?' This prompted him to say, 'Quite a change of career you've had,' to which the vicar replied, with a smile, 'Yes. Straight from Mammon to God.'

'Did you . . . you know . . . get a sudden call . . . as it were?'

The Reverend Martin Vigar gave a self-deprecating smile.

'Nothing as dramatic as a call,' he said. 'More of a whisper in my ear. I suppose, increasingly, over the years, I began to feel the need for a meaning to life, and particularly to my life.'

'And have you found that meaning?'

The vicar hesitated.

'It isn't as clear-cut as that,' he said. 'I am finding it. It is a process, a long process, not always an easy process.' He turned suddenly grave. 'I'm so sorry that my first visit to your lovely home should be for such a sad reason.'

'Thank you.'

He produced a sheet of paper and handed it to James, and again, it felt as though it would be a quote for insurance.

'The order of service. I think it's as agreed, but I thought we should check before it "goes to print".'

James looked through it carefully.

'Yes. That's fine.'

An imp in his head almost prompted him to add, 'I'll pay by direct debit, I presume,' but he resisted it.

'I had a very good talk with your brother Philip. He seemed a very nice man.'

'He's great.'

'That is so good to hear in this time of crisis for "the family".'

James was beginning to realise that there were a lot of inverted commas in the vicar's life.

'He emphasised that you are not in essence a religious family.'

James was careful not to fall into his catchphrase, not to say, 'I'm sorry.' He felt very strongly that this was nothing to apologise for.

'No, we're not. In fact, I'll be honest with you, after we'd

212

arranged all the details I wondered if we should have gone for a humanist service.'

'Ah. Yes. The woodland burial route. Well, let me reassure you, Mr Hollinghurst. This will be a Christian funeral service, but it will not be pious. It will be, if I may put it like that, "soft on God". Very low church. Very C of E, you might say. In my eulogy I will touch upon the message of eternal life, but I won't "rub it in".'

'Thank you. It sounds as if it'll be "just the ticket".'

No, James. Restrain the imp.

'We have a very good faith school round the corner from the church, and a lot of parents come to my services purely to get their children qualified for entry. I know that, and they know that I know it. I don't like it, it's not what I left Allied Dunbar for, but I live with it, and it does mean that I know how not to "over-egg the pudding".'

'Well . . . good . . . thank you. That sounds . . . just right.'

'So, the eulogy. That is, I presume, the lady in question on the pianoforte.'

'It is.'

'She was beautiful. Truly beautiful.'

'Thank you.'

'You must be devastated.'

Yes, I must. Go away, imp!

'Yes.'

'This is never easy, and I know you are going to give "that personal touch", but I wish not to sound too remote, that can be so very depressing. I was at a service once where the vicar said, "We can only imagine all the kind and thoughtful acts that he made in his life, being nice to waiters, stopping the car to let little old ladies cross the road," and his widow interrupted, "He didn't drive." So embarrassing.'

'Deborah did drive, and she drove fast.'

'Perhaps that is something that, in view of the manner of her death, we should skate over.'

'True.' James approached three words that he would find difficult to utter with a straight face. That imp again. 'More tea, vicar?'

'Do you know, that would be most welcome. I always think of myself as a "one-cup man", but these interviews are never easy, and the throat is dry.'

While he was pouring the tea, James was desperately trying to think of tales about Deborah that would illustrate her qualities and would be suitable to relate at a funeral, but all he could think about was the Peckover Drain. A suitable epitaph for Ed, perhaps, but a strong indication that Mike had murdered him. Mike had denied that they had caught perch in 'the something drain, picturesque Dickensian name'. He had denied all knowledge of it. Why should he have denied this if the drain didn't have a sinister connotation for him?

He realised that the Reverend Martin Vigar was speaking.

'Sorry,' he said. 'I was miles away.' Round about a hundred miles, probably.

'I understand. It's a difficult time for you. No, I was just saying that I'm not so much looking for those amusing anecdotes that always sound slightly forced in the mouth of a vicar. I just want to get things right.'

James pulled himself together and began to talk about Deborah's family, her time on the farm, her love of riding, her education, her first-class degree, her fine mind, their first meeting in the stifling dry heat of dusty Malta (leaving out her trips along the corridor to his bedroom). He spoke of the early days of parenthood, of the family holidays, of how perfect a son Max had been, irritatingly so to Charlotte sometimes, in the days before she walked out.

He told the vicar how Charlotte had disappeared without trace for more than three years before she made that one phone call to say that she was all right. He didn't think he could have told of these things if he hadn't been in touch with Charlotte again, and even now he could barely speak of them without breaking down. There was a crack in his voice, he was on the edge of an emotional precipice, and he wasn't helped by the hugely solemn face the vicar suddenly put on as he began these revelations.

He talked about his hope that Charlotte might come to the funeral.

'Her boyfriend, Chuck—'

'Chuck?'

'I know. I know . . . hopes to be able to persuade her to come.'

'Ah. Perhaps I ought to know whether she is there. Perhaps, right at the beginning of the service, I could give you a look, and you could give me a little nod or shake of the head, and, if it's a nod, perhaps also give some indication of where she is sitting.'

'No. I think that could be disastrous. I just wanted you to know, but I think it has to be absolutely low key. It's very sensitive. She's very sensitive.'

The Reverend Martin Vigar looked as if he felt thwarted of a potential big moment, but he agreed.

'As you wish.'

James continued his tale of Deborah, her love of the art gallery where she had worked five half-days a week for more than ten years, of her eye for a picture, of the fact that she found some beautiful object that she just had to buy almost everywhere she went. 'She could go to a car boot sale in Swindon and come back with something by Fabergé that some ignoramus was selling for fifty pee.'

'Excellent, but I won't use the word "ignoramus" if you don't mind. In God's eyes there are no ignoramuses, or should that be ignorami?'

'Well, actually it was my word. She would never use it. She had in abundance what is sometimes called Christian charity although I think the adjective is often entirely inappropriate.'

As he continued to talk of Deborah's many virtues, James again began to feel that he was on the verge of breaking into tears. Ever since she had died he had wanted to cry for her, he had been shamed by his inability to do so. Now he was having to fight his tears off.

There was no way he was going to break down in the presence of the Reverend Martin Vigar.

As he walked slowly up the stairs to Helen's apartment, James's heart was beating like a hummingbird's.

The evening sun was no longer shining through the double doors that led in from the street. The dull stained glass and the dark purple carpet gave the stairway an ecclesiastical gloom which did nothing for his peace of mind.

He knocked thinly, reluctantly on her door, and then ran a hand through his rebellious hair. He caught himself doing so and hurriedly took the hand away, even though he had only been doing it out of habit and not because he really cared about his appearance at this dreadful moment. Deborah had once told him that this habit was the most futile of all his futile gestures. As soon as he had finished, his hair always went back to wherever it wanted to be at the time.

The door opened, and there she was, pale and perfectly formed. They kissed each other on both cheeks. They always began with this formality, so it won him a brief moment before their world crashed.

'Drink?'

'No, thank you.'

'Did I hear correctly? Did James Hollinghurst actually refuse a drink?'

'Yes, I . . . I . . .'

'James! What's wrong?'

'I . . . I . . . I'm afraid this is the . . .' His throat was parched. He could hardly get the words out. 'I'm afraid I . . .' To blurt it out like this seemed so insensitive, so cruel, so crass, but he felt that if he didn't he might lose his nerve and wouldn't be able to say it at all. 'I'm afraid I . . . can't carry on with this relationship any more, Helen. It's over.'

'What?'

There was no anger yet, just disbelief. She simply couldn't take in what she was hearing.

'What's happened, James?'

'Nothing's happened. I . . .' I just don't love you any more. He couldn't utter those words. They were too cruel. 'I don't know how to put it. I find that I just . . . can't carry on. That's all.'

'All? All? You bastard!'

'I don't think I can argue with that description.'

'It's fucking Deborah, isn't it, and your fucking guilt? That's right. Frown. You don't like women swearing, so unladylike. You're pathetic, James. You've just climbed out of the primeval swamp.'

'Helen, I can hardly protest about your swearing tonight. I don't blame you.'

'You don't like my using the F-word in connection with the precious Deborah, though, do you?'

She came at him then, began raining blows on his chest with her fists. Then she reached towards his face and he turned his face away from her.

'You're frightened. No, you're not. You're turning away because you're terrified I'll mark your face, and everyone will see, and they'll know we've been having a row, and then they'll know that there's an us to have a row, and it'll all come out.'

She was still hitting him, and he was still cowering.

'Two black eyes. That'd ruin the dignity of the memory of bloody Deborah's death, wouldn't it?'

She stopped hitting him then. She flung herself on the chaise longue and burst into tears.

'All those cheap hotels in Bridgend and Kilmarnock. All those secrets. All those lies. And I never complained. Not once. And now this. Thrown over. Tossed aside. Why? Because you never loved me. You loved having a mistress. You loved having a secret. It made your grotty little life in packaging seem interesting.'

'It wasn't like that.' He wanted to say, I loved you, but he couldn't bring himself to use the word in the past tense, it sounded so bare.

'It was exciting when I was the forbidden fruit, but when there was the prospect of my being in a bowl in the centre of the dining-room table every day, it was a different matter.'

He reached out to touch her, to show a sign of affection, to show that he cared, but he didn't dare. He knew how hollow she would think it.

Had she really had no inkling, on Sunday, no premonition about why he had failed in bed? I don't fancy you any more. Couldn't say that. I suddenly found, to my astonishment, that the prospect of making love to you was completely unappealing. Couldn't say that.

There was so little that he could say.

'I had no idea that this was going to happen,' he said. 'I'm as shocked as you are.'

218

'Oh, big deal. Shocked, are you?' she wailed. 'Poor you. My heart goes out to you.'

'I didn't mean it like that. Clearly, some of the things you're accusing me of must have some truth in them, or this wouldn't be happening, but I would never have set out to do this. And I actually never promised you anything.'

'What bollocks. I accepted that you'd never leave Deborah. I didn't want to be a marriage breaker. We neither of us thought she would ever die. She was the nearest thing I've ever come across to somebody being immortal. But when she did die, well, I think I had a right to assume . . .'

Her indignation tailed off into silence. She was sitting up straighter now, and her tears had almost stopped. James perched himself on the end of the chaise longue.

She turned to him and slapped him, just once, a stinging blow on the cheek.

'I hate you,' she said.

'I actually don't blame you.'

'And please, please, don't say that you sometimes hate yourself.'

He had just been going to.

'I don't hate you,' she said in a much softer voice. 'I wish I did, but I don't. I love you, fuck it, and I probably always will.'

'Oh, no. No. Please. I'd rather you hated me than that.'

'Perhaps I'll kill myself. I'd get some pleasure out of thinking how ashamed and guilty you'd feel.'

'Please don't do that.'

'I won't. I'm not brave enough.'

He reached out again and this time he did touch her on the shoulder, but he didn't dare do any more than leave his hand there. She didn't respond but she didn't remove his hand.

'You men and your consciences, oh, God, you're a

219

menace. If you have a conscience, for God's sake why didn't you stick to the straight and narrow. I wish I'd never met you.' She paused. 'That isn't true. God, I wish it was.' She turned and looked him straight in the face, and said, much more quietly, 'I still can't believe this conversation is happening.'

'If it's any consolation,' he said, 'neither can I.'

'The men I've not gone out with because of you. Damien from the flat upstairs. Padraig from Accounts. Gunter that I met in Ulm who was oh so charming and Continental and sophisticated and so good in bed.'

He felt a bit shocked at that. But what right had he got to feel shocked? Sometimes he hated himself. No!

'We didn't go to bed. I was just trying to shock you. And I succeeded. Though what right you've got to be shocked I do not know. We didn't go to bed not because he didn't want to but because I refused. What a stupid woman. I refused because I wanted to be faithful to you. I was never unfaithful, James.'

'Well, nor was I.'

'You went to bed with Deborah.'

'She was my wife.'

'And I thought it was women who were supposed to be illogical.'

She blew her nose fiercely, then stood up and went to the mirror.

'Oh, God,' she said. 'I look terrible.'

'You couldn't.'

'Please.'

'Sorry.'

'So, Sunday was our last supper. No disciples except for Judas. Now just go, will you?'

She was standing by the window now, looking out on London with eyes that saw nothing. He walked towards her.

220

He wanted to touch her, kiss her, hug her, even just run his hand along her arm. He wanted to console her, apologise silently, anything, something.

'Don't touch me,' she growled, in a desperate low voice that chilled him to the marrow.

Wednesday

Airports always made James edgy, and Heathrow was the worst of them. It wasn't just the possibility of terrorist attacks, though that was always there, just below the surface. It wasn't just his own concerns, his worry over whether Max's plane would be delayed. It certainly wasn't the fear that the plane would crash, his brother was a statistician, after all, and he knew how unlikely a crash was, statistically. It was more that the air crackled with tension, with the fear of some, the bewilderment of others, the excitement of many, the joy of reunion, the sorrow of parting, the disobedience of trolleys, the weight of suitcases, the length of queues, the drabness of cafés, the blankness of officials, the constant appeals over the public address system for latecomers to join their flights so that you ended up worrying about people you would never meet, the capricious progress of time, so slow when you wanted it to move quickly, so fast when you wanted it to dawdle.

He had got there too early. He always did. The drive had been horrible, even though there had been little on the roads at that early hour. His head had felt as if a band had been tied round his forehead and just above his ears. His sleeping pill (the last but one) was still affecting him. He shouldn't have been driving.

He'd gone to bed the moment he got home, suddenly revolted by the thought of drinking on his own, suddenly repelled by the possibility of alcohol. He'd felt utterly exhausted, but he'd known that without the pill he wouldn't have slept a wink.

At twenty-five past six the arrivals board notified him that Max's plane had landed. A brief thrill suffused his body. Soon he would see the reassuring bulk of his son, his splendid, beloved son.

But still there, beneath the thrill, was the throbbing tension of the airport, and beneath that tension were the more personal worries that afflicted him this sunny Wednesday morning. His fear of the funeral and of the eulogy that he had committed himself to make. His pride and fear over the speech that he would be making in a few hours' time at the lunch to celebrate the fiftieth anniversary of the foundation of Globpack UK. He'd arranged for Max to attend. He didn't know if this was a mistake, if Max would be interested. He was a little ashamed because he knew that he was motivated by pride, the pride he hoped he would be able to feel in his son, the pride that he hoped Max would feel in him when he saw how successful he was, how popular, what a good speech he was making. And beneath that slight shame was the deeper shame, his shame over Helen, his horrified replaying of the final scene last night. And lurking there, in the depths, was the ever-present thought of Charlotte, the agony of her loss in part assuaged but in part deepened by the knowledge that she was there, in South London, at the end of a phone line, so near and yet so far. And in those murky depths now, after yesterday, was the growing suspicion that a man he knew well had plunged a knife into the stomach of another man he knew well, last week of all weeks. Didn't he have enough to respond to without having to think about that?

He stood there, among the crowds, surrounded by chauffeurs of private hire firms holding up boards with names on them that were probably misspelt. They couldn't possibly deduce, from his appearance, what he was going through, and he wondered if, beneath their passive, bored exteriors similar maelstroms of fear, guilt and loss were whirling.

He tried to calm himself down by running through the speech that he would be making later that day. 'Good afternoon, ladies and gentlemen. What a great privilege it is to be able to talk to you on this great occasion, the fiftieth anniversary of Globpack UK.' He was aware that his lips were moving, people would think he was slightly cracked, well, he was, so it really didn't matter. 'When I was asked what I did by people at cocktail parties . . .' No. Not cocktail parties. Too period. Made him sound eighty years old. 'When I was asked what I did by people at parties . . .'

It was no use. He couldn't concentrate.

Where was he? Come on, Max.

James had wondered if Max, supremely practical Max, who was cool in a way that was distinctly uncool, would have come with hand luggage alone, and would have been through ages ago. Now he began to wonder if he had been detained, if his bag was at this very moment being searched, if they would find substances – he couldn't articulate the word 'drugs' even in his thoughts – in his luggage. Maybe Max had changed in his months in Canada, got in with the wrong set, told him a load of lies in their phone conversations and in his emails. It was unlikely, but in his present state anything seemed possible to James. Maybe there's something rotten in me, he thought, well, I know there is, but maybe that something rotten has infected Max as well as Charlotte. Maybe he would lose the Max he loved as he had seemed to lose the Charlotte he loved. Maybe Max would have a ring in his nose now and a tattoo visible on his chest, and a face pinched and poisoned by substances, maybe he'd be swaying slightly, perhaps just from drink, good Lord, he of all people could hardly blame his son if he'd turned to drink in the long Canadian winter, oh, where was he, look at that clock, it's whizzing round, he should be here by now, he's missed the plane, no, he'd have phoned, he can't phone, he's lying in a drunken stupor in a cubicle in a Gents in Montreal Airport, he's yet another troubled young person in this troubled world. This is ridiculous, control yourself, man, get a grip.

Standing there in that crowded airport, people charging around on all sides of him, James felt more alone than he had ever done in his life. No Deborah, no Helen, no Jane, Charlotte only accessible through Chuck, now he was losing Max. Something had happened. Come on. Materialise through that door. Oh, God, look at all those people, pushing their absurdly laden trolleys. Tired, weary, frightened, confused, happy, excited, ugly, pretty, united only by their Maxlessness.

Where are you?

He had definitely missed the plane. There was no doubt of that now.

And then there he was, as solid as ever, as solid as a tree, his lumberjack son, his pride and joy. Immediately all his doubts seemed ridiculous. They hugged, long and hard. Max's body felt as firm as . . . yes, an oak. He had filled out. He was tough. He was the most treelike man James had ever met. It was impossible to imagine any career for him, except in forestry.

The words they spoke to each other were the words of cliché. So sad the reason, yet so wonderful to see you. But the feeling of paternal and filial affection that passed between them, that was no cliché, that was rare.

The phone was ringing as they entered the house, and there was no reason to think that he shouldn't answer it.

'I hate you. I hate you.'

He recoiled. Max heard Helen's loud, screeching, ugly voice, looked at him questioningly, worried, amazed. There were no screeching, ugly voices in his young world.

He signalled to Max to go, to go upstairs. 'Your old room,' he muttered. Max gave him another questioning look, James gave a pathetic shrug as if he didn't understand who was ringing, Max left the room, and all the while Helen was screeching, and it was he, James, who had done this, he who had reduced a lovely thirty-five-year-old woman to a child in a tantrum.

'I'm sorry,' he said wearily, 'I didn't hear any of that, we've just got back from the airport.'

'We?'

'Max and me.'

'Oh, the wonderful Max. Such a lovely son to his dad. Such a bore to his dad's friends. Max this, Max that, Max the other.'

'I am not that sort of father, Helen, and you are doing yourself no favours with this approach.'

'Oh, belt up, you pompous bastard.'

'I see no point in continuing this conversation.'

'Listening, is he, on the other phone, your precious wonder?'

'He isn't that sort of person.'

But maybe he is?

'I've said I'm sorry, Helen, and I can really say no more. There's no point in this call.'

'There is. I thought it only fair to warn you.'

'Warn me? Of what?'

'That I'm coming to the service tomorrow.'

His heart sank.

'Helen!'

'When the vicar gets to that bit where he asks if there are any objections, I'm going to object.'

'Helen! That's weddings. You can't object at a funeral. It's a done deal.'

There was a brief silence, and then her tone changed abruptly.

'Oh, God, sorry, you'll think I've lost my mind. I haven't slept.'

'I'm sorry.'

'I suppose you slept like a log.'

'Only with the aid of a sleeping pill. I was very upset too.'

'Then why do it?'

'Because I had to. You can't feign love.' That was, almost, I don't love you any more. But she was forcing him to say it. The silly bi— no, he couldn't think of her as that, she wasn't, oh, God, he was horrified to hear her like this.

But she was calmer now.

'There's no point in talking, is there?'

'No.'

'Sorry I was hysterical.'

'That's all right.'

'I am coming tomorrow, though.'

'Oh, Helen.'

'I am. And I'm going to make a scene.' A hysterical edge was returning to her voice. 'I'm going to tell them all what a bastard you are. Fucking wonderful James Hollinghurst, the polystyrene prince. I'm going to show them the truth.'

'Well, OK, I can't stop you, if you want to. It won't do you any good.'

'No, but it'll do you harm. And I'll feel good.'

'I doubt it, afterwards.'

'Oh, you know everything, don't you?'

'I know almost nothing. But I do know this. If it's guilt I'm feeling, as you think, your behaviour won't half rid me of that. In fact, it'll make me really glad I've left you, because I'll know what you're really like. Right now, Helen, this phone call, I don't think this is what you're really like. But I promise you, if you do come and make a scene, I promise you, I will never forgive you, and what's worse, you will never forgive yourself.'

'Oh, bollocks.'

She rang off, leaving him with a feeling of shame that he had won that last verbal round by so wide a margin.

He went upstairs. Max had almost finished unpacking. They looked at each other. For a moment neither spoke. Then Max asked, 'What was that all about?'

'In a minute. In a minute, Max. Are you hungry?'

'Starving. The food on the plane was pap.'

'English breakfast?'

'Fantastic.'

'I'm quite proud of myself,' said James as they went down the stairs. 'Even with all that's been going on, I remembered to get things in, after I'd seen the vicar yesterday, in case you wanted a good old English breakfast.'

Max's unanswered question, What was that all about?, hung in the air over the bacon, eggs, sausage, black pudding, mushrooms and baked beans. It was still barely half-past nine. It had been a long, long morning.

When the breakfast was finished, James cleared away the things and returned to the kitchen table.

'Are you sitting comfortably?' he said. 'Then I'll begin.'

The man who only yesterday had collected his white linen suit from the dry cleaners where, he hoped, they had

231

removed all trace of his visit to the hotel near Diss, was eager that the business over the lost wedding ring could be sorted out quickly. He was keen to see some of the sights of Belfast. Over the years all the tales of violence and trouble had led him to picture the city as a sad and dangerous place, but he knew that this was no longer so, if it had ever been. He had pictured Afghanistan as a land so torn by conflict that no civilised life could survive, until he had discovered that they had quite a successful cricket team, and he had realised how distorted his picture must have been. He was sure it would be like that with Belfast.

'Yes, sir? How can I help you this fine morning?'

The man behind the counter looked eminently suited to this drab office with its bare little room, its counter with reinforced glass, and, beyond the counter, its pigeonholes that stretched from floor to ceiling, almost all of them holding dead letters. His face was pale, as if he hadn't been allowed out to see the sun for several years. His drab pale clothes seemed covered in dust. He matched this dusty little place at the end of the postal road, this undertakers' parlour for lost letters and dead packages. He looked like a lost soul.

'I . . . um . . .' He just had to hope that the man was more a man of the world than he looked. 'I . . . um . . . a few days ago I did a rather stupid thing.'

'Which of us cannot say that he has done the same?'

'Um . . . yes.' He had the feeling that he was in a very foreign country. 'Quite. I invited a lady out to lunch in a hotel. I booked a double room in the hope that the meeting might lead to more than lunch.'

'I catch your drift, sir. I can see which way this is going.'

'Good. Good. Thank you. But . . . um . . . since the lady was married . . . I am not, my wife died a few years ago . . .'

232

'I'm sorry to hear that, sir.'

'Thank you . . . I gave a false address.'

'You're not the first, sir, and you won't be the last.'

'Thank you. Anyway, I had on my wedding ring, and I suddenly thought it . . . I don't know . . .'

'Tactless.'

'Yes. Exactly.'

'No need to look surprised, sir. We are not all ignorant peasants over the water, whatever your jokes may say.'

'Oh, no, please, I wasn't thinking that. Clearly not. And I don't make such jokes, let me assure you.'

'You wouldn't of course, sir.'

'The ring is extremely valuable to me. It's the most cherished gift my beloved wife ever gave me. You'll realise how excited and anxious I must have been to have forgotten it. Maybe you can understand that I feel guilty about my carelessness. I need it back.'

'Well, now, I'll have a look for it, sir. So what was the address you gave?'

Oh, God.

'Lake View, 69 Pond Street, Poole.'

'One might have thought that the hotel would have been alerted by the watery overkill.'

'There are a lot of foreign workers on hotel reception desks in England.'

'We live in a restless world, sir. Everyone thinks the grass is greener the other side of the rainbow. Listen to me philosophising. It's this place, sir. This office. This job. I feel sometimes as if I'm at the end of everything. Well, I'll have a look for your little package, sir.'

'Thank you.'

Please, please find it. Then all this will be over, and I can go and see the sights. People who have been to Belfast recently speak of a pleasant atmosphere, good restaurants, a spectacularly wonderful pub which no one should miss. Could do with a drink or two. Tomorrow will be stressful. Tomorrow is the funeral of the woman I love, love, love.

'Here we are, sir. Arrived this morning. You're early on the case, I must say.'

'Great. Fantastic.'

'Do you have some identification on you, sir?'

'I certainly do.'

He handed the man his driving licence.

'This is not the name on the package, sir.'

'No. I told you. I gave a false name.'

'You told me you gave a false address, sir. I didn't realise you had given a false name as well.'

'I'm sorry.'

'Well, I'm sorry, too, sir, because rules do not permit me to give this package to anyone except Mr J. Rivers.'

'But Mr J. Rivers does not exist.'

'I know. And therein lie the horns of our quandary, sir.'

'Surely you believe my story?'

'I believe that I do, sir. I do indeed.'

'Well, then. Look, I've told you how important this is to me. I've come all the way to Belfast.'

'I know, sir, but I have never met you before, sir, I don't know you at all, and I might be wrong. The criminal mind is devious. Criminals do not look like criminals. Terrorists do not wear T-shirts that state, "Watch out. I am a terrorist." And you yourself have told me that you gave a false name and address, so, with respect, sir, it is proved from your own mouth that you are capable of dishonesty. This is Belfast, sir, a city that has emerged from a nightmare and now lives on hope, and there is no way that I, a simple postal employee, could risk my career, my job and perhaps the safety of my fellow citizens by handing a package to any man other than the addressee. I'm very sorry, sir, but that is the one rule that governs my whole life.'

Globpack's chauffeur drove them smoothly towards the hotel where the luncheon was to be held. James put a consoling hand on Max's shoulder, and his son gave his hand a tiny, reluctant squeeze. It had been a hard morning for Max, learning about his father's feet of clay. Perhaps it had been the morning during which he had entered into full adulthood for the first time.

At last James had felt the seductive pleasure of confession that he'd hoped to find with Jane. At last he had experienced the cleansing power of telling the truth, the diminution of guilt by admitting it. But only for a moment. Halfway through his tale of his affair with Helen he'd begun to feel guilty for telling Max about his guilt. He'd begun to have an uneasy feeling that it would have been better for Max if he had never lost his respect for his father, and, above all, never found out about how he had misled and let down Max's beloved mother. And to tell it now, of all times, the day before the funeral, and all in the interests of his own self-respect.

By that time it was too late. It was a tale half told, and tales cannot be half told.

It had been difficult to persuade Max to come to the luncheon. Max was angry with him, sulky and withdrawn. But as the morning passed, slowly at first, so that they seemed to have hours of awkwardness to negotiate, and then in a sudden rush, so that they had been getting ready in a hurry that almost verged on panic, he had seen Max beginning to come to terms with his new picture of his father, and he had felt that the truth was important, and that, in the long run, he might have done Max a favour by educating him so painfully in the complexities of human goodness and badness, that it might be no bad thing for Max to have a less perfect role model. He knew of many children whose lives had been blighted by their failure to live up to their image of their parents.

As he thought about Max now he found himself being sucked back into the imagery of the forest. Max had swayed like a tree in a gale, but his roots had stood firm. As they walked into the hotel, giving a nod to the smiling commissionaire, he felt absurdly proud of his son. Tall, erect, solid but with no surplus flesh on him, his round face serene again after the anguish of the morning, Max cut an impressive figure.

The Champagne Reception – it was Prosecco actually, but that was the only concession to the economic crisis – was held in a cavernous room with a huge chandelier. There must have been almost two hundred people there. There were representatives from Bridgend, Kilmarnock and Birmingham, some of whom he would see again tomorrow at the funeral. There were notable guests from the wider world of packaging. There were a few particularly loyal and important customers. And of course there was Dwight Schenkman the Third. From the moment they entered the huge room with its roar of conversation, James could see Mrs Dwight Schenkman the Third, tall, slender, her hair exquisitely dressed by the best man in Birmingham and gliding towards him through the packed ranks of the packagers like a swan crossing a lake studded with moorhens.

Her name had gone again, despite all his efforts to capture it for ever. Why hadn't he prepared himself for this moment? Wait. He'd created a little mnemonic to aid him. An e at the end of a cake instead of the beginning. Brilliant. But then he realised that his precious mnemonic wasn't much use if he couldn't remember the name of the cake. Eccles cake?

236

Nobody was called Cclese. Oh, God. Battenburge? Nobody's called Battenburge, and it doesn't even begin with e. Idiot. Eclair? Claire! Wow! That was close.

'Hello, Claire.'

'Hi, James. How good to see you.'

'You look wonderful, Claire.'

'Thank you.'

'Claire, this is my son, Max. Max, Claire Schenkman.'

'Hello.'

'Well, hi, Max. My, my, Max, aren't you a fine young man?'

James could actually feel the wince that Max managed to stifle.

'I think I owe my good looks to my father, Mrs Schenkman.'

The boy will go far, thought James, and he felt a sudden lifting of the burden of responsibility that had been hovering all morning. He didn't need to watch over Max at this gathering. He could throw him in at the deep end, and he would swim.

He refused alcohol, and was just slightly galled to witness his son's surprise.

'Can't drink when I'm making a speech. Got to stay sharp.'

Dwight Schenkman the Third bore down on him like the leading ship in his wife's flotilla, shook his hand as if it was an irritation that needed to be got rid of, and said, 'I think it's no exaggeration to say that the whole global packaging industry admires your courage and your devotion to duty, James. You are literally an inspiration to us all.'

The reception seemed to last for ever. James sipped his orange juice and fielded endless words of sympathy. It seemed that no man in the history of packaging had ever lost such a wonderful woman. He knew that if he began to think seriously about this loss that he had at first not been able to feel and later had not allowed himself to feel he would be unable to make his speech.

At last they were called to the restaurant. The *Mauretania* Room, naturally, had been decked out with a nautical theme. There were paintings of famous liners on the walls, the windows were portholes, the top table was referred to as 'The Bridge', and the wine racks were in lifeboats.

The tables looked elegant. There was an orchid on every table. This function, planned last year, had taken on a symbolic quality. It was a Farewell to the Age of Extravagance. It was a Celebration on the Eve of Battle, the battle for economic survival. The *Mauretania* sailed over a watershed that day, from the rich Land of Plenty to the rock-strewn Island of Austerity.

James had schooled himself into a reasonably confident public speaker, but he was suddenly overawed by the scale of the event. As the luncheon progressed – smoked salmon pâté, steak-and-kidney pie (mushroom and cashew nut pâté and broccoli and pumpkin bake for vegetarians), orange crème brûlée, he began to feel more and more nervous, he longed for the drink that he had denied himself, he wished that he could taste the food which on another day might have seemed thoroughly average, he saw Max talking easily to men twenty years older than him, and thought, He is a tree among saplings. He shook his head at this thought, and the lady sitting next to him, the wife of a descendant of the man said to have invented the egg box, said, 'Oh, dear, why the sudden shake of the head? What swiftly abandoned thought crossed your mind there?' and he couldn't say, I am trying not to fall into the habit of considering my son in purely arboreal terms, so he said, 'I just realised that something I was going to say in my speech might be a rather serious faux pas,' to which she replied, 'Oh, say it. Do. Speeches are usually so boring,' after which she coloured slightly and added, a little too late, 'Though not yours, I'm sure.'

During the comfort break he went into a corner of the hotel and quickly read through his speech. He intended to speak it without notes.

As he heard himself being introduced, he was shaking. He could not have produced his notes, because they would have rustled in his hands.

At last it was time to stand up, and suddenly all his nerves left him, as if to say, We didn't mean it. We were teasing. We just wanted to keep you up to the mark.

'Ladies and gentlemen,' he began. 'It is a great privilege to me to speak to you, as Managing Director, on this the fiftieth anniversary of the formation of Globpack UK. What a landmark that is.

'I have a confession to make. As a young man, I didn't seek out a career in packaging. When other boys were saying, "I want to be an engine driver," I wasn't saying, "I want to pack things." At parties, when I said, "I'm in packaging," I saw the clear eyes of attractive women cloud over. I noticed men looking round to calculate in which direction they could most usefully escape from me. Once, in Droitwich, I told people that I was a lion tamer. In a moment of self-doubt and discontent in Chelmsford I actually pretended to be an accountant.

'I often thought about what other career I would enter into, when my real life began. And then, as I made my slow journey towards maturity, I realised that this *is* my real life. I see myself now, ladies and gentlemen, as a member of a dwindling elite class. I am a manufacturer. All of us in Globpack work for a firm that makes things. True, the things that we make aren't ends in themselves, they are designed to go round other things, but those other things are all things that people somewhere have made, so instead of bemoaning the fact that what we make is in no way glamorous, because it isn't an end in itself, we should think of how wide, how varied, how global, our involvement in manufacturing is.

'Packagers of the world, stand together. Stand tall. If people at parties prefer to talk to lawyers and estate agents, that's their funeral.'

Funeral. The word stopped him in his tracks. Several people gasped at the gaffe. Tomorrow. Helen. Stanley. Charlotte. Waves of worries. Hold on. Keep calm. Where were we? Notes. Get the notes out. No. No. His hands were shaking too much. Rivulets of sweat running down his back. Silence, too long a silence. Embarrassment at the tables. Dwight Schenkman the Third with his huge mouth wide open in horror.

'If the world finds bankers and hedge fund managers more glamorous, so be it. But I actually sense a shift in public perception.' Yes. Yes. Back on track. The sight of Dwight Schenkman had pulled him back from the precipice. 'The people who make their money just by moving our money around are losing the respect in which they have been held in society. The nation is beginning to realise that if it can't continue to make things that it can sell, it is done for. It's easy to mock those who make mundane objects in even more mundane industrial estates on the outskirts of abominably mundane towns, but that would be wrong, so wrong. They are the bedrock of this particular stage of the endless process of industrial revolution, or industrial evolution.

'I have been given the task, which some may think is a poisoned chalice, of attempting to save Globpack's British manufacturing. I am thrilled, particularly at a sad time in my life . . .' careful, '. . . to be given this challenge, this opportunity.

'Let me explain, briefly I promise, the details of the task I and my committee face with regard to our factories in

Bridgend and Kilmarnock.' Indian restaurants, Pizza Huts, bare unlovely rooms, naked pictureless walls, naked Helen. 'I . . . oh, God . . .' Sweat settling cold on the back of his shirt. Dizzy. Hold on. 'Oh, God. No, no. I'm all right. Sorry.' Pity. Tension. Glass of water. Max white as a sheet. And then, calmly, he heard himself bravely painting a picture that wasn't grimly pessimistic. 'There are the first faint signs that increased wages in poorer countries, increased travel costs, moves to modernise and rationalise our production here, coupled with low inflation and quality considerations, are beginning to shift the balance, that firms may even be beginning to bring production back to Britain from abroad. Nothing has bedevilled British industry more than the manager/worker divide. There is no such divide in my mind. Let there not be any such divide in yours.'

On the final straight now. 'It's well known that we live in an age obsessed by celebrity. I am actually rather proud to be in an industry that, so far from seeking celebrity, avoids it totally. In my youth I collected cigarette cards. There was never a series called "Famous Packagers". There was no "Dan Dan, the Packaging Man" in the Happy Families card game. Very few people ever talk about our products. "I bought a lovely egg box today." "Really? Can't wait to see it. Anything in it?" "Yes, six eggs. They fit beautifully."'

Winning post in sight. 'There's a very fine novel called *What a Carve Up* by Jonathan Coe, in which there's a vanity publisher who sends the hero a Christmas present of the most unreadable books you could imagine. One of the books is *A History of Packaging in seven volumes – Volume 4 – The Styrofoam Years*. Ladies and gentlemen, I have no intention, when I retire, of writing *my* memoirs. There will be no book called *The Cardboard Jungle*, the latest packaging epic from James Hollinghurst. But when I retire, I will not feel ashamed of admitting that I have devoted my working life to our great industry. I look forward to the day when I'm at a party, and some attractive woman says to me, "What line are you in?" and I will say, proudly, "I'm in packaging," and she will reply . . .' He stumbled. Devon Loch. Aintree . . . That impulse to self-destruct again, like on the ship. Throw himself over the rail of the *Mauretania*. Destroy his reputation in an instant. Dwight Schenkman, his great mouth open even wider. Irresistible. 'And I will say proudly, "I'm in packaging," and she will reply, "I suppose a fuck's out of the question?"'

The words reached his mouth, his lips parted, he caught a glimpse of Max, and sense prevailed, almost to his disappointment.

It had been a long pause. Almost too long. Anxiety crackled throughout the huge room.

'And I will say proudly, "I'm in packaging", and she will reply, "Are you doing anything next Tuesday evening?"

'Thank you.'

He sat down, shaking from the narrowness of his escape, his shirt clinging to his soaking back. The applause rang out. There was cheering. He couldn't be certain that it was for the content of his speech rather than the context. He thought it was from relief that he had made it to the end, that he had saved them from corporate embarrassment.

It didn't matter. He had done it.

The man who only yesterday had put his cleaned white linen suit in the boot of his car ready to take to Oxfam because he never wanted to wear it again never quite made it to that fine pub in Belfast. After he'd left the office of lost letters he'd walked for quite a long while before he came to a street where there were taxis. He'd been pleased to walk. It had enabled him to work off some of the irritation that he felt for having brought about this ridiculous chase by his own stupid action.

He hadn't liked to ask the taxi driver to take him to 'a really nice traditional Irish pub I've heard a lot about'. The man might have taken him anywhere. Maybe his brother had a pub in the docks. He could have ended up dead.

'I just want to see Belfast,' he had said. 'Could you drop me somewhere nice in the centre?'

The driver had dropped him in Donegal Square, near the City Hall, and he'd walked in the sunshine, along the lively pavements, working off his anger, building up his thirst. Then he'd stopped a young couple who looked friendly, and had said, 'There are probably lots of nice pubs in Belfast, but somebody has recommended a fantastic one.'

'It'll be the Crown Liquor Saloon,' the man had said. 'That isn't *a* pub. It's *the* pub. It's one of the world's great drinking holes. There aren't many pubs with a Michelin star – in the section for sights worth a visit, not in the food section. I'd like to come with you, but the wife needs some tights.'

Suddenly, for the first time that day, the man who had so foolishly called himself Mr J. Rivers had felt a flicker of enthusiasm. So, he'd lost a memorial to his beloved wife, but that was as nothing compared to his loss of her love and company three years ago. No, he would write the ring off to experience and the folly of telling lies, and sink a few pints of the black stuff in the Crown Liquor Saloon.

Then, just as he approached the pub, he'd had an inspiration. If he could produce a real Mr J. Rivers, perhaps he could get the ring back. Immediately this seemed extremely important again.

He'd found the main post office, hunted through the Belfast telephone directory, and found that there were three people in it called J. Rivers. One had turned out to be a woman, so that had been no use, because the package was addressed to *Mr* J. Rivers. A second hadn't replied. The third had not only replied but, on hearing the sad story, and being asked if he could help him and save the day, had announced, with surprising fervour, that he could, and had arranged to meet him on a specific bench near the City Hall in half an hour.

This must be him now, walking towards the bench in such a straight line and with such purpose in his stride that it would strike fear into the heart of any man.

'So here you are, you miserable sinner,' the man said. 'So here you are, and you ask if I can save you. Yes, sir, I think I can, since you have telephoned and expressed a wish to be saved, and to want that, sir, is to have already won half the battle. Yes, sir, with the aid of Almighty God, who is so pleased that you have sought help this day, I can save you. And I have these for the aeroplane, sir. Six copies of our magazine, the *Watchtower*.'

In the car Max said, 'Not easy.'

'Not easy, Max.'

There was silence for a few minutes. It wasn't quite the companionable silence of father and son.

'Did you get on all right with people?' James asked at last.

'Yeah. Cool.'

James realised that conversation was not going to flow. He was also just a little disappointed to hear Max saying, 'Cool.' He'd have preferred some colourful expression of enthusiasm picked up from the lumberjacks of Canada. Globalisation was going too far.

Their car dropped them off at King's Cross, where they discovered the unwelcome news that Stanley's train from Durham was ninety-five minutes late.

King's Cross station sat sourly, blackly, resentfully at the side of the refurbished St Pancras, with its champagne bar and its statue of Sir John Betjeman, lover of railways, women and champagne, not necessarily in that order. The bar at King's Cross was closed as the station underwent major restoration. It needed it.

The long champagne bar at the edge of the Eurostar platforms under the superb glass canopy of St Pancras station was thriving in the champagne weather. They found two seats and then a blush came to Max's stolid face, the blush of a man who, it was sometimes difficult to remember, was still only twenty-two. But when he spoke it was in the manner of a man of forty, and what he said astonished James. He said, 'Let me get you a glass of champagne. I think you need it.'

James knew that Max didn't particularly like champagne, but that he had the style not to spoil this rare occasion by ordering himself a beer. They sat there, father and son in a silence that *was* now almost companionable, sipping their champagne in this cathedral of travel. The Eurostar trains slid off silently exactly on time. It could almost be Switzerland.

James had a funny feeling that Max would never again refer to what he'd told his son that morning, never again mention Helen either by name or even by implication. He knew Max didn't approve. How could he have approved? He didn't want him to approve. All he wanted was for them to continue to be father and son together, and to know each other for what the other was.

Every time he thought of Helen, he wondered if he'd hurt her so badly that she *would* make a scene at the chapel. Desperately he hunted for something else to think about. Charlotte. Not exactly a relaxing alternative, but he needed to do something.

'I wonder if I should ring Chuck,' he said.

He'd filled Max in on his conversations with Chuck in the car on the way back from Heathrow.

Max had wept and said, through his tears, 'Sorry, Dad. It's jet lag. I'm tired.

James had said, 'No. Cry. It's all right. It's good to cry.'

Max hadn't realised that he was shedding James's tears by proxy.

'Max,' he said now, 'if I do ring Chuck, to find out what the chances are of Charlotte coming tomorrow, do you want to have a go at chatting to her?'

Max thought for quite a while before answering.

'Dad, it's been five years, she was just a kid. I don't think I'd know how to talk to her. Not on the phone. It might all go wrong. I don't think I should talk to her unless there seems to be no hope of her coming. What I'm saying is, I suppose, I'd rather not.' Max paused. James could see that he wanted to say more. 'Is that awful? I long to see her. That's different.'

James reached across and stroked Max's shoulder. He could see that it wouldn't take much for him to start crying again.

'I'm not good on phones,' Max continued. 'All my friends talk on them all the time. They text before they clean their teeth.'

James realised that there were huge gaps in his knowledge of his son as well. It occurred to him that maybe there was something deeply lacking in him as a father.

'I think I—' he began, only to be interrupted by a loud announcement about the next Eurostar train. He waited impatiently. At last the announcement ended. 'I think I will ring.'

James could feel his heart beating almost dangerously fast as he dialled. He thirsted for Charlotte to answer.

'Yep?'

Funny. It was almost like hearing a reassuring friend. He realised that he was relieved that Charlotte hadn't answered . . . unless it meant that she was incapable of answering the phone. Oh, God.

'Hello, Chuck. How are you doing?'

'Pretty cool, James. How about you?'

'Yeah, pretty cool.'

'Cool.'

'Chuck, I'm just . . . you know . . . wondering . . .' The tension was barely tolerable. He felt sick with longing. '. . . wondering what it's looking like . . . tomorrow-wise.'

'Yes, James, I think it's looking pretty good.'

Relief poured through James. He was glad he was sitting down.

'Yeah, she says she'll come. To the church, anyway. I don't know about the house, maybe there'll be too many people, but the church, yeah, it's looking good.'

'That's fantastic, Chuck.'

'Yeah. Great.'

'You might tell her that Max – that's her brother, he's sitting here with me now, we're on St Pancras station waiting for her great-uncle Stanley who's coming down from Durham – Max has just said he's longing to see her.'

'OK. Cool.'

'You might tell her that it'll all be very informal and we'll all be spilling out into the garden if the weather's still hot.'

'Cool. You guys have a good evening and don't worry about Charlie. I'll get her there.'

'Thanks. Thanks very much, Chuck.'

'James?'

'Yeah?'

'Don't be shocked.'

'What?'

247

'How she looks.'

'Oh. Right. Thanks.'

Oh, God. What has she done to herself?'

'Chuck?'

'Yep?'

'Thanks.'

In the end, back at King's Cross, the train was a hundred and two minutes late. The delayed passengers streamed down the platform under the grimy roof, some almost running towards appointments, for which they were already hopelessly late, others exhausted and resigned, but of Stanley Hollinghurst there was no sign. Then, when the stream thinned into a trickle, they saw him. He was walking between two young people who were each carrying a large suitcase. He was striding out boldly for a man approaching eighty, and holding himself ramrod straight, but the impression of vitality was let down by a pronounced limp in his left leg. With his dazzlingly green corduroy suit, far too thick for the weather, and the unruly wiry curls of his excessively long white hair, he looked like a maverick retired anthropologist and lecturer who was going to seed, not to mention slightly mad, from living on his own too long. This was because he *was* a maverick retired anthropologist and lecturer who was going to seed, not to mention slightly mad, from living on his own too long.

'These are my new friends,' he shouted as he approached them. 'Lee and Ellie. Who says young people have no manners? Who says civilisation is at an end? Not so, it turns out. Not so.'

Lee and Ellie put the two cases down, and everyone shook hands, and Ellie said they must be on their way.

'A pleasure to have met you, sir,' said Lee.

James and Max picked up one case each.

'God, they're heavy,' exclaimed James, and even Max winced with surprise.

'I don't travel light,' said Stanley, strolling beside James and Max as they struggled with his ancient cases, which had no wheels. 'It doesn't look good. An interesting couple, young Lee and Ellie. He's pure Saxon, she's pure Norman, don't often get that. They asked me if it meant that they'd be happy. I said I had no idea. Funny how people don't know how to read faces. Such a pity. Pity my book's out of print. Bastard publishers.'

Stanley's book *The Physiognomy of Tribes* had enjoyed a modest reputation in tribal physiognomy circles in the nineteen seventies.

'A hundred and two minutes late,' he complained, as they joined the back of the taxi queue. 'A hundred and two minutes. Personally I'm delighted that before many years have gone the line will begin falling into the sea. My, you've turned out tall, Max.'

'Thank you, Great-Uncle Stanley.'

'Oh, don't call me that. It makes me sound ancient. Stanley will do. Don't you work with trees? You're beginning to resemble a tree. Careful, boy.'

'I'll try to watch out for that danger, don't you worry, Stanley,' said Max drily.

James was shaken to hear Stanley echo his thoughts about Max. He changed the subject back to the line.

'I don't see how the line could ever fall into the sea, Stanley. From what I remember Peterborough and York and Co. are miles inland.'

'Further north. Beyond Berwick. Practically on top of the cliffs. One day, whoosh. Splosh. We apologise for the late running of the eleven o'clock from Edinburgh. This is due to its falling into the sea with considerable loss of life including the bloody catering manager or whatever they call him this week who couldn't stop rabbiting on about his bacon sodding sandwiches with or without tomato every time I wanted forty winks. Sad about Deborah. Best of the bunch.'

'I'll tell you what got me,' said Stanley in the taxi. 'We became late. Vandalism to overhead cables. Silly place to put them. Should put them underground. So, when it became clear that we were going to be more than an hour late, and that compensation would be due, what happened? Did all the other trains wait behind us in an orderly fashion as they should do in a land that loves queuing? No. The bastards send the next three trains on ahead of us, so they won't have to pay compensation to all of them, as if this was Italy, where they've too much sense to queue. They held us in stations, and I saw the other trains overtake us. Nobody else saw them. They were too busy talking on their Loganberries. The days of looking out of the window are over. Every man is an island, carrying his world with him. And they kept apologising for the delay, sorry for any inconvenience. Brazen hypocrisy. They were now causing the delay and they couldn't give a monkeys about the inconvenience, they hate us almost as much as I hate them. Charles'll be devastated. He always fancied her, you know. Oh, yes. Shouldn't wonder if . . . no, sorry. Shouldn't have said that. Not that I did quite say it, but you know what I mean. Almost slipped out, as the careless bishop said to the actress.'

As the front door closed on the unassumingly elegant Georgian house, James felt that this really was the beginning of the end. The clans were gathering. The countdown to the funeral had begun.

Stanley and Max were going to occupy the two single bedrooms on the second floor, with the main guest bedroom reserved for Charles and Valerie. Stanley had pooh-poohed the idea that two flights of stairs might be difficult for him at his age. 'I'm not eighty yet. I'm no age.' Now James wished that he had put Stanley on the first floor. He might well have a heart attack, lugging that suitcase upstairs. Even Max was struggling with the other one, the one that still had a purple label announcing *Deck 7*.

James didn't dare put the case he'd been carrying on the bed, in case the bed collapsed. He dropped it onto the floor, and the old house shuddered. He collapsed exhausted into the room's only chair. His arms ached and he couldn't get his breath. A dreadful thought had occurred to him. Maybe Stanley was aiming to stay longer than the planned two days. Maybe he was planning to stay a month. He had luggage enough for a month.

'Um . . . are you . . . um . . . still planning to . . . um . . .' he gasped, '. . . to . . . um . . . stay for . . . two days, was it?'

'Yes. It's long enough. Don't like staying in people's houses any more. I worry in case I fart when I go to the loo in the night. Old men's bodies don't belong in other people's houses. Why do you ask?'

'Well, your cases are so terribly heavy, and you've two of them. What *have* you brought?'

'Clothes for the funeral. Clothes for a change in the weather.'

'There hasn't been a change in the weather for ages.'

'The weather never changes till it changes. That's the thing about weather. Books. Several books.'

'Several? Will you have time to read?'

'You don't know. And you don't know what you'll want to read. Bring one book, you aren't in the mood for it, you ruin a good read by reading it at the wrong time. Unfair to the author. A ham.'

'A ham?'

'Yes. A carving knife.'

'A carving knife? What have you brought a carving knife for?'

'For the ham. Are you an idiot? What else would I carve it with?'

'You're planning to eat a ham, secretly, in your room?'

'I'm not planning. I hope it won't be needed. But you've probably never even boiled an egg in your life, I don't know what I'll get, I'm not taking the risk.'

'Even all that's not going to fill two suitcases.'

'No, well, I didn't want to admit this, not after you and Max have lugged the blasted things up two flights of stairs, but I've just put in a few heavy things to fill them up. It's a question of style.'

'Style?'

James was uncomfortably aware that in his conversations with Stanley he was apt to end up just repeating odd words like a bewildered parrot.

'I was brought up in the halcyon age of travel, when vast amounts of baggage trailed behind every Englishman worth his salt. I remember my father telling me very firmly that half-empty bags would not impress the porters.'

'There aren't any porters. There haven't been any porters for years.'

'I realise that.' Stanley sighed and suddenly looked his age. 'I'm out of touch.'

There was a ring at the door. James hurried off downstairs.

It was Charles and Valerie. Charles was carrying one small, elegant bag. Valerie looked tired. It was Charles who had travelled round Europe giving concerts, but it was Valerie who looked tired.

James made tea, and produced a lemon drizzle cake. As he brought it out he recalled something Deborah had said.

'That's the thing about James. He seems in a world of his own, and suddenly he produces exactly the thing you want.'

It was strange, but as each day passed he found that he was beginning to think more and more of his times with Deborah, little odd things, a remark, a laugh, a rebuke.

They sat in the garden, Deborah's garden, in the shade, sipping their tea, and eating their lemon drizzle cake. James had produced tiny forks, for the cake. He wanted there to be no diminishment of style because of Deborah's absence.

But Max took his sliver of cake in his great gnarled hand.

'Nothing pansy about eating cake with a cake fork, Max,' said Stanley.

Max blushed.

'Not a pansy, are you?'

'How did the concerts go, Charles?' asked James somewhat too fast.

'No need to change the subject, Dad. I'm not embarrassed,' said Max. 'I'm not actually, Stanley. I rather wish I was. Then I could sing "The Lumberjack Song".'

The allusion was lost on Stanley, who didn't watch comedy on television in case it made him laugh.

'No, but how did the concerts go?' asked James.

'Oh, you know, not bad,' said Charles.

'They were a triumph, Charles,' said Valerie.

Charles gave his wife a look of unmistakable irritation.

The phone rang. James started to get out of his chair but without any enthusiasm.

'I'll go,' said Max.

He bounded towards the house with the stored energy of a man who hasn't chopped down a tree for two whole days.

'Charles did the Schumann in Helsinki,' said Valerie.

Charles gave Valerie another look, less irritated but still not quite pleased.

'I've told James,' he said.

'Yes, but he may not have told Stanley,' persisted Valerie.

'He hasn't,' said Stanley. 'Nobody tells me anything. They don't when you're old.'

'I did it for Deborah, and I told the audience that I was doing it for her,' said Charles. 'They liked that.'

Stanley gave James a meaningful look.

Was there really anything in it? James tried not to think about what Stanley had said in the taxi, but it had been said, it couldn't be unsaid, and, for all that it was ridiculous, it nagged him.

Suddenly a dreadful thought struck him. The phone call might be from Helen, hysterical once more. Oh, God. He should have answered. He stood up, began to walk towards the house, but at that moment Max returned looking utterly unflustered.

'It was Uncle Philip,' he said. 'He said he'll join us at the restaurant.'

'The restaurant?' said Charles, perking up.

'We're going to a Turkish restaurant tonight,' said James hastily. 'Not far. Very cheery. Well, I couldn't face cooking.'

'Of course not,' said Charles, 'and Turkish food's very good.'

'A million people will drown in Istanbul when the sea levels rise,' commented Stanley. 'You wait.'

Charles ordered the meze. It was natural that he should do so. He was the one who went to Turkey. He was the one who had been cheered to the echo in Istanbul.

He ordered aubergine purée, beetroot salad, garlicky cucumber yoghourt, broad beans in olive oil, stuffed vine leaves, potato balls, stuffed mussels, runner beans with diced mutton, and tiny fish rather like whitebait that weren't on the menu. 'They've always got little things that aren't on the menu for those that know,' he said.

Valerie looked sour and James could guess at what she was thinking. None of them know what hard work it is for me, left at home, having to compete with all this, having to satisfy his jaded international palate. He wasn't feeling his usual unalloyed warmth for Charles. Perhaps there was something in what Stanley had hinted.

Philip arrived just as they were ordering their drinks, mainly red wine. 'Sorry I'm late,' he said. 'These conferences don't half go on. Sometimes I think talking about global warming creates so much hot air that it could heat five medium-sized towns.'

After the wine had arrived, and they had raised their glasses to each other, Charles said, 'Um,' so meaningfully that they all looked at him expectantly. 'I . . . look, throw this out if you like, please feel free, but I had an idea. I played the Schumann in Helsinki. The piano concerto. The one Deborah loved.'

Stanley gave James another meaningful look. James glared at him.

'I played it for her, really, and I told the Finns, and they loved the thought, and I gave it everything I'd got . . . people said they were very moved . . . so I wondered . . . everybody's emotional, we can't just sit around talking all night so . . . should I play some of it tonight, back at the house, for her? It wouldn't be quite the same, without the orchestra, but I have done it before for friends, and it sort of works. What do you think?'

'I think that's a wonderful idea,' said James.

'Honestly?'

'Honestly. It's ages since you've played for us, anyway.'

'Fantastic.'

Oh, Stanley, thought James, stop giving me meaningful

looks, you evil old man. You've planted the thought, it's there, it isn't going to go away, you don't need to give me meaningful looks.

The meze arrived, there was barely room for everything on the table. Stanley and James made sure that the red wine flowed, and Max turned to it after two beers. The restaurant had filled up. It was loud and cheery, and the smiles of the waiters never wavered. James wondered if the others had all forgotten they were here tonight because of a funeral.

Over the lamb kebabs, the stewed lamb, the cabbage rolls with minced lamb, and the baked red mullet (without lamb, thank goodness – Charles had chosen the main courses without consulting James, who didn't much like lamb) the conversation turned back to global warming, as perhaps it was bound to do.

'Probably this isn't the right moment to talk about this, Philip,' said Charles, 'but, you know, we got talking a lot in Copenhagen, where they had such an abortive conference on global warming last year, and there are such different opinions about it, but come on, you're the expert, how great is the real threat from global warming?'

'It *isn't* the right moment, Charles,' said Valerie.

'Don't feel it isn't the right moment because of me,' said James. 'I'd be delighted to have my mind taken away from why we're all here.'

Philip clearly didn't want to use his expertise to be dogmatic on this social occasion. He said that he was just one of many experts, and they didn't all agree. James pressed him for his personal opinion, and he said that he thought there was a real risk, if not a certainty, that the human race would destroy its own life on this planet well before the end of the century.

'Good job too,' said Stanley. 'It's a rotten planet. Time it went. You all talk about the threat of global warming. I talk about the promise of global warming.'

'Oh, Stanley!' said Valerie.

'I know. I'm wicked,' said Stanley complacently.

'That is just the trouble with evil,' said James. 'I keep hearing of judges and magistrates telling people they're evil and they seem to think it'll upset them. Don't they realise it's exactly what these people want to hear? That's why you can't deal with evil or ever conquer it, all you can do is encourage goodness and hope it wins the battle. That's why I believe you can only beat people like the Taliban with ideas, not guns.'

'Well, I think the battle between good and evil is maybe a bit heavy for tonight,' said Valerie.

A waiter poured more red wine, liberally and unequally, including into the glasses of those who didn't want it, so that they had to order another bottle. It's the way of waiters all over the world.

'I didn't say I was evil,' said Stanley. 'I said I was wicked. But, yes, I'll be gone and I think man deserves the catastrophes that are coming. Most parliaments in the world are built at very low levels. The politicians deserve to drown, and one day they will. I just wish I could be there to see it.'

'Oh, for God's sake, Uncle Stanley, your perversity is so tedious,' exploded Charles. 'You've fallen in love with your image. The eccentric academic.'

'And you, of course, aren't in love with your image at all, are you?' said Valerie.

'What image is that, my darling?' asked Charles icily.

'The famous artist, of course.'

A pink spot had developed on each of Valerie's pale cheeks.

'I didn't choose to become famous,' said Charles with an infuriating smile. 'It was sheer talent.'

James looked across at Valerie and his heart sank. Oh, Valerie, the pity of it, he thought. You are the only woman at the table with five men successful in their fields, and you cannot rise to the occasion. Where is the spark of yesteryear? Taken, James, by my distinguished husband, and spread among his fans. The reply that Valerie's tired eyes gave to the question he hadn't actually asked shocked James.

'I'm the person here who's going to be most affected by global warming,' said Max suddenly, 'and I haven't said a word.'

They all turned to look at him and a very slow blush crept over his large, owlish face like a sunrise. He took a quick sip of his wine and they could see that he was choosing his words very carefully. 'I wasn't terribly bright at school,' he said. 'I didn't connect. I think I was a big disappointment to Dad and especially to Mum, but in the forests of Canada I've done the connecting that I failed to do and the teachers failed to do at school, and I want to say this. I wish we wouldn't place so much importance on the different opinions about global warming, because I think that, whether or not it's going to happen isn't the point, the point is that not to act is a horrendous gamble, and, lousy though it may be, this is the only planet I've got, Stanley.'

Stanley had the grace to look somewhat abashed.

'The point is, as I see it, that the things we'd do to combat global warming are things it's good to do anyway. We're destroying the planet's resources, we're using them up, we just have to find alternative sources of energy anyway, we have to solve the population problem anyway, we have to stop cutting down the rain forests anyway, we have to reverse the pollution of the oceans anyway. Sorry. It probably wasn't the right moment, but I had to say it.'

258

James felt a surge of pride in his son, but no emotion could be without sadness for him on this night, and the pride led to a feeling of shame. Max had been very quiet all evening, and James had wondered if he was over-awed in this company, or merely jet-lagged, or just had nothing to contribute. Now he realised how little he really knew his son, and this led on, of course, to thoughts of Charlotte and the abyss that always hovered near his heart. He knew nothing of Charlotte's last five years. He could have known so much more of Max's.

They wandered back slowly from the restaurant through a London that had been transformed by the fine weather, past restaurants and pubs and cafés that were spilling out onto the pavements. Everywhere people were strolling and talking. If they had been better dressed it could almost have been Italy. James found himself wondering how much the cold and gloom of the British climate had contributed to the nation's character. Had upper lips only been stiff because they had been frozen? Would global warming free up the people of this strange island for one last brief era of junketing before the apocalypse came to wipe them off their planet?

The great, amorphous city was alive with noise, with chatter, with laughter, much of which sounded coarse, and with singing, most of which sounded drunken. It seemed as if nobody else in the great wen was facing any sadness the next day. James felt, as he had so often felt, that he was out of step.

Even in the shady ground floor of the house it felt warm. There was no breeze. James opened a bottle of chilled white wine, dropped three ice cubes into a glass of water and put it on the piano for Charles. Stanley plonked himself onto the chaise longue, Max sat tactfully in the straightest of

259

the chairs, Philip sat beside Valerie on the sofa, and James took the high-backed armchair. Nobody spoke. Charles had often played, in this room, over the years, but this was different. The atmosphere was just slightly eerie, somewhat artificial, as if they were posed for a photograph. James sensed a sudden tension in the room, a stiffness, an embarrassment, as if they all thought what a wonderful and utterly suitable idea this was, but all wished that it wasn't actually happening.

Usually Charles just plonked himself at the piano and began. But on this emotional evening he had felt the need to leave the room to compose himself, so now he had to make an entrance. But the living room of a Georgian terraced house in Islington is not the Albert Hall, and the family looked at each other and had no idea which would be the more absurd – the applause of a massed audience of five or an entrance in total silence. They opted for a smattering of embarrassed applause. Charles gave a little bow and a half-smile.

'Thank you,' he said. 'I think that the music speaks for itself, but for those of you who do not know Schumann's piano concerto . . .' he stared at Stanley as he said this, and then gave a little, less severe look towards Max '. . . I need to explain that it was written for his beloved wife Clara, a better pianist than he, though a less good composer. It's an emotional piece, subtle and elegant, written for a woman he loved. What could be a more effective memorial for a woman like Deborah? I wish I could have an orchestra here to give the full effect of this marvellous piece, for the musical conversation between piano and orchestra is one of its great strengths. Sadly, however, though a successful businessman, James isn't rich enough to be able to afford a house with a large enough room. What I am playing tonight is really just my patched-up version of the piano part, but I think it carries the spirit and meaning of the piece, and I like to think I have given it its own unity, its own integrity. Lady and gentlemen . . .' he smiled at his pedantry, '. . . Schumann's piano concerto.'

He sat at the music stool, stroked his beard thoughtfully, pulled down his cuffs, wiggled his fingers, held his hands just above the keys, appeared to go into a trance, and began.

James was absolutely determined to listen to the music to the exclusion of everything else, to savour every moment of his brother's brilliance. But listening to music is a talent in itself, and he didn't possess it. He knew that the music had emotional meaning, as opposed, he assumed, to narrative meaning. He felt that he must let himself go blank, devoid of thoughts and above all of words, so that he could just feel the emotions, but he found that he couldn't feel an emotion without knowing and describing to himself in words what that emotion was. Birds, he believed, could do that. Animals, he was certain, could do it. Why not he? He heard himself saying to himself, Ah. This is optimistic. Oh, now a touch of fear creeps in. And then the floodgates of his mind were open. He found himself looking at the other listeners and wondering how they were reacting. On the surface Philip seemed all sensitive concentration, but for all James knew he might have been wondering where to go on his holidays. He felt like an inferior being, lacking artistic understanding, solidly unmusical, and consoled himself only with the thought that this was not obvious to anybody else. He found himself watching Valerie, and he had a feeling that beneath her bourgeois serenity a great battle between pride and resentment was being fought. He noticed that Max's eyes were closing and opening, closing and opening, closing and opening, as he fought a long agonising battle against jet lag. For minutes at a time James hardly heard the music. Then he would

261

jerk himself back to it, as if he also was fighting jet lag. He would try again to empty his mind, and fail. Then he noticed that Stanley was fast asleep, utterly oblivious to this great performance. There was Charles playing his heart out, playing superbly (how did he know that it was superb? Did he know enough about music to know that it was superb?) and, out of his audience of five, one was fast asleep, one was fighting jet lag, one was reflecting on the fact that one was asleep and one was fighting jet lag, one had heard it all a thousand times before, and only one, Philip, was really appreciating it (he hoped). It was in danger of becoming a fiasco. Then Stanley snored, just once, loudly. His snore woke him up. He looked round the room, having no idea where he was, remembered, grimaced, saw Valerie glaring at him, sat up straight, listened with exaggerated attention. Charles hadn't appeared to hear the snore, he powered on, delicately, subtly, strongly . . . well, James was certain that he was being delicate and subtle and strong. Within about ninety seconds Stanley was fast asleep again, and Max was losing his battle against sleep and embarrassment. Now James could hardly concentrate on the music at all, for fear that Stanley would snore again.

At last what should have been a joy, a memorable artistic experience, was over, and he had hardly experienced it at all.

There was a moment's devastating silence, then Philip called out, 'Bravo,' and began to clap. James clapped too, Stanley woke with a jerk and clapped vigorously, Max also came to and began to applaud in a slightly embarrassed way. Valerie joined in the clapping and smiled, but James didn't think that her eyes were smiling.

Because there were so few of them they clapped for slightly longer than was necessary, and Charles bowed and bowed again and bowed yet again, and James felt certain that there were tears in his eyes.

'I . . . um . . . thank you,' said Charles. 'Thank you. Thank you so much. I . . . um . . . I don't want to risk boring you . . .'

'Never,' called out James. He felt he had to.

'. . . but if you're up for it I would like to play one more piece. It's—'

'I'm sorry,' interrupted Stanley. 'I'm not a late bird any more, and I've had a long journey and a big dinner, and I am bushed. That was wonderful . . . wonderful, Charles . . . simply wonderful . . . I enjoyed every minute of it, but I am for my bed.'

He clambered awkwardly out of his chair.

'I'm awfully sorry,' said Max, 'but the jet lag is beating me. I'm absolutely gutted, Uncle Charles. To sit here and listen to you playing the piano just for us, what an experience, but my eyes kept closing, I'm knackered.'

'I understand,' said Charles, looking as if he didn't understand at all, looking quite angry in fact. James couldn't remember ever seeing Charles angry before. 'I understand. Any more would be too much. I'm over-egging the pudding. It's probably a fault of mine.'

'No, please,' said Philip. 'I think one more piece would be just great.'

'James?' prompted Charles.

'Yes, it'd be wonderful, Charles. A privilege. I'm not looking forward to trying to sleep . . .'

'Well, that's what I thought.'

'And we are all perhaps a little bit overwrought, not surprisingly . . .'

'Well, that's what I thought.'

'And so I think conversation is a little bit of a dangerous activity tonight.'

'Well, that's what I thought.'

'So, please, play for us.'

'Well, if you're sure.'

My God, how much more sure do I have to say I am?

'I am sure.'

'Good. That's fine then.'

'Well, if you'll excuse me,' said Stanley, 'I'll see you in the morning. If the waters haven't risen and swamped Islington.'

He left to a chorus of 'goodnight's and 'sleep well's. As he reached the door he met James's eye and flicked his head in the direction of Charles in yet another meaningful glance.

'Stupid bugger,' said Philip the moment he had gone.

'Absolutely,' said James, 'but if you really want to do something to raise awareness of the risk of global warming, you could do worse than to use him. Put him on the telly, saying, "You're all going to drown, you bastards, and you deserve it." He would at least shock people, and, human nature being what it is, we are tragically ready to get bored by do-gooders.'

'Well, I'm off to bed too,' said Max. 'And I'm really sorry. I feel mortified.'

'Oh, don't,' said Charles. 'It's only music.'

James wished Charles hadn't said that. And he wished Max hadn't said that he was mortified. He was twenty-two. He was too young to be mortified. He was too young to use words like 'mortified'.

'Um . . . well spoken in the restaurant, Max. Fantastic,' said Philip.

Max mumbled his thanks and made an awkward exit, suddenly looking the young, inexperienced man that he was.

'Now are you still absolutely sure?' asked Charles.

'Yes,' said Philip with emphasis.

'Right. Well, I thought it might be rather interesting to

compare Schumann's concerto with another concerto written by a man who admired and was frankly influenced by Schumann's concerto. I refer, of course . . .'

James loved that 'of course'. Charles knew that there was no 'of course' about it to anyone but himself.

'. . . to Grieg's piano concerto. Again, emotion, feeling, subtlety, but this time expressed in a Nordic way rather than a Central European way, or are such regional differences only in the imagination? Let's see, shall we? And of course once again you are not getting the full effect, we haven't an orchestra, but once again I venture to say that I think I can make it into some kind of artistic whole. Lady and gentlemen – well, at least the men are still in the plural – let us say, "Lady and Brothers," Grieg's piano concerto.'

There are only three of us, thought James. This time I cannot afford to let Charles down. This time I will concentrate utterly, I will be sensitive to every nuance, I will be worthy of my brother.

There were tears in Charles's eyes. I'm sure of it. Of course he won't have slept with Deborah. Stanley's a wicked old man, unhinged, twisted, on the way to being deranged, why should I even listen to him?

Concentrate on the music. Oh, Charles, your playing is so lovely. Oh, I so wish I could do that. And this is a lovely slow piece, elegant, passionate, building towards a climax, so Nordic, or is that just my imagination?

Valerie doesn't look like a woman who's getting much.

What kind of an unsubtle thought is that, in the middle of a piano concerto? I am utterly unworthy of your music, Charles.

But she doesn't look loved.

It was Charles that Deborah was going to so eagerly with her red shoes. He knew it. He'd been blind. She had been planning to go on his musical tour with him. Or maybe there had been no tour, maybe the tour had just been a cover. He'd had to go on it anyway, or be found out. He'd been spending nights in lonely beds in European capitals, crying for his lost love in a way that James could not. Stop it. Back to the music. Concentrate.

He closed his eyes, furrowed his brow, tried to let his mind go blank, and suddenly there it was, filling his head, at last his head was filled with nothing but the music, rich, beautiful, powerful, spiritual, strong, rising to a climax, ending.

It was over. He'd heard almost none of it. He clapped like mad.

Philip was clapping like mad too. But Philip had understood it. Perhaps all along it ought to have been Philip that he should have wanted to be.

It had never occurred to him to want to be himself.

Charles took his bows and they clapped and clapped and Valerie said very firmly, in case Charles was contemplating an encore, 'That was a lovely little concert, Charles.'

'Fantastic,' said Philip. 'Well, I must be off back to Leighton Buzzard.'

'I'll see you to the door,' said James.

At the door Philip said, 'Well, that was wonderful.'

'Wonderful.'

'A great artist improvising on the work of two great composers, and all in your living room.'

'Incredible.'

'A privilege to be there.'

If only I had been.

'Absolutely.'

James held out his hand. Philip shook it and then, impulsively, hugged his brother for the second time.

Now at last the tears flowed. He shook with silent sobs, soaking his pillow. The bed stretched vast and empty on

266

both sides of him. He felt lost, tiny, utterly lonely. Now at last he missed Deborah with every bone in his body, as he waited for his final temazepam tablet to kick in. He put his arms round where she should have been, and gave the air a kiss that was meant for her.

Thursday

He was woken by the phone at ten past eight. At first he thought it was his alarm ringing and tried to switch it off, but then he realised that it wasn't switched on. Then he grabbed at the phone and knocked over his glass of water, soaking the edge of the bed. Not a good start to a difficult day.

Not a good omen.

He managed to pick up the phone just one ring before it would have gone onto the answerphone.

'Hello.'

His early-morning voice sounded like a hoarse crow's.

'Hello, James, it's me.'

This was too much too early.

'Helen!'

'Have I woken you?'

No more lies. There was no need for lies any more.

'No. I'm at my computer, checking on my emails before anyone else gets up.'

'James, I'm ringing to apologise for all the awful things I said yesterday.'

'Oh, that's all right.'

Oh, that's all right? What sort of a reaction is that? Come on, James.

'It's not all right. It was dreadful of me. What sort of woman must you think I am?'

'I know what sort of woman you are, my darling.'

Ouch. My darling? No. It's with just having woken up, but really, that's dangerous.

'Oh, James, I miss you.'

I miss you. No. Well, I do, but at the same time I know that I won't. But, James, whatever you do, don't say it. Look what that 'my darling' has done. It's made it intimate. It can't be intimate. It's over. I didn't want it to be over. I wouldn't for the life of me have ended it if there was a chance that it wasn't over.

'Are you still there?'

'Yes. Sorry. Thoughts are sort of flashing around, sort of not quite yet sorted out.'

Say something to show that it's still final, James, something to deactivate that unwise 'my darling'.

'Anyway, thank you for phoning and saying that, Helen. We had five great years. I really don't want it to end in bitterness for either of us.'

'I wouldn't dream of coming and ruining the service. I couldn't.'

'I know.'

He hadn't known. The relief flooded in

'James, I've done a lot of thinking. I think I can understand your . . . um . . . I don't know how to put it, really . . . your thinking on this. Your fear.'

'My fear?'

'Yes. That a great affair, a fantastic sexual adventure, would slide into an ordinary sort of marriage, an affectionate existence. We had an intensity that can only exist when you're up against it, in snatches, in crises. The excitement we felt

272

was a drug. We'd die without it. When you said "my darling" just then I thought, maybe there's still a bit of hope. There isn't any, is there?'

Hard not to prevaricate. Hard not to say, I'd never rule anything out. No. Be strong.

'No, I don't honestly think there is.'

Oh, God.

Go now. Ring off. You've said enough. It's over.

'I've . . . um . . . I've decided to try to be positive.'

Good. That's good.

'Good. That's good.'

It was a relief for once to be able to say what he was really thinking.

'Don't think I'm getting over you or anything. Don't think I'm happy. I'm devastated.'

'I know, and if I say, "I'm sorry," it sounds pathetic, but I am.'

'But I already feel that this is a watershed for me. I've . . . um . . . I've decided not to hang about. I've . . .' He was surprised to hear a touch of coyness entering her voice. 'You remember I talked about a man I met in Germany.'

'Gunter from Ulm who was so charming and Continental and sophisticated.'

'Don't mock, and my God, you have a memory. Well, I've written to him and I . . .' Her voice began to crack. 'Bye, James.'

She rang off hurriedly before the tears began.

James stared at the phone, put it to his lips, kissed it, then slammed it down abruptly. Then he made love to Helen for the last time, fiercely, briefly, nostalgically. Afterwards he felt flat and soiled. It was extremely unpleasant to feel flat and soiled after sex, but on this occasion his very flatness, his very soiledness – was there such a word? – gave him a

273

brief sensation of excitement. He had done the right thing. A new life lay ahead.

He pulled himself to his feet, ambled over to the window, and drew back the curtains on yet another glorious sunny morning. The calm of the Georgian street matched a new feeling of calm in his heart, a feeling of which he was a little ashamed, because he knew that it was caused by his knowledge that Helen wasn't coming, that his behaviour was not going to be revealed to the congregation, that his reputation was not going to be destroyed in front of all those he knew and loved. A strange, almost optimistic feeling crept over him, a feeling that something important would happen today, something would change, and that, hard though it was to imagine it on such a day, it would be a change for the better. Then the worries that had consumed him before the sleeping pill took effect returned. Would Stanley let the side down? Would he break down during his eulogy? And, above all, would Charlotte come, and, if she came, how would she look, how would she behave, how would she be?

The house was quiet. Nobody was up. All four of his house guests had travelled yesterday, and travel is tiring. He'd have liked a shower, but the noise of the pump might wake somebody up, and he wanted them to remain silent for as long as possible. The morning of a big funeral is an excruciating time. The minutes pass slowly. Tension rises remorselessly. Everything has been arranged. There is nothing to do. To be sad is to pre-empt. To be happy is to be insensitive. No mood is appropriate.

If no mood is appropriate, it must be good to let one's mind go blank. As he began to prepare breakfast, James managed just that, achieving with ease what he had so dismally failed to manage while listening to Charles's playing last night.

To float around in one's dressing gown, to prepare breakfast for one's guests, that was a luxury. James the Provider.

There are few more comforting roles. He laid the distressed pine table in the kitchen thoroughly and slowly, putting out butter, jam, two kinds of marmalade, two kinds of honey, a basket for toast, jugs of orange juice, tomato juice and mango juice, two types of cereal, two brands of muesli, a jug of semi-skimmed milk, a jug of soya milk, salt, pepper, mustard, brown sauce, bowls, plates, knives, forks, dessert spoons, teaspoons, napkins. On the marble worktops he put eggs, bacon, sausages, black pudding, tomatoes and mushrooms, all ready to be cooked. On the Lacanche cooker with its five hobs of different sizes and its gas and electric ovens he placed all the pans necessary for the cooking of a full English breakfast. He was more than James the Provider. He was James the Widower whose Competence would Astonish Everybody. He was James the Bereaved whose Stoicism was Admirable. He had roles to play, and he would play them very slowly. With a bit of luck breakfast would last most of the morning.

Breakfast had lasted a long time, and much of the rest of James's morning had been taken up with showering and shaving and getting dressed in clothes that reflected the tragedy of the occasion but were not excessively sombre. He had tried to tell as many people as possible that Deborah hated the sight of large numbers of people dressed in black. He himself was wearing black trousers with a striped shirt, a dark but not black tie and a burgundy jacket.

Then people began to arrive. The caterers came first, ready to prepare a light snack for those who were coming to the house before going on to the crematorium in procession behind the hearse.

'I wonder if I could have a quick sandwich,' suggested Charles. 'I'm going to get down there early. I need to compose myself.'

'An appropriate term,' commented James.

'Yes, I suppose so.'

'I'll come with you,' said Valerie, and it was a statement, not a suggestion. 'I see so little of him, James. I have to grab him when I can.'

James could see that Charles didn't want her to go with him, but didn't know how to say this, and soon they were off in a taxi, absurdly early, it seemed to him.

Soon after they had gone, Fliss arrived, with her husband Dominic, who was an industrial relations consultant. James found him unimpressive, but he must have something. He was in demand across half the globe.

'So sad,' said Dominic, as he shook James's hand with that slightly sweaty handshake that James dreaded. James always wondered if all his flesh was slightly wet and, if so, how Fliss could bear to touch him. 'I felt so helpless, James, that was the awful thing. Fliss needing me, and there I was in bloody Indonesia.'

Unfair to take it out on poor old Indonesia, thought James absurdly.

He led the way into the living room.

'Stiffener?' he suggested. 'Sherry, wine, whisky, gin? Long, harrowing day.'

Dominic glanced at the clock, which was showing two minutes past eleven. He hesitated.

'Or is it too early?' prompted James.

'No, no,' said Domnic hastily. 'I don't think one would do any harm. Sherry, please. It's a terribly underrated drink, but it's going to make a comeback.'

'Fliss?'

'G and T would be good.'

'Coming up.'

Smelling the drink the moment it was poured, Stanley clumped downstairs and accepted a whisky. Max soon

276

appeared and asked for a beer. James reminded him that they would be a long time out of range of a toilet, and he changed it to a whisky.

'I'm really upset about my hair,' said Fliss, and Dominic raised his eyebrows towards heaven. 'My girl's on holiday, and the other girl just doesn't understand it at all.'

'It looks really good,' said James.

'That's right. Tell her,' said Dominic. 'Not that she'll listen.'

'It won't make much difference to Deborah, that's for sure,' said Stanley.

There was a rather dreadful silence, to which Stanley seemed oblivious. He raised his glass.

'Well, cheers, or is that not what one says on these occasions?' he said.

To James's relief the doorbell rang at this moment. It was the Essex lot, the Harcourt clan. Fliss's and Deborah's brother Chris, his wife Tessa, and Malcolm and Monica Harcourt, the parents of Deborah, Fliss and Chris. Malcolm and Monica, known affectionately throughout Essex farming circles as 'The Ems', were extremely bronzed after their holiday. Malcolm apologised for it, and James had to agree that it made them look out of place. They always did, with their old-fashioned, patched-up clothes, but today the inappropriate suntans made them stand out even more than usual. There was no room for any gradation of grief on those teak outdoor faces. Malcolm had passed the two farms on to Chris now, though he still helped, and indeed had a great deal to do at harvest time. The holiday had been in preparation for this ordeal, for ordeal it had become to Malcolm, and there were people who said that Chris put too much upon him at his age. James noticed that morning that, beneath the suntan, there was the first faint hint of frailty in Malcolm.

As the Harcourts entered the room, Stanley gave a low whistle and said to Max, 'Pure Viking. Amazing. Well, not the younger woman. Strong touch of the Norman there, if I'm not mistaken.'

Max smiled inwardly at Stanley's phrase. He didn't think Stanley ever really thought that he was mistaken.

As James poured the drinks for the Essex lot – whisky for the men, sherry for Monica, dry white wine for Tessa – the last of the calm that he had managed to build up over breakfast melted away. He felt an icy blast of danger, the danger that before the day was out the family would discover how much less than a perfect husband he had been. And this brought him back to Helen and the knowledge that, while her generous phone call that morning had been a huge relief and blessing, its very generosity was kick-starting his feelings of guilt again.

Then Philip arrived having fetched Mum, and the little gathering was complete. Conversation proved somewhat sticky, and James chucked a polite stone into the silent pond.

'How's the harvest looking?'

'Bad,' said Chris.

'Always he says, "Bad." He's such a pessimist,' said Tessa. She still had the black brooding beauty that had once made her a frontispiece for *Country Life*. She came from a County family and was always quick to point out that the County wasn't Essex. 'I am not an Essex girl,' she would say without humour. She had three dogs. People said that she loved them more than she loved Chris, and that she loved money more than she loved them. People said that she was disappointed that Chris wasn't more ambitious and grasping. People said that it was her meanness that prevented Chris from hiring harvest help and easing the burden on his struggling father. But then people said a lot of things. James had once dreamt that he was making aggressive love to Tessa, on a piece of waste ground strewn with rubble, in a city ruined by war. Ever since then he had tried not to look at her, and he was trying not to look at her now.

'Well, if it's a bad harvest, it's obviously bad,' said Chris, 'but if it's a good harvest, the price will collapse, so that's bad too. All harvests are bad now, thanks to our friends the European Union and the British Government.'

'If the temperature rises three degrees, there won't be any harvests at all,' said Stanley.

'Thank you for that,' said Chris.

There was an uneasy silence. Philip decided that it needed to be broken, and said the first thing that came into his head. Also, it has to be admitted, he was rather fond of showing that he knew about things in other people's fields.

'I heard that it looks like a wonderful year for barley.'

His remark was not the soothing influence that he had anticipated.

'Our family *can* talk about other things than crops, you know,' said Fliss.

Mum leapt in now, and James was briefly proud of her, even though he did think that her bright, almost garishly yellow outfit was carrying his instruction not to be sombre slightly too far.

'We saw two bullfinches in a garden just after Philip had driven out of the flats,' she said. 'They really are such beautiful birds.'

'Don't talk to me about bullfinches,' said Chris. 'Destructive little buggers. Strip an orchard in an hour.' He caught sight of Tessa's face and realised that he was not living up to her standards of social grace. 'I'm sorry, Mrs Hollinghurst,' he said. 'That was rude of me. But my friend Rod from agricultural college had such trouble with them on his fruit farm. They helped to ruin him. I'm not rational about bullfinches, I'm afraid.'

What *are* you rational about? asked Tessa's spoilt, disappointed, absurdly beautiful face.

'Orchards are a red rag to a bullfinch,' said Max. His only joke of the day seemed to pass entirely unnoticed, and he blushed.

'Time for a little something to eat, I think,' said James.

As they walked towards the kitchen, Malcolm edged himself close to James.

'I'm so sorry, chap,' he said, in his Essex way. 'So sorry. Sad for us all, but for you, tragic.'

James felt spectacularly awful.

'Thank you.'

'Families, eh?'

'Absolutely.'

Over their sandwiches, taken standing up round the table in the kitchen, James organised the funeral procession. He would go in the first car behind the hearse, with Fliss and Dominic. The Essex four would go in the second car, and Max, Stanley, Philip and Mum would go in the third car.

Mum made a face at him, signalling to him to follow her, and left the kitchen. He excused himself and followed.

'What is it, Mum?'

'I'd like to go in the first car, with you. There's room.'

'Well, yes, there is, but I just thought, you aren't a blood relation, the Harcourts are.'

'That stuck-up Tessa thing isn't a blood relation, she hasn't got any blood.'

'No, she isn't a blood relation, but I was thinking of the Ems. I just thought it might be more tactful if you went behind them.'

'I see. Tact's more important than a mother's love. I understand.'

'Oh, Mum. You'd be with Philip. You're his mum too.'

'You're the one who's just lost a wife. You're the one who you might think would need a mum's support.'

'Mum, I would love your support. I just didn't want to be selfish. Anyway, it's no problem. I'll change it.'

'I don't want to make a fuss.'

'Mum, you're making a fuss.'

'No, I mean, I don't want you to change things. I don't want you to do anything.'

'Well, what did you call me out here for, then?'

'To tell you how your mother feels about things.'

'Right. Well, now I know how you feel so I'm going to change things, so there. And actually I can do without all this, Mum.'

He strode back into the kitchen, followed at some distance by his mum, who crept in.

'Slight change of plan,' he announced. 'Mum feels, and she's right, of course, that she ought to be at my side in my moment of grief. She'll come in the first car.'

'You do right, chap,' said Malcolm.

So that was how it was, and very soon the black cars arrived outside, and they made their way to them.

As the cortège slipped slowly past the Georgian terraces, James felt uneasy. He wished now that he had been more proactive, had stamped his personality and his wishes on the proceedings, rather than going along with the traditional ritual proposed by Ferris's Funeral Services. There was no point now in this ritual. Nobody took any notice of them. In the olden days people had stood on the pavement and taken off their hats as the processions passed, but now nobody had a hat to take off, except for one woman on her way to get a Tube train to Wimbledon, and there was no other appropriate gesture to be made, so the procession was just an embarrassment, especially to other road users.

Luckily James didn't see that at the first mini-roundabout

a white van, with the legend *'Geoff Noblet* – the *name for meat'* on its side got skewered into the procession, and stayed in it, for the traffic coming in the other direction was heavy and in any case Geoff Noblet was blissfully unaware that he was in the middle of a funeral cortège. Then two police cars came screaming up behind them, sirens blaring, and the whole cortège had to pull over to let them get by.

On and on they went, five vehicles in dignified procession: hearse, sombre black car, Geoff Noblet – *the* name in meat – and two more sombre black cars. Progress was slow, and James began to get that crematorium nightmare, the fear that they would miss their slot.

The mourners were beginning to assemble, and were standing around outside the crematorium building in the hot sunshine. Black was the predominant colour, but a few people had heeded James's wishes and dressed more colourfully.

People stood in groups of their own kind, as birds and animals do. Cambridge friends in a small huddle. Globpack people in a larger huddle, including Declan O'Connor and Rod Avery, who had fallen in love with each other in the accounts department and moved away to hairdressing, where they felt more comfortable. Deborah's girlie friends in a more glamorous huddle. Philip's four children and their wives and partners. Married couples from the various stages of James's and Deborah's social life eyed each other warily, knew that they should know each other, but weren't quite confident enough in their powers of memory to venture towards each other. Everyone was tense. They all, seeing people from various aspects of the lives of James and Deborah, felt an echo of their original shock. They shouldn't be here on this lovely summer's day. Deborah shouldn't be dead. It was against the natural order of things.

The previous funeral ended early, it must have been a

skimpy affair. Only nine people emerged from the chapel, some of them elderly and tearful, others young and spiky-haired and imprisoned in suits that were too small and hadn't been worn for years. Nobody watching could fail to feel sad at the sight of this evidence of a lonely life and death.

Charles made his way briskly into the chapel, with Valerie following in his slipstream. Slowly, a little uncertainly, not quite sure if it was yet time, people edged their way nearer to the doors. Everyone was a little anxious about getting a seat, for the place was going to be crowded, but nobody wanted to be seen to be anxious. It wasn't quite dignified to be worried about having to stand, on such an occasion as this.

'If you'd kindly wait just a moment,' said a crematorium official with a half-smile, 'we are just putting reserved notices on seats for the family. Thank you for your patience.' He looked at his watch. Where were the family? They were cutting it fine.

A lady emerged from the chapel, gave the all-clear, and the official stepped aside and waved the mourners in. The first few hesitated, none of them wanting to be the first to go in. This was England, the Land of Hanging Back.

Charles didn't look up from the piano as the first people entered. He was in a different world. The eloquent, beautiful notes of Grieg's 'Notturno' from the Lyric Pieces, Op. 54, softened the severe Victorian chapel with its dark stained-glass windows, its frowning statues and its lifeless rows of pews.

Outside, the procession made its appearance at last, minus Geoff Noblet – *the* name for meat. They *had* cut it fine. James's nerves were shredded already, and the service hadn't even begun.

Just before the procession pulled up outside the chapel, a couple hurried round the corner, close to the wall of the building, as if trying to creep in without being noticed. The young woman was thin, almost emaciated. She had a ring in her nose. Her clothes were long and dangly and made for someone larger, and her complexion was as white as fresh snow. She looked as if all the blood had just run out of her. The man was much older, his clothes slightly ragged, his face looking lived-in, and lived-in by somebody rather disreputable and not altogether clean in his habits. They slid into seats near the back. Charlotte had used up all her courage by coming at all. She was trembling. Her companion held her hand and pressed it.

Four solemn men carried the coffin slowly up the aisle. Behind it James couldn't help wondering how much of Deborah had remained to be put in the coffin. Beside him, Max looked more like a tree than ever. He had set his face in a wooden mask that hid all emotion.

James walked slowly into the chapel and down the aisle. He longed to look straight ahead. He didn't want to see the massed faces of his friends and colleagues, all looking at him to see how he was bearing up, how he had taken it, whether his grief had marked him, whether his hair had turned white, whether he had lost weight, all suffused with that strange mixture of sympathy and curiosity that congregations feel at funerals. But he had to force himself to look, force himself to face their stares. He felt sick with apprehension as he hunted for Charlotte. He found her straight away. His heart soared and sank all at once. She was there. She had come. She looked so ill.

She was looking straight ahead, for which he was grateful. Now he could look straight ahead, and did so fixedly. The family took their places, the vicar stood facing them.

Charles, not to be hurried, continued playing, leaving the vicar with egg on his face.

At last Charles brought Grieg's splendid 'Notturno' to a close. A sudden deep silence rolled round the chapel. Charles walked, with slow, erect dignity, to the seat reserved for him. Valerie shuffled over to give him the room his importance demanded.

'Before we start our service of thanksgiving for the life of Deborah, who was a much loved woman as can be told from the size of the congregation here today,' began the Reverend Martin Vigar, 'James has asked me to tell you that you are all invited back to the house – you'll find the address in your order of service – for refreshments afterwards, and he really would like you all to go, the more the . . . well, not the merrier exactly, but the more people who go to share memories of Deborah, the more pleased he will be.'

Suddenly his tone changed, and he said, 'Let us pray,' in a deep, sonorous voice.

As the vicar led them in the prayers and responses, James felt shocked. Gone were all traces of Allied Dunbar. In their place was his love of God, and, even more powerfully, his love of himself. James realised that he was a frustrated actor, a luvvie of the lectern. This was what he had given up his salary and his commission and his bonuses for, not for scantily attended services and parents forced into hypocrisy for their children's sake but for the moments when a full church hung on his words, when every eye was on him and he abandoned his tactful stoop and stood tall. His mouth was suddenly full of plums. What had been a hint of singsong was now a threat that at any moment he might burst into extracts from *The Sound of Music*. This was not the man he had booked. This was not the performance he had asked for. This was not 'light on God'. He felt cheated. And the pity of it was that the man wasn't even a good actor. He was playing a vicar, and it was a cliché, and he was playing it badly, while in his own persona, with its hint of the financial consultant of yore, he had been quite interesting and far more likeable.

The coating of significance that had so suddenly entered the vicar's voice robbed his first prayer of all significance for James. Its pretension stripped the words of all meaning. When the congregation uttered their first solemn and fervent 'Amen' he found that he couldn't utter the word. He just couldn't do it, and this was a shock for which he was entirely unprepared.

Now they were standing for the first hymn. The organ boomed out.

> *'All things bright and beautiful,*
> *All creatures great and small.'*

The singing was good. James loved hymns, and he sang along too. His singing was flat, but hearty. He was singing for Deborah. He was singing with his beloved son at one side, and his brother Philip, suddenly promoted into being his favourite brother, at the other side. The three of them were as one, expressing in song their love of Deborah. James was surprised to hear a catch in Philip's voice.

But all the while, below the surface as he sang, James's thoughts were churning. He was having a revelation. He didn't believe in God. He didn't believe that Deborah was on her way to heaven. He didn't believe that he would ever meet her again. He felt devastated, yet still he sang.

> *'How great is God Almighty,*
> *Who has made all things well.'*

More prayers followed, and he just couldn't bring himself to utter the responses. This shouldn't really be such a shock. He hadn't been to church once in the thirty years since he had left school, except to attend weddings, christenings and funerals. He hadn't once given serious thought to the question of religious belief. There hadn't been any need for spiritual feeling in the world of packaging.

Every time there was a response spoken by the congregation he could detect above all others the voice of Dwight Schenkman the Third. Beside him, Max was mumbling, and he sensed the moment when Max noticed that his father wasn't joining in.

He realised with a sense of shame and horror that he had done no thinking about the form of the service. Naturally Deborah and he had not yet made any plans for their funerals, and the shock had taken him entirely unawares. How he wished now that he had held a humanist funeral, with a woodland burial. How Deborah would have liked the thought of her body, in the earth, giving sustenance to some of the lowliest creatures in nature's cycle. How stuffy all this was. Why why why hadn't he thought more deeply about it?

And now here was the Reverend Martin Vigar starting on his eulogy. Fair play to him, he didn't pretend to have known Deborah, and he related the facts of her life accurately and with less pomposity than he had employed in his prayers. His delivery became a little more natural. But it still felt as if he was talking about somebody James had never met, had only heard about. He spoke of Deborah's pride in her fine son Max, and her deep sorrow at the disappearance of her beloved daughter Charlotte.

A humorous note crept into the vicar's voice like a mouse into a platter of cheeses as he related a vaguely amusing anecdote with which James had primed him. No, James wanted to cry, don't signal the joke, you'll kill it, frail thing that it is. He closed his ears to it, he couldn't bear to hear it, but he did hear the faint flitter of laughter that passed through the congregation like a breeze through a spinney, rapidly stifled as the Reverend Martin Vigar slid back into evangelism. He ended on the note that, just as James would in his house in less than an hour's time, Deborah would look forward to welcoming them all during the eternity that was to come.

James hardly heard a word of the next prayers. He didn't believe in God. He didn't want to be here. He didn't want to talk of Deborah in this building. She had gone for ever. He had been unworthy of her. It was too late for him to make it up to her.

'James will now say a few words about Deborah, striking a more personal note than I was able to do.'

He stumbled from his seat, walked uncertainly towards the lectern. He hadn't touched a drop, but people would think he was drunk.

He couldn't believe how crammed the pews were, and there were even people standing at the back. The faces of the mourners were blurred, except for Charlotte, sitting there like a ghost (but where was Chuck?), and Dwight Schenkman the Third, ramrod straight and huge, a quarter-back in a convention of dwarves. He must speak. He had been silent with these images too long. People were getting uneasy.

He pulled himself together, and began.

'The vicar has told you that we met in Malta,' he said, 'when we were both holidaying with our parents. What he hasn't told you, because he doesn't know it, is what we did in Malta. We were all staying at the same hotel, and when our parents were asleep . . . how can I put this tastefully, as befits a chapel? We experienced some very interesting nights, and none of them were Knights Templar.'

'You didn't!' exclaimed his mum, almost under her breath, but clearly audible in the deeply silent chapel. Another titter ran through the congregation, and James almost smiled, but he feared that hysteria would follow if he let himself go. He looked very stern, and the titter fizzled out. But his mum was blushing like a beetroot.

'I'm afraid we did,' he said. 'It was love at first sight. There was nothing sordid in it. We've had such a happy life, and I must be thankful for that. In a few minutes you will all, I hope, come to our house. When you do, have a look around you, at what you see. I bought some of it. To be more precise, I bought one of the decanters, the Chinese vase in the hall, and a hundred and ten bottles of booze. Everything else in the house was bought by Deborah. I was told the vase was Ming. I paid two hundred pounds for it. I took it to the *Antiques Roadshow*. It was a fake, worth fifteen pounds. I never bought another antique. But Deborah never came back from anywhere without something. It might just be a Victorian pepper pot. "It looked so lonely without its salt cellar. I had to give it a home." Everywhere she went, she saw something that wasn't happy being left on the shelf. If she saw a Dresden dog, its eyes followed her round the room. When things were a bit slow in packaging, I sometimes drove round all the bypasses to avoid passing any antique shops. Later I realised, such was her eye, that I needn't have worried. Everything she bought turned out to be worth more than she had paid for it.

'We never had a dog, they're too great a tie and she couldn't have faced leaving it at the kennels. We did have cats but they all get run over in Islington. She loved animals, though. Even rabbits, which is odd in a farmer's daughter. Sometimes we'd go out for a day in the country. "Oh, look at that poor horse, James. It's got no company." "Oh, dear, one of those sheep is very lame, James." "I think that jackdaw's hurt its wing, James." We'd get home and she'd say, "Well, that was a lovely day," and I'd say, "I'm really depressed."

'She was a great cook. She made the best beef Stroganoff

this side of the Urals. And always so neat and elegant. She didn't sweat onions, she perspired them. She . . .'

His voice cracked. Tears were beginning to trickle down his face.

'She . . .'

He couldn't go on. He couldn't fight against it.

'I wasn't worthy of her,' he wailed.

A murmur of embarrassment rumbled through the congregation.

He needed to confess. Here. Now.

No. Don't.

But he had to.

'I . . . I did . . . I . . .'

Should he confess? Would she want him to? The tears were streaming now.

'I'm sorry. I can't . . . I can't . . .'

He began to stumble back towards his seat.

'I'm sorry. I'm so sorry.'

Max, mature beyond his years, came out and put his arm round him and helped him back to his seat.

'Let us pray,' thundered the Reverend Martin Vigar.

During the next short sequence of prayers and responses, James managed to pull himself together, but how he longed for the end of all this.

'Felicity Parkington-Baines will now read a poem in memory of her sister,' intoned the Reverend Martin Vigar.

James hadn't always seen eye to eye with Fliss, they had never been truly warm together, but he hoped with all his heart now that she would do this well and with dignity. All his irritation with her melted away. He loved her in that moment in a wonderful, simple way, with a love that had no sexuality in it. Sadly, this was the best form of love.

He needn't have worried. She had been building herself

up for this moment for days. In her elegant black-and-white outfit, with her hair far more successfully styled than she believed, she looked, if not as lovely as her sister, a pleasantly attractive woman in early middle age.

'I'm going to read a poem by Christina Rossetti,' she said in a clear, strong voice.

James expected that it would be 'Remember Me', often chosen at funerals, but it was a slightly more ambiguous piece. Fliss read it slowly, not rushing to get the ordeal over as so many people do.

> 'When I am dead, my dearest,
>   Sing no sad songs for me;
> Plant thou no roses at my head,
>   Nor shady cypress tree;
> Be the green grass above me
>   With showers and dewdrops wet;
> And if thou wilt, remember,
>   And if thou wilt, forget.
>
> 'I shall not see the shadows,
>   I shall not feel the rain;
> I shall not hear the nightingale
>   Sing on, as if in pain;
> And dreaming through the twilight
>   That doth not rise nor set,
> Haply I may remember,
>   And haply may forget.'

As she walked back with slow dignity, Fliss cast just a fleeting glance towards James. Was it his imagination, or was there a challenge in it? Had she chosen this particular poem, which struck him as beautiful but inappropriate, as her way of telling him, 'You shouldn't be having my sister cremated. You should have had a woodland burial.'?

Already he knew that before long he would start to find her irritating again.

The vicar announced the second and final hymn. The congregation stood. It was almost over now.

> *'Rock of ages, cleft for me,*
> *Let me hide myself in thee . . .'*

James sang, treating the words as noises rather than as things with meaning. Max gave him a look and a fond but tentative half-smile. They sang together, father and son, strongly, lustily, tunelessly, meaninglessly.

The hymn ended, they sat, they bowed their heads, the vicar spoke. The meaning of his words no longer got through to James. There was a clank, and the machinery began, the coffin began to slide away, he couldn't look, he feared what he had joked about earlier, that a pathologist would rush in and shout, 'Stop.' He had a sudden, bright, heart-rending image of a peaceful woodland glade, a bamboo coffin, a nightingale singing without pain (it struck him as cruel that the nightingale in the poem had needed to be in pain just for the sake of a rhyme – strange to think this now, but anything was better than thinking about what was happening).

She had gone. It was over. Charles was moving towards the piano, but otherwise all movement was stilled.

The Reverend Martin Vigar walked slowly towards the congregation, began to walk down the aisle through the middle of them, looking rather as if he was Moses and they were the Red Sea. He nodded to James, the nod meaning, 'Follow me, my son.' Charles began to play one of Brahms's lovely Intermezzi, Op. 117. James came out of his coma and began to walk, trying not to look at the congregation, trying not to fall, for he was barely conscious of any link between his thoughts and his feet.

He was outside, the remorseless sun was still shining, he was shaking the vicar's hand, the vicar shook his hand as if it was a wet sock that needed ringing dry.

It was over.

He longed to sit down. There was no strength in his legs. But he couldn't sit down. He had to greet people, thank them, be nice to them, share his grief with them and their grief with himself. And they were not just any old bunch of people, these were virtually all the people that he knew and cared about in the world.

It was over. He had the feeling – unjustified because we cannot know what is to come, but a comfort at this moment – that nothing quite as bad as that funeral could ever happen to him again. And the strength began to come back into his legs. He was alive still.

The crematorium official approached.

'I'm so sorry,' he said. 'I have to ask you to move away from the doors. The next lot's waiting. They'll need access. I'm so sorry.'

It wasn't fair to blame the man. He had a most unattractive task, but really, 'The next lot's waiting,' what a way to put it. That's what we were, 'the last lot', the lot that has to be got out of the way. And now we come to lot number seventy-three, Deborah Hollinghurst. Oh, for that woodland glade.

James and the vicar led them away from the entrance to the chapel. James could still hear the official saying, 'If you wouldn't mind,' and, 'So sorry.' It reminded him of the priest in the Sistine Chapel shouting, 'No photos. No flash,' at regular intervals, killing the moment.

He found himself shaking hands with friends, colleagues, acquaintances, relatives. He heard people saying astonishing things – 'Nice service,' 'Well, that went off well,' 'Well done, James,' 'She'd have been pleased,' 'The vicar was good.'

Were they just being polite, or had they been to a different funeral? Were there two chapels side by side, and they'd gone to the other one? Other people said things that seemed more honest. 'Brave of you, chap,' from Malcolm. 'Bet you're glad that's over,' from Ursula Norris. 'I'll be thinking of you,' in a voice near to tears from Roger Dodds.

The dark cars were waiting, the drivers standing respectfully beside them, looking as if they longed to go to the pub.

'I'll see you all back at the house,' James called out. 'Please come. Please do come.'

And all the while he was looking for that white face, that wreckage of what had once promised to be so beautiful. Charlotte's face. He mustn't let her go. He mustn't let her slip back off to the shadows.

He found Max.

'Max,' he said urgently. 'I must talk to Charlotte. I doubt she'll come back, somehow. Can you go in my place in the first car, and get the show on the road? Of course you can, and the caterers will know what to do.'

'What about you, Dad?'

'I'll find my way. I'll get a taxi. With Charlotte, I hope. You can do it, chap.'

Max smiled.

'Thanks, Dad. Can I just have a quick word with Charlotte?'

'Yes, of course.'

There she was, slipping round to the side of the chapel as if she couldn't bear to be seen by the mourners. Well, that suited James. He didn't want their stares either. This was a deeply private moment. There was a middle-aged man with her. James wondered who he was. Max approached his sister purposefully, then stopped, said, 'Hello, Charlotte,' rather awkwardly, then moved forward to kiss her. She withdrew instinctively, then bravely held her ground and allowed herself to be kissed with almost no contact on one cheek. She gave a half-smile. Max said, 'Hi. I . . . um . . . I have to go. See you, Charlotte.'

'See you.'

Her voice was tiny.

Max walked away, back towards the massed mourners.

'Hello, darling,' said James.

He kissed her very gently, as if she was made of porcelain. She accepted the kiss but didn't return it. He could see that the beauty she had once promised the world had not entirely gone. It might, yes, it really might still be there, one day. He wanted to hug her. He wanted to hug her long and hard. He wanted to relive fifteen years of love. He wanted to fill five years of emptiness. He wanted to do it all at once. It wasn't possible.

She smiled, a little more confidently than she had smiled at Max. It made her look fifteen again, but her smile was as fragile as a butterfly, and when it had died she was twenty and anorexic and stunted by drugs and with a ring through her nose again.

'Hi,' said the man at her side. His complexion was faintly yellow, and his face was lined and crumpled, like a piece of blank paper that has been forgotten on a sunny windowsill. He smiled. His teeth were faintly yellow too. 'I'm Chuck.'

James was astonished.

'Ah. Somehow I thought you'd be . . . younger.'

'So did I. It doesn't happen, does it? I'm fifty-three, and I'm in the lift that's going up. Don't ask me what I've done with my life.'

'I won't. You're here now, you're with my daughter, and all I'm interested in is what you do with the rest of your life.'

Chuck gave him a serious look. James's remark had clearly surprised him, which wasn't surprising. It had surprised James too.

'Wow,' said Chuck. 'Cool. You are one cool dude, James.'

This surprised James too. He had never been described in such terms before.

'Dad . . .' Charlotte stopped. She looked as if calling James by that simple word had been an exhausting struggle. 'Dad . . .' She repeated it a little more confidently, as if she was exploring how it sounded. 'I don't think I can come to the house.'

'Too many people,' said Chuck.

'I agree,' said James. 'Far too many. A lifetime of people. I don't mind about the house.'

'Honestly?' asked Charlotte.

'Honestly.'

She smiled again. This smile looked a little more natural, as if she was beginning to remember how to do it. Her teeth looked reassuring. He realised that when he had last seen them they had had braces on them. James felt – it seemed inexplicable at this moment – a sense of optimism. If it was too strong to call it a moment of hope, it was at least a moment when hope was a possibility, when there could be hope of hope.

'I want to see you again,' he said. 'I want to see you again very soon. Max doesn't go back till Tuesday week. He'd love to see you properly.'

'I'd like to see him.'

He was pleased to hear this, but he noted that she had not echoed his use of 'love'. He ought to go slowly.

He couldn't go slowly. He wasn't that sort of man.

'Darling . . . oh, Charlotte. Oh, Charlotte . . . what made you leave us? Can you tell me?'

Chuck frowned. James sensed that all the colour would have drained out of Charlotte's face, if there had been any colour there.

Chuck put his arm round Charlotte's tiny waist. James

could see that he had to do it very gently, so as not to crush her. She was so thin.

'It's all right, Chuck,' she said. 'I saw you in Porthcawl, Dad.'

James reeled.

'Porthcawl?'

'With that woman. On the beach.'

James was too astonished to feel shame.

'In the sea.'

'Oh, God.' James had a vision of Charlotte in all her youthful innocence. Oh, God. 'Were you one of those children building sandcastles?'

Charlotte gave a much more adult smile.

'Not quite. I was fifteen.'

'Well, what *were* you doing in Porthcawl?'

'What were *you* doing in Porthcawl?'

'I was on business.'

'It didn't look like business.'

James sighed.

'She's called Helen. She was the only person I was ever unfaithful to your mother with. We . . . I've known her for five years. I broke it off this week. Oh, Charlotte, I'm sorry.'

Charlotte shrugged. It wasn't a nice shrug. There was a long way to go.

'But what *were* you doing in Porthcawl?'

Charlotte smiled, and, like the shrug, it wasn't very nice.

'The father lived there.'

James felt as if there was no air left on that hot afternoon. He had the greatest difficulty continuing to breathe. Slowly the shock subsided. Chuck caught his eye, and gave a sympathetic wince. He raised his great eyebrows at Chuck, asking the question. Chuck shook his head emphatically and looked shocked.

'I was three months pregnant, Dad, and neither you nor Mum noticed. You didn't really care, did you?'

'Charlotte!'

'Oh, you did, but you didn't. You know what I mean. Your fucking packaging. Mum's fucking gallery. Your fucking friends. Mum's fucking golden girls. Mum's fucking bridge. Your fucking meals. Your fucking claret that you sniffed like a dirty old man. Our fucking holidays with all that fucking sightseeing.'

Chuck winced at each swear word. James didn't mind the swear words. He winced at each truth.

'That's how I saw it, Dad. I was fifteen and horrid. I still am.'

'Horrid?'

'Fifteen. I couldn't talk to you. You hadn't even noticed I wasn't still a little girl.'

'Oh, Charlotte. This is . . . this is . . . What happened . . . to the . . . ?'

'I had an abortion. I so wish I hadn't. I so wish I hadn't, Dad.'

Charlotte met his gaze, defiantly.

'Well, that's it. That's it. That's your precious little daughter.'

All the care Helen and I took within thirty miles of the house, within thirty miles of Guildford, within thirty miles of all the places that might trap us, and we got caught out in bloody Porthcawl.

James looked round. The last mourners were drifting away, and the last mourners for the next funeral were drifting in. Soon they would be alone, in the sunshine.

'I ought to go,' he said. 'I have a houseful of mourners to contend with. My fucking friends, Charlotte, and their fucking friends. Oh, God, I don't want to go. I don't want to leave you now I've found you. I won't go. Let's go and

298

have a drink. Who cares about them? I'm one cool dude, after all.'

He met Chuck's eyes and they almost shared a smile.

'You gotta go,' said Chuck. 'We'll see you again, now we've seen you, won't we, Charlie?'

Charlotte nodded.

'OK. But . . .' Should he say it? He wanted to, but did he mean it? He had to say it, and say it now, for fear that later he wouldn't mean it.

'Would you consider coming to live with me?'

They looked at him in astonishment.

'Both of you, of course.'

They looked speechless.

'Don't answer. It's far too soon.'

'Are you serious?' asked Chuck.

'Utterly. I wouldn't ask it otherwise. My offer. My promise. No questions about Chuck's past. No questions about Charlotte's missing years. No snide remarks about tattoos or rings through noses. You can eat with me when you want or on your own when you want or not at all though I don't recommend it.' He gave them a stern look. A serious tone entered his voice. 'Now. Your promise. Well, two promises. The first is for both of you. No drugs in the house at all. I know what drugs do. I don't want you to have any anywhere. I probably can't stop you outside but I can in the house, and, believe me, I will. Break that rule, and you're out. The second rule is for you only, Chuck.'

James looked very stern. Chuck looked slightly anxious.

'What's coming?'

'Never call her Charlie. Her name's Charlotte. She's a beautiful girl. She's my beautiful daughter, and she has a beautiful name.' He had hoped to finish the sentence without emotion, as a cool dude would, but his voice gasped into tears, and he turned away, sobbing.

As he walked away, he raised one hand in farewell. He didn't turn round.

He walked briskly, glad of the exercise, the physical activity releasing at least some of his tension. He couldn't believe what he had just offered. Not that he regretted it. He was shaken as he thought of how his life might be disrupted. Shaken but not frightened. He felt that he would be able to rise to the challenge. He felt a little flicker of optimism again, a feeling that he was going to be able to make a new start, a feeling that he might at last, rather late in the day, be able to fulfil the full obligations of fatherhood.

He had passed through the gates of the crematorium now. A taxi passed him, and he didn't hail it. Another one was coming. He didn't hail that one either. He didn't want to go to the wake. He didn't think he could face all those people today.

He had to. Whoever heard of a widower not attending his wife's wake? His three great worries had been about his eulogy, about Helen and about Charlotte. He had nothing left to fear.

All over the house people would be wondering where he was. And they were all his friends, there to comfort him, there to share what at last he had recognised as his grief.

He looked round for a taxi, but now, when he needed one, there were none to be seen. He began to feel desperate. He began to want to run. He began to break out into a sweat. He needed to get home.

At last a taxi appeared.

At the house, only two people noticed that he wasn't there. Dwight Schenkman the Third wanted to drown him in long sentences of sympathy and admiration. Marcia wanted to offer him her body without actually saying so. But otherwise, those crowded into the living room might have thought he was among those who had slid inexorably into the kitchen, as certain people always do at gatherings, there to linger in what they thought of as the heartbeat of the house. And the people in the kitchen, grabbing the canapés before anyone else, might have thought he was among those spilling out into the elegant little garden. The caterers were dispensing drinks and canapés very efficiently, people were huddling among their own kind. Some of them would continue to huddle, others, as the drink began to ease their tension, would start to circulate and introduce themselves to people they didn't know. Everything was exactly as it would have been if James had arrived.

The man who today was not wearing a white linen suit was listening as Gordon Tollington described in every detail the tasting menu at the Fat Duck. He omitted no herb, he ignored no spice. His listener felt so full just listening that he waved away the offer of a smoked salmon blini. But he was listening with only half his mind. The other half was busy trying to remember where he had seen a particular woman before. She was middle-aged, vaguely shabbily dressed, shapeless and charmless rather than ugly. He felt that she had the aura of a woman who had never gone to bed with a man. She was in among the Harcourts standing at the far end of the narrow garden, beside a statue of Pan that Deborah had been unable to resist in Winchester, and she was staring at him, which was disturbing. He really did feel vaguely alarmed, and all the more worried because the feeling was so vague. He associated her with an unappetising smell of overcooked meat. The remembered or imagined smell of the meat was all the more unpleasant when compared with the delights still being described so eloquently by Gordon Tollington.

It was when she turned to smile at somebody – insincerely,

301

it seemed to him – that he saw her double chin and remembered. When he had last seen it there had been a splodge of tiramisu upon it, in a hotel restaurant near Diss. He had noticed what a sloppy eater she was. He disliked sloppy eaters.

She was walking towards him. She had a strange smile on her face. There was no humour in the smile. He felt a stab of fear.

'Excuse me, Gordon,' he said. 'Fantastic, amazing stuff, beautifully described, I almost feel as if I don't need to go there now, but I just have to speak to this lady. Sorry about this, I'll catch you later, I'd love to hear about the puddings.'

'No problem. They're worth hearing about, I can assure you.'

He turned away from Gordon and faced the woman. He felt an irrational dislike of her, her slightly plump face, her baggy body. This feeling made him uneasy. He was a civilised man, a quietly generous man. He didn't have irrational dislikes.

'It is, isn't it?' she asked.

'It is what?'

'You are . . . him.'

He wasn't going to make it easy for her.

'Well, yes, I'm me, if that's what you mean.'

Nothing pleasant could come out of this.

'No, I mean, it's you. You are who I think you are.'

'Madam, how can I have any idea who you think I am?'

'You're the man I saw in that hotel, near Diss.'

'I was in a hotel near Diss, yes, and I remember you now. You had a blob of tiramisu on your chin.'

She flushed slightly.

'Oh, dear,' she said. 'I was . . .' A strange expression flitted across her face like the shadow of a bird. 'I was lunching with my friend.'

She spoke the word 'friend' rather coyly, and he realised that he had been wrong in thinking that her bitterness was in part because she had never been to bed with a man. It was because she had never been to bed with a woman.

'I had the impression you were waiting for somebody,' she said.

'Oh?'

'I wondered if it could have been a woman.'

'Don't you think that's my business?'

'Well, I just wondered if it might have been Deborah. It was on the road close to the hotel, and on that very morning, that she had her crash. It occurred to me, when I heard about the accident, that you might have been waiting for her. But then, although I thought I recognised you, I couldn't place you. Then today it all clicked. We met at Felicity and Dominic's twentieth wedding anniversary party, in Guildford.'

He didn't remember, but he decided to pretend that he did.

'Yes. I didn't like you then either.'

Unwise, he thought, as he walked abruptly away from her.

But it isn't always possible to be wise.

James didn't enter the house by the front door. He didn't want anyone to witness his late arrival. He scurried along the path on the eastern side of the house, and drifted into the garden, hoping that he would look as if he had just drifted out of the house. He appeared to have been successful, and was soon mingling with the throng. At least forty people were standing around among the ferns and grasses and statues, most drinking wine, one or two beer, a few tea or coffee. Two smart young ladies were taking round trays of canapés. Already, the buzz of conversation was such that it was hard to believe that this was a funeral wake. The reception was going well. It was everything he had hoped it would be. Because he had missed that first half-hour – the thawing solemnity, the cautious return to some kind of normality after the service – its aura of good cheer stabbed him in the heart.

Dwight Schenkman the Third had spotted his late arrival, and now he and Claire tacked through the throng to greet him.

'James, I have to say this to you,' said Dwight. 'You probably won't welcome it. You English tend to shrink from praise, and you think we Americans overdo it.'

'Not at all. Not at all.'

'But I have to say it. You'll have to take it on the chin. I have realised, these last few difficult days, what a man of integrity you are.'

'Thank you, Dwight.'

'We have to be going in a minute.'

Hurrah!

'Oh, I'm sorry to hear that.'

'A man of rare integrity, James. I have so admired your commitment to your people in Bridgend and Kilmarnock.'

'Thank you.'

'I hope with all my heart that you will be able to come up with evidence that will enable me to pursue a policy which will give you gratification in this matter.'

Was he right to detect an underlying threat there? Was he right to find significance in the fact that Dwight had said 'your people' and not 'our people'?

'I hope so too.'

'But enough of Globpack. Today is all about Deborah. We are going to miss her so much, James.'

'So much.'

'But we know that our grief, painful though it is, is but

a trivial thing compared to the immensity of your grief. I want you to know that we are with you all the way, James.'

'All the way.'

'Thank you.'

James endured Dwight's global handshake, and rather enjoyed being allowed to place a soft kiss on each of Claire's lovely soft cheeks, and then they were gone, and he began to move to the edge of the garden in order to take a deep breath, as if he was an otter breaking the surface to take a gulp, and there was Marcia steaming down on him. His mother's phrase, There's no peace for the wicked, came to him and he thought, Oh, God. Mum. I mustn't neglect her.

But Marcia was first in the roll of duty.

'Hello, Marcia, you look very glamorous.'

No!!

'Thank you. I took ages working out what to wear. I don't have much dress sense.'

Don't draw attention to it.

'Nonsense.'

'I tried to look, as I know you wanted, not too drab and glum.'

'You've succeeded.'

'Without looking tarty.'

Sadly, you could never do that.

'And I know of course I'll see you in the office during the rest of my month's notice.'

Oh, God.

'But, James, I want to say, when all this has . . . well, you know . . . but . . . in time . . . when you've . . . you know . . . because, I mean, at first you'll be . . . you know . . . devastated. I mean, I remember how I felt when Ronald died . . . and he was only a hamster . . . what I'm saying is . . . you know where I live, you have my number, I'll be there.'

305

'At the end of the phone?'

'Exactly.'

'Thank you, Marcia. Thank you very much. How's the . . . how's Willy the Wombat coming on?'

'He's coming along pretty well. I'm getting lots of ideas. I thought he might be employed by the UN to save the world from a great crisis. Or he might lead all the animals in London Zoo in a big revolution type of thing. He might have amazing powers and get called Superwombat. I mean, I haven't really got going on it yet. I think early on an author has to explore all the parameters.'

'Great. That sounds wonderful. I can see you holding court in the Ivy in years to come.'

'Do you mean that?'

He realised, to his amazement, that he did. Who could tell? He felt a wave of true affection for this sunburnt, shapeless young woman. He felt an urge to say something really affectionate, something to give her hope. He resisted it.

'Well, keep at it,' he said. 'I must go and find my mum, Marcia. Duty calls.'

He kissed her on both cheeks.

James didn't know it, but his long day's journey towards his mum was going to be interrupted by several more encounters.

He felt that he had seen her before. You wouldn't have described her as beautiful. The word 'pretty' wouldn't have come instantly to mind. Attractive? Yes, well, very definitely if one thought of it as opposed to unattractive, but even then, while she was attractive, you wouldn't necessarily have described her as such. When he thought about her, later that evening, after she had gone, James found himself using a very odd word. She was complete.

She was talking to a couple of the Glebeland girls, just in the garden, but close to the back door, and he remembered where he had seen her – in the photograph of all the Glebeland girls that he had found. He would have to pass her to enter the house to find Mum. Their eyes met for just a moment, it was nothing dramatic, just a brief connection. She turned away from the other two girls, and he suddenly knew who she was. She was Grace Farsley, the girl who got away, went to Rangoon or somewhere, married a tea planter or something equally Victorian, was never seen again. Deborah had lost all contact with her, had regretted it often, had asked the other girls about her, some of the other girls hadn't liked her, had thought her stand-offish, Deborah had thought only that she was reserved, Deborah had really liked her, and Deborah had almost never been wrong about people (except Constance Thrabnot, but we needn't go into that).

'It's good to meet you. Deborah often spoke of you.'

'Really?'

'She wondered what had happened to you. She longed to see you again.'

'Well, I'm amazed. Well, that's . . . well, it's nice, in a way, but it's also rather awful. Because now I feel so sad that I never will. I haven't been back in England that long, and I had no way of contacting her either. And then on Saturday I saw the announcement of her death in the paper. I was devastated. I was very close to her once. So of course I felt that I must come.'

'I'm glad you did.'

'I thought you were wonderful today, James. Yes, yes, I can see it on your face. You're ashamed you couldn't see it through. Honestly, James, when that vicar's voice has faded into oblivion, I'll still remember the true emotion of that moment.'

'Yes, Grace, I'll agree there. It was true.'

'I think Deborah was very lucky.'

Oh, Grace, Grace, did you have to say that? Oh, the burden of my secret.

'So you . . . um . . . didn't you . . . this sounds terribly Somerset Maugham . . . marry a tea planter and go to Rangoon?'

'I married a surveyor and went to Penang. The humidity turned the surveyor sour and he became cruel to me. That was a bit Somerset Maugham.'

'You didn't keep up with the Glebeland girls?'

'For a while. I liked them, but there was a problem. I hated Glebeland, and they all loved it. Well, it's nice to meet you.'

She shook his hand and turned back to the girls, but it didn't seem like a rebuff.

He walked along the corridor that led into the house from the garden, just as Mike came out of the living room. There they were, face to face. He hadn't even noticed Mike in the church. In fact, so much had been going on in his emotional life that he had completely forgotten about Mike and his hardening suspicions. But now, coming face to face with him so unexpectedly, he was utterly shocked. He was shocked to see him looking smart, wearing a jacket and tie, his hair neatly brushed and almost certainly washed. He was shocked at his certainty that, respectable though Mike looked now, he was a murderer. He came out in goose pimples all over his skin, and he flinched instinctively.

And Mike saw him flinch.

Mike stood stock-still. He looked at James in astonishment. Their eyes couldn't avoid each other's, and there wasn't time for the eyes to hide their messages.

'You know!' breathed Mike in startled amazement.

'I do now,' said James in a low voice, trying not to sound grim.

Just five words, and nothing would ever be the same between them again. Mike came towards him, and it was all James could do to avoid flinching again. But Mike walked straight past him, out to the garden. James leant against the wall of the corridor, momentarily too weak to stand unaided. For a moment he thought he would pass out, then he knew that he wouldn't. His heart was slowing down. He became capable of movement again.

He went out into the garden, searching for Mike, though not knowing what he intended to say if he found him.

But Mike was nowhere to be seen.

It took him a while to pull himself together. It took a while before he felt capable of plunging back among his guests. He walked tentatively, almost shyly, into his own living room.

Surely nothing more would tear him apart today?

A woman whom he didn't know immediately detached herself from a group of Harcourts and buttonholed him.

'I'm Dorothy Harcourt,' she said.

'Ah,' he said meaninglessly. He didn't think that he had ever heard of her.

'I'm one of the Gloucestershire Harcourts.'

'Well, how do you do? How are things in Gloucestershire?'

Careful, James. But there was something about this woman, something to make you want to be sarcastic, something to make the flesh crawl.

'I have something to tell you. I wondered whether I should tell you or not.'

'Obviously you decided that you would.'

Her skin was the colour of Wensleydale cheese, her hair clung limply to her scalp as if frightened of sliding off, but in her eyes there was glittering, ferocious life. James felt instinctively alarmed by her inner fires.

'I decided that I must tell you for your own good.'

309

'Why does that alarm me so much?'

'I have a slight psychic gift, I put it no higher than that. I don't wish to have it, it can be disturbing. I sense, James, that you are a troubled soul. I smell guilt.'

'I really don't know where this is leading.'

She smiled smugly. It was a smile to curdle milk. This was a very sad soul, and, unlike most sad souls, there was something about the woman that repelled all sympathy.

'I know men. Perhaps I should rephrase that. I know of men. I sense – correct me if I'm wrong – that you have been . . . disloyal? . . . unfaithful? . . . in some way. I sensed it in your eulogy . . . your very moving eulogy. I sensed that you were about to admit to something, and couldn't.'

'Perhaps you could speed this up a bit, tell me where it's leading. There are lots of people here that I wish to speak to.'

'Of course. I am just explaining why I think what I have to tell you may make you feel better. Your wife was not the saint that she is usually painted.'

James tried to look unconcerned. He didn't want to give this woman the satisfaction of knowing how much she was disturbing him. But he could feel the blood, which had only recently returned to his face after the shock of his confrontation with Mike, draining away again, and a spasm of hideous pleasure crossed the woman's face as she saw this.

'Oh?'

'I was lunching with a friend . . .' James saw in her eyes a hint of the wild hatred that was consuming her. '. . . Well I *thought* she was a friend . . . in a hotel near Diss last Wednesday. The day that Deborah died.'

'Go on.'

'Your brother was lunching there too.'

Suspicion hardened instantly into certainty.

'He was clearly waiting for somebody.'

'How can you possibly know that?'

'He kept looking towards the door. It wasn't at all an interesting door.'

As Dorothy talked on, James couldn't avoid casting a quick glance round the room. He saw Philip, looking at him rather anxiously, and tried to give him a reassuring smile. Beyond Philip he saw Charles. The great man was leaning on the piano, as if to remind people who he was. He was holding court, in his usual genial way. He always claimed to be embarrassed by the attentions of his fans, but in that moment James realised that he loved them, that he thirsted for them and drank them. This vicious, nosey, wretched, lonely, twisted woman was telling him how she had 'happened' to look into the hotel's visitors' book, how somebody called Mr J. Rivers had booked in and given an absurd address that was clearly false. 'I'm certain it was him. There wasn't anyone else it could have been.'

James disliked this woman so much that he could hardly get the words 'thank you' out, and indeed he didn't know whether he was grateful or not. He moved off, making his way past Roger Dodds and the Hammonds – no sign of Mike – and past a little bunch from the Kilmarnock factory. He could see that they wanted to speak to him, he didn't want to offend them, God, social responsibilities were wearing. 'See you in a minute,' he said as he went past them.

Philip was approaching him. He didn't want to speak to Philip just now.

'She's told you, hasn't she?' said Philip.

'What?'

'That woman. That dreadful woman. She's told you.'

James was astounded.

'You know about it?' he said.

'What do you mean?' Philip looked puzzled for just a moment, then ploughed on. 'I'm sorry, James. Sorry that you've had to find out. I don't see why you ever had to know, not now that she's dead.'

James had been so certain about Charles that realisation was dawning only very slowly.

He stared wildly at Philip.

'You! It was you?'

'Well, what did you think? Didn't she tell you?'

'She only said, "your brother".'

'Charles? You thought it was Charles? Oh, James. Is there somewhere we can talk?'

'Our bedroom. My bedroom.' He gave a twisted smile. 'Deborah's bedroom.'

In the bedroom, James stood looking out over the apparent normality of Islington. He felt shredded.

Philip came in very slowly.

'So you thought she was talking about Charles?' he said, shaking his head as if he still didn't quite believe it.

'I'd begun to think he was in love with Deborah.'

'Oh, I think he was, but I think he could only express it in music. I don't think Charles is a very sexual person.'

'Really?'

'Well, I hate to say this, I'm very fond of them both, but Valerie doesn't look like a satisfied woman. Music is a life substitute for Charles, which is why despite his great success he isn't really happy.'

'Charles isn't happy?'

'I don't think so.'

'I feel as though I understand nothing. I feel as though I'm swimming in fog. So it was you!'

'You still sound surprised. Even at this very serious moment in our relationship I feel slightly piqued that you don't think of me as sexy. I do have four children, James. Four more than Charles, as it . . . no, don't go there.'

They were circling round each other, waiting for the moment to pounce.

James pounced first.

'How could you, Philip? How could *you*? *You*. Of all people.'

'Oh, God, James. I'm sorry.'

'It's a bit late for that.'

'Well, I'm not honestly sure I am, anyway. I mean, I can't honestly say I wish it hadn't happened. I was in love with her, James.'

'Did you go to bed with her?'

'No.'

'But would you have done . . . that day?'

'Who knows? I certainly don't.'

'Well, how long had this been going on? Come on. Tell me.'

'Not long. We had a couple of meals when you . . . you know . . . were away with . . . her.'

James felt the floor shift beneath his feet. So it really did happen.

'You knew about Helen?'

'Is that her name? Yes. We knew there was someone.'

'Deborah knew?'

It was a scream of astonishment and pain. James's legs began to give way. He tottered onto the bed where he had slept with Deborah for more than twenty years.

'She didn't know when, where, how, but a woman knows a thing like that, James.'

'Oh, God. Why did she . . .? Why didn't she . . .?'

'Who knows? Who knows, James? I didn't know her that well.' It was Philip's turn to give a cry of regret, muted, but still passionate. 'And now I never will.'

His long, stern, statistician's face crumpled into

313

inconsolable grief. He sat on the other end of James's marital bed, and wept.

'Oh, for God's sake, Philip. She was my wife, not yours,' snapped James.

He strode out of the room, slamming the door.

He leant against the banisters at the top of the stairs. He thought of all the people milling around downstairs, the hum of their conversation growing with each drink and each passing moment, as they appeared to turn their backs on their sadness.

He'd made three enormous discoveries in a matter of minutes. He'd learnt for certain that Mike *had* murdered Ed. He'd discovered that his beloved brother Philip had been intending to cuckold him. He'd found out that Deborah had known about Helen. That was the one that shook him to the core. That was the one that meant that every moment in his life with Deborah in recent times had not been as he had thought it was. How could he walk down the stairs and join the throng? How could the stairs remain solid and not crumple?

He squared his shoulders, drew himself up to his full height, and went downstairs to perform the duties of a man at his wife's wake.

James could see his mum looking in his direction; he really didn't want to ignore her, but he couldn't walk past Fliss without stopping.

Fliss just stood there, waiting for him to come to her, clocking every delay, making a list in her mental Filofax of everyone he had spoken to before he spoke to her.

He kissed her on both cheeks. She barely responded, but gave a half-smile.

'Brilliantly read,' he said. 'Very moving. Honestly, Fliss, really well done.'

She thawed visibly. Really it wasn't so difficult, and in

the ease with which he could thaw her he realised how insecure she was, and he felt the return of that affectionate love he had experienced in the chapel.

'I didn't want to do anything too obvious,' she said.

'Quite right. Deborah would have loved it.'

'Oh, thank you. I do hope so.'

'I'm sure so.'

He wasn't sure really, he had no idea what Deborah would have thought, but did it matter?

'You didn't think my hair let the side down?'

'Your hair? It's fine.'

'I don't like it.'

'It's great.'

He found himself wondering if Fliss also knew of his adultery. He could hardly bear the thought that she might. A great surge of contrition and regret swept through him. Well, James, he told himself, you shouldn't have started down that road if you couldn't accept the consequences. A ridiculous phrase crossed his mind. If you can't stand the cold, don't sit in the fridge.

Fliss gave him a quick little kiss, which astounded him. So it didn't look as if she knew. He had a sudden vision of people as packages: the skin was the paper, the contents were a secret until opened, but even then, the thoughts were unreachable. No pathologist could open a man up and say, 'He's secretly envious of his father.'

James shook his head to rid himself of these thoughts, which were not helpful to conversation. He really must stop thinking about pathologists. He smiled at Fliss and felt an astonishing warmth towards her. He realised now just how insecure she had felt in Deborah's presence. Pretty, but not as pretty. Liked, but not as liked. Stylish, but not as stylish. He hugged her impulsively, saw the surprise and even slight alarm in her eyes.

315

'We must all keep in touch,' he said. 'We must keep Deborah's memory alive together.'

'We'd love that,' she said.

'Good.'

A moment of peace, into which Stanley limped like a rusting dredger.

'Oh, Lord,' said James. 'Here comes Stanley, who's also going mad, but without the excuse of strain.'

Stanley raised his glass of red wine and said, 'Groans.'

'Groans?'

'It's my new greeting to friends on sad occasions. The opposite of "cheers".'

'Oh, very good, Stanley.' James raised his glass, which contained only water. 'Groans.'

'Groans,' echoed Fliss, and gave a slight giggle, happy to be in on a joke, however slight, that she understood.

Stanley turned to her, and asked her, 'Fliss, are you at all interested in your roots?'

'I have to be nowadays,' she said. 'I have them coloured every eight weeks.'

His mum had watched his efforts to get to her with quiet amusement inappropriate to the occasion. Not that she wasn't sad. Like everyone else, she had liked, even loved Deborah. But her fondness was tinged with a little secret difficulty. In her heart she had been just a little jealous of Deborah and just a little envious of James. There had been happiness in *their* marriage.

Inevitably, her mind today had wandered back to her husband's funeral, to the quiet relief that she had felt during the service and the wake, in her release from his infuriating blend of solicitous physical attentiveness and cold mental cruelty, and the sudden sense of anticlimax that she had felt that evening, when the guests had gone and only her three sons remained, and she had begun to understand, if dimly yet, that she had also been released from her role, the protection of her boys from their monstrous father.

Freed from their father, they had been released to fly out into the world, all at once, as if they were three red kites in a breeding programme. They hadn't been cruel, they had done their best, but, almost overnight, everything had changed. They had no longer needed her. Now she had needed them. She had never really recovered from the shock, never again been quite the woman she had been before. She knew it, and hated it, and couldn't change it.

Today she saw it all, in James. She saw that he was frightened not to rush towards her, but she also saw that he was reluctant to face her. She saw that she had begun to drift, over the years, into the sort of mother that sons dreaded visiting. She also saw that, with James now alone, with Philip still alone, with Charles not as happy as everyone thought he was, she still had opportunities to play a role. Whether she was still able to play it she wasn't sure, but today, while she definitely had a role – the widower's mother – she would begin the attempt. And the role was, in truth, very simple. It was to become a nice old woman, to age gracefully. If she could pull it off . . .

But there was an added little potential for drama in the role today. Every time she saw James looking towards her, she put on her disapproving face. How astonished her sons would have been if they had ever discovered that she practised this look in the mirror in her bathroom. Now, as she watched him leave Fliss, hug her (amazing), and slowly traverse the last few feet across the carpet, giving the impression that it was a really difficult ascent that he was making up the North Col of his own living room, she set her face into rock, into hurt granite, and waited for him to arrive.

'My poor darling boy,' she said. 'What pressure they all put you under, my love.'

Oh, but how she enjoyed the look in his eyes, the astonishment that he couldn't quite hide.

James was two people now, a schizophrenic. If he'd been a flat, he'd have been a duplex. On the upper floor, a widower, a host at a wake, a grieving husband. On the lower floor, a confused man, a shocked man, a man on the rack.

The wake began to break up. He said goodbye to the Bridgend gang. Thank you for coming, boys. *Charlotte had seen, seen, seen him with Helen in Porthcawl.* See you in a couple of weeks, boys.

And he said goodbye to the Kilmarnock contingent. *Helen had been to Kilmarnock. Deborah had stayed there, though not in the same hotel. But she had known, known, known.* Goodbye, lads. Thank you for coming. Challenges ahead, but we'll meet them.

Tom and Jen Preston. Sorry you missed Wimbledon. Really, it's of no account. *Charlotte looked so ill, ill, ill. Smiled, though, at least once.* It's been a great send-off. We'd have hated to miss it.

Marcia wanted to kiss him on the mouth, but he managed to avoid this. *How many times had Philip kissed Deborah on the mouth?* Good luck with Willy the Wombat. Thanks. Don't forget what I said. I'll always be there. I won't forget, Marcia. But he would.

The Glebeland girls, leaving, as they came, in a gaggle. *Had Deborah told them that she knew he was having an affair? Had Deborah, among the girlie laughs, been sad, sad, sad?* He hadn't spoken much to them, because, in truth, he was a little abashed by their gagglehood. Thank you so much for coming, girls. We couldn't not. Deborah was one in a million. Oh, how very true. Grace Farsley not leaving with you? No, she said she'd stay on a bit. Interesting.

The six members of his newly formed committee at Globpack. *Deborah had met them all, and all the time she had known, known, known.* Challenges ahead but we won't mention them today. No, quite.

Sandra Horsfall from the Dorking days. *He'd once walked with Mike on Box Hill, near Dorking. He'd gone on a ramble with a killer!* Sorry I didn't get to talk to you, Sandra. Me too, James. Kiss kiss.

Callum, son of his old school friend, and Erica, whose tattoos he still regretted. *I'll have to get used to tattoos, if Charlotte and Chuck come to live with me. Oh, I hope, hope, hope they do.* We must meet, go to exhibitions, show you modern artists that we like. I'd love that. I really would.

Roger Dodds, the Hammonds and the Meikles. Have you seen Mike? *What's he going to do now that he knows that I know? Shut me up? Kill me? Knife me?* No, he seems to have just disappeared off the scene. Odd. *Disturbing.*

Fliss and Dominic. You've seen her off most beautifully, James. *Oh, Fliss, did you have to put it like that.* You must come over to dinner. *What would you think of Chuck?* I'm going to have to learn to cook. You can be my guinea pigs. I hope we won't have to eat them. *That's the nearest you've come to a joke in all the years I've met you, you boring bugger.* Oh, very amusing, Dominic.

Gordon and Stephanie Tollington. We must get together and have a really fabulous meal. *I couldn't care less if I never eat in another fine restaurant in my life. Been there, done that. I have something worthwhile to do now. Save, save, save my Charlotte. Some lies are so unimportant that they aren't worth avoiding.* That would be lovely.

Grace Farsley.

'I hope I haven't outstayed my welcome,' she said, colouring ever so slightly. James found the blush quite unexpectedly charming and exciting.

'Not at all,' he said, and he couldn't help smiling, though there was nothing in particular at which to smile.

'I've had such an interesting time. I've heard so much about Deborah, I feel it's almost as if I've filled in the missing years.'

'That must have been rather moving.'

She'd be good with Charlotte.

'Very. I've just had a chat with your uncle Stanley. He asked me how long ago my family left Hungary.'

'I didn't know you had Hungarian connections.'

'Well, no, nor did I. Do you think he knows what he's talking about?'

'I've no idea.'

'He *is* rather drunk.'

'Oh, Lord, is he? That's all I need.'

'I told him I had almost no idea about my family tree, and he said, "Don't you want to know who you are? Why are people so lacking in curiosity? Why are they so disappointing? Why are they so stupid?"'

'Oh, good Lord. Oh, I'm sorry.'

'I didn't mind.'

She smiled. She had good teeth.

'Well, I must be off,' she said.

She gave him a quick, warm kiss on one cheek.

'It's not going to be easy for you,' she said. 'You'll be in my thoughts.'

He watched her walk down the short path to the street. He was far enough away from her to notice for the first time that she had good legs. He watched her until she was out of sight.

The caterers had put some food aside, in the big fridge-freezer, for the family to eat after everyone else had left. Suddenly James found himself incapable of doing anything more.

The day's events had exhausted him utterly. He sank into a kitchen chair. He wasn't even able to be James the Provider.

Philip the Capable took over, got the food out, arranged it on the kitchen table, opened bottles of good Côtes-du-Rhône, under James's instructions. He poured a glass for James. James looked him in the eye, and felt for a moment too tired to be angry or resentful. He had a lot of thinking to do. He wasn't ready for it yet. And Philip, he could see, was taking care to be entirely unemotional. Whatever was going to happen between them, there was no hint of it now.

James raised his glass.

'First of the day.'

'Really?'

'Might not have stopped if I'd started. Didn't want to be drunk at my wife's wake. Wouldn't have been seemly.'

That word again.

After a glass of wine, after ten minutes, sitting in the chair like a zombie, James felt slightly better. Philip offered to put food on his plate for him, but he roused himself to stand and suddenly realised that he was starving. He hadn't got round to eating anything, not so much as a canapé.

He piled the food onto his plate – ham, tongue, pâté, prawns in mayonnaise, sweet herring, hard-boiled egg, tomato, sun-dried tomato, an artichoke heart, a spicy pepper, lettuce, chicory . . . he stopped, this was getting ridiculous. But oh, he was hungry.

They sat round the circular mahogany table in the cool, north-facing dining room. James, Philip, Charles, Valerie, Max, Stanley and Mum. On the sideboard stood several elegant decanters that Deborah had rescued from their lonely, unloved, sideboard-starved existence in antique shops from Cornwall to Northumberland.

Nobody spoke. Everyone was too drained to accept the responsibility of making the first remark. Everyone except

Stanley tried to eat with a degree of delicacy. They were ashamed of how hungry their grief and emotion had made them.

Then Stanley bowed his head towards his plate, his fork poised to spear a prawn. The fork slipped out of his hand, his head slipped onwards and sank onto his plate, splattering mayonnaise onto the smooth tabletop. He gave a single, vast, shuddering snore.

'I think we're going to have to get him to bed,' said James.

'He'll be heavy,' warned Philip.

'We've four strong men,' said James.

'Um . . .' said Charles.

As ums go, it was a rather powerful one, and they all looked at him. It was impossible to see whether he was blushing, under all that hair.

'I'm afraid under my contracts, in this age of Health and Safety, I have guaranteed not to indulge in any physical activity that might be risky. I've a big tour coming up. I just can't risk it.'

'We can manage,' said Max.

It was almost a shock to hear him speak. James realised that he hadn't spoken to him or even been conscious of seeing him since he had asked him to take responsibility for the wake just after the service. In a way this was a compliment. Max could be trusted. He didn't need to check up on how he was doing.

'I can take his head. I'm pretty used to weights in logging. And Dad and Philip can take one leg each. We won't need you, Uncle Charles.'

Valerie tried, not entirely successfully, to hide a tiny smile, a smile that said, you, the mighty Charles, the centre of all attention, will not have enjoyed it being pointed out by your nephew that you are surplus to requirements.

Max went to the back of Stanley's chair and put his hands

round the old man's bent shoulders. James and Philip slid their hands under his mighty buttocks. The three of them lifted the elderly, forgotten author of *The Physiognomy of Tribes*. Stanley rose from his chair like an old car pulled from a river. James took hold of his left leg while Philip maintained a hold on his buttocks. Then Philip let go and moved his arms hurriedly to Stanley's right leg. His inert body lurched for a moment, then they steadied him. He gave a low moan, stirred, but did not wake.

'May I suggest you don't take him up two flights?' said Charles. 'We can go home tonight. It would be more sensible. I've been thinking of suggesting that, anyway. I've lots to do at home, and then there's the next ridiculous tour planned by another maniac. Put him in our room. The bed's perfectly clean.'

Valerie blushed slightly as if this was an admission of sexual inactivity.

'I hardly think he'll worry about that,' she said.

They began to carry Stanley to the door.

'Just a moment,' said Mum.

She hurried over with her napkin and gently wiped the mayonnaise off Stanley's face. He stirred, grunted and gave a single immense cough. Bits of hard-boiled egg sprayed from his mouth. Mum reeled from his alcoholic breath, but she stayed to finish her task.

'There,' she said. 'A bit of dignity for the poor old boy.'

The three men carried the sleeping anthropologist very slowly up the first flight of narrow stairs, Max walking backwards at his head, James and Philip at his feet, a brother who had just discovered that he had been about to be cuckolded side by side and sharing a task with the brother who had been about to do the cuckolding, their bodies touching in the narrow space, their minds knowing that nothing in their changed relationship had yet been resolved.

The three men carried Stanley across the landing. Mum hurried into the main guest bedroom, and pulled back the sheets. The three men laid Stanley gently on the bed, loosened his tie and took off his shoes. Mum pulled the sheet up and tucked him in tenderly. He gave another huge single snore.

They tiptoed out of the room, leaving him to dream of Celts and cataclysms.

They returned to their food. James tried to eat, but his appetite had gone. He put his knife and fork down, although he still had plenty of food left, and spoke in a low, but, he hoped, not too earnest tone.

'I discovered something momentous in the chapel today,' he said. 'I discovered that I didn't believe in God. Belief in God has never been something I've thought about. I think I've been unbelievably lazy intellectually. I've drifted along, a non-churchgoer rather than a non-believer. Suddenly today I thought, I wouldn't dream of belittling other people's faith, but it doesn't make sense to me. I don't believe I shall ever see Deborah again in some strange unbodily form. We had an adventure. We had a story. And stories and adventures end.'

He glanced at Philip, whose face was a mask. He didn't know if he should be saying these things to him, but he had to. He couldn't carry the burden of his surprise on his own.

'I found I couldn't join in with the responses.'

'I noticed that,' said Max.

'I know. I noticed that you noticed. I felt so very close to you, Max.'

Max blushed with a pleasure that he tried unavailingly to hide.

James felt the need to continue. 'If there is no God, if we are not serving some purpose in life outside ourselves, the meaning of our life is the sum total of all our actions, and it's therefore even more important, not less important, that our actions should be good, as mine, I'm sorry to say, so often haven't been. Chaos without God? I don't think so. I daresay I'm not making much sense to you, but really all I need to do is make sense to myself.'

He took up his knife and fork, cut off a small piece of tongue, and began to eat it.

'I'm telling you this, because I need to, but I honestly think I'm too tired to debate it,' he said. 'Oh, Mum, you've got your don't-talk-with-your-mouth-full face on.'

'I can't help it,' said his mum. 'I hate the sight of wet food revolving in a mouth like clothes in a washing machine.'

'Sorry.'

He realised that this was the first 'sorry' he had uttered for quite some time. He tried to rally, take up his theme again, but it was difficult to get back to the meaning of life after a comment about wet food in mouths. Good old Mum. He felt very tired now. He looked across at Philip and felt that he too looked tired, and very strained. They must talk.

He saw Mum making when-are-you-going-to-take-me-home signs to Philip.

Philip saw them too and said, 'I think Mum wants to be taken home.'

'I'm not thinking about me,' protested Mum. 'I was thinking of you. You've got to go all the way to Leighton Buzzard.'

'We must be getting back too,' said Charles, who had been very subdued since his refusal to help putting Stanley to bed.

'Well, before you go, Philip,' said James, 'there's that little bit of business to discuss.'

Philip looked at him questioningly, then the penny dropped.

'Oh, yes,' he said. 'May as well get it over. Won't be long, Mum.'

'Don't worry about me,' said Mum defensively.

James led Philip upstairs to his little office at the back of the first floor, next to the house bathroom. He only worked at home when it was unavoidable, and the small, cluttered room had no sense of importance. There were papers on the chairs, papers on the floor, papers everywhere. Two crumpled handkerchiefs stood on top of a pile of invoices. As he cleared papers off the two adjustable swivel chairs, James could hear his father saying, of his bedroom, 'An untidy room reflects an untidy mind, boy,' and slapping him hard across the cheek. His father, even in his worst tempers, had never hit him hard enough to cause injuries. The tempers, it struck him now, had never been uncontrolled. They had been fuelled by cold, calculated cruelty. Mum had never had an inkling that their father ever hit them. And here they were now, the two younger sons of this vicious man, in this bleak, untidy room, here not to discuss, as they hoped those down-stairs thought, some abstruse financial fallout from Deborah's death, but a question of passion, their shared love of a wonderful woman.

'I feel as if I've been summoned to the headmaster's study,' said Philip.

'A very untidy, unmethodical headmaster,' said James. 'I . . . I need to speak to you about Deborah, Philip.'

Philip looked back at him impassively.

'Your face gives away so little, Philip. No wonder I got you wrong.'

'I'm a very private person.'

'I've been utterly shocked by what you told me today.'

'I can understand that. I suppose what I did was shocking.'

'I didn't say I was shocked by what you did. I said I was shocked by what you told me. I was shocked to think that

326

I'd made Deborah so unhappy that she could contemplate such a course of action.'

'Don't punish yourself too much, James. I think Deborah still . . . I think you and she still led a life that she found . . . well . . . oh, God, words, they're so much harder for me than numbers . . . that she found . . . I have to get the word right . . . bearable.'

'Oh, my God. "Do you take this woman and promise her a not intolerable life in sickness and in health?" "Bearable."!'

'Well, I'm sorry, but obviously she wasn't overjoyed at developments.'

'No.'

James noticed an unopened envelope on his desk. He took a paper knife from the box that held his pens, and ripped it open savagely. The little burst of savagery allowed some of his anger to escape.

'You're angry with me,' said Philip. 'I'm not surprised.'

'I'm not angry with you, you idiot,' said James angrily. 'I'm angry with myself.'

He pulled the contents out of the envelope as if removing the entrails from a rabbit he was skinning.

The envelope contained an invitation to a capital gains seminar in a hotel outside Pontefract four months ago.

The displacement activity had achieved its purpose. James was calm again.

'I've been thinking about this all evening,' he said. 'I've been talking and listening and all the time it's been there in my mind – you, Deborah, me. What I want to tell you, Philip . . .', he said very quietly, '. . . and I didn't intend to say it today, because I wanted to be absolutely sure that it's what I really think before I told you, but I do know, I've thought enough about it this evening, it's absolutely what I think. I'm so thankful it was you.'

'What?'

'I don't think either of us know what would have happened about all this if Deborah had lived, but it's a huge consolation to me that at the moment of her death she was happy, she was looking forward to the future, she was . . . oh, hell, why is this embarrassing, why am I so English, can't Stanley find any foreign blood in me to loosen up my emotions? . . . I'm pleased she was dreaming of a life with a good man.'

'Good God, James.'

'I know. But I mean it. Really.'

'Well . . . thank you . . . I'm . . . I'm really touched, James.'

'And not a hint of it on that mask men call your face. And there's Charles, awash with emotion most of the time, and how much of it is real?'

'Oh, some of it, I think.'

James stood up. So did Philip. They approached each other awkwardly, hugged briefly and rather stiffly.

'I think I'd have come to my senses and fought you for her, and who knows who'd have won, and it might have got nasty,' said James, 'but I really do mean it, my old bruv. I'm so very glad that, last Wednesday, it was you.'

And so, as the sun set over Islington, as the day approached its dying fall, James kissed his mum and told her that he and Max would take her out to a restaurant for Sunday lunch.

'Restaurants!' she said. 'Ten per cent service, and half of them don't speak a word of English. What sort of service is that, I ask you?'

James and Philip shared a brotherly smile. Good old Mum. She had been so sweet today, but it wouldn't have been right for her visit to end with a polite 'thank you'.

The two men were careful not to share more than a

328

brotherly smile. They were both acutely aware of Charles, wondering what they had been discussing upstairs and not quite liking to mention it this evening. They knew that, if they gave him a chance, he would ask them. They were aware that this was a new situation in their brotherly relations. James and Philip together, Charles excluded. Something had shifted – for ever.

Charles and Valerie drifted out to their car behind Philip and Mum.

Charles and James kissed and hugged, and Charles said, 'You're going to miss her so much, James. She was a wonderful, wonderful woman,' and James felt guilty at having believed for a moment that it had been Charles she had been driving towards with her red shoes at the ready. It was all words with Charles, perhaps because, in his professional, artistic life, words were so much less important than sounds. 'She was beautiful, she was kind, she was an angel.'

'Yes, come along, Charles,' said Valerie.

As he closed the door behind them, James realised a surprising thing. He didn't wish he was Charles any more.

He sat at the dining-room table, with Max, amid the wreckage of the impromptu family meal. The light was fading. A tiny corner of the wall was catching the sun as it set in the north-west. The sliver of light just caught the edge of the sideboard and one side of the decanter nearest the window. The decanter glinted and sparked with ever-changing reds and crimsons, while the rest of the room grew slowly darker.

'Drop more?'

'Just a drop.'

James knew that Max longed for sleep, and was only accepting more wine out of politeness. They sat there without speaking for several minutes, and this really was a companionable silence.

But as the silence stretched, James began to feel the urge to break it, and to break it with something meaningful, something emotional, something definitive, something that would summarise the state of play between them. But it was too late, he was too tired, Max was much too tired.

'I thought we might take Gran out for Sunday lunch,' he said.

'Sounds good to me,' said Max. 'The old Sunday roast.'

Max yawned loudly.

'Go to bed,' said James. 'Don't worry about me. I'm going out into the garden with my thoughts.'

'If you're sure.'

Max stood up, stretched like a dog, hugged James very briefly, and set off. As he opened the door, they could hear Stanley snoring prodigiously.

James, who almost never drank whisky, poured himself the equivalent of a pub triple measure of Lagavulin, added the same of water, and went out into the garden.

The last faint light was lingering in the western and northern skies. He sat on the cast-iron bench, beside the alabaster statue of Apollo that Deborah had been unable to resist in Chipping Camden. The far end of the garden was now almost entirely dark. When he had first gone outside, the security lights had come on every time he moved, and this had irritated him. He had gone back inside to switch them off. He didn't need security lights. There wasn't much risk of his being attacked in his own garden, in semi-serene Islington.

The funeral service, the wake, they spelt, in the modern word, closure. James knew that he had not yet quite achieved closure himself. He felt the need, alone there in his own back garden, to speak to his dead wife, perhaps for the last time. He didn't welcome this need. His recent past was a murky place, not pleasant to visit.

He fought against the need. He forced himself to think about the future, and felt again an unexpected sense of optimism, of hope, of – yes, and he couldn't believe that he could feel this today – of excitement.

What was his future? He would stay at Globpack until he had finished the task that he had been set. When that was over, whether successful or not, he would either leave Globpack or take a sabbatical and visit Max in Canada for a long stay. No, he couldn't do that if Charlotte came to live with him. Charlotte, Charlotte, Charlotte. He would do his utmost to save her life, whether or not she came, whether or not she stayed with Chuck. He would try to find, for Philip, the good woman that he deserved. Helen? That would be neat. No, no, she wasn't his type at all.

Helen. Regrets? Of course. He would miss her. But no, not the ultimate regret. He had done the right thing.

And Grace Farsley, why did he think of her? She was just an old friend of Deborah's to whom he had spoken twice, among many others. He had liked her. It was now that the strange adjective came to him. Every feature was pleasant. Her personality had seemed attractive, her mind had seemed clear, she had appeared to have humour, he felt that there was warmth and kindness in her soul. There was nothing extraordinary about any one aspect of her, but she was . . . well, there was that extraordinary word . . . complete.

Would his less than passionate memory of her fade in the coming days? Were his two conversations with her any more than the first indication that one day perhaps he would emerge from the shadows of recent events and be able to begin a relationship with another woman? He might never see her again. He knew that. He might meet her again, fall in love, and marry her. It wasn't important, not tonight, not yet.

331

Should he be thinking these things on the night of Deborah's funeral? Well, they were not that unseemly. They really were very gentle speculations. Too gentle to keep him away from his dear departed Deborah.

He found that he was on his feet, without having given his legs any instructions to rise. He found that he was walking right to the back of the garden, under the trees, where the earth almost never dried out, but it was dry now.

He stood on the dry earth, among the nettles and the foxgloves, and called out to his dead wife.

'Oh, Deborah, Deborah, my darling. I'm—'

He heard a cough. His blood ran cold. There was somebody else in the garden with him. He heard footsteps, rustling the dry plants. He heard a foot strike a stone.

'Sorry. I had to interrupt.'

He froze. Mike. It was Mike. Come to kill him, because he knew. Come to plunge a knife into his stomach, because killers always used the same method again, didn't they?

He could just see Mike reach into a pocket . . . and bring out . . . what? A gun? A knife? A shaft of moonlight reflected off something gold. James waited for the shot, or the plunge of the blade, wondered how much it would hurt, felt the involuntary clenching of his stomach, the fierce beating of his heart. But he knew, in that moment, and knew with blinding clarity that what he was frightened of wasn't death, but the anticipated pain, the moment when the instrument of death broke his skin, ripped through his veins, plunged into his heart. He wasn't at all frightened of ceasing to exist. He just felt sad.

They say that as you drown your whole life passes before you. As James waited to be killed it was his future that surged through his mind. He wouldn't be able to give Charlotte a home. Other men perhaps less committed would have to try to save Bridgend and Kilmarnock. He would never have the joy of witnessing Stanley's hangover tomorrow. Grace Farsley would never receive a reply to her letter, if indeed she wrote one. He would never open his front door and see, for the first time, the girl whom Max was going to marry.

This must be the worst thing about death. You miss the end of so many stories.

But no gunshot came. No knife was thrust into his midriff.

'I've brought your pen back.'

The words made no sense whatsoever to James.

'What?'

'You left it. I meant to bring it. I forgot. I went back for it. Sorry.'

The words were on a different scale. They were incomprehensibly trivial.

'Pen?'

'Your Mont Blanc. Your posh pen. You signed your autograph with it in my book. You forgot it. You were pissed.'

'Oh, God. Well, thank you for giving me the scare of my life.'

'I didn't mean to scare you.'

'Oh, no.' James began to raise his voice. 'You come up on me in the dark in my back garden. You flash what I think is a knife at me, and you say you don't mean to scare me shitless. Have you forgotten that I know you're a killer?'

'I am not a killer, James. I am not a fucking killer.'

A blackbird shouted its alarm at their raised voices and flew off.

'Well, what the fuck are you, then?' shouted James.

'I'm . . .' Suddenly Mike lowered his voice, became almost calm. 'I'm a man who killed.'

'It's a fine distinction.'

'Not to me, it isn't. I have to live with it. It is not at all a fine distinction.' Mike's voice rose steadily to a shriek. 'I cannot believe that you thought that I was going to kill you. Fucking hell, James. I'm your friend. Oh, you thought, "He's killed once, he's through the barrier, the second time will be easier, the third time easier still, nobody in London will be safe from the maniac."'

'Don't you bloody well shout at me, Mike. This is my garden. You're in my sodding garden. I was scared, very scared, and I don't give a toss about your fine fucking distinction, you've killed a man. You came up to me in the dark, silently . . .'

'I heard you in the garden, and as I walked up I realised you were going to talk to Deborah. I didn't want to overhear anything so personal. I coughed to stop you. Fucking hell, James, I must be the most sensitive and considerate serial killer of all time.'

It was as if all James's anger just drained away into the earth.

'Oh, I'm sorry,' he said. 'I'm sorry.'

What had happened to his hopes of a new dawn in which he never needed to say 'sorry'?

'Can we sit down?' asked Mike.

'Of course.'

'Can we talk about this quietly, calmly, without raised voices?'

'Absolutely.'

They sat on the cast-iron garden bench. It was already wet with dew, but neither of them noticed.

Mike told him how he had been deeply shocked to realise that James knew that he had killed Ed. He'd gone off, and gone for a drink at the pub at the end of the road. He'd decided to come back to talk to James, late in the evening, when everyone else might have gone or be in bed. He needed to know whether James intended to go to the police. Then, realising that if he stayed in the pub all evening he'd get hopelessly drunk, he'd decided to go home and get the pen.

334

'Well, thanks for that.'

'It's ridiculous, but I thought if I did something nice like bringing your pen back, it might influence you.'

'"I couldn't tell you he'd killed a man, officer. He'd just made me a very nice sandwich."'

James began to shake. He felt extremely cold, even on this warm, humid evening. He knew that this was the after effect of shock. He clenched his whole body in an effort to hide the shaking, but Mike could feel it.

'You're shaking. Oh, God, I really did scare you.'

'It's all right.'

And it was. And the funny thing was, beneath the huge relief there was just a tiny little voice of regret, a sense – ridiculous but real – that he had been cheated of his part in a great drama.

They both fell silent then. It seemed as if the conversation was over, but they both knew that only now was it reaching its most important point.

'So . . . um . . . I have to ask you this, James. What do you intend to do?'

'Oh, God, Mike. I don't know. I . . . can you tell me anything about why you killed Ed?'

'Yes. He laughed at me.'

'What?'

'I went to Roger's party. He was there. He seemed . . . contrite. I invited him back for a drink. A peace offering. We got rather drunk. I saw he wasn't contrite at all. He was pleased he'd ruined my life. He laughed at me, James. I lost my temper and stabbed him.'

James didn't know what to say, so he said nothing.

'I was drunk, of course. We both were. I was horrified I'd done it. I decided to conceal it. I didn't want him ruining my life twice.'

'I don't blame you.'

'Do you mean that?'

'I don't know. It was just a remark. Just what one says. Oh God. Oh God, Mike. I have to say . . . I really do have to say . . . I'm not saying anything really, but . . . I don't see what good it would do anybody if I reported you now. If I say "he deserved" it, it sounds as if I'm adopting the rules of the Wild West.'

'Thanks.'

'Don't thank me. I haven't actually said I won't, you know.'

'There'd be no evidence. They'd find it very hard to convict.'

An urban fox knocked the lid off a dustbin not far away, slicing through the night's silence, and in the distance, a siren spoke faintly of some other crisis in someone else's life.

Mike and James were silent for quite a while.

'What actually happened?'James asked at last. 'How on earth did you get rid of the body?'

'You aren't trying to trick me, are you?'

'No.'

'No. Sorry. Oh well.'

James realised that Mike was also yearning for the cleansing power of confession.

'It was easy. A chap I know's gone abroad for two years. I'm looking after his car, starting it every week, running the engine for a few minutes to charge the battery. He's not the sort of person to check the mileage. I wrapped the body in an old sheet and then in cardboard. It might not have stood up to close inspection, but you'd have been proud of me. I lowered the back seats of the car, and just managed to lift one end of the body into the boot, and then I slid it in. I was sweating buckets, but nobody saw me. His car has been thoroughly cleaned, as has my flat. There were no witnesses at any stage. The sheet and the cardboard went into landfill, and the knife is in a different watery grave, nowhere near the Fens or Acton. And I wore gloves throughout. It's funny. I always thought that one day I'd find something I was good at, and I have. Murdering. Not a gift I can ever use again.'

There was another silence between them, a silence which Mike might have broken by asking James for a promise, an assurance, and in which James might have given such an assurance. But neither did, and when James spoke it was to make a very different point.

'Mike?'

'Yes.'

'Thank you.'

'What?'

'Yes, I was scared. Of what I thought was the knife. But not of dying. On the day Deborah was cremated, you've brought home to me that I'm not afraid of dying. Thank you.'

'Well . . . what can I say?'

'Nothing.'

It was true. There was nothing more to be said.

They walked slowly round to the front of the house, and there they shook hands, solemnly. Neither had the faintest idea if they would be able to continue to be friends.

Mike walked away, suddenly brisk.

Then James called out.

'Mike?'

Mike stopped.

'Thanks for bringing my pen back.'

James wandered very slowly back into the garden. It struck him as extraordinary that he didn't find it at all extraordinary that he should be contemplating something as extraordinary as not reporting a murderer who had confessed.

Had the moment for speaking to Deborah passed? Had

Mike's interruption proved fatal to his intentions? No. The need was irresistible.

He walked back to the same spot, as if that was the only point in the garden from which she would be able to hear.

'Oh, Deborah, Deborah, my darling,' he repeated. 'I'm certain you aren't there. I'm certain that there is now no life in you in any shape or form. I'm certain that you are not in heaven. I'm certain that, even though I'm looking up into the sky, there is no heaven. I'm certain that this is a futile gesture, but then you always said that I was rather good at futile gestures. I'm standing at the end of the garden, among the nettles, in that bit we kept wild for the birds and the butterflies. It's a lovely night, the weather has been wonderful since you died. I probably look mad, I probably am mad, but I just had to speak to you. I just had to let you know that it was you I loved all along. It was. It was. I just didn't know it, fool that I was, fool that I am. Oh, and Charlotte came to your funeral. I so wish you could know that. She's going to come and live with me. I think. No, I'm almost certain. Oh, darling, I would love your help in dealing with her. It won't be easy. Oh, Deborah, we will miss you. I don't know why you didn't let on that you knew about . . . her. There's no need for you to know her name now. Maybe you thought it would blow over. Maybe you were happy to keep just a part of me. Maybe, like the French, you understood that a man could need two women. I'll never know now, and it doesn't matter. Well, that's about it. I . . . I didn't ever want to have to say this again, and I'm saying it now for the last time, I hope. I'm so sorry. I'm so sorry, Deborah.'

Now the tears streamed. He wandered slowly back to the bench, looked for his whisky glass, couldn't find it. It didn't matter now. He didn't need props now. Those days were over.

He looked up into the – not the heavens . . . heavens, no – into the sky. He was alone, alone with only the whole solar system, the vast galaxies, the unimaginable distances, the inconceivable immensity of it, and here mankind was on one piddling little planet, and he was of no significance on this planet, he wasn't even important in so-called Great Britain, he was just a speck in the vast sprawling city of London, he didn't even stand out in Islington, he didn't stand out in his street in Islington, damn it, until last Wednesday he hadn't even been the best person living in his house.

And now he believed – he wasn't arrogant enough to say that he knew – that there was no life after death. His time on this earth would be, in cosmic terms, laughably short. He also believed, therefore, that he was not serving some overall purpose outside his own life. He realised that the excitement that had surprised him a few minutes ago was not something that would be recognised as exciting by a lot of people in this world of ours. It was an excitement that would involve no death, no blood, not a pathologist in sight. It was an excitement that involved only himself and the most important part of his body. And it was not – and oh goodness how it was not, and oh goodness how until now it might well have been and almost certainly had been – his penis. It was his brain. Perhaps people ignored their brains because they were invisible. Perhaps if every time a man had a thought his brain grew large and erect, men would respect their brains more.

He felt excited, challenged, by his belief that his life was not serving God's purpose. It meant either that life was without purpose or that we must find our own purpose in it. He felt, with a surge of optimism, that without belief in a received purpose in life, he had the strength to make his own life purposeful, that indeed those who did not believe in God were in a stronger position to make their lives meaningful and responsible, because there was no divine being onto whom they could thrust the responsibility.

He sat on his cast-iron bench in the lovely garden that Deborah had built. He looked up into the vast universe, and could see nothing, not a star, because in the glow of lights over London it's not easy to see the vastness of space. But he knew that it was all there, in its immensity, and that Deborah's lovingly created garden had no more significance than a pinhead. But you can store all the words of *War and Peace* on a pinhead, and he felt encouraged by his knowledge of his insignificance, he felt freed by his puniness, stimulated by his unimportance, intoxicated by the brevity of his life. There was no reason for anyone to be pompous or self-important, to boast of success, to seek high office by low means. In the tininess of our lives compared to the infinite nature of space, in the brevity of our lives in the context of eternity, there lay freedom, release, and a need, oh, such a need if one really believed in this, to make the most of one's little life, and to try to bring something into the little lives of other people. It was worthwhile, however little, because those lives were so little. Goodness, that sounded preachy, but in view of the amount of preaching done to us in the name of God, why should a humanist be ashamed of one small sentence of good intent?

And the good intent that he so miraculously felt, this to him was the final and the biggest happening on this day of happenings. He could hardly wait, time sped by so fast, to begin the rest of his life, and he knew that there was nothing in this wish that was disrespectful to Deborah and her untimely death. He would remember her, and honour her in his thoughts, every day for the remainder of his little life.

A clock, somewhere over towards Stoke Newington, struck twelve. An owl, somewhere near Highbury, struck two in reply, or that was how it seemed to James. He had read of birds bonding unsuitably. Could an owl bond with a clock? Could it believe that it was getting a message of love every fifteen minutes?

He smiled, and he thought, even as he smiled, that it was odd, and perhaps a little miraculous, that he could still smile at the end of such a day as this.

He walked towards his sleeping, snoring house, and he realised that he felt – and this was strange too – as calm as he had ever felt in his life.

If you enjoyed this novel and would like to read more of David's books, why not take advantage of our special offer?

We are offering you the opportunity to buy three of David's brilliant novels for the price of two.

OBSTACLES *to* YOUNG LOVE

DAVID NOBBS

'Three mighty obstacles threaten the burgeoning love of childhood sweethearts Timothy Pickering and Naomi Walls. They are Steven Venables, a dead curlew and God.'

1978: Two lovers perch precariously on the cusp of adulthood. Timothy's life ambition is to take on his father's taxidermy business; while Naomi dreams of a career on stage.

Across the decades their lives continue to interweave, and occasionally cross — bound by the pull of intoxicating first love. But will their destinies ultimately unite them?

Nobbs's rare comic talent delivers a memorable and moving tale of love won and love lost. You will never look at the art of taxidermy in the same way again.

'**Thank goodness for David Nobbs!
He carries on the comic tradition of
P G Wodehouse with this marvellous
new book...**' Joanne Harris